THE RIVER, BY MOONLIGHT

"The River, By Moonlight," by Camille Marchetta. ISBN 978-1-60264-017-7 (softcover); 978-1-60264-018-4 (hardcover).

Published 2007 by Virtualbookworm.com Publishing Inc., P.O. Box 9949, College Station, TX 77842, US.

Library of Congress Control Number: 2007931220.

Manufactured in the United States of America.

The River, By Moonlight

A Novel

Camille Marchetta

FOR MICHAEL AND VICTORIA BELL

She left the web, she left the loom,
She made three paces thro' the room,
She saw the water-lily bloom,
She saw the helmet and the plume,
She look'd down to Camelot.

Alfred, Lord Tennyson

APRIL 1917

HENRIETTA

Nuala awakened her, coming into her room without even knocking, saying, "Sorry, missus, but there's a telephone call." For an instant, Henrietta clung to the comfort of sleep, to the pleasure of the dream she would not later remember. But Nuala would not let her be. "Missus," she repeated, "the fella says it's urgent."

The "urgent" did it, the word a brush fire in her mind, clearing it of everything but the fear it left in its wake. Alert now, Henrietta sat up and allowed Nuala to help her out of bed and into her robe and slippers. Ignoring the erratic thud of her heart cautioning her to move slowly, she hurried down the stairs, clutching the wooden banister for support, thinking as she went, It's Lily, something's happened to Lily; then, just as quickly, fighting back the rising tide of dread, telling herself, Don't be foolish. It won't be anything too awful. A wrong number perhaps. It was just past six o'clock in the morning.

The black candlestick telephone sat on the oak table in the center hall between the Tiffany lamp and silver desk set. The receiver was off the hook. Picking it up, she held it to her ear and said into the round mouthpiece, "Henrietta Canning speaking."

"Mrs. Canning? I'm Detective Malone. New York City Police Department." She could hear the beat of her heart, the rasp of her breath, the detective's voice, halting and apologetic, difficult to understand at times because of the crackling on the wire, telling her that at shortly before midnight a young woman had entered (that was the word he used, absurd as it was) the Hudson River from a slip at the Columbia Yacht Club at Eighty-sixth Street in Manhattan. "A vagrant walking along the New York Central tracks saw her go in," the detective said, though *jump in* was what he meant, Henrietta knew. "The man raised an alarm, and attempted a rescue, but . . . by the time he found her and pulled her back to shore, it was too late."

"What has this to do with me?" Henrietta asked. She was surprised by how calm her own voice sounded, and how faint, as if she were hearing it from a vast distance.

In the woman's purse, the detective explained, among other belongings, was a key to a room in the Pelham Hotel. "We found that the room was registered in the name of your daughter, I believe. Miss Lily Canning?"

"Yes."

"Do you know where she might be?"

Henrietta fought back the tears, the desire to scream. "In her room there, sound asleep, I should imagine," she said, her voice steady, confident. "There must be some mistake. Someone's confused the numbers."

"I'm afraid not, ma'am." When they got no response to their knocking, the police had entered the room, and the night clerk had absolutely identified its contents as belonging to Miss Canning, said the detective. He

2

sounded as if he would rather be talking to just about anyone but her, thought Henrietta. He sounded like a very nice young man. "Of course, there's always the chance the purse was stolen, and your daughter is . . . elsewhere."

"Yes. I'm certain that's it," Henrietta said, determined to grasp whatever straws blew her way. "No doubt she decided to spend the night with friends." Teddy and Alice, she thought. Lily's stayed over at their studio. Or she's with Edmund. If she were not so frightened, Henrietta would have laughed at the relief she felt at the idea of it when, at any other time, she would have been overcome with anger, and shame. Edmund!

"I'm sorry to have to ask you this, ma'am, and it may well be a waste of your time, but could you come to New York? Today, if possible? We have to try to identify the . . ." He had been about to say body, or worse, corpse; instead, he finished lamely, "the young lady." After again giving her his name, and his number, which Henrietta wrote down carefully with the pen from the desk set, he said, "If you'd let me know when you've made your travel arrangements, I'd appreciate it."

Her hand was barely shaking, Henrietta noticed as she replaced the receiver and put the telephone down; but then, however cynical experience might have made Detective Malone, it was not her custom to believe the worst until she must. The whole matter was undoubtedly a mistake, a ghastly mistake. Lily's purse had been stolen. She was with friends. She was safe. That was the only reasonable thing to think. Turning toward Nuala, who hovered anxiously near the steps leading down to the kitchen, Henrietta said, "They think something might have happened to Lily. Silly girl. Out gallivanting when she ought to be getting a good night's rest." Again her voice sounded very faint, very distant. Go back upstairs, get dressed, go to New York, she urged herself, but she could not seem to move. Please, dear God, she thought. Please. Don't let it be Lily.

"Missus?" said Nuala, her face drawn with concern. "Are you all right?" Usually she was neat as a pin, but not this morning, bundled as she was into her worn, too-big bathrobe, with her mop of red hair, put up

3

hastily, in danger of tumbling down. Standing there, she looked ridiculously young for the title of housekeeper, bestowed on her after the other servants, in turn, had died or retired or married, leaving her in sole charge of Riverhall, the Canning home.

"Yes. Fine. I have to go to New York," Henrietta said. Picking up the telephone again (to do what, at least since her husband's death, she always did at the first hint of trouble), she asked the exchange for Erich Roeder's number. He answered, thank goodness, not Violet, who would have been very cross indeed to have been awakened by Henrietta at that hour, though one would have thought a doctor's wife would long since have made her peace with having her sleep disturbed.

Though the local operator would have learned all she needed to know from the detective's call, had she given in to the temptation to listen, still Henrietta spoke as vaguely as she could manage, giving only as many details as needed for Erich to get the gist of the situation. When she finished, he said, "You're quite right. No doubt it's all a load of rubbish. And you, Etta, how are you?"

"Surprisingly all right," she said, though her voice caught on a sob. "I'm sure all will turn out well, but I do have to go."

"Not alone," he insisted, as she had known he would.

Spurred by the thought that he would soon be on his way, refusing Nuala's offers of help dressing and a hearty breakfast afterward, insisting on coffee only, though she had noticed lately that it made her heart beat even faster, Henrietta returned to her room, washed hurriedly, buttoned herself into her gray wool suit, pulled on her felt hat, and went back downstairs to the library to await Erich's arrival. She knew that he would come quickly, as quickly as he could make things right with Violet, and with his nurse, who would have to put off the patients scheduled for the day. Still, though she had barely time enough to finish her cup of coffee (freshly brewed and smelling delicious, but like acid in her mouth), it felt like an eternity until he appeared, his daughter in tow. "If I'm not to be

4

trusted to go off on my own," he said, his tone as light as he could manage, "I think it's best if Rosaline were to come with me to New York."

"But I must go," Henrietta said, for how was she to keep the awful fear at bay, if she wasn't busy doing something?

"I understand why you want to, my dear, but as your doctor, as well as your friend, I have to tell you that it would be beyond foolish, Etta. Think of your heart. You've had how many episodes in these past few months? All minor, to be sure, but you know exertion sets them off. Why risk another? If this is all rubbish, and I'm sure it is, think how Lily would feel to return home and find you ill again."

He went on about the strain of the journey and the inevitable unpleasantness of the police business, however happy the outcome. Not one to surrender easily, she stood her ground for a while, but finally, just as she had done when the call had come about her husband, Henrietta conceded. "How I let you bully me!" she said, though relief instantly swamped her irritation, for (if she was to be honest about it) she was only too happy to have Erich, her friend and protector from childhood, interpose his solid, comforting presence between her and heartbreak for as long as he was able, until there was no choice but for her to muster the courage to face it.

With her usual tact, his daughter had stayed out of the discussion, for which Henrietta was thankful, or she might have felt truly under siege. Though a little thing, and kind to a fault, Rosaline was full of spirit and could, as her father always remarked, argue the devil out of his pitchfork if she had a mind to. Now, she looked at Henrietta and said, "Shall we stop at Mrs. Allen's on the way to the station and ask her to come round?" Except for the solemn expression in her large gray eyes, Rosaline, in her apricot-colored dress with its matching hat and single jaunty feather, looked for all the world as if she were off on an outing to the city with Lily, not in search of her.

"No, I'd rather you didn't," said Henrietta. Her sister was the last person she wanted near just then. Edith always had to talk, to air her worries aloud. She could never resist adding her measure to any bushel of woe. "Nuala's all the company I need."

Without further protest she let Erich and Rosaline go, telephoned to the police detective to let him know they were on their way, and then went back to her room to change into her purple day dress (she refused to put on the black) before returning to the library to wait. For how long? she wondered. They planned to take the eight-thirteen train to New York from Minuit. It was just over a two hour journey into Grand Central, but it would take another half an hour, perhaps longer, to reach the police station. And then? Henrietta had no clear idea of what was to follow, or the amount of time needed to pursue the necessary inquiries, but she supposed she ought not hope to see them again until at least early evening. Meanwhile, it would be best simply not to think about anything, she cautioned herself. She took her sewing basket from its place by the armchair, chose a sheet of Egyptian cotton from among the items to be mended, and settled herself on the leather sofa, her back firmly to the window and its broad view of the Hudson. The day was certain to be endless, no matter how she tried to fill the time.

The sofa was not her usual seat, nor was she often to be found indoors on such a fine April day, with the sun, out at long last, trying to tease the forsythia into bloom and raise the first pink blush of spring on the dogwoods. A spry, athletic girl, she had grown into an energetic woman, an industrious housewife, one who always had to be doing something. At this time of year she should be in the garden, pruning and weeding, or, if not that, then traipsing about the countryside on some errand or other. Only when the weather was bad, or her heart was acting up, and she was forced inside, did she retreat to the library, but then it was in the armchair by the window that she always sat, and no matter the task she set her fingers, her eyes would inevitably find the river, a bolt of shimmering cloth in an ever-changing array of colors, unfurling between the graceful slope of the lawn and the rise of the Highlands across the way. Though not the busy thoroughfare it had been before the railroad had come

6

through, the river still bustled with the business of life, with barges and steamers, schooners and tugs, with fishermen in rowboats and millionaires on yachts, while motley freight trains, at this distance no bigger than a child's toy, wound around the mountains on the opposite bank.

Today, however, no matter how firmly she held to the conviction that all would turn out well, she could not look at the river, for it was not as if, having lived beside it all her life, she had failed to notice its treachery. And as she picked up a spool of white thread, snipped off a length, slipped it through the eye of the needle (at least she did not need spectacles yet!) and began to sew, taking one stitch and another, soon the sad memories breached the dam in her mind and came flooding in. She recalled the time (she had been how old then? twelve, perhaps?) when a sudden squall capsized a sailboat no more than a few hundred yards from shore. Driven indoors by the storm, she had been reading quietly in a corner of this very room, hoping that — if she kept still enough — her father would not send her away. She remembered the blissful serenity of the moment, the fire in the grate, the distant sounds of a door closing, of footsteps on the stairs, of scales drifting in from the parlor where Rupert, her brother, was practicing the piano. Then, for no particular reason (as he said later), her father had left his desk to amble over to the door that opened out onto the back porch. Lost in her book, his frantic call to "Quick, fetch Jonas" had caught her unawares and brought her back abruptly from France and the Terror, the shadow of the guillotine and Lucie Manette. As he headed off to get his slicker and boots, she had run to the garage to find the handyman while Rupert, hearing the commotion, came racing along the hall to join in the rescue attempt. A raincoat pulled on over her sodden clothes, Henrietta had watched with her mother and Edith from the shelter of the porch to where, at the bottom of the slope, Jonas and Rupert held her father by a rope tied around his waist, as he struggled against the wind and rain into the roiling water.

"Pray, children," her mother had said. "Pray with all your might."

Her father had managed to save only one, a boy of no more than ten. His older brothers, two of them, had drowned. And three years later, Mr. Muller, the baker, skating across the frozen river, returning from a visit to his married daughter on the west bank, had fallen through the ice, shocking everyone. "But no one knew the river better than him," the men of the town had murmured, shaking their heads in consternation, while the women carried casseroles of sympathy to the widow and gave thanks to the Lord for leaving their own husbands be, at least for the moment.

There were others, so many others, and their unwelcome shades flitted through Henrietta's memory now, when she wished least of all to think of them. But none had belonged to her. They had not been family, not beloved, not by her at any rate; and so, after the wakes, after the burials, after the words of condolence to the survivors, she had pushed the victims from her mind. She had let her pleasure in the river overcome her fear, though not her caution, of course. Thanks to her father, she too knew the river. In turn, she had taught what she knew to Lily.

Lily.

But she did not want to think of her daughter. She wanted only to sit, as if turned to stone, to a statue entitled *Mother, Waiting*, until Erich returned. When he told her what he had learned, what he had seen, then she would allow herself to feel: relief, God willing; or, if necessary . . .

With a resolute shake of her head, she looked up at the clock on the mantle. But surely it was later than nine-thirty? How slowly this day was passing, creeping from moment to moment like the sad old crone she was so much afraid of becoming, at the mercy of her failing heart, rambling about this great silent house. Though not yet, she reassured herself, for even now, at fifty-six, she sometimes caught a glimpse of the child who used to racket about the place, the girl whose mother used to beg her to slow to a sedate walk, to remember that she was a lady.

She took a final stitch and snipped the thread with her scissors. The sheet was done. Folding it neatly, she put it back in the basket, took out a torn petticoat, rethreaded her needle, and began again to sew, wishing, as

8

she always did when she was troubled, that her brother were still alive. Rupert had been as merry as sunshine. She could always rely on him for light no matter how dark the way ahead. But Rupert had been carried off by the same diphtheria epidemic that had taken her own baby, her first, a sweet little boy of two. She had lost another child a year later, an infant girl. It was pneumonia that time. Ill with it herself, Henrietta had prayed to God to take her as well since only death, she was certain, could put an end to the pain she felt. But that was not to be. Her will was too strong, Erich said, though that could not have been true, for surely then she would have died, so earnestly had she prayed for it. No, it was her husband who had saved her. Titus. It was his voice she had heard in her delirium, his will that had called her back. And now he, too, was gone, buried beside their babies in St. Mark's churchyard, a short distance away from Rupert, who lay beside his own stillborn child. Two years after his death, his widow had married an executive with the Florida East Coast Railroad and moved to Miami. She still kept in touch by way of letters and Christmas cards. Two grown sons she had, one an architect, the other a railroad man like his father.

Poor Rupert. All his dreams had come to nothing.

What she did not wish, Henrietta realized, not today at any rate, was for her husband's presence. Though often she longed for him, for the reassuring sound of his voice, for the smell of his cigar, for the touch of his hand on her arm as they walked up the aisle in St. Mark's for Sunday services, for his warmth beside her in bed even now, three years after his death, today she was content to have him lying in peace in the churchyard rather than in the city, seeing what he would see, taking the dreadful blow first, then having to return home, having to watch her face as he told her the awful news.

But perhaps the news would not be awful. More than you need will arrive at the door without borrowing trouble, her mother had always said. That nice detective, surely he had not meant to sound so certain? The police were still investigating. The purse might have been stolen. Surely, in

9

the end, it would turn out to be a case of mistaken identity? One often read about such things in the newspapers. It was not necessary to think the worst. She would not think it. She would pray instead; pray with all her might.

ℊ

The door into the library opened and Henrietta looked up anxiously. But it was only Nuala, a cap now sitting pertly atop her crown of braided hair, a ruffled apron covering the front of her new black uniform, the sight of which gave Henrietta a fresh surge of hope, for it was Lily who had insisted on taking Nuala into the city, to McCreery's Department Store on Broadway, just last month to buy it and a few other household items — new towels, tablecloths and napkins, that sort of thing. It was Lily who (though she usually never took an interest in such matters) had pointed out how worn everything had become since her father's death. Yes, she had. She had been quite passionate about it, urging her mother to throw away all the old things, to start afresh. It was impossible to believe that she would have cared so much about shabby linen if she had been planning to . . . to . . . no, certainly she would not have cared. She would hardly have noticed. "Yes, Nuala?"

"Are you sure, now, you wouldn't like a cup of tea, missus? And something to eat?" There was no trace of Nuala's usual smile and her green eyes, normally as bright as the shining tiles in her kitchen, were clouded with worry.

"No, thank you. I'm not hungry."

"You've not had a morsel of food all the morning."

"Don't pester me, Nuala!" She hated being treated like an invalid. She was not one, not yet.

"No, missus," said Nuala, standing her ground, "but then I wouldn't have to now, would I, if you'd be sensible about looking after yourself?"

With her high cheekbones, full mouth, and lovely fair skin (spoiled just a bit by a sprinkling of freckles), Nuala was really quite pretty. But her looks were never what one noticed. What commanded attention was her bearing. She had such dignity. For such a young woman she was remarkably self-possessed, which — had she not been so dependable, with such a lively sprit and good heart — Henrietta might have found irritating. As it was, she liked the girl. "I'll have something a bit later, I promise." Turning her attention back to her mending, Henrietta tried to look too busy to be bothered further, but Nuala remained in the doorway, not yet ready to leave. "There was something else?"

Nuala's head bobbed. "Mrs. Allen telephoned, wanting to talk to you."

Henrietta flung down her mending with an exclamation of annoyance. "I regret the day Mr. Canning ever let that devil's plaything into this house!" But Erich Roeder had installed one in his home; it was therefore only a matter of time before Edith and George would do the same; and Titus could never bear to be the last to have the latest innovation. So, the telephone had come to Riverhall. It was irrational, Henrietta knew, but she could not help blaming it for every scrap of bad news that had entered her home through its evil black body; and, since the day the call had come from that obscure hotel in New York to tell her of Titus' death, she could not hear its ring without a start of fear. "What did you tell her?"

"That you was resting, missus."

"Nothing else?"

"No."

"Good."

"Still, it might be a good thing if she was to stop by?"

"She didn't say she would, did she?" She really did not think she could deal with Edith just then, though ordinarily she enjoyed her company. Henrietta was truly fond of her younger sister. Edith might see disasters around every corner, but she was delighted when they failed to arrive, and kindness itself when they did.

11

"No. But she said you was to telephone to her when you felt up to it."

"I will. Thank you, Nuala."

The housekeeper started out of the room, but then turned back again. "Are you sure, now, you wouldn't be wanting just a bit of soup? I made it fresh this morning. Vegetable, it is."

Henrietta shook her head firmly and retrieved her sewing. She heard the door close. She was alone again, with nothing to distract her from her thoughts but her mending. I'll just finish this, she told herself. I can do it. One stitch, then another, small, even, just as she was taught.

When the petticoat was done, she took one of the pillowcases from the basket. Laying it across her lap, she adjusted the lace edging that had come loose. It was one from her trousseau, of the finest Irish linen, hand sewn by her mother. She would be amazed at how skillful I've become, thought Henrietta as she rethreaded her needle, after what a trial I was to her. Edith could sit for hours without fidgeting, but I always wanted to be on the river, skating with Rupert, fishing with Father.

It was a comfort to think of those distant days, the time when her mother and father, when her brother were all still alive, the time before sorrow had touched her. Oblivious to all the worldly problems, the sordid little secrets, of which even Minuit had its share, she had been a happy child: allowed to run wild, some people said, but that was far from true. Her parents were quite strict about most things, about the usual things, about schoolwork and household chores, about sitting still in church and minding one's manners. They had taken pride in their children's conduct, in their knowing how to behave in company, but they had also believed in fresh air and plenty of exercise. No, she had not run wild at all. She had run free.

It was different for Lily, of course. After the two babies died, it was only natural that she and Titus would want to keep an eye on her, keep her close to home, keep her safe. He was a devoted father, so unlike most men who hardly took any notice of their children until they came of age to be useful. Even when Lily was a baby, Titus had spent countless hours with her. It was he who had taught her to read, long before she started school, and to draw as well, since he had some talent for it, though piano lessons were left to Henrietta, who was considered quite accomplished, if not nearly so good as Rupert. In those days before phonographs, her brother had provided the accompaniment for dances at their parties and was sorely missed when he left for Harvard.

She had fallen in love with Titus, dancing with him as Rupert played, just a few days after her brother's return from Cambridge with his new friend in tow. In the course of their first term, the two young men had become inseparable, and from then on had spent a part of each vacation together, climbing, skiing, doing all sorts of enviable things forbidden to girls, always stopping off to visit each other's families between adventures. She remembered the excitement of their arrival that first time, the banging of bags against the moldings as the boys carried them upstairs, the welcome commotion in a house that had seemed so quiet with Rupert away, the laughter over dinner, her sister chattering, her mother looking flushed and happy, her father seeming delighted with the man his son had become. A few nights later there was an impromptu party, local friends invited in for refreshments and music. They had rolled up the rug in the parlor, and Rupert had sat at the piano to play, polkas and waltzes mainly, Strauss and Offenbach. Everyone was dancing with everyone, and she had not stood still a minute, for how she loved to dance! Titus had held out a hand to her and said, "Come on, Etta!" Though too young really even to think of such things (she was only fifteen), until then she had nevertheless taken it for granted that one day, inevitably, she would marry Erich Roeder. But it took no more than the feel of Titus' hand at her waist to convince her otherwise. Grateful that dancing had brought up her color so that he would not notice her blush, her eyes had dropped away from his. So this is it, she had thought. This is what it's like. Love.

Titus' feelings never had quite caught up to hers, though Henrietta chose not to think about that often, nor let it worry her when she did. She had got him, and kept him. Nothing else mattered. And how could she blame him for not falling head over heels for her, as she had for him? Now, she was considered a handsome woman, a matter of style and a certain acquired elegance of manner, but she had not been a pretty girl. Tall and angular, she had had then, she was certain, all the allure of a board. Her face was too narrow, her nose too sharp, her eyes unremarkable, her hair a nondescript brownish color, wiry and hard to control — a far cry from that notorious Lillian Russell, "the American Beauty" as she was called, whom Titus had found so entrancing. With little hope that he would ever return her love, the gawky Henrietta was grateful from the start just to have him treat her like a pal, as Rupert always did, accepting without comment her joining them (when household chores permitted), walking in the mountains, fishing on the river. Titus never even offered to help her reel in a catch, a gentlemanly lapse she had much appreciated. She did not like being treated as if she was helpless.

Henrietta had learned a lot about her future husband during those times, when he and Rupert, forgetting she was there, lost themselves in conversation. Unlike her own family, which numbered among its relations a signer of the Declaration of Independence, Titus' forebears were of much more humble origins. His grandfather, a blacksmith's son turned soldier in Wellington's army, had emigrated from England after the Napoleonic Wars left much of Europe an economic wasteland. After trying one thing and another, following opportunity as it beckoned, he had settled finally in Wyoming, where he might possibly have married an Indian woman; in any case, they produced several children together, one of them Titus' father, who (without doubt, though with some trouble) had managed to wed the local minister's daughter and become respectable. By the time Titus had set off for Harvard, his parents were long since dead; and though he was fond of his siblings, he said, he did not have much in common with them. His older brother had inherited the family ranch and raised horses he sold mainly to the army. One of his sisters had married the owner of a dry goods store, the other, the county sheriff.

While Rupert returned from visits to Titus' home in love with the west, with the grandeur of the landscape, the beauty of the horses, the strong character of the men, and the independent spirit of the women (one of whom he brought home as his bride), it was clear to Henrietta that Titus was always relieved to be once again in the east, near to the centers of culture, where he could see art, hear music, attend plays, date actresses (or so it was whispered), and enjoy the easy sociability of the many friends he had acquired. Though she could not help wishing sometimes that she were the reason for his preference, she knew it was not herself but — say — the prospect of seeing Edwin Booth play Othello that got him all fired up. His feelings for her, though they grew steadily over the years as he came to admire her character — and even her appearance, he said, calling her "a fine-looking woman" — were altogether quieter, which did not mean that they were any less genuine, or more likely to fade. Whatever others might say (not that they would, to her), he had loved her, Henrietta believed. He had certainly enjoyed her company, and she had agreed with his confident claim that they would have a good life together. He had known what he was doing when he asked her to marry him, as had she when she said yes, grateful that, however slowly, Titus had finally reached the point where marriage to her had seemed as desirable, as much in his best interests, as the law partnership offered him by her father.

Henrietta also had Rupert to thank for that. After getting his degree, her brother had decided that he was not at all interested in practicing law. He had taken it into his head to become a newspaperman, which seemed a peculiar and unsatisfactory choice to his family, who had no connection with newspapers beyond the reading of them. But Rupert would not be talked out of it, and off he went to the city, where, thanks to a few strings pulled by a relative of his mother's, he landed a job at the *New York Herald*. With the place held for his son in the law firm suddenly vacant, who better to fill it, thought Henrietta's father, than Titus, who was so soon to be his son-in-law?

A disturbing idea occurred to Henrietta. Could Rupert, who had brought Titus into her life, be responsible as well for bringing Edmund Farel into Lily's? Henrietta had never understood how it was that her well-brought-up daughter could have let herself accept the attentions of a stranger on a train, but suddenly she had a theory. In Lily's account of that unpropitious meeting, Edmund had let it be known at once that he was a newspaperman. Perhaps that had been enough for him to slip past her guard? Lily had, after all, been raised on stories of Rupert, her mother's dashing older brother, her father's best friend, who had made something of a name for himself in journalism before dying so tragically young. He had been a glamorous figure to Lily all her life, and perhaps some of that glamour had rubbed off onto Edmund?

The sound of a sob interrupted her thoughts: her own, Henrietta realized. She looked at the clock. Ten to ten. Well, at least the pillowcase was done, she thought, taking a final stitch. She picked up her scissors, snipped the thread, folded the piece of linen, and dropped it into the basket. It was all nonsense, of course, she told herself. Whenever did a handsome rascal need the aid of a ghost to make himself appealing to a susceptible young woman? And Lily had indeed been susceptible.

And whose fault was that? It was a question that posed itself when Henrietta's defenses were low, and as always it brought a rush of anger, followed instantly by fear, for the answer led where she had no wish to go. Hurriedly, she changed the direction of her thoughts. She let her eyes drift aimlessly from one piece of furniture to the next, from the closed door to the papered walls, covered almost completely by paintings in gilded frames — Lily's paintings. In a house with no shortage of delightful rooms, Henrietta had always liked this one best. It had been her father's library, and then Titus'. The parlor and small sitting room (the first reserved for company, the second for family) were in the front, facing out over the extensive grounds that lay between the house and the main road, but the dining room and library overlooked the river. Shortly after her husband died, Henrietta had taken the room over for her own use. She felt especially close to him here, and whatever her grievances (for she had some, even if she did not care to dwell on them), they were nothing compared to her love; and she imagined sometimes, as she sat in the chairs where he had worked and read and smoked his cigars, that she could feel some of his strength seeping into her failing body. At her weakest, she felt it was he, still, who kept her going, if not always for her own sake, then at least for Lily's.

Henrietta's father, Samuel Vanklieft, had built the house. From a small Dutch settlement, founded when Peter Minuit was governor of New Amsterdam, the town — thanks to its harbor, the natural beauty of its landscape, and, later, its limestone quarry and furniture factory — had grown into a prosperous community, still small but with a certain bustling charm, its commercial center the hub for a reasonably well-off working-class, an affluent middle-class, and a handful of wealthy New York stock brokers and bankers and industrialists who had built country homes (mansions really) overlooking the Hudson. Especially in the boom years after his return from the Civil War, Sam's law practice had profited from the presence of all three groups. He had quickly accumulated enough money to buy the land, a peninsula jutting out into the river a few miles north of the town, and to hire an architect, whom (according to all reports) Sam had driven nearly mad with his constant changes, improvements, flights of fancy. Riverhall, he had named the house. With cream-colored siding and turquoise trim, it had a pitched roof, steep cross gables, windows with pointed arches, and a single tower with a stunning view of the Hudson and the Highlands. Two covered porches ran the width of it, front and rear. It had hidden staircases, oddly shaped rooms, huge attics filled with the overflow of the family's life — a magical place to grow up.

Happily, as it turned out, her sister did not share Henrietta's love of their home. Though it was only two miles and a bit from town, Edith considered it too removed from the center of things and by far preferred her own grand Queen Anne house off Minuit's main street, a short walk, indifferent to weather, to the office of her husband, George's, insurance agency. Only from the top floor of the Allen house, in winter when the trees were bare, was it possible to see the river. For that reason alone, Henrietta could not have lived in it. Even when Titus and she were first married, their small cottage, perched as it was on a hill, had offered an unobstructed view of the water, and she had been happy there, until the loss of her babies. By then Rupert had died, her mother soon followed, and her heartbroken father, so it had seemed the happiest finale to that sad time for Titus to buy out Edith's share of the property. In the summer of 1891, a few months before Lily's birth, he and Henrietta had moved into the house.

Over the years they had made changes, of course. They had stripped the dark silk papers from the walls and replaced them with lighter patterns and colors. Keeping only a few mementos themselves, they had sent the heavy Victorian furniture off to Edith and George (and what they did not want, to auction), replacing it with pieces in the Art Nouveau style that was then all the rage. The gas lamps gave way to electricity. Central heating was installed. Yet, the essential nature of the house never changed. It never stopped being familiar, comfortable, loved.

There was a section of wallpaper coming loose, Henrietta noticed, just below the cornice, beside the door leading to the hall. And there was another, above the mantle. She frowned. She suspected that, should she look closely, she would see more signs of decay throughout the house. Titus would never have let things run down to this point, but ever since — when? his death? her own illness? Lily's? she had begun to ignore her responsibilities, to neglect the place. Lily was right.

Lily.

This time, with the name, images of her daughter came flooding into Henrietta's mind, not recent images, but ones of Lily as a baby, beautiful from the moment of her birth, with a long slender body, elegant fingers and toes, silky dark hair, and perfect features, the picture of Titus, even then, newborn. She was an eager, curious toddler, a rambunctious youngster, not really frail at all, except in appearance. There was such a look of impermanence about her; so pale, so ethereal did she seem, it was hard to believe that she had come to stay, hard especially for Titus. He worried about her so. Was she dressed suitably for the weather? Was the day too cold, or too hot, or too wet for her to go out? Was allowing her to play with other children a reasonable risk? Each time Lily had come down with one of the classic childhood illnesses, measles, chicken pox (there was no keeping her from those, no matter how hard they tried), he would regret the necessity of allowing her any playmates at all, even Rosaline, or Edith's girl, Florence. He had wanted to hire a tutor to school Lily at home, but Henrietta, unable to warm to that notion, suggested that they send her instead with Rosaline to Queen of Heaven, where the classes were small and the nuns very strict about matters such as personal hygiene. Initially Titus had balked, but when Erich introduced him to one of the sisters, who happened to be a trained artist, swayed by the prospect of lessons for Lily (who was showing promise, even at that young age) he had at last agreed. Much to Henrietta's relief. She was the first to admit that, yes, she did indeed share her husband's (perhaps excessive) concern for their daughter's health. How could she not, after losing two children? She was the one who had carried them within her for nine months, who had endured the agony of giving birth, who had suffered as Edith, as Violet Roeder, as all mothers suffered, but without the compensating joy of watching her child — her children — grow to adulthood. How could she not be frantic with worry for Lily? Yet, there was something in Henrietta that had rebelled at the idea of keeping her daughter a prisoner in her own home and made her wish for Lily the same simple pleasures, the same easy association with friends and family, the same wild delight in running free that she herself had experienced. Titus, who had come from an altogether different background, who had risen before dawn and worked side-by-side with his father and brother from the age of seven, who had got himself through school and to Harvard only by a supreme effort of will, saw things from another perspective, as was only natural, she supposed. To him, being a good father meant denying his daughter no luxury he could afford, and then some. It meant enriching her mind, encouraging her talent. It meant, above all, keeping her safe.

In the end, Titus was happy to concede that they had made the right choice, for — despite an occasional headache, and a moodiness when she reached adolescence that could not help but worry, and sometimes even exasperate, her parents — Lily's health in general remained excellent, her grades good, and her progress in art truly astounding. Her teacher, Sister Mary Eugene, had studied at the *Académie Julien* in Paris before entering the convent, and so provided a higher level of instruction than was usual in a town the size of Minuit. She was also experienced (or perhaps humble) enough to know when the time came to pass Lily on to another of even more formidable ability, Grover Watson, who had also studied in Paris, at the more prestigious *Ecole des Beaux-arts*, which was accounted by many to be the best school of art in the world, though Henrietta had heard the case made against it many times since. Lily had studied with Watson, who lived locally, for years, and though she eventually became impatient with him for reasons her mother could not quite understand, surely all her later success could be said to have come from those early experiences. And as Lily's horde of prizes grew, and Titus began to believe that she would achieve great things, that she would leave Cecelia Beaux and Mary Cassatt in her dust, Henrietta had taken a silent pride in knowing that she had been the one to open the door into a world that so delighted her husband and daughter. At least she had at first, until it occurred to her that Lily's obsession with art seemed to drive all thoughts of a more normal, a more complete and satisfactory life from her mind, until she noticed that her daughter was not, after all, happy.

But she had done her best, thought Henrietta; she had tried her utmost. She had opposed her husband many times for Lily's sake, though not head-on. That never worked, at least not for her, though their beautiful daughter could always manage it when her heart was set on something. But it had been far too easy for Titus to terrify his wife into giving up whatever plan she had in mind by reciting the many possible disasters that might result from it. Still, he was often away from home, looking after the affairs of clients who, though they might own houses locally, had mansions in the city as well, and extensive national interests in railroads and banks and the like. When he was gone, Henrietta would let Lily run errands with the housemaids. She would send her to Edith's, where there was always a crowd of children, to play with Florence and young Louis. She would pack a picnic lunch and take her and Rosaline hiking in the mountains. She had done what she could. She had taught Lily to row a boat and to sail. She had taught her to skate, to swim, and to fish. She had taught her to be fearless on the river.

But if you had a father who took you to and from school until you were well past the age of being able to manage it on your own; if you had a father who chose what books you read, what paintings you saw, what music you heard, what friends you associated with; if you had a father who made it a pleasure to share with him every thought, every dream; if you had a father who was, when all was said and done, determined to mould your mind to conform to his own, and had the charm to make the doing of it seem fun, then how could such a child develop independent taste, independent judgment? How could she learn to distinguish for herself between the shoddy and the priceless? How could she tell a rogue when she saw one?

The questions rose up and overwhelmed Henrietta's defenses, but the anger she felt now was directed only at herself. Despite her efforts, she had sent her daughter into the world unarmed. She had suspected it for some time, but had known it absolutely on the day that Lily returned home, her face radiant with happiness, her eyes full of something that looked very much like triumph, to announce that she had married (married!) Edmund Farel, a newspaperman she had met on a train a few weeks before.

21

Of course, she had what seemed to her a reasonable explanation for her behavior. Though often a bit freer in her manners than generally approved of, Lily conceded, she did not make it a practice to attach herself to strange men on public conveyances, adding — in an attempt to comfort — that she probably would not have spoken to Edmund at all had Rosaline not been there. The girls often traveled to New York together, to spend the day shopping along the Ladies' Mile on Sixth Avenue, visiting the uptown galleries and museums, stopping to dine before catching a late train home. And that day (early last October, only six months before), Henrietta had sent them off with a lighter heart than usual, for though Rosaline was to return that evening, Lily meant to stay on for a series of meetings at a gallery about an exhibition of her paintings scheduled for the spring. The exhibition was the only thing for which she had shown any real enthusiasm in the two years since Titus' death, and it had eased Henrietta's own sorrow to see her daughter getting on at last with her life. So much for mother's intuition!

Though they hadn't noticed him at first, Lily said (though it was hard to imagine how that was possible since he was one of the handsomest men Henrietta had ever met, if not quite so handsome as Titus), she and Rosaline had somehow, quite naturally, fallen into conversation with Edmund, who was sitting across the aisle from them on the train. He had seemed so polite, so proper, so deferential, and yet so easy, it had not occurred to them that they were doing something their parents (or, in Rosaline's case, her husband) might not consider quite respectable. When they reached Grand Central, Edmund had said good-bye without suggesting they continue the acquaintance, to which, of course, they would have said no, though Lily admitted that she was sorry to think she would not see him again, for even Rosaline thought that, except for William, he was not only the most attractive, but possibly the most interesting man she had ever set eyes on.

That would have been that, a chance encounter quickly over, except that Lily had run into him again later that afternoon. This second meeting had seemed so providential, so fated, that when Edmund suggested they dine together, she could only say yes. And since the evening went so very well, delightfully in fact, she had said yes again to lunch the next day, and then to dinner. And so it had begun.

Why Lily kept these meetings secret was not hard for her mother to understand, when she finally learned of them. Certainly she would have insisted that Lily bring the young man home to conduct his courtship under Minuit's watchful eye. She would have been fretful, wary, overprotective. No matter how hard she had tried not to, she would somehow have spoiled her daughter's fun. She would have been unable to help herself. But two weeks after their meeting, when they made the decision to marry, why had Lily not come then to tell her mother? Perhaps she would have suggested that they wait a while, a few months at least. Would that have been so terrible? Titus and she had known each other for years before they married; and, when they did, they were by then secure in their feelings and confident that, whatever storms lay ahead, they would be able to weather them together. There was much to be said for patience, though Henrietta supposed that these days, with the world in such turmoil, the war in Europe, the protests at home, everything changing so quickly, one could hardly expect young people to appreciate that.

But only a month or two, would it have been too much to ask? It was barely enough time to plan a wedding. And surely Lily would have preferred a proper one, with all its luxuries — the elaborate trousseau, the silk gown, the church ceremony, her uncle George to give her away, family and friends to join in the celebration, her mother weeping tears of joy?

"We wanted to be married, that's all. We wanted to be together. A big wedding seemed beside the point. Unnecessary," Lily had replied when her mother put those questions to her as calmly as she could manage. "After all, I'm not a girl anymore. I'm twenty-five. And I didn't want to wait, even a little while."

"It would have made me so happy to see you walk down the aisle in St. Mark's."

"I know, Mama, and I'm truly sorry, but this is what Edmund and I wanted, and it was our wedding, after all."

There was no point continuing the discussion. Recriminations would accomplish nothing, Henrietta had realized as shock and disbelief gave way slowly to the hope that this might be good news, an occasion to celebrate, a daughter married, grandchildren to come, Lily settled and happy at last. It was a hope that Henrietta had persisted in clinging to, for what was there to fear in Edmund Farel, a well-mannered young man, every inch the southern gentleman, gainfully employed, conspicuously devoted to his new wife? It was simply a matter of putting the best face possible on what, after all, was a fait accompli, on what might indeed be a very good thing. And so Henrietta had welcomed Edmund into her home. She had sent out announcements, held a reception, and introduced him to her family and friends. She had even tried to love him, and though she had not succeeded in that (there was hardly enough time, for the marriage ended as quickly as it began), she could not help liking him. He was so very charming.

What bitterness Henrietta had allowed herself to feel was directed at Rosaline who admitted, when asked, that she had known of Lily's meetings with Edmund, and of their growing attachment. From the first, Lily had confided in her. "I can see that you're hurt, Aunt Etta," Rosaline had said, "and indeed I'm very sorry for that. But I really couldn't have told you. I gave my word to Lily. I couldn't break my promise." Though typical of Rosaline, it was nonetheless difficult to accept in the circumstances.

If only, instead, Lily had taken Florence into her confidence, though that was hardly likely. Lily was no fool. She would have known Florence was incapable of keeping such a secret. She was too (if one were to be honest about it) jealous of her prettier, more indulged cousin. Poor Florence, always having to play second fiddle, not only to her younger brother, but to Lily as well. It could turn a girl nasty, if she did not have the character to ignore the slights. Edith and George were much to blame for that, for doting so obviously on Louis. And though Henrietta, feeling

24

sorry for her niece, always did her best to be generous, to be affectionate with her, it was not easy. Florence had been a prickly, difficult child, and was a solemn, self-absorbed young woman, quick to take offense, eager to find fault. Whenever Lily had one of her "spells," when finally her world fell apart, when she was so very ill ... oh, why dress it up in fine clothes now? When Lily had her breakdown, beneath all Florence's expressions of concern had run a steady stream of satisfaction. She had seemed almost to gloat. Rosaline, on the other hand, had been genuinely distraught, blaming herself for the part she had played in Lily's trouble. But by then Henrietta had forgiven her, for she had realized that it hardly mattered who had known what, and when, for all of them would have been equally helpless before Lily's obstinacy.

Dear Rosaline. How like her it was to be the first to offer to help, even now when she had a husband and three young children of her own to care for. Without her, she could not have got through the long weeks of Lily's illness, Henrietta was sure, for whenever she had been at her wit's end, feeling unable to cope for another moment, Rosaline had reliably appeared to keep Lily company, to jolly her along, providing Henrietta with an infusion of hope, as well as a needed respite.

How odd that suddenly those weeks no longer seemed so terrible to her. Sitting here now in her comfortable library, her back to the river, her sewing basket at hand, trying to keep herself from imagining worse horrors, those weeks seemed almost . . . well, not pleasant certainly, but bearable. Yes, completely bearable. At least she had known where Lily was, no farther than her room at the hospital, or reassuringly nearby — upstairs in her studio; in the parlor, playing the piano hour after hour; just here, in the armchair by the window, watching the soothing flow of the river.

Henrietta looked toward the door. If only Lily would come through it, if only she would cross to the sofa, her beautiful face looking flushed and excited, or anxious and tired (it hardly mattered), lean down to kiss her mother's cheek, and say, "Poor Mama, were you worried? I'm such a trial to you, aren't I?" Then, Henrietta would happily live through the long weeks again, once, twice, over and over, if only . . .

$$\mathcal{L}$$

Putting aside her sewing basket, Henrietta picked up the *Hudson Tribune* from the table where Nuala always placed it, and settled back again, determined to read so as to fill her head with problems other than her own. But there was no comfort in that. The paper was filled with news of the war that, after years of ignoring, then resisting, and finally preparing for, the United States was at last about to enter. She scanned the text of President Wilson's address to the Congress, calling for a declaration of war: "... the day has come when America is privileged to spend her blood and her might for the principles that gave her birth ..." Noble sentiments, but would they do to comfort a mother for a slain son? Well, some mothers perhaps. Not Henrietta Canning.

Please, dear God, she prayed, don't let it be Lily.

Impatiently, she put the newspaper aside and looked at her hands. They were covered in print. She would have to go wash them.

As she opened the library door, the tall clock in the hall struck ten-thirty. Had she imagined it, or had the last few minutes passed more quickly? Erich and Rosaline would be at Grand Central by now. Henrietta could see them, in her mind's eye: Erich in his navy wool coat and bowler hat, Rosaline with her apricot feather bobbing, hurrying through the station's main concourse, past the towering pillars, oblivious to the gilded constellations hanging in the vaulted turquoise heavens above, making their way quickly up the marble staircase to Vanderbilt Avenue, where they would find a taxi to take them to the police station. They would certainly take a taxi. Erich disliked the subways and the elevated trains. Dirty, noise-belching contraptions, he called them.

The brilliant gold light that flooded through the leaded glass panels of Riverhall's front door into the wide hall in the early morning hours had

26

turned a milky white with the movement of the sun. The house was quiet, quieter than it usually seemed with Lily not home. There was an unnatural stillness in it, as if it too were waiting. But, no, she was imagining it, for now she could make out the sound of voices coming from the kitchen: Nuala talking to someone. The knife-grinder perhaps? It was Tuesday, his usual day. Or the grocer's boy making a delivery? Oh, what does it matter, thought Henrietta with an exasperated sigh, surprised that even for a moment she had mustered the interest to wonder about anything so trivial as the normal running of her household. With a practiced gesture, she lifted her skirt out of the way and started up the stairs, then stopped as she heard a door open. Looking over the banister, she saw Nuala watching her from the end of the hall. "Yes, Nuala?"

"I heard you moving about, missus. I thought you might be wanting something."

"Nothing, thank you. I might lie down for a while." Nuala nodded approvingly and Henrietta climbed another few steps, then looked over the banister again. The girl was still watching her. "I thought I heard voices."

"It's Deirdre. She brought the pot back Mrs. Allen borrowed the other week."

"You didn't tell her," said Henrietta. Deirdre, Nuala's sister, worked for Edith, who (always resourceful) had gone herself to one of the employment agencies to which girls were directed after completing the immigration formalities on Ellis Island. She had hired them on the spot.

"Not a word. She thought I looked a bit sorry, but I told her it was on account of a glass I broke, and not being sure what you'd say."

"As if I'd care about that!"

"No, missus, but it was what came into my head. And I did so break a glass."

Henrietta almost smiled. "How old are you now, Nuala? Nineteen?"

"Twenty, last November."

Five years younger than Lily, thought Henrietta, that's right. "And you've been with us four years?"

"A few months more, missus."

"How young you were when you left home," said Henrietta. It was always a wonder to her how Nuala and her sister had managed.

"Nineteen-twelve, it was. We needed the work. And Dee was older, by a year."

There had been no Titus in Nuala's life, or Deirdre's, to shower them with every comfort. Yet here they were, alive, working, happy enough. Or so both girls seemed. "You're happy, Nuala, aren't you?" It would be awful if the girl was miserable, thought Henrietta, and she had not noticed, for it was true that she sometimes missed what was right under her nose.

"Oh, yes, missus. I mean, not today, but you know, in the general run."

"Good. I'm pleased to hear it." But was she telling the truth? Henrietta hoped so. "Would you bring me some water? That's all I'll be needing." Gathering her skirts again, she continued slowly up the stairs.

The door to Lily's room was closed, as it always was whether or not she was at home. For a moment, wanting to believe in miracles, Henrietta was tempted to open it and look inside, as if the power of her wishing it might actually conjure her daughter doing nothing more dangerous than sitting in the wicker chair by the window reading the *Saturday Evening Post*.

But no, she was being silly. She had kissed Lily good-bye days ago, exchanging all the words of caution she wished to utter for a single compliment.

"Oh, you always think I look a treat," Lily had replied, smiling. Then, smoothing the jacket of her smart new suit, she had added, more seriously, "but I do hope Darius Menlo agrees with you." The purpose of the trip, and her new wardrobe, was to "wow" the gallery owner into granting her every wish for the exhibition that was now just weeks away. "You mustn't worry while I'm gone. I'll be perfectly well. And I will telephone."

"See that you do," Henrietta had replied with mock sternness. Standing on the front steps, a smile fixed firmly on her face, she had watched as Jonas (still ramrod straight, but moving much more slowly than he used to) stowed Lily's portmanteau and box easel in the car, the Packard that Titus had bought the year before he died. Her daughter had climbed into the front passenger seat. Then, as the handyman took his place behind the wheel to drive her to the station, Lily had turned one last time to wave.

Bye, dear. Bye.

How was it possible, wondered Henrietta, forcing herself to walk past the closed door, that she would never see her daughter again? But as quickly as the thought entered her mind, she ushered it out. The purse might have been stolen. She would not mourn until she knew, beyond a doubt, that there was nothing else to do.

Continuing on, she went past the guest bathroom and down the hall to what had once been her parents' bedroom, then hers and Titus', now hers alone. Set above the library, overlooking the river, it was a large room, furnished with the delicate maple bedroom set that had replaced her parents' massive mahogany one. She remembered how happy she had been the day the Herter Brothers' furniture van had arrived, how she had stood with Titus in the doorway, directing the delivery men where to set the bed, the vanity table, the armoire, the chest of drawers. The sun had streamed into the room, lending everything a rosy glow, picking out the colors in the Wilton carpet. A sailboat, gliding past on the river below the window, had shone in the light as if glazed with enamel. From downstairs had come the sound of eight-year-old Lily practicing the piano. All the bad times had seemed to be past. Only pleasure, only joy, lay ahead.

Opening off the bedroom was a large tiled bathroom, one of four in the house, perhaps Samuel Vanklieft's most luxurious modernism. Entering it, Henrietta washed her hands while trying to avoid looking at herself in the mirror above the porcelain basin; but, inevitably, her gaze lifted and she saw hazel eyes full of anguish staring back at her, an oval face pale with pain, a halo of coarse brown hair, streaked here and there with gray, escaping the pins with which she had secured it that morning: herself, though barely recognizable. Usually she looked much younger than her years. Now she seemed to have aged eons in just a few hours.

Turning away from the disturbing image, Henrietta dried her hands on the spotless white towel and left the bathroom. Had she any right to rail against God now, she asked herself as she went to the bed and carefully turned back its cover so as not to wrinkle the pale green satin. After all, she had had a remarkably happy life — not without its sorrows, of course; but having Titus near had helped heal even the worst of her grief. She was so fortunate to have married him, and not just because of his good looks and compelling presence, though certainly those had attracted her to him (and so far as she could see every other woman, old or young, whom he met), but because he had, in his way, been an admirable husband, making her feel always that, no matter where his interests took him, his heart remained with Lily and with her. It would have been difficult to find anywhere, she was certain, a more devoted family. And if she and Titus had sometimes disagreed (and what married couple did not?), if she could not always quite like his friends, or be easy in her mind about just what he got up to when absent from home (nothing very much, he had assured her, and — lacking evidence to the contrary — she had believed), if they had occasionally differed about what was best for their daughter, their disagreements had been, more often than not, settled with few cross words exchanged; and if the settlement had usually involved Henrietta's giving in to her husband's wishes, well, wasn't that the way of most marriages? Though, she had to admit, not Edith's. There it was poor George who did most of the conceding, Edith who had the will of iron.

What she ought to be, as her mother had told her many times, as the Reverend Moreland often preached from the pulpit at St. Mark's, was grateful to God for His goodness. He had showered her with blessings, so many that she could hardly be said to have earned them. She understood that. So, what right had she to complain if He should choose now to allot her another burden of grief?

No, she had no right to rail against God, thought Henrietta, though she was not certain that would stop her should Lily fail to return safely home.

But of course she would. She was safe, and well. Erich and Rosaline might even have found her by now. Perhaps at any moment the telephone would ring, this time to bring good news.

Sitting in the slipper chair, Henrietta leaned over to remove her shoes. She would not undress further, she decided, in case she should need to go to the telephone. Her fingers struggled with the buttons, and she got the first shoe undone. Then, as she started on the second, she felt the familiar pain in her chest. Her breath grew short. Her head began to spin. This had happened the night before as well, and she had gone early to bed. It was happening more frequently, without doubt.

She heard a knock on the door and Nuala's voice calling her, but she was unable to answer. Lifting her head, she straightened her spine and sat gasping for air.

The door opened and Nuala entered, carrying a tray with a pitcher of water and a glass. "Has the pain come on, missus?" she asked, setting the tray down on the chest of drawers. "You did take your medicine this morning?" Henrietta managed a nod as Nuala hurried to the bedside table, opened a drawer, pushed aside the Digalen, and picked up the glass tube of glycerine trinitrate. "Something just for the pain, so." Hurriedly, she opened it, shook one of the tablets into Henrietta's hand, stood watching as her mistress slipped it under her tongue, and then knelt to unbutton the remaining shoe. "You'll soon be feeling better," she said. Standing, she waited for signs that the pain had eased. "You want help off with your things?" she asked, when Henrietta at last seemed able to rise from the chair.

"No, I'll stay as I am, thank you." Leaning heavily on the girl, Henrietta made her way across the short distance to the bed and sank into it, resting her head on the soft pillow, letting Nuala lift and straighten her legs and pull up the blankets to cover her.

"I'll sit with you," said Nuala.

Henrietta shook her head. "I'll do fine," she said firmly. She remembered then that Lily had telephoned the night before and Nuala had not awakened her. "You must call me if the telephone rings."

"Yes, missus."

"Wake me, if I manage to sleep."

"I'll do that," said the housekeeper, and Henrietta could tell from the bleak look on her face that she, too, was remembering the missed call. "Well, then," Nuala said, moving the pitcher and glass of water to the bedside table, "I'll be back in a while to have a look in." Taking the tray, she went out the door, closing it gently behind her.

For weeks now, Henrietta had thought her heart might stop at any moment. She had been expecting to die, not wanting to exactly, but thinking how fine it would be to see Titus again and her babies, Rupert and her parents. She had thought that, since she could hardly expect to go on indefinitely, now might be as good a time as any to take her leave, with Lily well again and excited about her show, her life full of promise. But now Henrietta knew she could not die, not yet, however tempting death might seem at this moment, offering an escape from the pain, which — if it came — would be far worse than any she had experienced before. And this time it was not Titus calling her back from the brink, but herself. For as long as she could muster the strength, she would have to go on. Whatever the news Erich brought with him from New York, she would have to be here, for Lily, to take care of her as she had from the moment of her birth. No matter what her own wishes, Henrietta could not escape that duty.

"Oh God, please, sweet Lord, don't let it be Lily," she murmured. Her eyes closed. No, she could not escape. Not yet, she thought. Not yet.

ERICH

A s a medical man, even one who practiced his profession in so quiet a backwater as Minuit, Erich Roeder had observed as much of human suffering as a person should have to bear. When he thought of the mothers he had seen die in childbirth, the stillborn babies he had held in his arms, the children claimed by scarlet fever and pneumonia, men and women drowned, choked, stabbed, shot — dying even as he tried to save them with all the desperate effort of his combined knowledge and skill — he wondered how the weight of all he had seen and done (or failed to do) had not yet managed to crush his spirit. But here he was, at fifty-eight years of age, looking hardly worn at all by the troubles he had witnessed, the troubles (he sometimes feared) he might have caused through ignorance, bad judgment, or just plain bad luck. He was resilient; there was no doubt about that. After a few profane words for the Deity and a display of bad temper directed at anyone who happened to be still alive and within reach, he would take himself to a quiet place, pour a soothing glass of brandy, light a cigar, smoke it to the last inch, then retire to bed early and awake in the morning ready to face the next ordeal. In a day or two he would be himself again, a cheerful, vigorous man, with graying hair and moustache belied by a youthful demeanor, a kind-hearted fellow, one who had mastered the art of encouraging optimism without offering false hope — which is what he had tried to do with Henrietta Canning that morning.

But had he gone too far? he wondered. In a general sense, he deplored lying, especially to patients, which among other things Etta was, and he would have thought less of himself had he resorted to it for his own benefit. He had come to believe, however, that in particular cases telling, if not an outright lie, something less than the truth was a sensible way to proceed. (Do no harm — that was the first law of his profession.) By encouraging her to believe that the report of Lily's death was a terrible mistake, he had meant to throw his dear friend a life raft, one that would keep her afloat until she mustered the strength to make for shore when the truth became finally, incontrovertibly known. Over the course of the day, the two possibilities — that Lily was alive, that Lily was dead — would fight it out in Etta's mind, hope battling with despair, until she grew used to the awful idea, so that if, in the end, he returned to her with bad news, she would be able — just — to bear it.

For himself, Dr. Roeder had little hope that the drowned woman would not be Lily, or, given her history, that her death was in any way accidental. Still, he clung to that buoy, small as it was, during the long train journey into New York City. Whatever good sense had to say on the subject, it was one thing for a medical man to accept the probability of suicide in the case of a disturbed stranger, another for a family friend, one who might be said to stand in place of an uncle, to believe that someone whom he had watched grow from a lovely child to an intelligent, talented, glorious woman, might choose to take her own life. It was too terrible a prospect to face before one was made to, before one had reviewed all the facts, before one had seen the body. Yes, until he had seen the body, he would not cease to hope.

Sitting opposite him in the train compartment, a look of determined brightness on her face as she pretended to be engrossed in a magazine, Rosaline, too, was refusing to give in to despair, the doctor noted with some pride before burying his own nose in the *Hudson Tribune*. But there was no refuge to be found there. It was full of the news of America's imminent entrance into the war, the anti-German feeling that had been building since August of '14 revved up to a fever pitch. Not that the Kaiser didn't deserve every epithet uttered against him, but still it was disturbing to read the hateful propaganda directed at an entire people, his people, no matter how tenuous the connection. He threw the paper down with an exclamation of disgust.

Rosaline looked up anxiously from the magazine. "What is it, Papa?"

Several times over the past month or so, he had experienced some pain he could not quite conceal; and though he had assured them it was only indigestion, his wife and daughter persisted in worrying about it, which was not to be wondered at, he supposed, as his father-in-law had died of stomach cancer. His trouble was not that, he was certain; though even if it were, there was nothing to do about it. "This damn war!" he said. A look of relief flashed over Rosaline's face, followed by one of resignation. She's tired of my lectures, he thought, but still he could not resist launching into another. Someone had to tell young people the truth. The American newspapers, with their lies about "Hun" atrocities, could not be relied upon to do it, if the recent story in the *Times* about spies poisoning Red Cross bandages was anything to go by. For that matter, the German language newspapers (and even the *Fatherland*, which was published in English) were so filled with pro-German propaganda that they could hardly be said to be any better.

"Surely a point of balance can be found?" The doctor did his best to keep his voice low, his temper under control. "Surely it's possible to deplore Germany's militarism without demonizing its people? They are, after all, a hardworking, industrious, cultured lot. World-renowned poets, philosophers, scientists, composers have come from their stock. You and your brothers must remember that."

Their mother, his wife, had been born in Germany and emigrated with her family in the 1870s, when she was a child. His own ancestors had come to America a good deal earlier. A distant great-grandfather had arrived at the time of the Revolutionary War in a contingent of Hessian soldiers fighting with the British. Press-ganged into the army when no more than a boy, treated brutally, for him war had not been a matter of principle, but of necessity. So when the Continental Congress, in July of 1776, offered tracts of land to any Hessian who would desert, he had taken the offer and settled in Pennsylvania. One of the sons in the next generation had migrated to upper New York State, and Erich Roeder's own father, after serving as a surgeon in the Union Army, had moved his family to Minuit to start a medical practice. After completing his studies, Dr. Roeder had joined him there. His brothers had gone west, to Oregon and Washington. His sister had married and moved to Albany.

Previously, the doctor's interest in his family's history had always been more academic than passionate. He viewed himself as a complete American, for his roots in the country's soil spread far and deep. But since a German submarine had sunk the British ship, the *Lusitania*, with so many United States citizens aboard, the tenor of the war coverage in the newspapers, the comments by politicians, the casual remarks of friends and acquaintances who had no reason to think that he might have cause for offense, the use of hate as a weapon of war, above all, had got his back up, had made him return atavistically to some previously unsuspected core of his being, had made him want to set the record straight. And there were his sons to think of, his two boys, Marcus in medical school, and Henry still at university. Who knew what this would mean for them, this anti-German feeling, or this declaration of war?

He pushed the thought away. Somehow, surely, he could manage to keep them safe. "What's the world coming to," he asked, "when a man can't even order sauerkraut at Luchow's? Liberty cabbage! What a load of rubbish!"

Rosaline confined her responses to agreeable nods of her brown head (the feather in her hat bobbing along in concert), and an occasional murmur of what could be taken for either sympathy or assent. A small woman, still slender despite her three children, she had an air of sophistication remarkable in someone who rarely left the town where she was born. And had her mother not been such a beauty, the doctor was convinced that Rosaline's looks would receive far more credit. As it was, it was allowed that she was pretty, with a heart-shaped face, flawless complexion, a straight nose, a dimpled chin, and clear gray eyes that regarded her father now with an intelligent and engaged look, though he still could not be sure she was listening to him. He hoped she was, not entirely because he had a thing or two to teach her, but because his tirade might distract her, might keep her thoughts from Lily, for at least this little while; and so with no encouragement, but practiced eloquence, he continued his rant until the train arrived at Grand Central Station.

"We can take a trolley, if you'd rather avoid the subway," said Rosaline, as she and her father joined the stream of passengers moving along the platform.

Clearly, like himself, today even his intrepid daughter had no wish to be underground, trapped in some dark hole. "No, no. We'll take a cab," he said.

They made their way quickly through the vast pillared concourse and up the broad staircase to Vanderbilt Avenue. Grimly conscious of the purpose of their trip, unlike many of their travel companions, perhaps in town for a day of shopping and an evening at the theater, they paid no attention to their surroundings. Even Dr. Roeder, who had not been to the city in some time, had no thought to spare for the magnificence of the station, a veritable palace of commerce, now barely four years old.

37

Outside it was cool and brisk, but the sun shone. A boy in a peaked cap, round-collared shirt, and bow tie shouted the morning's headline, selling the *New York Herald* from a stack he held under his arm. The war, that's all anyone was talking about; and everywhere one looked were flags and recruitment posters and young men in uniform.

A line of black taxis sat in a row at the curb. Dr. Roeder waited impatiently for the two women ahead, fashionably dressed with skirt hems just above their ankles (a mother and daughter on a shopping expedition, he guessed), to get into the first cab. He ushered Rosaline into the second, and gave the driver the address of the police station where they were to meet Detective Malone.

"It might take some time," warned the driver. "Traffic's the worst I've ever seen. Mrs. Belmont's leading a motorcade, trying to drum up enlistment."

As the cab rattled west, then turned north on Fifth Avenue, Dr. Roeder sat quietly observing the passing world. Lately he had come to think of Minuit as bustling, a sign of how provincial he had become, he realized now. The streets of New York seemed to him to be teeming. There were horse drawn carts stacked with goods, electric trolleys jammed with passengers; there were taxis, automobiles, people everywhere; and what once had been exclusively an avenue of palatial homes, grand hotels, and soaring cathedrals, now boasted some of the finest shops in the city housed in flamboyant new buildings, their stylish fronts, in a rare display of patriotism, draped in American flags.

"How changed everything is," he commented finally.

"Yes," said Rosaline. "New buildings seem almost to spring up over night."

How strange, thought the doctor, that even the young should notice. Wasn't it usually old fogies like him who felt as if the world were spinning out of control?

As the taxi passed the spot where Madame Restell's old house had once stood at Fifth Avenue and Fifty-second Street, its presence an affront to her respectable neighbors, another dram of the doctor's determined optimism seeped away. A notorious figure in his youth, the madam was an abortionist who had made a fortune out of her unlucky patrons, then slit her throat in her own bathtub when the vice squad took her dare and went after her. A horrible way to die, he thought. Horrible. Far worse than drowning.

"Some of the buildings are quite pretty, though, don't you think?" continued Rosaline, pointing to the facade of Schumann's Sons, a jewelry store.

"Too pretty, if you ask me," replied her father, regarding with a frown the curved iron balcony of the offending edifice, the awning projecting above the door like some odd medieval headdress. A handsome limestone front with a few supporting columns, that was about as fancy an architecture as he liked.

Apprehension growing with each tick of the meter, father and daughter lapsed into silence. By the time the taxi reached Central Park South, fear lay heavy on the doctor's heart. Then, he had a comforting thought: if Lily was alive, she would by now have returned to her hotel and discovered the uproar her absence had caused. She would have telephoned to her mother. Yes. His heart lightened again. The taxi turned onto Broadway, then onto West Sixty-eighth Street, and stopped at the station house. The doctor helped his daughter out and paid the driver. Taking Rosaline by the arm, he hurried her up the steps and inside. Yes. By now someone would have phoned Detective Malone with the news, and he would appear before them smiling a relieved, apologetic smile, sorry to have caused so much unnecessary trouble.

When the detective came out to greet them, however, his face was grim, and Dr. Roeder felt the surge of hope recede. Malone's eyes were heavy with fatigue, not just from lack of sleep, the doctor suspected, but with the accumulated burden of interviews like the one he was about to conduct. Not more than thirty-five, he was clean-shaven and wore a navy suit, a celluloid collar, and a plain necktie. His features were strong, his manner firm; his handshake was that of a confident man.

After the introductions were completed and excuses made for Henrietta's absence, the detective said, "If you don't mind returning here with me later to deal with the paperwork, we can talk in the car, on the way to the . . . " He hesitated, and then continued, "On the way to view the deceased. It might save time."

"It would, I'm sure, if there's been a mistake."

"Yes," said Malone. "Please, if you'll come this way." He murmured a few words to a sergeant seated behind the high oak desk and then led Dr. Roeder and Rosaline into a narrow corridor, past closed doors, and out of the building into an alley where a police car stood waiting, its driver leaning against a black fender. Malone cast a disapproving glance at the man, who hastily stubbed out his cigarette, buttoned his uniform collar, and opened the rear door, offering a hand to Rosaline to help her in. The doctor sat next to her. The driver closed the door and got behind the wheel. Malone climbed into the front seat beside him.

"The morgue is still at Bellevue?" asked the doctor, though he knew perfectly well it was. He simply wanted to establish his credentials.

The detective turned, cast a quick look at Rosaline, as if trying to assess how she would handle the coming ordeal, and then said, "Yes, it is."

"I interned there."

Rosaline reached for her father's hand, but otherwise betrayed no emotion. She was, after all, his daughter. She could always be relied on in a crisis, which was why he had finally given in to her arguments and allowed her to accompany him.

The police car rattled downtown along Broadway, passing endless automobile dealerships. Lily's cousin, Louis Allen, worked in one of them, the doctor remembered. Poor Louis. He would take Lily's death very hard. And there was the massively ugly Olympia Theater. He had taken his wife there once, to see . . . what? He had forgotten, but he recalled that they had dined in the restaurant afterward, and Violet had admired the roof garden. He really ought to bring her to the city again, sometime soon. She enjoyed going to see a play every now and again.

What a street of memories this was! They passed the Casino Theatre, where he and Titus Canning had gone (before he had stopped accompanying Titus on his jaunts) to see first Lillian Russell, and then Evelyn Nesbit perform. A veritable Venus she may have been, drive men to murder or what you will, she couldn't hold a candle to Lily, that Evelyn Nesbit, thought the doctor. Rosaline is pretty enough, but that Lily! What a beauty the girl was!

Is, he corrected himself. Is!

"I've been wondering," the doctor heard Rosaline say, "about the man who tried to rescue . . . the young woman. Is he all right?"

"Yes," said Malone, turning his head. "No worse for the ordeal. We dried him off, cleaned him up as best we could. Got him a new suit." He ventured a grin. "Well, it may be it isn't exactly new."

"It was a brave thing to do, plunging into the river like that."

"Drink makes a lot of fellows foolhardy."

"Well now, detective, there's many a fellow living rough, you'd think no better than an animal," said the doctor, irritated by the man's smug self-righteousness. "But as often as not they come from good people. Once they might have been clean living, hardworking, as sober as you or I, before whatever calamity it was struck. Before the drink got them."

"We had a talk with him, in case there was more to what happened than he let on," replied the detective, ignoring the doctor's appeal to a common humanity.

"You think he might have had something to do with it?" asked Rosaline, relief and horror mixed equally in her voice.

"It's our job to look at a situation from every angle, ma'am. But I'm confident that everything was just as he said. He would hardly have waited around otherwise. And the lady's purse was still wrapped around her wrist when the police arrived. There was money inside it, a tidy sum. It's doubtful a man like that . . ." The detective cast a brief look at the doctor and then continued, "A man so down on his luck, would have let it be, had his intentions been in any way dishonorable." The range of those possible "intentions" made Rosaline shudder. "Her effects are at the station house," continued the detective. "Her clothes, the money, a few pieces of jewelry. A lapel pin, a ring, nothing very grand."

The sort of things any young woman might wear, thought Dr. Roeder, anyone at all.

"There were no other witnesses?" asked Rosaline.

"There was a dance going on at the yacht club, but no one there seems to have noticed a thing."

Ah, yes, thought the doctor. Louis Allen belonged to the club, along with several other young men from Minuit. Trust Rosaline to remember that.

The car continued down Broadway, past R.H. Macy's, turning east on Thirtieth Street, moving toward First Avenue and Bellevue Hospital. Not only had Dr. Roeder interned there, it was where he had met his wife. She had caught his eye one day while visiting her father who was there for some minor surgery. Such a lovely thing she was, small, slender, exquisitely fair, and quiet, very different from Henrietta. Not so much smitten as curious about his reaction to the girl, the intern had made himself attentive to the family; and, taking him for a poor struggling student, they had in gratitude invited him to their home on East Eighty-seventh Street one Sunday for "a goot meal," as his future mother-in-law had called it. By the time he realized their mistake and put them straight, he had determined to marry Violet, which (given what turned out to be his irreproachable background and bright future prospects) had delighted her parents. It was a confusion they had all laughed about for many years afterward. He and Violet sometimes still had a good chuckle over it.

The doctor sighed. He had never regretted marrying Violet, never. He had put away the hurt of Henrietta's preferring Titus to him and got on with his life. He had been a good husband, he liked to think. Certainly Violet frequently said so, however much she sometimes seemed to resent

42

the claims others made on his time (though what she expected a doctor to do about that, he had no idea). He had been a good father, indulgent perhaps, but firm when it counted. And he had succeeded at both without sacrificing his friendship with Etta, for he did not consider his feelings for her to be in any way in conflict with those for his wife and children. And for Etta's sake, however repelled he sometimes was by her husband's behavior, the doctor had been Titus' loyal friend as well, keeping his secrets to his death, and after.

It all suddenly came back to him, the last time he had run just such an errand for Henrietta: the house off Gramercy Park, the discreet stone front, the opulent interior, the half-dressed girls in the parlor, the worried madam, Titus lying naked on the silk sheets in the "Turkish Salon," dead of a heart attack. He could not say that it had been easy, but the doctor had stifled his anger, his disgust. He had let pity carry the day. And no matter the rumors, never had he let fall a hint, not even to George Allen, that the "hotel" to which he had gone to fetch the dead Titus home had been a bordello.

Did Etta ever suspect, wondered the doctor, to what lengths he sometimes went to protect her?

"Here we are," said the detective.

For the first time in his life, the sight of the hospital's massive brick edifice rising up before him struck fear in Erich Roeder's heart. Following Detective Malone along the bleak corridors, the last vestige of hope left him, leaving in its place not despair, but acceptance, so that when at last, with the detective and the coroner beside him, he stood looking at the unfortunate young woman lying so still, her beautiful dark eyes closed, her hair a black nimbus surrounding a face with the pale sheen of death on it, her bare shoulders rising as cold and white as marble out of the cloth that covered the rest of her slender body, he was filled only with an overwhelming sadness.

"Is it Lily?" asked Rosaline.

43

The doctor had asked her to wait at the entrance of the viewing room until he was certain. He turned to her now and said, "Yes, it's Lily." The purse had not been stolen. There had been no mistake. He extended an arm, and Rosaline came and stood within its circle.

Grief welled in her and streamed from her eyes as she regarded the face of her friend. Reaching out a hand, she touched the bruise on the right temple; then, leaning forward, she kissed the cold cheek. "Oh, Lily," she murmured.

"I'm sorry," said Detective Malone. His voice was emotionless, polite.

"Indeed, very sorry," said Nelson Carter, the somehow inappropriately big and blustery man who was the coroner. He had been a classmate of Dr. Roeder's in medical school, which was a blessing, for his help was needed.

The doctor tightened his hold on his daughter. "Thank you," he said. And at that moment he remembered Lily as she had been once, not quite fifteen years old, the summer she had painted the portrait of him that now hung above the mantle in his parlor. He had posed dressed in his best black suit, seated in a wingback chair, his hound Gertrude at his feet. "Mind you make me look distinguished," he had told her.

"As distinguished as if Sargent himself had painted you," she had replied, laughing, so full of life and confidence, a stained smock covering her flounced white dress, dashing forward, brush extended, to place a stroke of paint on the canvas. And indeed it had been a wonderful portrait, so good that it had taken first prize at the next County Fair.

Who would have thought that beautiful girl would come to this?

A private word with Nelson Carter left Dr. Roeder assured that no mention would be made of suicide. There was no moon that night. In the dark (the doctor suggested, and the coroner concurred), the sole witness, who had not been quite sober, might easily have mistaken the circumstances. Lily's death could very well have been an accident. In any case, in the absence of a note, in the absence of any confirmation of a distraught state of mind, it was impossible to prove otherwise.

Presuming further on his acquaintance with Carter, Dr. Roeder made use of his office to make the arrangements for Lily's body to be taken back to Minuit; and when that was done, after thanking his friend for himself and for Henrietta, he and his daughter returned with the detective to the station house. There, Rosaline was able to identify Lily's tapestry purse, the ruined sketchbook, her butterfly pin, the opal ring her parents had given her for her fifteenth birthday. When the doctor had signed the necessary papers, Malone turned the items over to them along with Lily's money and her clothes, all bundled into a neat package. Again, he expressed his sympathy.

"One more thing," said Rosaline, to forestall his ushering them out. "The man, the one who tried to save Lily? We would like to thank him."

"Do you have any idea how we might go about finding him?" asked the doctor, keen to do the right thing now that Rosaline had reminded him.

"We put him in a holding cell," said Malone, "in case we needed to ask him more questions. There's no other way to keep tabs on a vagrant," he explained. "Turn your back and they've gone."

He left the room, and the doctor and Rosaline sat silent for a while, waiting. "This is all so unreal," said Rosaline finally. "I can't believe any of it is happening."

"It's the shock," replied the doctor.

"Damn Edmund Farel! Damn him!"

The doctor said nothing. Though normally he might have argued that — however much he disliked the wretch — Lily's behavior, not just this last bit of madness, but even her hasty marriage and its sorry aftermath, could not all be laid at Farel's feet, at the moment it seemed best to be quiet. There would be time enough for further postmortems in the days, even the years, ahead. He reached across the space between their two straight-backed chairs and clasped the hand picking at the fabric of the apricot dress. "Now, my dear, we've a long way to go yet. You must hold on."

Withdrawing her hand from his, Rosaline opened her purse, took out a linen handkerchief, and dabbed at her eyes and nose. "There," she said, hazarding a small, tight-lipped smile.

Hearing the door open, they turned to see Detective Malone and, shuffling into the room behind him, a tall reedy man with the stooped frame and gaunt look of one who has gone for too long without wholesome food. He had a long face, its paleness exaggerated by a sparse gingery beard and hair to match. He looked to be about forty, though he might have been far younger. In his practice, the doctor had seen too many people aged beyond their years by the hardness of their lives.

As the doctor and Rosaline got to their feet, the detective closed the door, leaving a uniformed policeman on guard in the hall, though that hardly seemed necessary. "Here he is," said the detective. "Daniels. Roland Daniels." He turned to the vagrant. "These are the folks I was telling you about, Dr. Roeder and his daughter, Mrs. Schuyler."

The suit found for Daniels looked worn and far too large, the trousers pooling around his battered shoes, the sleeves of the jacket extending to his fingertips. The hand he extended to the doctor in greeting was rough, but delicate in shape, the nails jagged and lined with dirt.

"We're friends of the family, my daughter and I. We'd like to express to you our gratitude, and that of Lily's mother. I only wish your efforts had succeeded."

"It was very brave of you," said Rosaline, offering her hand to the man, "to go into the river like that, after her."

Daniels wiped his hand on his jacket before taking Rosaline's, and then said, "Was that her name? Lily? She looked a lovely girl."

"She was," said Rosaline, her eyes again filling with tears.

46

"I couldn't be sure at first what was happening. There was no moon, you see. I went closer to have a look." He turned his head away and said, "I did what I could, but it took too long."

"We're very grateful you tried," said the doctor.

"It's too bad, it is," said Daniels, meeting the doctor's eyes. His sorrow seemed genuine, heavy. He seemed weighed down by his failure to prevent yet another story being added to the world's collection of sorry tales.

The doctor rummaged in the package the detective had given him and extracted the damp bundle of salvaged bills. "This doesn't come near to matching our appreciation of your . . . heroism, that's the word for it, but we'd like you to take it, if you would. It's what was in Lily's purse when you pulled her from the river."

"Ah no, I couldn't," said Daniels, taking a step back. For a moment, he seemed to inhabit a former life, one where valorous deeds were not uncommon, where pride prohibited acceptance of a reward for what, after all, had been the only right and decent thing to do.

"Come, man, don't be foolish," said the doctor, his hand outstretched. "Lily has no more need of money, and I'm sure you can make use of it."

"I wish you would take it," said Rosaline, "if only to make us feel a little better."

Need overcame scruples. Daniels shrugged his narrow shoulders, stretched out his hand, and took the sheaf of bills. "It will come in handy, you're right about that," he said. "My thanks to you both. It's most generous of you. Most generous." Then, all vestige of his past disappeared, and he was once again only a vagrant, albeit a mannerly one.

The doctor turned to Malone. "You won't be needing him anymore, will you? Your investigation is closed?"

The detective hesitated a moment, and then said, "Yes, it's closed." He turned to Daniels. "You get along with you now," he went on, adding, an afterthought, "You've earned yourself a bit of leeway around here, but see you don't go taking advantage of it." He extended his hand to the surprised man, who shook it, and then shuffled out of the room through the door Malone opened for him. "He can go," he told the waiting policeman.

"We should be going, too," said Rosaline. "We've taken up quite enough of your time." Malone murmured a few last, halting words. The doctor thanked him for his efforts on their behalf and shook his hand, as did Rosaline who offered him a smile and said, "You've been very kind. Thank you."

He's anxious for us to be gone, thought the doctor, as Malone ushered him and Rosaline out of the station house. And who could blame him? A sad case, yet not a particularly interesting one to a detective. There was no mystery, no excitement, only the reality of a death, and the ordeal of having to cope with grieving family and friends. He would go home to his wife, home to a railroad apartment, the doctor imagined, simply but nicely furnished, up in Washington Heights, or across the river in Brooklyn perhaps. When she asked, he would tell her that nothing much had happened at work that tour. Nothing much. Just another dead woman, a suicide, no matter what the coroner's report said. Not a prostitute this time, or a pregnant girl, curiously enough, but a well-brought-up young woman, a beautiful woman, with everything to live for. Why, the wife might ask. Only God knows, the detective would say.

Only God.

It was hours since they had eaten, and then only breakfast, buttered toast and some coffee, before they had rushed off to see Henrietta. They ought to have been hungry, but, when the doctor and Rosaline stopped for a bite to eat at the Plaza Hotel, neither of them could do more than push their food listlessly around on their plates. Surrounded by the marble columns of the Tea Room, the tall palms in their Chinese pots, the clusters of women, the husbands and wives, the dating couples, the family groups in their best city clothes, in the midst of such normalcy, Dr. Roeder was aware of a nebulous feeling of unreality. He might just have awakened from a nightmare, or drifted off into a pleasant dream.

The hum of voices rose around them and mingled with the sound of the string quartet playing on the dais at the far end of the room. Something by Brahms — a German, thought the doctor with some satisfaction. War hysteria had apparently not found its way into this staid haven of upper-middle-class pleasure, at least not yet; and though some of the talk must surely revolve around the war, there was no evidence of fear in the faces he could see from his vantage point. Even the few young men of fighting age looked more excited than worried, except for one, but the cause of his distress seemed to be a lover's quarrel. The young woman sitting opposite him, a lovely thing in a smart astrakhan hat, was spitting fire. Were they engaged? wondered the doctor. Newly married?

He looked across the table at his daughter and thanked God for her. She had caused him few moments of grief in her life. Indeed, he could count them on one hand: that winter she had come down with pneumonia, the time she and Lily had taken the rowboat out on the river without permission, the day she had gone off to join in a suffrage march, here in the city. Not that he was against women getting the vote, by no means, but he had feared the potential for violence. Needlessly, it turned out. Though boisterous, the march had proceeded without serious incident, and Rosaline had returned home unscathed, if even more ardently devoted to the cause than before. She was strong-willed, his Rosaline, and vehement in defense of her beliefs, though far too levelheaded to be labeled rabid. She had courage coupled with good sense, compassion with sound judgment. She was everything a father could wish for; and today he could not help wondering why it was that he had been so fortunate, not just in Rosaline, but in his boys as well, while Henrietta, as good a woman who had ever breathed, as tender and caring a mother, had been made to

49

suffer so much, losing two children, then bearing Lily, only to endure her depressions, her follies, and now finally this, her death.

Rosaline felt his glance and looked up from her plate. "Sitting here it's hard, isn't it, to believe that all's not well with the world?"

"You're a good girl," he said.

She returned his brief smile with a frown. "It has nothing to do with goodness," she snapped. "You above all people should know that. There was never a better person than Lily."

"She was indeed very special."

"You were always hard on her."

"Now that's too strong, Rosaline."

"Even before the business with Farel."

Frequently, when Lily was the subject of conversation, Rosaline reminded her father of Sheba, their cat, back arched and spitting whenever anyone tried to get within reach of a new litter. His daughter was fiercely protective of her friend, whom she had always known to be, despite the bravura, so much weaker than herself. "I worried about her, that's true enough," he said. And with good reason, he thought. From adolescence, Lily had suffered from migraines and bouts of depression. At times, she would be high-spirited and full of mischief; at others, withdrawn into herself, saying and doing little, or nothing, for days, weeks, sometimes months. In those periods, she was so tentatively present that it was possible to be sitting next to her and forget she was there. When "herself," however, like her father, she had an electric quality — she could light up a room — though even then she was inclined to spend far too much time in that studio of hers, with sticks of charcoal and tubes of paint, when she ought to have been enjoying herself with people of her own age. Still, the doctor could not help but admire her diligence, and her talent, or resist the temptation to cater to both. He had once spent a considerable amount of his leisure time teaching her anatomy, a necessity, she had insisted (and she could not have been more than fourteen, at the time), if she hoped to make any progress in drawing. "And I worried about her influence on you," he continued, to Rosaline. "And with good cause, you'll have to grant me. Lily could be very reckless. But I couldn't have loved her more if she were one of my own."

Rosaline sighed. "I know. Forgive me, Papa. I'm just so . . . How could she have done it? Especially now, with her show about to open? She was looking forward to it. I know she was. She was excited, optimistic. Everything was so much better than a few months ago. Then, I might have understood it!" She stopped, and then continued more quietly, "No, I wouldn't have, not even then."

"You know what Lily was like, swinging on the moon one minute, crouching at the gates of hell the next."

"Will the exhibition go ahead now, do you think? I have to confess that I don't quite understand what she was getting at in some of her recent paintings, but . . . well, she was so eager to have them shown."

"I don't know what's usually done in these circumstances. I'll talk to Etta. And to the gallery, if she likes. I'm sure something can be worked out."

"I hope so. Lily would be just devastated to have it cancelled." Rosaline stopped, and then went on. "Oh God, I really can't believe it." She gave her father a bleak look and said, "What could have happened to make her do such a thing?"

Indeed, that was the question now. "Do you know . . . has she . . . has Farel been anywhere around?" he asked.

Rosaline's gray eyes widened. "No! At least, Lily never mentioned him. Not in months anyway. You don't think—"

The doctor shrugged. "I don't know what to think." He felt the familiar pain in his gut. Glancing at the remaining food on their plates, the remnants of sandwiches and cakes, he beckoned to a waiter. They were clearly not going to eat any more. "We should go," he said to Rosaline, "if you've finished."

"Oh, yes," she replied. "I've never felt less like eating in my life."

51

By the time they left the hotel it was mid-afternoon and the sun hovered behind them, wrapping Grand Army Plaza in a golden haze. In the park across the way it fell invitingly on the budding trees, and on any other day the doctor might have suggested a ride in one of the horse cabs still used to take visitors on excursions. Today, however, carrying the detective's neat bundle in one hand, he took his daughter's elbow with the other and, dodging a brand new Maxwell with an obviously inexperienced driver, together they crossed to the opposite sidewalk and continued down Fifth Avenue, past the Vanderbilt mansion, very like a grand French chateau dominating the entire block. As they turned onto West Fifty-sixth Street, the light vanished and a chill filled the air. At the entrance to the Pelham Hotel, though a young man in a handsome blue uniform snapped to attention to open the door for them, they paused as if stopped by an invisible barrier. Then, gathering their courage, they proceeded inside.

The Pelham was an elegant nine-storey building, its facade a combination of limestone and brick, with twin columns supporting a balcony cornice at the front. Originally an apartment hotel for bachelors, after the turn of the century it had opened for more general use. It was where Lily had lived with her parents while studying at the Art Students League, and where she had stayed afterward whenever in the city, until recently, when she had given it up in favor of the Gotham or the Astor, which had the virtue of being totally lacking in associations, pleasant or otherwise.

"I should have known something was wrong when she said she was staying here again," murmured Rosaline to her father. "But I thought it was a good sign that she felt ready to return."

"We all did," said the doctor, though he wondered how he could have missed all the warnings, for surely there must have been some, little cries of distress that neither he, nor anyone else, had heard.

The lobby was small but attractive, its parquet floor covered by an Oriental rug. Scattered across it were groupings of lounge chairs covered in brocaded silk, occupied by guests drinking tea, reading newspapers, smoking cigars, cigarettes, pipes, cheroots, a haze of smoke hovering in the air above their heads. From the coffered ceiling hung brass chandeliers with globes of amber glass. A massive flower arrangement stood on a table beside the staircase, and on the wood-paneled walls hung landscape paintings. One of them, near the front desk, caught the doctor's eye. It was a small painting of a familiar scene, the Hudson from the vantage point of the Cannings' back porch. Sure enough, when he looked closely, there was Lily's signature in the right-hand corner. The doctor turned to Rosaline, who stood studying it. Finally, she said, "The owner asked for it in lieu of a week's rent when Lily was here as a student, he liked it so much. He got a bargain, don't you think?"

"You got yours for nothing," teased the doctor. A similar painting, featuring the same view, but in winter, hung in Rosaline's parlor. It showed two young girls, splashes of viridian and rose in a brilliant winter light, at play on a cottony hill that billowed in soft folds down to the river, a solid expanse of gray-green ice butting against the snow-covered mountains opposite.

"It was a birthday present," said Rosaline, with a pretense of indignation. And, caught for a moment in the memory of that happier time, she gave him her first genuine smile of the day. "Though she gave it very grudgingly, I have to say. You know what she was like."

Indeed, Lily had never liked to part with her paintings. She had clung to her work until the last possible moment, trying relentlessly to make it better, never willing to accept less than the very best from herself. Given a few more years, she would have learned, as he had, as everyone must to go on living any reasonable sort of life, the necessity of compromise, the blessing of it. Perfection, after all, was an attribute only of God, and any human aspiration to it bound to fall short. To do one's best, yes, always. But to accept one's limitations, there was freedom in that, and peace.

At the desk, they explained their business to the clerk on duty. He called for the manager, a Mr. Locke, who had heard from the night staff of the appearance of the police at the hotel in the early hours, and of Miss Canning's mysteriously empty room. Nonetheless, he seemed shaken to have her death confirmed. He was short and stocky, with sand-colored hair and a neat moustache. His frock coat looked fresh and new, as if worn for the first time that day; his shoes were polished to a high sheen. "Such a lovely young lady," he said, his voice quavering with emotion. There was a quality in his distress the doctor could not quite put his finger on. "Why, only yesterday . . ." Locke told them of his last sighting of Lily as she left the hotel the previous evening, just before he went off duty. She had sailed past him looking lovely as always, smiling, calling him by name, wishing him a good evening, and asking to speak with him in the morning — that very morning. Clearly, Locke would have liked more details. He would have liked to know how she had come to be walking alone in Riverside Park late at night, how she had managed to fall into the river and drown. "What a terrible thing," he said.

"Yes," agreed the doctor, "a dreadful accident." And that's what it would be, except to the very few who must know otherwise, an "accident," not only to still the gossip, but also to allow a Christian burial. Etta's heart would break for certain should Lily be denied a service at St. Mark's.

The manager offered to accompany them up to the room, but, when the doctor insisted there was no need, he escorted them only as far as the elevator, where he turned them over to a man in the hotel's blue livery. As the elevator rose to the sixth floor, the operator cast a few curious glances their way, but said nothing, hesitating even to offer a word of sympathy; and, once he had pointed them in the right direction, he closed the elevator's brass door quickly, anxious to get away.

"That Mr. Locke is a little in love with Lily," said Rosaline, following her father along the corridor.

"So that's it," he said. "I knew there was something."

"Men were always falling in love with her." There was not a hint of resentment in Rosaline's voice. "Even when we were children, the boys used to get up to all sorts of nonsense trying to attract her attention. She was so beautiful."

"That was hardly a blessing, as it turned out."

"I don't think she even noticed."

"Oh, she noticed all right. She just didn't care." After all, what room had there been in Lily's life for any other man as long as Titus was alive? And, to do him justice, his adventures had always taken second place to his daughter. He had been not only her father, but her friend, her mentor, her companion. And all the eager young men who had come courting, the young knights determined to win the princess in the tower, had found themselves defeated, and not as much by the father's stern condescension as by the daughter's complete lack of interest in their plumes and sabers, their good looks and sparkling ambition. None of them could shake Lily's satisfaction with the life she already had: the financial comfort, the doting parents, the safe haven, the time to paint. If she had longed for anything more, the doctor had sometimes suspected, it was not for a husband, not for children, but for a talent greater than the one she possessed. Her involvement with Farel had shocked him as much as everyone else.

"Here it is," said Rosaline, stopping in front of the door to Lily's room.

Dr. Roeder took the key the manager had given him, turned it in the lock, and led the way through the door and small foyer into a parlor overlooking the street. It was furnished simply, with a sofa and armchairs upholstered in a flower pattern, matching draperies, a sideboard against one wall, and a small lace-covered dining table between the front windows, some apples in a glass bowl on top of it. Lily's box easel, which she never traveled without, leaned closed against one of the dining chairs. The police had barred anyone from entering, even to clean, and so everything was just as she had left it. There were newspapers in a basket on the floor near the fireplace, a small photograph of Titus and Henrietta in a leather frame on the mantle, and a few magazines on a side table. The door to the cooking closet was slightly open, and the doctor could make out the sink and gas range behind it.

Adjacent to the parlor were the bedroom and bath, and here, too, there was ample evidence of Lily's occupancy: clothes strewn about, the closet door ajar, a pair of shoes and some boots on the floor, a portmanteau beside them, a strand of pearls draped over the ornate frame of the dressing table mirror, her satin jewelry case left open, her toiletries still in the bathroom. The rooms looked as if whoever inhabited them had stepped out only for a while, with every intention of returning.

"Oh, my," whispered Rosaline, sinking onto the dressing table stool. "She couldn't have planned it. She couldn't have! It must have been an accident, just as you said."

"Did I?" asked the doctor, but then he remembered he had used the word in his conversation with the manager, Locke. Well, why not let Rosaline believe it an accident, if that would make her feel better? The truth once again seemed a luxury, one likely to cause more harm than good; and, if he felt the need to cling to it himself, there was certainly no necessity for him to inflict it on anyone else. "Of course she didn't plan it," he said.

But when Rosaline's eyes met his, the doctor knew that there was no hiding from the truth for her either. With a shake of her head, she said, "Lily might not have gone to the river thinking she would never come back. But it wasn't an accident."

"We don't know for certain what happened, my dear. Of course, we'll have to tell Etta what we suspect," he said. "Though I wish to God it wasn't necessary. As for everyone else, you understand, the less said, the better."

She nodded. "Yes. As few people as possible must know."

Though the police had already searched and found nothing, no letter from Lily to her mother, no word to anyone, still the doctor cautioned Rosaline to keep an eye out for a note as she packed Lily's belongings into the portmanteau. While he gathered up the personal items Lily had left scattered about, he had a good look around the parlor himself; and though he had not really expected they would find any sort of communication from her, when they had finished, Dr. Roeder nevertheless became aware of a gnawing sense of disappointment. However intriguing the human mind might find mysteries, it found them intolerable as well, racing to the end of murder stories to discover the villain, worrying any problem through sleepless nights — through centuries, if that's how long it took — to solve it. And while it could hardly matter in any concrete way just why Lily had decided to take her own life, still it would be a relief to know, and a comfort to Henrietta to have an explanation, however painful it might be to hear.

"Did Lily keep a diary?" he asked his daughter as they retraced their steps to the elevator, a bellman following behind with the portmanteau and boxes.

"Not that she ever mentioned. No, I'm sure she didn't," said Rosaline. "She hated writing anything, even a letter. Oh . . ." she added in a whisper, then went on, the anger that she had directed at others once or twice during the day now finding its true object, "but you'd have thought this once she might have made an exception. Didn't she think of us at all?"

"I don't suppose so. If she had, things might have turned out differently."

They took the elevator back down to the lobby, where Mr. Locke insisted on escorting them outside. "If I can be of any assistance to you, please let me know," he said, as the bellman strapped Lily's things into the taxi's luggage compartment. Refusing the doctor's offered tip, the manager added, "I was very fond of Miss Canning. Never a complaint from her. Always a kind word to say. A gracious lady. If you think I might, I'd like to write to her mother. I have the address on file."

"I'm sure Mrs. Canning would appreciate it," said Rosaline.

"Then I will," he said with great seriousness, as if committing himself to a daring act. He helped them into the taxi, closed its door, executed a small bow, and turned to reenter the hotel.

As the taxi pulled away from the curb, a giggling Rosaline turned to her father. "Definitely in love."

"Without a doubt," said the doctor, joining in the laughter. It felt good to laugh, no matter how slight the cause.

"Do you remember that funny little boy . . . what was his name? The one who lived over near the limestone quarry? Ned? Yes, that's it. Ned. Do you remember how he used just to turn up at Riverhall? Lily insisted it was because he was hungry and Aunt Etta always gave him something to eat. As if Mama wouldn't have done the same! Or Mrs. Allen, though it's hard to think of any boy having a crush on Florence. She was so horrid to everyone!"

"Now, dear, there's no need to be unkind," the doctor said reflexively. Over the years, he had often found himself having to mediate when conversation turned to Florence.

"Oh, she's much nicer now," conceded Rosaline. "But she was always jealous of Lily, who didn't have an ounce of conceit in her. Not one! Why, I could never get her to admit that Ned walked all the way to River-hall only for the pleasure of seeing her, and was no doubt late home to his perfectly adequate dinner. How I used to tease her!" she said, laughing again, but this time the sound turned quickly to a sob. She turned her head into her father's shoulder. "Oh, Papa!"

He took her hands in his and held them, hoping to offer some comfort with his touch, for as great as his own sorrow was, he knew it could not compare to Rosaline's. The girls had been close, as close as sisters. No, he corrected himself, even closer, because their relationship had not come from an accident of birth, but from choice. They had chosen each other as children, and the bond forged between them when they were as little as two or three, playing with their china dolls and tea sets, had survived the usual childish spats, had outlasted separations, had even withstood the rival claims made by family, by marriage. Nothing, no one, in all their lives had been able to part them, until this. Was it any wonder that Rosaline was finding it difficult to believe that Lily would willingly go off and leave her behind forever? Rosaline could not have done it. Loyalty would have held her back, loyalty and love.

But Rosaline had been blessed with an essentially happy, optimistic temperament. Depression had never laid its heavy hand on her heart. Despair had never sucked the breath from her body. She was someone who could be relied on to find the one flower in any field of weeds. The doctor thought of Lily as she had been four months before, listless, unhappy, her skin dull, her clothes hanging from her too-slender frame, her head bowed under the weight of the terrible thoughts she would share with no one. How could Rosaline, how could anyone who was not Lily, understand what it had cost to live with such a burden? How could any of them judge whether, if similarly afflicted, they would have been able to pay the price?

$$\mathcal{L}$$

On their way back to Grand Central Station, they made one more brief stop, at the offices of the *New York Times*, where Rosaline waited in the taxi while Dr. Roeder went inside to place the notice of Lily's death. Afterward they continued on, arriving at the station in plenty of time to make the five-twenty-two train.

"There's no need for a porter," said the doctor as he tipped the driver. "We can manage." He handed the hatboxes to Rosaline, and picked up the portmanteau and box easel.

Outside and in, the station was a bedlam of activity, with newsboys crying their headlines, young men engaged in heated conversations, commuters returning home after a day in the city, travelers setting out on a journey, friends and lovers and family members seeing one another off. The ticket queues in the main hall straggled back almost to the information booth. The doctor checked the board for the number of the departure gate, and then led the way through the crowd. He thought of Etta and his heart sank at the ordeal that lay ahead.

"Poor, poor Aunt Etta," said Rosaline, echoing his thoughts.

He saw a newsstand and stopped. The war figured in the headlines of all the evening papers. There were quotes from the president's speech, updated reports about the sinking of the steamship, *Aztec*, by torpedo boats, speculations about conscription. He bought several newspapers and some magazines. They would need distraction on the long train ride home if they hoped to arrive in any fit state to deal with Henrietta.

It was fifteen minutes before their departure time, and they went directly to the train. The day had exhausted them, as well as the subject of Lily. They had nothing left to say to one another and retreated behind the newspapers, exchanging them without a word when they finished, the doctor hoping that the small item in each, about the drowning of an unknown woman, would escape his daughter's notice.

The train made its way slowly north, following the course of the Hudson, stopping from time to time to set down and pick up passengers. Spuyten Duyvil, Tarrytown, Peekskill . . . Flags snapped to attention in the evening breeze. Recruitment posters pinned hastily to the walls fought the wind to get free. At Garrison, the doctor looked up to gaze across the river at the imposing hulk of West Point. He thought of the vital young men now training there who, hoping for glory, in the name of patriotism, would soon have to face the horror of battle and the possibility of death. He thought of all the young men scattered across the vast country, his sons among them. Oh, dear God, no, he thought. I will fear no evil, he prayed, for thou art with me. Thy rod and thy staff, they comfort me. He looked at Rosaline, but her eyes were closed and she appeared to be dozing, a copy of *Collier's Weekly* open in her lap. Surely goodness and mercy shall follow me all the days of my life.

At last the train arrived in Minuit. The doctor awakened Rosaline, and they disembarked in a flurry of passengers. Refusing the stationmaster's offer of help, they made their way across the cobbled street to where Dr. Roeder had parked his Studebaker that morning. They traveled the distance to Riverhall in silence. When they reached the house, he stopped the car in the gravel drive in front of the porch steps. Still wordless, he and Rosaline got out, collected Lily's things, mounted the steps to the front door, and then, dreading what was to come, hesitated a moment before the doctor finally reached for the knocker.

The door was flung open so quickly that Nuala might have been standing in wait for them. She stepped aside to let them in, looking anxiously from Dr. Roeder's face to Rosaline's, and back again. The doctor shook his head.

"Ah, no," said Nuala.

"Where's Mrs. Canning?" he asked as he set down the portmanteau and box easel.

"In her room. She went up again not half an hour ago for another lie down. She was that tired, after sitting all the afternoon, staring into space. I'll go wake her," she said.

"Let me," offered Rosaline, dropping the hatboxes onto the settle, but she had made it only to the third step when Henrietta appeared at the top of the stairs.

Her hair was awry and she was shoeless. Her eyes were glazed with fatigue. "I heard the knocker," she said. "Did you bring Lily home?"

"Etta . . ." said Doctor Roeder, hurrying past Rosaline. "I'm sorry."

Henrietta swayed back and forth on her bare feet. Reaching for the banister, she whimpered, "No . . ." Then again, "No, no, no . . ." A moment before the doctor reached her, she sank to a heap on the landing, buried her face in her hands, and filled the house with muffled wails.

As Rosaline raced up the stairs to join them and Nuala stood her ground weeping, the doctor sat next to Henrietta and pulled her into his arms. "Etta, I'm so very sorry." It occurred to him that now, having lost both Titus and Lily, whom she had loved and relied on beyond all others, it would be always to him she turned when troubled; and while he could not help but appreciate the irony of it, nor completely repress his shameful pleasure that at last he had got what once he had wanted beyond all things, what he mostly felt was pain. And at that moment he would gladly have sacrificed this final victory to have been spared the burden of delivering to her, his old friend, his dear love, this heart-breaking news. "Yes, Etta, cry. It will make you feel better," he said, though he knew it to be untrue. "Cry . . ."

NUALA

It was a terrible thing, an unbelievable thing, may God have mercy on the poor lady's soul, thought Nuala, standing there at the bottom of the stairs, listening as Dr. Roeder told Mrs. Canning, as gently as anyone could tell such things, what he had seen and learned that day. Holding the weeping woman, he said that Lily was now at peace in the House of the Lord, and that should be at least some comfort to her mother. They were words, only words. Nuala, who had seen her own mother mourn the death of a son killed in the endless skirmishing over Home Rule, knew that the missus would not be soothed by them, not at first, no matter how religious she was, though of course it was possible that Protestants differed in this way, too, from the wildly grieving Catholics of her experience, who shouted for retribution and took vengeance when they could.

Another of her brothers, Seamus, had shot one of the murdering soldiers ("executed" him, he said, for his crimes) and fled the country, the first of them to come to the United States. Two sons her mother had lost, when all was done, and a husband before, Nuala's Da, head groom at the largest estate in the county, kicked to death by one of Lord Falconer's mad horses. And for all that Dr. Larkin said it was her liver, it was grief that had worn her mother down, Nuala was sure of it. It had killed her and changed her children's lives beyond imagining, sending Liam, the oldest of them, off to join Seamus, who had found work on a horse farm in Kentucky, bringing the girls, six months later when their brothers sent the fare, to settle in New York.

"Would you fetch Mrs. Canning's shoes, please, Nuala," asked the doctor; and, as she slipped past the seated figures on the landing, she heard Rosaline whisper how her own heart was broken.

"Oh, my dear, how will we ever bear this?" Mrs. Canning sobbed in reply.

After Nuala returned with the shoes and helped Mrs. Canning on with them, the doctor coaxed the woman, now weeping more quietly, to her feet and down the stairs.

"Come," said Rosaline gently, taking her arm, guiding her toward the library.

Nuala wiped her eyes with a quick movement of both hands, dried them on her apron, and murmured the doctor's name. He turned to look at her. "The missus hasn't had but some coffee all day," she said. If anyone could get her to take food, he would. "I've some soup that only needs heating."

"Yes, bring it, please. I'll see that she eats something," he said. "Be with you in a moment," he called after the retreating figures of his daughter and Mrs. Canning. Stopping at the hall table, he picked up the telephone. As Nuala hurried off down the stairs to the kitchen, she heard him speaking first to the operator and then, his voice hushed almost to a whisper, to his wife, telling her that the news was not good and that he and Rosaline would stay until Henrietta was settled for the night.

Nuala had left the electric light on, and, as she entered the kitchen, she felt a brief flash of satisfaction at the orderliness of the room, not a thing out of place, the cooking pots — bright as new pennies — hanging from their racks. She had spent the long afternoon hours, while Mrs. Canning had sat so worryingly still in the library, in a fever of activity, cleaning and polishing, trying to ignore the waiting silence of the house.

Because of the slope of the hill, the kitchen was entirely above ground and bright for most of the day, then flooded with light in the late afternoon when the sun sank to the west. It had a gas range, an icebox, fitted pine cabinets and countertops, and a large plank table where Nuala often sat shelling peas or stringing beans. It was here she took her own meals, or sat chatting over tea with her sister when Deirdre called in on an errand from the Allens, or served up a bit of cake and some coffee to the tradesmen, if there was time. The grocer's lad fancied her, she knew, but though he was good-looking and then some with his mop of yellow hair and wicked blue eyes, he was a bit on the young side and not established well enough to suit her. When she married, she wanted to step up in the world.

After putting the soup on to heat, she took the loaf of freshly baked bread and began cutting thick, wholesome slices. It was all very well having mean slices for fancy sandwiches, but Mrs. Canning needed something more substantial tonight, something to help keep her strength up, for she would surely be needing it in the coming days. Assessing the contents of the icebox, Nuala decided she would make an omelet; and, after cutting the baked ham into pieces, she added them to the bubbling butter in the pan, whipped the eggs into a froth, spooned them in along with pinches of salt and pepper, and then folded the thing as it set into a perfect omelet, the color of sunlight on a summer afternoon, rich and golden. But something green was needed, and lettuce was not to be thought of as it had begun to soften. She put the omelet in the oven to keep warm, took the leftover spinach from the icebox, and, after putting it on the range to reheat gently, she hurried up to the dining room to lay the table.

When all was ready, she knocked on the library door and, without waiting to be asked, threw it open. Rosaline was sitting on the sofa next to Mrs. Canning, holding her hand. Seated in the armchair, Dr. Roeder was leaning toward them, saying something about how only the Lord could know for sure, and how only He could judge.

Then, the three pairs of eyes turned toward her, and Nuala said, "Supper's ready, if you come along so to the dining room." For the moment at least, she noticed, the missus had stopped crying.

"Thank you. We'll be right there," said the doctor.

Not waiting for them to gather themselves together, Nuala scurried back along the hallway and down to the kitchen, transferred the reheated spinach to a serving dish, took the omelet from the oven, and returned with both to the dining room, where the doctor was helping Mrs. Canning into her usual seat, to the right of what once had been her husband's place. Rosaline sat beside her, and the doctor across from his daughter. When they were settled, Nuala served the soup from the tureen she had earlier left on the sideboard.

"This is excellent, Nuala," said Rosaline, after tasting a mouthful. She turned to Mrs. Canning. "Do try some, Aunt Etta. It's awfully good."

"Made fresh this morning, it was," said Nuala.

"Etta, you must eat something," said the doctor when Mrs. Canning still hesitated.

"Yes, I know," she said. "I just don't seem to have any appetite." Nevertheless, she took one mouthful, and another.

"Good," said the doctor. "Now, try some bread," he urged, offering her the basket and the dish of butter.

Mrs. Canning did as she was told, and Nuala felt another surge of satisfaction. She had been right to speak to the doctor. "I'll be going," she said. "Just ring, when you need me," she added unnecessarily as she slipped out the door.

Too upset herself to have eaten more than a few scraps during the day, Nuala found now that she was ravenous. Back in the kitchen, she ladled some of the steaming soup into a bowl and cut a good slice of the bread and spread it with butter. After finishing the first bowl, she took another. It was good, she thought with some pride. Her mother had been cook at the Falconer place, and Nuala had helped her from the time she was six, maybe before (it was hard sometimes to set a date to some of the things she remembered). She had learned a thing or two in those years, and more since she had come to work for the Cannings. From the time of her arrival at Riverhall as a housemaid, she had pored over recipes marked in books and tucked away in albums, generations-worth of family favorites she found on the shelves in the kitchen. To those she had added ones she liked the sound of from the *Ladies Home Journal*. Whenever she got the chance, she tried them. Now, young as she was, she would not hesitate to match herself against any cook in Minuit. For that matter, she had had a meal or two in restaurants in New York City that she thought could not hold a candle to one of her own.

As she savored the soup, into her mind came the memory of the first meal she had prepared for the Cannings. Rebecca, who was then cook, was off for the day, and Nuala had served up a rabbit casserole, which she had thought was a particular favorite, given the tattered state of the recipe. The missus and Mr. Canning had pronounced it delicious, but Lily had refused to taste it. She must have been near twenty-two by then, and too old to be sent from the table, though her father looked sorely tempted to try. It was no different from eating chicken, he had told her, and if she had no qualms about the one, then it was pure foolishness to refuse the other. Which made perfect sense, but Lily had refused to back down, eating only the vegetables and bread. She could be that stubborn when she took a notion into her head. So could Nuala, in truth; but, grateful for Mr. Canning's support (for surely he had stood firm against his daughter only as a kindness to herself), she had judged it wise, in future, to avoid cooking anything that might be considered a family pet — to everyone's relief, she was sure.

Nuala had been with the family less than two years when Mr. Canning died, but she had taken his passing hard enough, harder than she would have expected on such short acquaintance, maybe because she had seen so much of death already, maybe because it was impossible for any woman not to be a bit taken with him, so handsome he was. But, in truth, his looks were the least of it. There was a daring quality to him. He seemed more like one of those cowboys who turned up from time to time in the illustrated magazines than a respectable lawyer, though he could be as grand as the next man when he liked. With her, though, he was always courteous, always kind, always careful of her feelings. He had encouraged her to better herself, to think about the future, to plan for it, above all to educate herself, even lending her books, ones that he thought she might enjoy, some plays by J.M. Synge, a volume of poems by William Butler Yeats, that sort of thing. They were not always easy reading, and she had occasionally exaggerated her enthusiasm when Mr. Canning asked her how she liked them, but sometimes . . . oh, yes . . . sometimes, the words seemed to touch her soul. "I will arise and go now, and go to Innisfree . . ." And wouldn't she love to do that, Nuala had thought. It sounded a lovely place.

For her library card, though, it was Lily she had to thank, recalled Nuala as her mind ran on. Such a small thing, a library card, and yet, to her, getting it had seemed a marvelous happening, young as she was at the time, and at Riverhall for just a few months. There had been more servants in the house then (the cook and another maid, as well as Jonas, the handyman, with extra help brought in when needed), so that her presence was not always as necessary as now; and, since Mr. Canning did not like his daughter going anywhere on her own, it was Nuala's job to accompany her into Minuit when he or Mrs. Canning could not. The two girls would walk when the weather was fine, or bicycle, or take the pony-and-trap, calling in at Burdett's Emporium, the dry goods store, where Lily would buy gloves or trimming lace or stockings, while Nuala flirted a little with Joseph, the owner's son. At the confectioners, they would stop for Mr. Canning's favorite chocolates and a treat for themselves. Often they would drop by to see Rosaline, or go to the Allens' where Lily would visit with her cousins, while Nuala sat in the kitchen with Deirdre, talking over the latest news from their brothers in Kentucky and their auntie in Portnoo, or exchanging information about their new lives in this vast country. That was Nuala's favorite destination, for she did not feel so lonely when she was with Dee, but the small white-frame building that was the local library ran it a close second. It was not that Nuala had such a love of reading, or any great interest in the life of the mind, but she did have ambition, and she suspected that it would take knowledge (maybe even more than money) to help her get on in the world. To her, the books in the library seemed like a passport, not to the realm of ideas, not to the world of romance, not even to the kingdom of God, but to a comfortable future and a secure life, what she wanted above all else. She was not certain how these books would help get her to where she wished to go, but she felt instinctively that without them she might find the way ahead full of pitfalls she had not foreseen, obstacles she could not get past.

"You know, you really should have your own card," Lily had said. She had noticed how Nuala still went on browsing among the shelves long after she had finished gathering novels for her mother and, for herself, whatever new books on art the elderly librarian had managed to acquire. "Then, on your free afternoon, you may come and spend as much time as you like, without me hurrying you along."

Wondering how it was that she had not thought of such a grand idea herself, Nuala had filled out the form provided by Miss Goodrich. Then, with her new card tucked in her pocket and a copy of Isabella Beeton's *Book of Household Management* clutched to her bosom, she had followed Lily out of the library and down the stone path to the road. The gratitude Nuala had felt that day did much to counter, from then on, the grievances she was inclined to collect against her beautiful young employer, for though Lily was unfailingly polite in her demands, she had the right to make them; and with the best will in the world it was hard not to resent, a little at least, someone who had everything, yet failed to notice how lucky she was. "Thank you ever so much, miss."

Lily had smiled and shrugged, "The library's free, and it's for everyone. He may be a terrible old scoundrel, but we should at least be grateful to Andrew Carnegie for that."

"Oh, I am, Miss Lily."

"He gave the initial grant, and Mrs. Dowling, bless her, supplied the rest."

Mrs. Dowling was a rich widow who often came to Riverhall for dinner. As for Andrew Carnegie, just about everyone in the world had heard of the man who, after years of accumulating millions by means that would shame the devil, had sold his company and then, to the amazement of all, had proceeded to give most of his money away. It was such a peculiar thing to do, Nuala had thought. Giving to charity was a duty, and should she be rich some day (as she sincerely hoped to be), she would not shirk it, of that she was as sure as could be; but she would keep the lion's share of her wealth for herself, and her children. "If it's him we have to thank for the library, it's a grand thing he did."

"It was indeed. And Mrs. Dowling, too." A bright autumn day it had been, with the sun shining, and the air crisp with a light wind, and the leaves on the turn, so that, as they retraced their steps along Beech Road back to Riverhall, the woods had stretched to either side of them in rippling waves of scarlet and gold and the deep green of pines. "You know, Carnegie came to this country from Scotland, an immigrant like you," Lily had continued. "He was poor, but ambitious. It didn't take him long to move up in the world."

"He was hardworking, I expect."

"Oh, he was that. Without doubt."

"Do you suppose, miss, that a man, or a woman if she can find a way to get on, can be kind and . . . moral, like, and still make something of themselves?"

"Certainly, I do. Why, just look at my father. There's not a better man alive. And he's done very well."

"Oh, he has," Nuala had replied quickly, for Mr. Canning was successful, that was true enough, though not, to be fair, fabulously rich like Andrew Carnegie. "He's a fine gentleman."

They had walked on in silence for a bit, but then Lily had said, seemingly out of the blue, though she must have been brooding on it, "Ambition can be a terrible curse, I think. Yet without any, what would we do? Be content to sit on the back porch, sipping tea, watching the world sail by? And would that really be so awful? Sometimes I'm not at all sure."

For a moment, Nuala had wondered how to reply, or indeed if she was meant to, but then had said what she thought. "Not if it made a body happy, Miss Lily. It takes all kinds to keep the world going. But if it's not in a body's nature to be content with the little things, then I expect there's nothing for it but to be going after the big."

At that, Lily had laughed. "Nothing for it, indeed."

A very odd conversation, Nuala had considered it then, and later she could not help but think of it at those times when Lily refused to leave off painting even to eat, or indeed when she herself, her chores done and with a few moments at last to call her own, sat dreaming in her tiny room of the grand life she meant one day to have.

♋

A bell rang, and the sound recalled Nuala to her solitary place at the kitchen table. Mrs. Canning and her guests had finished their meal and wanted her. Hurrying up the stairs, she thought about the rice pudding she had made the day before, wondering if perhaps she could offer that, as really there was nothing else suitable for dessert on hand, just a bit of cheese. However, when she entered the dining room, she saw that Mrs. Canning was already on her feet. "I need to lie down," she said when she saw Nuala.

"I can stay the night, if you like," said Rosaline, sounding worried.

"No, no," said Mrs. Canning quickly. "Nuala and I will manage. You run along home to your babies. You've been away from them too long, as it is."

"If you're certain . . ."

Mrs. Canning forced a reassuring smile, and then turned to Dr. Roeder. "You, too, Erich. You've been kindness itself. But I mustn't take advantage of your good nature."

"As if there's any question of that!" said the doctor, studying her in his careful way, as if preparing to make a diagnosis.

"I'll be fine," said Mrs. Canning. And she did indeed seem more in control of her emotions.

He studied her a moment longer and then said, "Yes, I'm sure you will, Etta. You've always been a strong and courageous woman."

"Have I?" She thought it over for a moment. "That's not how I've felt, let me tell you."

They started out of the dining room, the doctor and Rosaline on either side of Mrs. Canning. Trailing a little behind, Nuala turned to look back over her shoulder and do a quick survey. A bit of the omelet was left, but no spinach, and the bread was gone. To get the food cleared, these plates and her own washed, the dining room and kitchen put to rights, it would take her no more than an hour, she estimated.

"Let me at least come upstairs with you," Rosaline was saying as Nuala caught up with the group.

"If you like, dear," said Mrs. Canning. She hesitated a moment, and then added, "Erich, it seems I have one more favor to ask. If you would, tell Jonas. I don't think I can manage it myself tonight, and he ought to know."

"Of course. I hope the poor man hasn't gone to bed yet."

"Ah, no," said Nuala. "I told him you might be needing him."

The doctor smiled at her kindly. "You can always be counted on to think ahead."

Nuala blushed, and Mrs. Canning said, "I don't know what Lily and I would do without her." Then, her voice breaking, she whispered, "Oh dear Lord, I can't believe it."

"No," said Rosaline. "None of us can." She touched Mrs. Canning's arm. "Come, Aunt Etta."

Mrs. Canning nodded. Holding her skirts with her left hand, the banister with her right, she began to climb the steps. "Goodnight, Erich. Thank you."

"Goodnight, my dear."

"Nuala?"

"I'm right behind you, missus." She smiled a goodnight to the doctor, but he had left off watching them to go out the front door, heading for Jonas' quarters over the garage.

"It's time he was retiring," said Mrs. Canning when she reached the top of the stairs and paused to catch her breath. She meant Jonas. "But he won't hear of it."

"I suppose he likes to keep himself busy," said Rosaline. "And with no family to speak of, now that Rebecca's gone . . ."

Jonas had told Nuala the story (many times, in truth) of how Mrs. Canning's father had caught him pilfering fruit from the greengrocer and offered him a job. Just twelve years old, and a bit of a scamp, he had not meant to stick it long, but Rebecca had come to Riverhall a few months later. When old enough, they had married, and that was that.

"Work gives him a reason to get up in the morning, he says, when I raise the subject. Though I find reason enough, even now when I can't manage half of what I did before. Most people do. . . ." She fell silent, and Nuala knew her thoughts had turned again to her daughter.

Walking slowly to accommodate Mrs. Canning's pace, the three women made their way down the hall, past Lily's closed door, which drew their eyes for a moment before they moved on. "If you could help me sort through Lily's things," said Mrs. Canning to Rosaline. "I'm sure you'll know better than I what's to be done with them."

"There's time enough later to think of that. And you know all you have to do is ask when you're ready," said Rosaline. Reaching out, she opened the door into Mrs. Canning's room. "Oh, how lovely it is, the prettiest bedroom I've ever seen, like something out of a fairytale. That's what I thought the first time I saw it, when I was just a little girl. And I still do."

The bed was awry, and Nuala frowned. She had not had time to fix it when she had come to fetch Mrs. Canning's shoes, and she did it now, plumping the pillows and straightening the satin with a few deft movements, before turning down the covers. "There," she said. "That's better so."

"Nuala does like everything to be in perfect order," said Mrs. Canning.

Settling her into the slipper chair, Rosaline smiled a little and said, "As if you don't!"

"Oh, no. I don't mind really if things are a bit of a mess. My mother was convinced I'd be a hopeless housekeeper. I was thinking about that earlier today. What a wild creature I was, once upon a time."

"So my father's mentioned."

Mrs. Canning smiled. "Yes, he'd know. Though I think it's fair to say I settled down to be a good wife and mother." She leaned forward in her chair and reached for Rosaline's hand. "I was a good mother, wasn't I, Rosaline? God knows I tried. I did my best." Her voice, so soft a moment before, had become urgent.

Rosaline dropped to her knees in front of her. "You were a wonderful mother. No one's ever had better. And Lily always said so."

"Did she?"

"Yes, always," said Rosaline firmly. "You mustn't blame yourself, Aunt Etta. There was nothing more you could have done. Nothing!"

74

"So I keep telling myself." She sat for a moment with her head bowed, her eyes closed, her hand clasped in Rosaline's. A shudder racked her body. Then, her eyes opened again, and she said to the anxious woman crouching before her, "I'll be all right. You go along now, dear."

"Are you sure?" asked Rosaline, rising slowly. "I can stay. William and Dora can manage the children between them."

That would be the day, thought Nuala. Young Will was a rascal. The twins were little demons. And as for Dora, their nanny, even saying boo to a goose was beyond her, Nuala was sure. No backbone at all, that woman.

"I'll be fine," said Mrs. Canning. "I'll be sound asleep before you reach town."

"If you promise—"

But she reached for Rosaline's hand again. "Can you think why Lily would have gone there?" she asked. "Do you think she was meeting someone? Louis is a member of the yacht club, isn't he?"

"Lots of the local boys are. But Louis would have telephoned if he knew anything. He's going to be dreadfully upset, poor thing." Stooping she kissed Mrs. Canning's smooth cheek. "Try not to think too much tonight, Aunt Etta. It will only cause you pain." Then she turned to Nuala. "You needn't bother coming down. My father and I will see ourselves out."

Nuala nodded. "I'll lock up later."

"I'll be back in the morning," said Rosaline. "As soon as I can get away." At the door, she hesitated and turned to look back at Mrs. Canning.

"Go," she said, and when Rosaline stepped into the hallway, closing the door behind her, Nuala knelt at Mrs. Canning's feet and began to undo the buttons of the shiny black shoes. "I feel so helpless tonight. Not able to do for myself."

"We all need a hand from time to time. There's no shame in that." The shoes off, Nuala removed Mrs. Canning's black cotton stockings, so much finer than her own, and helped her on with her slippers.

75

From downstairs rose the hush of voices, and then the sound of the front door opening and closing again, the doctor and Rosaline leaving. "They're gone," said Mrs. Canning, sounding suddenly forlorn.

"They'll be back before you know it." Helping her to rise, Nuala undid the buttons of the dress, slipped it off over Mrs. Canning's head, and untied the strings of her corset. Before she took sick, she had never allowed anyone, except her husband of course, to see her in a state of undress; but now, whenever her heart was acting up, she had no choice but to accept help. Nuala, knowing how much Mrs. Canning minded the enforced intimacy, always tried to make it as easy as possible for both of them, keeping her touch light and quick, averting her eyes so as to see as little as possible of her employer's pale body emerging from its shell of clothes. She was still slender and surprisingly firm for one so old, fifty and more, Nuala had heard it said. Her own mother had never reached such an age, but had looked years older all the same.

Once wrapped in her cotton nightgown, Mrs. Canning sat again, this time on the stool to the vanity table. Nuala took down her thick hair, brushed it smooth, and braided it loosely, while her employer kept her eyes tight shut, as if afraid of catching sight of herself in the mirror. Then, when she went into the bathroom (insisting she needed no help inside), Nuala quickly tidied the bedroom, hanging up the dress, putting the shoes in their place in the closet, the corset in its drawer, the underwear in the basket with all the things needing to be laundered the next day, something she would have to find time to do.

Coming back into the room, Mrs. Canning seemed to lose her balance. She recovered it immediately and, when Nuala rushed to her side, said, "I'm not an invalid," a touch of impatience in her voice.

"No, missus. But you're not all that steady on your feet, just at the minute. You don't want to be falling."

Ignoring Nuala's hand, Mrs. Canning walked slowly but steadily to the bed. "There, you see," she said, sinking down into it. Settling against the pillows, she swung her legs up.

"Would you like a bit of hot milk? Or some of that medicine the doctor gave you a while back to help you sleep?"

"No, thank you, dear. Nothing." She closed her eyes. "I don't want to sleep. I want to lie here and remember Lily, while I still can, before she begins to fade the way my husband has. You know, sometimes I can't quite see his face. I have to look at his portrait, or a photograph, to remind myself what he looked like."

"It's the same so with my mother," said Nuala, pulling up the covers and tucking them in around Mrs. Canning. "And the only photo I have is that old, I can't be sure it's her no matter how hard I look."

"You'd think we could do a better job of remembering the people we love."

Nuala stepped back from the bed and looked down at Mrs. Canning's sorrowful face. "Well, now, I expect forgetting is God's way of making us get on with our lives, for would there be any point living, if all we did was sit and grieve over the past?"

"You think God cares how much we grieve?"

"Oh, missus!"

"How can He, when He sends so much pain to plague our lives?"

"It's on account of original sin, there's all the pain and suffering in the world." It was a mystery to Nuala what Protestants believed, but every child in Ireland knew that much. "But, sure, He would never send us more than we have the strength to bear."

"You believe that?"

"Oh yes, missus. I do. With all my heart. And I believe that if we accept all our sorrows with courage, He'll be rewarding us in heaven."

"And if we don't? If we're cowards and run from them? What then?"

Nuala hesitated a moment, not certain how to answer. She had never seriously thought about the matter before. The optimism of her youth, reinforced by her experience so far, made her take for granted that, when troubles came, she would deal with them, triumph over them. But others, she was coming to learn, did not have her strength, her determination.

Others collapsed like stick figures in the wind at the first hint of trouble. "We have to rely on His mercy, missus," she said finally. "That's what the priests are after saying."

"His mercy," she echoed, though Nuala was far from sure whether it was agreement or doubt she heard in her mistress' voice. Mrs. Canning's eyes closed, and soon a trickle of tears crept out from under the closed lids. "She drowned, you know."

"Yes, missus."

"In the river. She drowned."

Nuala felt the tears starting in her own eyes. "I'm that sorry, missus, truly I am."

"Do you remember the day when Lily and Rosaline took the rowboat out without telling us?" She opened her eyes, wiped away the tears with her hand, and looked at Nuala.

"It was before I came."

"Yes, that's right. Long before. The girls were no more than twelve at the time. What an awful day, it was," Mrs. Canning went on, though no matter how terrible the day, the memory of it seemed to bring her some comfort. "We thought they were playing in Lily's room, but they didn't come when called for lunch; and then Jonas found the rowboat gone. We were frantic with worry, all of us. We took the sailboats out, Titus and me in one, the doctor and Jonas in another. We tacked up and down, searching both shores, for hours it seemed. Every time I saw a bit of something washing toward us, my heart flew right into my mouth. . . . We found them finally, in that small cove two miles north of here. Rosaline was asleep. Lily was drawing. Completely oblivious to the time, they both were. I was so happy to see them safe, I can't tell you. It may have been the happiest moment of my life, finding them there, alive." She smiled the first genuine smile of the day. "Titus was in such a rage. He took Lily's drawing supplies away from her for a month."

Though Nuala and her employer often chatted, mostly what they talked about was the house, or Nuala's family. Mrs. Canning was always good about asking after Dee and what the news was from her brothers. They had never had a conversation like this, and Nuala felt a little out of her depth, afraid of saying the wrong thing, of making matters worse. "I'm sure Miss Lily didn't like that," she said finally, after considering a number of responses, most of them to do with Mr. Canning's not having been nearly hard enough. In her opinion, he had been inclined to molly-coddle his daughter. Nuala would have got a good hiding had she ever frightened her mother so.

"I've always loved the river," said Mrs. Canning. Suddenly, her body shook again with sobs. "How will I ever bear to look at it now?"

Nuala moved quickly to the dresser, took one of the linen handker-chiefs from the drawer, and returned to the bed. Sitting on its edge, she gently wiped Mrs. Canning's face. "There," she said. "You should be quiet, missus. It won't be doing your heart any good, your taking on so."

"I want to die, Nuala. I do." Her voice rose and shattered in a wail. "I want to die, and I can't!"

"You will, missus," said Nuala, "all in God's time."

"Oh, Lily, darling . . ."

On the bedside table was a half-full pitcher of water. Nuala reached for it, poured a glass, and, when Mrs. Canning's sobbing eased, said, "Here, take some of this. Do you have any pain?" she asked, watching worriedly as the woman sat up.

"No," she said. She took a few sips, returned the glass to Nuala, then again rested her head against the pillow and closed her eyes. Putting the glass back on the table, within easy reach, Nuala rose slowly. Mrs. Canning's eyes shot open. "Don't go."

"There, I won't," said Nuala, resettling herself on the edge of the bed. She picked up the hand lying on the comforter. "I'll stay till you sleep." Once a strong hand, able to wield a spade in the garden, handle the tiller of a sailboat, haul up a net of shad from the river, it had grown weaker and soft — though not yet quite soft enough for a lady's, its neatly rounded nails (at least since Mrs. Canning's illness) a result of Nuala's manicuring, another skill she had acquired since coming to Riverhall. Some days there seemed to be no end to the chores she was expected to do — look after the house, care for Mrs. Canning, fetch and carry for Lily — not that she minded in the general run of things. The Cannings were fine people and treated her decent, far better than the Allens treated Dee, she knew, though her sister never complained. While Mr. Allen was always a gentleman, handy with his thank-yous, Mrs. Allen was one of those worriers for whom nothing could be done well enough; and when Florence was about, things only got worse, for she had a belittling tongue. She could make a person feel that small, while Lily was just the opposite (when she took any notice at all, that is), always trying to build a body up, treating everyone she met, no matter their station, like an equal. In any case, it was not in Nuala's nature to resent work, or to shirk what needed doing. And if it had seemed to her sometimes a peculiar state of affairs that she should be so intimately looking after Mrs. Canning when she had a daughter of her own in the house, well, Nuala liked the woman a great deal, though she had not expected to, for the only knowledge she had of being in service was the experience of her mother, who at bottom had despised Lady Falconer for the coldhearted, light-headed hussy that she was. Besides, Nuala was glad enough of the money she was paid for doing it, and grateful for what that money gave her. It was a thrill to be able to buy something pretty for herself from time to time, for Dee on her birthday, for her auntie and brothers at Christmas. Even better was simply to watch it accumulate in the account she had opened in the bank in Minuit (over two hundred dollars, so far), to feel herself to be a woman of means, one who did not have to kowtow to a living soul, a woman with a fine future before her.

Mrs. Canning lay awake for a long time, her eyes closed, their lids fluttering. She's thinking of Lily, thought Nuala. She's calling up memories, watching them (as Nuala herself did sometimes) like she would a movie. Well, maybe that was to the good, if it kept her quiet, if it brought her comfort.

Nuala loved the movies, but, as the nearest picture palace was in Poughkeepsie, she did not get to go as often as she liked. The last movie she had seen, she remembered, was *The Cure* with Charlie Chaplin, and that was with Lily, only a few weeks before, when they had traveled to New York to get, among other things, some new uniforms for Nuala. That day, Lily had sailed through McCreery's, through Arnold Constable's, B. Altman's, Lord & Taylor's, on a tide of good humor, spending money with no thought for thrift, until they were both laden with packages. Afterward, they had stopped at Child's for something to eat, and then, dismissing the idea of returning home just yet, Lily had declared they would go to a movie. Nuala herself might have preferred something with Mary Pickford, but she did not like to say; and, after all, she had enjoyed the treat mightily, though not as much as Lily, who had watched Chaplin's drunken antics with the delight of a giggling schoolgirl. It had been a relief to see her like that, so happy, after those long months when her face had seemed unacquainted with a smile, when she could hardly be coaxed into doing anything more than sit by the window and stare out at the river. That day, it had almost been possible to believe her dark times were over forever.

Well, now they were, for sure.

Finally, Mrs. Canning's eyelids grew still, her breathing slowed. Hardly breathing herself, Nuala slipped her hand from the sleeping woman's, rose from the bed, and made her way quietly across the floor, leaving the lamp on, closing the door after herself. The bell rang in her bedroom as well as in the kitchen, so she would know if she was wanted in the middle of the night.

Downstairs, Nuala locked the front door, tidied the library and turned out the lights, then went across to the dining room, where she cleared away the remnants of supper, swept up the crumbs, and when all was as it should be, turned out those lights and the ones in the hall. Returning to the kitchen, she transferred the leftovers to storage bowls, placed them in the icebox, washed up the dishes, scrubbed the pots, cleaned the range, wiped the table and countertops, and gave the floor a quick mop. It was after eleven by the time she finished, and she would have to be up by six, if not sooner, should Mrs. Canning not sleep through the night. Yet, tired as she was, Nuala did not climb the back stairs to her third-floor bedroom, but took her canvas coat from the peg by the kitchen door and went outside. Passing through the small stone courtyard where sometimes, when the weather was good, she sat looking out at the river as she shucked corn or polished silver, she opened the gate, went past the herb garden, and took the path leading to the porch steps. Her boots were wet with dew, she noticed as she settled herself in one of the rocking chairs; she would need to polish them before she slept. There was a wind coming from the northwest, chasing wisps of cloud across the sky, and she pulled the coat closer about her.

The moon lay nestled in a hollow of the mountains on the opposite shore, its rays falling to highlight the rough water with silver. Overhead, clusters of stars stretched as far as she could see like salt crystals spilt over a piece of black velvet, the same stars, she reminded herself, that she used to wish on back in Portnoo what seemed like another lifetime ago. Only there, it was the sea she had sat beside, with the surf roaring in her ears and the spray misting her face, and her wishes had been a young girl's, for then she had wanted nothing more than Jamie Ryan's love.

How small and tame this river seemed in comparison, its tempests nothing to the gales that had sometimes whipped the boats of the village men back to shore with the night's fishing half done. Jamie Ryan had died on such a night, his boat capsized in a storm, his body washed up to the beach a week later. She was only fourteen at the time and, truth to tell, she doubted that Jamie had ever thought of her as anything more than a wearying child, always underfoot. But she had known her own heart and had thought it would break with the pain of losing him. Afraid of making a fool of herself, she had stayed away from his funeral, pleading illness, which was not so far from the truth. She was sick indeed with grief. She had lain in her bed all the day and wept for weeks afterward, while her mother, who suspected how it was with her, let her be, and her sister and brothers took care not to tease.

Jamie had been her first and, so far, her only love; but then, who else was there with his darling face, his winning smile, his way with a song — or his prospects? Unlike so many of the men Nuala knew, he never drank more than he ought, and everything he put his hand to had brought him success. Until that night. It was a pity, it was. Still, her heart had mended quickly enough, when all was said and done. She had got on with her life, though to this day Jamie Ryan seemed to have free access to her thoughts, coming and going at will; and she never did think of him without a pang of sorrow, of regret for what might have been, for he would have taken note of her eventually, she was sure of it: there may have been prettier girls in Portnoo, but not many, and not a one of them had her spirit, not even Dee.

How different her life might have been had he lived, thought Nuala, sitting on Riverhall's porch, rocking gently back and forth in the chair. Perhaps she would have remained in Portnoo, married Jamie, had little ones, and now be keeping her own cottage tidy instead of working for the Cannings and each month depositing a bit of pay in the bank. Would that have done for her? she wondered. Or would she have been ground down eventually by the poverty of it all, as her mother had, by the ceaseless backbreaking work, with never a penny to spare for something to add a little brightness to life? Would she have come to resent Jamie and the endless parade of children, one after the other, year after year? Would she have grown restless and dreamed of running off to faraway places?

So many questions, and none with any answers she could be sure of. What she did know, and for certain, was that she liked the life she was living now, no matter how long or how hard she worked, for it left her feeling full of hope. Her future seemed bright with promise.

Looking out over the water, watching the play of moonlight on the river, Nuala thought again of that fierce storm, of Jamie fighting to live until he had no strength left and the sea took him. She thought of Lily sliding into the river's dark water.

What was the truth of it? Nuala wondered, trying to piece together the whispered fragments of conversation she had heard that evening. Had it been an accident? Had Lily somehow managed to fall heedlessly into the river she had lived beside all her life without harm? Even without knowing that stretch of the Hudson near Eighty-sixth Street, Nuala doubted it, for to be walking all alone near the river in the middle of the night was strange enough, but then to stumble by some mischance into the water? Lily? Why, even in that unlikely event, she would have swum right back to shore and climbed out.

But perhaps she had been murdered? The thought sent a chill through Nuala, and she dropped her chin into the collar of her coat. Perhaps Edmund Farel, that snake, had arranged to meet Lily there? Perhaps they had quarreled? Perhaps he had struck her, knocked her unconscious, thrown her senseless body into the river? "If I can't have you, no one else will!"

Ah, no. She had been reading too many stories in *The Police Gazette*. Too handsome for his own good, he may have been, with a lazy smile and soft drawl that could stop your breath, but Farel could have begged on his knees for Lily to meet him and she would not have done it, she was that finished with him. She never wanted to see him again, so Nuala had heard her say and never doubted that she meant it. Not that her voice was so fierce when she spoke, for that might have meant she still loved the man; but rather it was as cold as the North Sea in winter. It was as if her heart, at least the portion that Edmund Farel once claimed, had turned to ice. Besides, the doctor, when talking to Mrs. Canning on the stairs, had said something about a witness. Surely, if it had been murder, the man would have said. Unless he had done it, of course. But then, would the police have let him go? And an accident, the coroner had called it.

So, why then had the doctor spoken of God's judgment?

No. Chase which notion she would, there was no escaping the truth — Lily had killed herself. Mrs. Canning and the doctor and Rosaline could speak of an "accident" all they liked. And why not? It could have been, for all anyone would ever know for sure. And what could they do but insist it was that, or think of the scandal? She would not say anything to anyone, decided Nuala, not even to Dee, for it was not her place to interfere, but the truth was plain as homespun cloth. Lily had done herself in.

Nuala remembered a time, a Sunday it was, a few weeks back (it must have been in early March, the first fine day after a spell of bad weather) when Mrs. Canning had sent her to fetch Lily, who was walking along the bank at the bottom of the garden. Coming abreast of her, Nuala had seen such a look of longing on her face as she stood there, looking out over the water, that she had grown anxious, though she could not have said exactly why, for Lily always studied the river with such a fierce gaze when thinking how to paint it. Hearing her name called, she had turned like someone waking from a deep sleep. A moment later, though, she was hurrying happily away from the icy green water, back to the house as if she had not a care in the world beyond being late for church. Nuala had dismissed her fear as foolish, and had not thought of the incident again until now.

What must it be like, she wondered, to want to die? She could not imagine it. As heartbroken as she was to lose Jamie, she had not thought of following him. When her brother was killed, she had mourned him, and though sick with grief when her Da had died, and her mother, she had never wanted to take her own life. Never! She had prayed to God only for sleep, for a place to hide from the anguish in her mind, the fire in her heart, a place to gather strength to face the torment of the next day, and the next. In time, she had learned that even the worst torment fades, to flare only now and then, a sudden sharp pain, gone almost before its cause is remembered.

Her life had been too easy, that was Lily's trouble. Beautiful and admired for it, pampered and petted, the way made smooth before her, she had only to speak a wish to have it granted. A new dress, a piece of jewelry, anything money could buy—her parents had denied her nothing; her friends had fawned all over her; even people who resented her for her looks, her money, her talent, could not help admiring her. Was it any wonder that she had gone to pieces when her father died, when her marriage went wrong — even before that, truth be told, whenever life was not to her liking, for when had she the time, or the need, to develop the strength of character, the strength of will, that would have seen her through trouble and out the other side?

Nuala felt a wave of contempt rise in her, rise and break over the memory of the young woman of whom she had been fond, yes, but — she admitted it—jealous, too. Contempt and anger. How could Lily, who had everything, so foolishly have thrown it all away? She who had never had to lift a finger, not even to tidy her own room, or make her own bed! It was a sin, it was, and she would burn in hell for it, burn for all eternity.

But no sooner had the thought come than Nuala pushed it away. She felt tears on her cheeks, turning cold in the night air. God forgive me, she thought. Lily had been good to her. Like her father, she had encouraged Nuala's ambitions and respected her opinions; she had treated her, more often than not, like a friend. Where was the right in second-guessing the Lord, in begrudging the lady the life He had seen fit to give her? Envy, too, was a terrible sin.

Looking up at the night sky, her heart full of sorrow and remorse, Nuala suddenly caught sight of a star shooting across the heavens and then dropping sharply behind the great shoulder of hill at the river's bend. And letting go of the last of the anger, the jealousy, she prayed. May eternal light shine upon her. May she rest in peace.

All at once Nuala's spirits lightened, for she was young, and alive, with a future spread long and wide before her. Ah, let my sorrows be small and my joys great, she prayed. Let the years bring me riches of love and money. Let me live till old age and die happy. Let me not be afraid.

Rosaline

The Schuylers lived at 15 River Road, in a brick Georgian-style house set in a pretty garden, a short walk from the Hudson. Except for the old Wild Goose Inn at the end, the rest of the buildings on the cobbled, tree-lined street were private dwellings, modest in size, many dating from the colonial era, most in excellent repair, with tiny front yards that later in the spring would be a riot of colorful blooms. Since this was the oldest part of the town, and on the far side of the railroad, which had come through in the middle of the last century, these homes did not command the high prices of the newer, and larger, Queen Anne or Gothic Revival houses off Center Street, where Rosaline's parents lived, among those of Minuit's more affluent citizens who did not choose, or were not quite wealthy enough, to own estates on the river. William had bought the place for a song two years after their marriage with money he had saved himself, and the delight Rosaline took in it had as much to do with her pride in their independence as with the house's elegant façade and gracefully proportioned rooms; and while some might think it too small (she sometimes did herself), she loved it, and never returned to it without a rush of pleasure, and never with more gratitude than on that night when she said good-bye to her somber father and hurried up the brick walk to the front door. She let herself in with her latchkey, removed her coat and hat, hung them on the bentwood rack in the hall, and noticed with relief the light in the parlor. William had waited up for her.

His head was bowed over the *Hudson Tribune*, his face grim. Hearing her step, he looked up, dropped the newspaper on to a side table, and rose out of the armchair. "You look all done in," he said.

"So do you."

"It's this damn war." He moved across the Turkey carpet to meet her.

"Papa talked about nothing else all the way to New York." As he put his arms around her, suddenly anxious, she looked up into his pale face, hanging so high above hers. "You're not thinking—"

"No," he said, stooping to kiss her, "War *is* the problem, not the solution to one," adding, as he guided her toward the sofa, "Even if there is a draft, married men won't be called."

"Thank God for that, at least." She sank into the soft velvet cushions, settling herself against him as he sat beside her. "The children?" she murmured, her eyes closed.

"Sound asleep. And Dora, too, I imagine." He kissed the top of her head and said, "Won't you tell me about it?"

She opened her eyes again, and turned a little so that she could see his face. "It was a nightmare that wouldn't end," she said. "It still hasn't."

"Your mother told me it was Lily—"

"Yes. Oh, William, it was awful!"

"Sweetheart," he murmured. "I'm so very sorry."

88

"To see her like that, in a police morgue . . ." She began to cry, softly at first, and then in loud, choking sobs. William said nothing, but she could feel his chin on her hair, his chest against her back, his arms wound tightly around her, trying to console her as best he could with his touch.

Her husband (such a comforting word, "husband") was tall and reed-thin, with skin so fair it appeared translucent. Even she, and she loved him very much, did not imagine that anyone in the world, but herself, would consider him handsome. She had, right from the first, when she met him at the Allens', where George Allen, who was his insurance agent, had invited him to a birthday party for Florence. Sometimes, Rosaline even thought William beautiful, with an ethereal quality that seemed to her almost angelic. His hair was curly and the color of ripe hay, his eyes a light brown when lit by good humor, though the color would deepen with anger or passion or, as now, with concern. He had a long, narrow face, and delicate fingers that could assemble a model sailboat for his son or repair a broken doll for one of his daughters with astonishing grace and speed. His hands were gentle, and his touch, as light as a butterfly's, drove her almost mad with pleasure when they made love. At first, when she stood beside him, she had thought they made a ridiculous couple, with him towering over her so, but she had long since ceased to care. He was the best man she knew, absolutely the best, without her father's temper, or Titus Canning's arrogance, without any truly hurtful qualities at all. His faults (and that was perhaps too strong a word for them) were small ones; and if she was driven particularly mad by his tendency to forget that she, and the children, and the entire rest of the world, existed when he had his nose buried in a book, leaving her sometimes to shout the house down to get his attention, once she did have it, there was no one in the world more considerate, more loving, or more amusing than he. William taught at the local high school, and Rosaline believed him to be a very fine teacher indeed.

"I've needed to do that all day," she said when she could speak again. She felt William move and, a moment later, he handed her his handkerchief. Taking it, she wiped her eyes, blew her nose. Her head felt as stuffed with feathers as a pillow. She could hardly breathe.

"You shouldn't have gone."

"I couldn't let Aunt Etta. Or Papa go alone, for that matter."

"There was no question of that," said William impatiently. He had offered to accompany his father-in-law to New York that morning, but Rosaline would not hear of it.

Now, with a stubborn shake of her head, she said, "I had to go. And I'm not sorry I did. I feel sure Lily would have wanted me there." Rosaline felt quieter, though a weight of sadness still pressed on her heart and the tears kept trickling from her eyes in a steady, unstoppable flow. From time to time, she dabbed at them with the handkerchief as, choosing her words carefully, conscious of the pact she had made with her father, she recounted for William the events of the day: the long train journey to New York, the interview with the detective, the visit to the morgue, the meeting with Lily's would-be rescuer, the packing-up of her room at the Pelham, the evening with Henrietta. "Poor Aunt Etta," she said, "I don't know how she'll survive this."

"She won't have an easy time of it, that's for certain. But she's a strong woman."

"I'm sure Papa didn't think she'd make it through the winter. And I doubt she would have, if Lily hadn't needed her. But now . . ." Her breath caught again on a sob.

"We'll all do our best to help her through. Your father especially. And you. You mean a great deal to her. Perhaps it will be enough."

Her eyes dropped away from her husband's, down to the square of linen her fingers were playing with aimlessly. "If only I hadn't spoken to Edmund that day! It was I, you know. I was the one dazzled by him, by the chance to talk to a real writer, at any rate. I encouraged him. Actually encouraged him!"

"Now, Rosaline," said William, "you can't go blaming yourself."

"What a mess I've made of things. I should have said more to discourage her. I should have told Aunt Etta. Perhaps if she had known, she could have stopped Lily marrying him. I still can't understand how I was so taken in! Sometimes I think it was that southern accent. It made him sound such a gentleman. And I used to believe I had such good instincts about people."

"The point about scoundrels, sweetheart, is that they do take people in. That's their chief talent. They use what assets they have—looks, charm, intelligence—and Farel had an abundance of those, to dupe people. Even those of us who couldn't quite like him . . ." William could not resist a smile. "I mean us *men*, of course. We never thought he meant any real harm." None of them knew for certain (Lily had been stubbornly dumb on the subject) why her marriage had come to such an abrupt end, but they took it as given that the fault lay entirely with Edmund.

"I hate him," Rosaline said. She looked William squarely in the eye and repeated, "I hate him."

And though she had a thousand times heard him lecture their son (for uttering the same words) on the virtue of Christian charity, all William said to her was, "I'm sure you do. You hold him responsible for Lily's death because you don't wish to blame her."

"Blame her? Why? It was an accident! I only meant—" She stopped. She could not lie to him. She went on softly, "She killed herself."

"Yes."

"Oh God, how unhappy she must have been! And I thought she was better." William reached for her again and pulled her close. "God forgive her," Rosaline said. She was weeping again, uncontrollably. "God forgive her. . . ."

❧

When she was — at least for the moment — drained of tears, Rosaline went up to see the children, little Will in his own small bedroom under the eaves, the twins sharing another next door. She had so much anchoring her in this world, she thought as she studied her offspring, finding them beautiful beyond words. Leaning down to straighten the covers around them, she kissed their silky cheeks, sniffed the fresh talcum smell of their small bodies, the apple fragrance of the shampoo Dora had used to wash their hair, and felt almost weak with love. She could never, not if she had anything to say in the matter, leave them, not for any length of time, not her babies, not William, not her parents or brothers. If God wanted her, He would have to send an army of angels to bring her to Him, and she would fight like the very devil all the way there.

Had that been Lily's trouble? Rosaline wondered. Had the ties that moored her to the world been too few and too fragile to hold? Her father was gone, her mother failing, Edmund sent packing, and no children to need her. The future might indeed have seemed bleak to her.

Yet, no one got through the years unscathed. No one went without his portion of woe. And most people managed to survive, some even to triumph over their troubles. Lily was still young, and so lovely, and very dear. Surely it should have been possible for her to hope, to *believe*, that the winds would change, as they always did, that life would come about, that happiness lay just around the next bend in the river.

But who was she to judge, thought Rosaline, making her way back down the narrow stairs. Though she sometimes flailed at the constraints of her life, bemoaned the lack of time and her inability to get everything she wished done, gave way to anger and (if she was to be completely honest) a hateful self-pity in the face of thwarted ambition, still her demons were small ones and tamed with comparative ease. She was not given to headaches, to moods, to periods of depression, as Lily had been all her life. More than that, Rosaline had been spared — until today — any truly great sorrow. It yet remained to be seen how she would deal with one, whether she would go all to pieces, or somehow keep from spinning out of control. She found herself praying again, this time not for Lily, but for herself, asking God to give her the strength to bear the coming days, the strength to be of comfort to Henrietta while not neglecting the children or William, the strength to endure her own grief without giving way to bitterness.

Though William certainly could not be counted on to notice any neglect, she thought, entering their bedroom and finding him sound asleep. A smile managed to push its way through the sadness weighing on her, for though his ease dropping off could be exasperating, when they did not drive her mad, she found her husband's foibles endearing.

In another mood, she might have banged about, hoping to wake him, but instead she moved quietly around the room, taking her nightgown from under her pillow, laying it across the back of the vanity chair, then sitting to remove her shoes and stockings. Rising again, she unbuttoned the apricot dress and took it off. It had cost her entire clothes allowance for spring, and she would never have thought to buy it, had Lily not urged her on. "It looks as if it were made for you," she had said. "Do take it, or you'll think of nothing else from now to summer, and regret it every minute." Normally, Lily did not really care so much for clothes herself, no doubt because she looked well, even stylish, no matter what old thing she put on; but that day, just a week or so after her release from the hospital, she had claimed to have nothing decent to wear and uncharacteristically had bought two rather expensive outfits. Her mood was so good after all those months of depression that Rosaline could not bear to dampen her friend's spirits by turning practical herself; besides which, she had loved the dress and wanted it desperately. Now, she would never be able to wear it again, she thought, as she hung it in the wardrobe. It would always remind her of Lily, and of this awful day.

She slipped on her nightgown, picked up her drawers and stockings, threw them in the laundry basket, then folded the chemise and corset and put them away. William had not done the same with his things, which lay wherever he had dropped them, but this was so usual an occurrence that Rosaline hardly noticed the surge of irritation she felt as she picked up after him. Many of the people she knew left this tidying to be done by their servants, but she never did. For one thing, aside from Dora, who was occupied almost totally with the children, the Schuylers only had one girl to help in the house, Minnie, who came in for a few hours each week-day morning. They could not afford more, and even with the three women working full out, there was never enough time to do all that was necessary to keep the household running smoothly.

If only William could be made to understand that, he might be more inclined toward neatness, thought Rosaline, walking down the dark hall to the bathroom, her felt slippers soundless against the flowered carpet, grief trailing her like a beggar held at bay by whatever random thought she could grab to use for a shield. But of course her husband did understand. It was just that, however much of an effort he made when reminded, he could not be counted on to remember that where he dropped his socks or left his papers could be an inconvenience to someone else. His mind was occupied with other things, higher things, like the battle of Thermopylae or the conquest of Gaul. History was his passion — aside from herself and the children, his great passion. It was that passion, doubtless, that made him such an excellent teacher, and surely there was no greater call-ing than to teach, to mold the minds of children, readying them to face the challenges of the world in which they lived. Only by studying history, William often said, could mankind learn how to build on past glories and avoid past mistakes. He believed this war represented just such an error, a retreat into barbarism that he had once considered unthinkable in the second decade of the twentieth century.

Yes, he was an admirable man, thought Rosaline, washing the day's grime from her face, never complaining when she was away from home on suffrage business, nor minding when her organizing duties ate into time that some other husband might have insisted be spent on her family. He was as ardent a supporter of the suffragist cause as she, which was just as well, as it was unlikely their marriage would otherwise have gone on as happily as it did. And though William was inclined to point out that it was no one's fault but hers if she left herself with only odd moments to spare for her writing, she could hardly blame him for that as she mostly agreed, despite having no idea what to do about it.

But could either of them be said to have progressed far enough along the path of equality between the sexes, she wondered as she brushed out her brown hair and plaited it, if both still felt it was her duty to pick up his discarded clothes? But then, she knew from her own experience with the Cause how long a time it took to move from principle to practice. Meanwhile, the truth was, she adored William, and while she did regret not having gone on to Vassar as she had planned to do before meeting him, and sometimes fell into a welter of self-recrimination because the book she wanted so desperately to write was still nothing more than a jumble of notes, she was, at the same time, happy to be a wife and mother. She would not have traded William and the children for the world.

Her toilette completed, Rosaline returned to their room, joined William in the carved mahogany bed, and, reaching out a hand, turned off the lamp. Settling herself under the covers, she adjusted the feather pillow beneath her head and closed her eyes, hoping that sleep would come quickly.

It did not. Though she could feel exhaustion pulling at her body, trying to drag her down into the restful darkness, grief clamored again for attention, and her wide-awake mind teemed with fragments of unrelated thoughts and vivid images, not just the awful ones she had witnessed that day, but long-ago memories of Lily, who came romping through her head with such vitality that for a moment it seemed absurd to believe that she was gone, forever. How narrow it was, the line between the living and the dead, how hard to grasp the finality of crossing it. How could there now be nothing, when only yesterday, a matter of such a few hours, there had been so much beauty, so much talent, so much life?

She wished she could wake William. She wished she could be sufficiently modern to be able to ask him to make love to her. It was not just the comfort of the act that Rosaline craved, but the mindlessness, consciousness overwhelmed in a flood of sensation, of pleasure. She wanted to forget everything, to put aside sorrow and guilt, to lose herself for a few precious moments in bliss.

There were women who could ask, fast women, who could approach a man on a street, in a hotel, on a public conveyance, and offer to give him pleasure for a price. What was that price? she wondered. Not in terms of sin, the loss of God's love, or of one's own self-respect, those costs that ministers (and mothers) tended to dwell on, but the actual monetary sum involved in the transaction? It would differ according to the woman, of course, those with looks or talent or intelligence to barter being able to command a far higher price than some poor girl soliciting on a street corner. At night, in certain sections of the city, coming out of a restaurant or theater, Rosaline had seen some of the latter, scrawny things in rags, sisters to that poor Mr. Daniels, unclean and undernourished. It was difficult to imagine anyone wanting to pay them even a few pennies for the use of their bodies, but men did. Some men. William would not know how much, but her father might. As a doctor, he came into contact with all sorts. But she could hardly ask him. Nor was she certain she could gather the courage to raise the question even with Mrs. Hurley, one of the area's leading suffragettes, though it was just the sort of detail that she often seemed to offer as proof of one thing and another having to do with the exploitation and subjugation of women.

Turning in the deep feather bed, Rosaline snuggled against her husband, hoping, since she could not sleep, that he would wake, as he sometimes did, and want to make love to her, though she supposed that was unlikely tonight. Even if he woke as ardent as she wished, he would control himself, out of a sense of what was right, out of respect for her, imagining that she might consider lovemaking, in the circumstances, distasteful. And how could she tell him otherwise? As progressive, as understanding, as appreciative of his passionate wife as William tended to be, he would not, she was certain, be able to fathom her strange state of mind. She hardly did herself. Still, she moved even closer to him, pressing

96

spoon-fashion against him, dropping her arm across his body. If he woke, they could at least speak; but his breast continued to rise and fall evenly beneath her hand, and his breath kept its steady rhythm. She could smell the apple scent of his hair, feel his shoulder under her chin, his back against her breasts, his comforting warmth.

And all at once there came the memory of herself in a gingham dress, lying propped against a tree, writing furiously in her notebook. Pausing to think, she had looked out from under the wide brim of her straw hat at the river sparkling in the sunlight, at a rowboat pulled half onto the shore, and Lily sitting cross-legged beside it in the tall grass, her sketchbook in her lap, the pencil in her hand moving furiously. "Don't move," she had called. "I've almost got you." And Rosaline had sat so still that, lulled by the hum of insects, the sound of water lapping, the wonderful lethargy induced by the sun's warmth, she had dropped off to sleep.

She had that sketch somewhere. Lily had given it to her after all the fuss had died down.

Lily.

No, she mustn't think of her any more, not tonight. Only of the sun and the river, of William's warmth and the scent of his hair. She tried to breathe as he did, in concert with him, softly, in and out, in and out, in and . . .

After a restless night of fitful sleep, Rosaline came wide awake at six-thirty, her usual time for rising. For an instant, as her eyes opened to the familiar sights of her bedroom, she believed it was a normal morning, that all was well with her world. Then she remembered, and the pain came again, as sharp as when she had seen Lily in that morgue, lying there so still and white. Lily was dead. She had killed herself.

Rosaline's eyes felt swollen, her head ached, and she would have welcomed another hour or two of rest; but, though Dora and Minnie could certainly manage without her, she doubted sleep would come again and forced herself from the bed. In any case, she had too much to do that day to waste any of it in hiding. Putting on her slippers and dressing gown, she gathered up her undergarments and, leaving the window curtains drawn and William still asleep, made her way down the hall to the bathroom. She locked the door and started the bath water running. Catching sight of herself in the mirror above the basin as she brushed her teeth, she was dismayed to see the face staring back at her almost as pasty white as Lily's had been, and then grimaced with distaste at her vanity. What did she care how she looked? What did it matter? Her heart was broken. She had lost a friend. A sister. There was no one in the world she felt as close to as Lily, in some ways even closer than to William. She and Lily, after all, had known each other longer, had shared their lives almost from the day they were born, had shared their secrets since they could speak. They were the repository of not only their own, but of each other's memories, a tangle of shared experiences and whispered hopes. Now, who was there with whom she could talk the secret language they had devised when they were twelve? Or laugh about her adolescent crush on Charlie Anderson, her brother Marcus' friend? Whom could she count on now to remind her of what she had forgotten? It was as if Rosaline had lost a part of herself.

Tears stung her eyes, but she fought them back. She did not want her children to see her looking distraught. For their sake, for her own, for everyone's, she needed to keep hold of herself. Rinsing a cloth in cold water, she pressed it to her eyes and held it there until she felt prepared to face the day.

Resisting the temptation to linger, she hurried through her bath, and then released the stop so that the water drained away as she dried herself with a thinning towel. It had been part of her trousseau and, really, it was time to replace everything, but the money was always needed more urgently elsewhere, for repairs to the house, shoes for the children — there was always something, she thought, allowing her mind to rest for a moment in a matter she knew to be of no importance at all. She put on her dressing gown, rinsed the tub, replaced the stop, turned on the taps, and returned to the bedroom to wake William. "I've started your bath, darling," she said, throwing open the curtains. He flung an arm over his eyes and murmured something unintelligible. "It's nearly seven," she said insistently. Getting her husband out of bed was often as difficult as reclaiming his attention from a book he was lost in reading. She went to the bed and pulled the covers back. "William, you know you won't like it if you're late to school."

"Oh, very well," he murmured, opening his eyes. He sat up, not yet quite awake, and smoothed his rumpled hair. There was a crease in his cheek where it had pressed against the pillow. After a moment, he looked at her. She could see the change in his eyes as he, too, remembered. "Are you all right? Did you get any sleep at all?"

"Some," she said, nodding.

His nightshirt fell about his knees as he got out of the bed. Putting his arms around her, he rested his chin against her hair. "And I slept like a baby," he said guiltily.

"You always do." For a minute, she rested against the comfort of his body. Then, she pulled away. "Hurry," she said, "or the bath water will overflow."

Left to herself, Rosaline took a black wool skirt and white cotton blouse from her wardrobe and finished dressing. Sitting at the vanity, she unbraided her hair, brushed it out, and rolled it into a loose bun on the back of her head. As she fixed it with a few last pins, she saw, reflected in the mirror, the door opening and her son on the threshold. Still in his nightshirt, his feet bare, he was looking very worried. Turning, she held out her arms to him. "Good morning, Will."

He ran across the rug and flung himself at her. "You never came home last night," he said accusingly.

"But I did. I'm here, aren't I?" She gathered his body to her, kissed his shiny hair and his nose as he turned his face up to look at her, the worry not quite gone from his eyes. "And I kissed you goodnight, before I went to bed, you and the girls, but you were so sound asleep you didn't feel it, did you? Well, here's another," she said, moving her lips to his cheek.

Will was seven and tall for his age, though not slender like his father, nor delicate like her. He was broad and sturdy, with light hair that would darken with age and hazel eyes usually alight with mischief. If he could be said to resemble anyone, it was his grandfather, even to the expression on his face at the moment, which reminded Rosaline strongly of the times she had been reprimanded by her parent for turning up late to dinner.

"You're not going to be out again today, are you?"

"Yes. I promised Aunt Etta I'd visit, and I may have to stay with her a while, not only today, but for the next few days as well."

"But, why?"

Rosaline hesitated a moment, considering her answer, and then said, "It's on account of Aunt Lily. She's gone away, and Aunt Etta is feeling very sad and lonely."

"But she's only gone to the city, for just a few days," he said. It was what Lily had told him before she left.

"It's for longer, I'm afraid."

"But she never said a proper good-bye."

"No, she didn't," agreed Rosaline. "It was very thoughtless of her." Yes, that was the word, *thoughtless*. If only Lily had thought of anyone but herself, and her own unhappiness, she could never have done what she did. If only she had thought of her mother, of Rosaline, of the children, of how they loved her, of how they would miss her!

"And so I'll say when she comes home!"

It seemed futile to put off telling him what sooner or later he would have to know. "Aunt Lily's gone to another home, Will. Home, to God. She won't be coming back to us."

"Never?"

"Never."

Tears filled Will's eyes and spilled down his plump cheeks. The unfairness of life was more than he could bear. "But she always brings me a present when she comes!"

Appalled, Rosaline did not know how to reply. Then, looking up, her eyes met her husband's. He was standing in the doorway in his dressing gown, his hair damp from his bath, a look of amusement on his clean-shaven face. She began to laugh. A moment later, William joined in.

Her son looked at her suspiciously, and then turned to his father. William got himself under control and looked down at the boy in just the way, Rosaline imagined, he would regard a student he wanted to set on the right path. "We'll all miss Aunt Lily's generosity and kindness," he said. "Just as we'll miss seeing her lovely face, and spending time in her company. She was always good fun, wasn't she?" Will nodded solemnly. "We'll all miss her for many reasons, and feel sad because she's no longer here with us. But we mustn't forget to be happy, as well, that she's now in the best of all possible places, in heaven with the Lord."

But was she? wondered Rosaline. In the circumstances, which would triumph — God's justice or His mercy? In either case, how could she have laughed? A moment before it happened, she would not have thought it possible.

"And with His angels?" asked Will.

"Yes," said William.

"Will they'll teach her to fly?"

This time, Rosaline managed to stifle her laugh. "I certainly hope so," she said. "Now, hurry and dress, or you'll be late for school."

Will removed himself from her arms and raced out of the room past his father. "Dora said we're having pancakes for breakfast," he called. "I love pancakes," he added, as if that fact had somehow previously escaped his parents' notice.

Coming into the room, William removed his dressing gown, flung it on a chair, and began to dress. Rosaline got to her feet and automatically picked it up. "I'll put it away," he said, not impatiently, but as if eager to do her some service, however small, and this one, having been called to his attention, would do as well as any.

"I've been thinking," said Rosaline, oblivious to his words, hanging the gown in its place in his wardrobe, "if only Lily had had children . . ." She let the words trail off.

William shrugged. "She might not have thought of them," he said, "any more than she thought of you, or her mother, or anyone. We don't know what it's like to be in the grip of such despair."

"No," said Rosaline. "Thank God, we don't."

When she finished tidying up, she went up the stairs to the nursery floor. As she hurried along the hallway to the twins' room, Will came hurtling past her, fully dressed in his short pants and long socks, starched white shirt and brown jacket, on his way down to breakfast, which, from the bangs and rattles drifting up from the kitchen, Minnie had already begun to prepare. "Don't run down the stairs," Rosaline called after him. "And be sure to hold on to the banister."

"Yes, Mama," said Will dutifully, lifting his chubby hand to the railing and slowing his pace a fraction.

"And don't eat all the pancakes!"

He thought this hilarious, and the sound of his giggles followed her all the way to her daughters' room, where she found Dora trying to wrestle the girls into their dresses. They were a handful, Helen especially, though Emily ran her a close second. Slender and fair, they were the spit and image of their father, all arms and legs, far too tall to be only five years old. Rosaline's fear was that they would continue to grow until they were as tall as William, towering over their brother and every other man of their acquaintance, though if any young women could cope with that eventuality, Rosaline was certain her twins could. Nothing seemed to daunt them. They were fearless, the two of them.

"Mama, Mama," they called, seeing her in the doorway, Helen pulling out of Dora's grasp, both of them hurtling across the room to her.

"Hello, darlings," she said, stooping to kiss them, noticing that the nanny's face was unusually sober as she greeted her. "Good morning, Dora," Rosaline replied. "I expect Will told you?"

"Yes. I'm so sorry."

"Thank you. We all are. It's going to be a terrible few days," she added, turning her attention back to the girls who were clamoring to be noticed.

"I fell," said Helen, yanking up her skirt to show her mother a bruise on her thigh.

Rosaline commiserated with her, and with Emily over an invisible scratch on her arm, then admired the drawings the twins had done in her absence, crayoned scrawls "for Aunt Lily," Helen told her. It was Lily, of course, the twins had to thank for the crayons and the paper, Lily who had spent endless hours with them, since they were old enough to hold pencils, encouraging their feeble efforts, as her father had once encouraged hers.

"But Will said she's not coming back," added Emily, sounding suddenly aggrieved.

"No," said Rosaline. "Aunt Lily's gone away." She took a breath and added, "She's gone to heaven."

"But when will we see her again?" asked Helen.

"Someday," said Rosaline, taking refuge in theology. "But not for a very long time."

"Then do put these away and keep them safe," said Helen, gathering up the drawings and handing them to her mother, "so we can show her when she comes."

At a loss for what else to say, Rosaline took the drawings, put them on the top shelf of the bookcase with the others being saved for one reason or another, and then helped Dora with the fidgeting girls, buttoning the straps on their shoes, adjusting the bows on their dresses, the ribbons in their curly blonde hair, until they resembled little angels, an image that could last as long as an hour, if all went well. "I don't think they really understand," said Rosaline as she and Dora followed them out of the room.

"They're very young, ma'am," replied Dora. She was, as always, wearing a dark blue dress and a starched cap perched on her gray-streaked hair. A small, plump woman, originally from Boston, she looked a great deal like Queen Victoria, Rosaline always thought, though in fact she was a gentle creature, quiet, unassuming, barely able to manage the children, but such a welcome relief after the tartar of an English nanny who had preceded her that neither Rosaline nor William was anxious to find fault. The girls loved her, possibly because she was no match for them; and even Will never seemed to mind when she fussed.

"They're going to miss her so."

"Oh, yes," said Dora. "At first, though I expect they'll forget her soon enough," she added sadly, as if foreseeing how little her own eventual exit would matter to the children.

Forget Lily? Rosaline's heart twisted in her breast. Her children forget the sweet, generous "aunt" who had doted on them from birth? How could that be?

The girls went with Dora to join Will in the kitchen, while Rosaline entered the dining room, where William had already taken his place at the table. Though she had made a valiant attempt to have the family eat all meals together, in the end it had turned out to be easier on everyone to have the children take breakfast with Dora and Minnie, and for William and herself to enjoy a few moments of peace together at the start of the day. Weekends, however, were another matter. Then, they ate all meals together, though they were as likely as not to be at William's parents, or hers, for dinner. The Schuylers lived in Kirkby, about ten miles away. If the weather was good, it was a pleasant outing with the children to visit them. William had purchased a Ford a few years before especially for that purpose, although they occasionally made longer journeys, last summer as far as Rhode Island to see the Atlantic Ocean.

Over a breakfast of oatmeal and buttered toast and good strong coffee (black and unsweetened), Rosaline and William took refuge from the thought of Lily in the morning paper and a discussion of the news — the uselessness of Senator LaFollette's threatened filibuster against the resolution of war, the doubtful truth of reports concerning German spies in the State Department, the way her father even now must be fulminating against such nonsense. There was an especially worrying item, since it called up concerns close to home, about the College of Physicians and Surgeons' decision to push forward the graduation date of the next class of doctors, making them available as early as possible for service. "Marcus will be called, I suppose, though he hasn't finished his residency yet," Rosaline said. She did not know how her parents, or herself for that matter, would bear it, if her brother went to war. "And even if he's not, he'll volunteer. He'll want to be in the thick of it."

"He'll want to be where he can do the most good, that's certain," said William.

They were interrupted by the sound of crying coming from the general direction of the kitchen, but had barely made it out of their seats when Helen threw open the door and flew into the room, her twin and Dora hot on her heels. Tears were streaming down the girls' faces.

"What's wrong?" said Rosaline, her eyes checking for injuries. "Have you hurt yourselves?" There were no bruises, no scratches, no torn clothes, not even an untied ribbon.

"No, no," said Dora reassuringly, trying to grab hold of Helen. "They're not hurt."

Helen pulled away from Dora and looked at her mother accusingly. "Will said Aunt Lily's dead."

"Like Tiger," added Emily. Tiger, the cat, had died of old age a few months before.

"He said we have to dig a hole—"

"And b-b-bury her!"

"Will!" shouted William, throwing his napkin down on the table and hurrying from the room, leaving the girls to Rosaline.

"I'm sorry, ma'am," said Dora. "I couldn't shush him."

Rosaline's head began to ache. Why had she been so vague earlier? Why had she not just told them the whole truth, instead of leaving that to Will?

"I called Will a liar," said Helen defiantly. She had been told never to do that.

"You shouldn't have."

"He is!" insisted Helen.

"Come here, the two of you," Rosaline said gently, then signaled to Dora that it was all right for her to go. From the hallway came the sound of Will's voice, protesting to his father that he had only confirmed what the twins had already been told, that Aunt Lily was going to heaven, and it wasn't his fault if they were upset about having to bury her first. It was only the truth. While William tried to convey to his son the notion of subtlety and respect for the feelings of others, Rosaline took a napkin from the table, wiped the girls' faces, and tried to explain. Later, she had no clear memory of what she said, only that, by the time she returned them to Dora, the twins had seemed comforted, convinced that Lily, although gone, was still with them, like the guardian angel in one of their bedtime stories.

It had taken them only a few days to get over Tiger's death, recalled Rosaline gloomily; and she could not remember the last time the cat's name had cropped up in conversation, hardly ever after the first week or so. Yes, it would be the same with Lily, and the inevitability of that made her want to weep.

Leaving the table, she went into the hall and waited while William gathered his things and took his chastened son by the hand. As he did each day on the way to the high school, he would deposit Will at Queen of Heaven, into the care of Sister Seraphica, a sweet young nun who managed the second-grade well enough most of the time, though it had to be said she sometimes failed to keep Will and his friends in line.

Rosaline stood on the doorstep and watched as they went hand-in-hand down the short walk, past the beds of budding azaleas and clusters of tulips, and out through the gate into the street, away from all the "girls" at last, William carrying his worn leather schoolbag, jammed to bursting with books and papers, Will holding a smaller version that he had begged as a birthday gift. It was a sunny morning, though with a chill in the air and a breeze blowing in from the river, which Rosaline turned to look at when her husband and son had disappeared into the tunnel under the railway tracks. At the end of the street, beyond the inn, was a small park with wooden benches facing the water, a Civil War Memorial, and a bandstand where there were concerts in summer. Today it seemed, as it often did, a tranquil, happy spot, and the river no more than a wide stream, incapable of harm, though Rosaline knew better, of course. Dora had strict instructions never to let the children wander out of her sight.

"Mama," Helen called.

Rosaline hesitated, her eyes held by the view, by its mesmerizing combination of beauty and danger.

"Mama!"

Shivering a little, she turned away. Before setting out for Riverhall, she had to spend a little while with Dora and Minnie discussing household matters, and with the twins, if she hoped to escape without too much of a fuss; and there were those letters she had promised Mrs. Hurley she would write. "I'm coming," she called, and stepped back inside the house.

Despite the chill, Rosaline decided to walk to Riverhall rather than take the Ford, which William had taught her to drive in a series of combative lessons. Skirting the center of town, following Potter Lane to Apple Hill, she made her way through the April morning over the railway bridge and north along Beech Road, high above the river that ran like a silver ribbon threaded through the screen of trees. As she followed the familiar route, she felt herself fighting not only the wind, but an awful dread. Not even when Lily was sick had she felt this way. Even then, she had looked forward to spending a few hours with her best friend. But now, instead of pleasure, the prospect of seeing Lily again brought only pain.

At Little Neck Road, Rosaline crossed back over the railroad, followed the elm-lined causeway to the Riverhall gates, then continued on along the graveled drive, around the oval stand of birches just coming into leaf, past the old cedar tree, and up the steps to the porch. Nuala opened the door for her. "You never walked!" she said when she caught sight of Rosaline's mud-caked shoes, her flushed face, the tendrils of hair escaping from under her hat.

"I don't know why I thought it would be a good idea."

"Well, give me those shoes. They need a good cleaning. Mrs. Canning's in the library," she added as she took Rosaline's black wool coat and felt hat, hanging them on the wrought iron stand near the door.

"Did she sleep?" asked Rosaline, sitting on the settle to remove her shoes.

"She says so," replied Nuala, sounding doubtful. Her own face was unusually pale, with blue smudges of shadow under her eyes.

"And you? Did you get any rest?"

"As much as you, I expect," said Nuala, with a grimace. "It's an awful business, this. Would you like some coffee? And a bite to eat? You'll be needing something after that walk."

"Just some coffee, please. I'd love a cup." She handed Nuala her shoes.

Nuala nodded and set off for the kitchen. "I'll get these right back to you," she said, as Rosaline, in her stocking feet, started down the hall to the library.

"Aunt Etta, dear," she called as she entered.

The curtains were drawn, casting the room into twilight. Only the desk lamp was on, shedding a small circle of brightness over Henrietta, who was seated at the large oak desk, fountain pen in hand, writing, her address book open in front of her, sealed envelopes bearing her flowing script lying in a pile to one side. Looking up, she said, "Oh my dear, how kind of you to come so early. I expected the twins would keep you occupied for a good while this morning."

"They did try," said Rosaline, crossing the room to the desk. She put a hand on Henrietta's shoulder and leaned down to kiss her cheek. "How dark it is in here," she added, moving away from the desk toward the windows.

"No, no," said Henrietta. "Turn on the lamps, if you like, but don't open the curtains."

"I won't, if you'd rather I didn't." And Rosaline went instead to the lamps, turning each of them on, giving the room the comforting glow of evening. "That's better."

"Yes," murmured Henrietta politely, "thank you, dear," giving Rosaline the clear impression that she had preferred the gloom. She was writing notes, she explained, as she could not bear the thought of calling everyone who needed to know of Lily's death. "I haven't even telephoned to Edith," she said. Jonas would deliver the notes when she was done. "He took the news hard," she added. "He and Rebecca both doted on Lily."

"Everyone did," said Rosaline, though she knew it was not quite true. "Let me at least address the envelopes for you." Drawing up one of the side chairs, she sat across the desk from Henrietta. For a while, the only sound in the room was the scratching of the nibs against the heavy cream-colored paper. Then, Nuala came in with a tray laden with coffee and a plate of buttered bread, which Rosaline did not refuse in the hope that her eating might encourage Henrietta to do the same.

"Fresh baked, this morning," said Nuala encouragingly before leaving again.

Rosaline urged Henrietta to try some, which she did, setting it aside after only a few bites, returning her attention to the note she was writing. After a moment, she stopped and tore it to pieces. "What can I possibly say to Reverend Moreland?" she asked.

Rosaline knew very well what she meant. This woman who had never in her life spoken an untrue word, beyond the usual social flatteries meant to be kind rather than to deceive, now had to tell a lie of cosmic proportions. Moreover, she had to tell it not only to family and friends, but to her minister, flinging the lie in God's teeth, so to speak. Was it any wonder that she hesitated at the prospect? Yet, what was the alternative? Lily refused a Christian burial, put in the earth somewhere beyond the churchyard, away from her family, in some unsanctified grave? It was unthinkable. And surely it was hard enough that she would have to stand before her Creator, perhaps had already stood before Him, with such a sin on her soul without subjecting her to the censure of the far less compassionate citizens of Minuit?

"Why, you must tell him what you know for certain," said Rosaline firmly. "And mention the coroner's verdict."

Dropping her pen, Henrietta buried her face in her hands.

"Would you like me to write him? Or perhaps you'd rather telephone?"

Henrietta was silent for a moment, but finally she lifted her head and, looking steadily at Rosaline, said, "I can't speak to him. Not yet. I don't wish to speak to anyone. But I really must write the note myself, I suppose. I would be grateful, though, if you could go with me later to see him. To make the arrangements. You'll know better than I what Lily would want."

"I'm sure she'd want whatever would please you."

Her face bleak, Henrietta nodded, and Rosaline realized how foolish she had sounded. As if anything about this sorry affair could possibly please anyone! Reaching across the desk, she took hold of Henrietta's hand. After the months of inactivity brought on by her illness, it was smoother than it had ever been in a lifetime of rowing and sailing and tending her garden, but still surprisingly strong as it returned Rosaline's clasp. "We must keep in mind," she said, "however much we're suffering, Lily is at peace."

"Yes," said Henrietta. "I'm keeping hold of that thought." Then her eyes welled with tears. "Oh, but when I think of the life she might have had . . ." Impatiently, she shook her head and, withdrawing her hand from Rosaline's, dabbed at her face with a handkerchief she took from the pocket of her black silk dress. "I'm all right," she said. "I just need to keep busy." Picking up her pen, she began to write. "We had better finish these."

In another half hour, they were done. As Henrietta sorted the envelopes into a basket, Rosaline went to the mantle and pulled the bell cord; and, in far less time than it should take to get from the kitchen to the library, Nuala was at the door, Rosaline's shoes in her hand. "Yes, missus?" she said, her eyes going immediately to the tray, taking note of how little had been eaten.

Henrietta extended the basket to Nuala. "If you'll give these to Jonas? He's waiting."

"He is," she said. "In the kitchen so, these twenty minutes." She handed the shoes to Rosaline and took the basket, making room for it on the tray. Picking it up, she started for the door.

"It might be a help to him if you went along," said Henrietta. "So he won't have to keep getting in and out of the car."

The girl looked back, ready to refuse, but Rosaline said, "I'll be here." She finished tying her laces. "There's no need to worry. We'll be fine."

"All right then."

"And please tell him that I'll be needing the car later. I have to see Reverend Moreland."

"Yes, missus," said Nuala, with a nod of her head; she left the room, closing the door after her.

III

"His arthritis has been acting up," said Henrietta, referring to Jonas, "with all this damp weather."

A silence descended, a terrible void that for a moment neither Rosaline nor Henrietta knew how to fill. They moved from the desk to the sofa and chairs arranged around the large fireplace. Above the mantle hung a still life of Lily's. It was of the house, set back behind the giant cedar tree in the front garden. There was hardly a picture left that she had not painted, thought Rosaline, only a few landscapes that Mr. Canning had done, all rock and bright light, nothing like Lily's work at all.

Henrietta settled herself on the sofa, and Rosaline sat nearby in an armchair. The two women looked at each other bleakly.

The clock in the hallway struck the hour, and Rosaline glanced at the one on the mantle. Only noon, she thought. How was it going to be possible to get through this day?

Finally, Henrietta said, "Tell me about the children." Rosaline hesitated. It seemed wrong somehow, gloating, boastful, to speak of them, but Henrietta must have read her mind because she went on, "Really, it would cheer me up. They're such little imps. Always up to something to make me laugh."

That was true enough. After the urge to scream had passed, or the desire to spank, one really could not help laughing. She launched into an accounting of their latest peccadilloes and even managed, in the next quarter hour, to bring more than one smile to Henrietta's face. But then her attention began to flag, and Rosaline, noticing that she was again looking very tired, said, "Now, that's enough of that. William says I can talk about the children all day without stopping to draw breath, but I've learned to have a little pity for others, especially when they're looking as done in as you, Aunt Etta. Wouldn't you like to rest for a while?"

"Yes, I think I would. For a few minutes." Though instead of returning to her room, she said, she preferred just to stretch out on the sofa.

Rosaline helped her to remove her shoes, offered her a needlework pillow to rest her head on, then covered her with one of the crocheted throws (all Henrietta's handiwork) that lay in a basket beside the hearth, ready for those times when even central heating could not quite take the chill from the room.

"You needn't stay," she said. "Nuala will be back soon."

"I'm happy to," replied Rosaline. Henrietta nodded and closed her eyes.

The *Hudson Tribune* lay untouched on the table, but Rosaline had read it already. In any case, she had had enough of war news for the moment. Regretting that she had not thought to bring her knitting (she was making a sweater for William), she moved quietly to the bookshelves and browsed among the volumes, looking for something that would occupy her while she waited. Though not a huge collection, it was an interesting one. In addition to Titus Canning's law books, there were volumes of drama, from ancient Greek to modern day; and of poetry, by Shelley and Bryon, Whittier, Longfellow, and on through Tennyson and Yeats to Robert Frost and Edgar Lee Masters. There were leather-bound editions of Shakespeare, Carlyle's *The French Revolution*, Gibbon's *Decline and Fall of the Roman Empire*, and a number of works of fiction, including novels by Dickens and Scott, by William Dean Howells and Henry James, by Edith Wharton and Willa Cather, even a copy of Upton Sinclair's *The Jungle,* as well as collections of short stories by O. Henry and Guy de Maupassant. She pulled one by the latter down from the shelf, settled back into her chair, and began to read, randomly choosing "The Jewelry," feeling herself, at its end, unsettled by the dubious morality of the tale (for surely one ought to find the virtuous wife the more sympathetic woman?), yet wishing that she could write like that, with such attention to detail, with such clarity and elegance, wondering what sacrifice she would be prepared to make to secure her own husband's comfort. Would she be brave (or foolish) enough to surrender her honor? She closed the book and sighed. If she could just find a way to demonstrate to William how much she loved him, for one never knew. If Lily could be snatched away so quickly, then so, too, could he, so could everyone she cared for, with no warning. It was a terrifying thought.

Henrietta whimpered and pulled the throw closer around her, but she did not wake. Laying the volume of stories aside, Rosaline sat studying the sleeping woman's face. It was so familiar to her, and dear, hardly lined at all, a lovely face, so she had always thought, though Henrietta did not have the air of a beauty, that womanly aura commanding deference, an aura that Rosaline's own mother possessed, carrying herself as if she were a queen and the rest of the world her court, there to do her bidding. Not that Violet Roeder was in any way demanding, only expectant, and she was rarely disappointed. Her sons, her son-in-law, friends of her husband, waiters in restaurants, men everywhere, presented with her fragile blonde loveliness, could not do enough to please her. And though it was hard to be the plain daughter of such a beautiful mother, even Rosaline could not help loving her, for there was not a shred of meanness in her. When she spoke, it was usually to say a kind word about someone. Only her father, it seemed to Rosaline, though clearly devoted to his wife, took her looks in stride, apparently oblivious to his good fortune in having married such a catch. He treated her well, but matter-of-factly. He was always much more gallant with Henrietta. Was that because they had been friends from childhood? Rosaline wondered. But surely, in that case, his manner would have been even more offhand?

She sighed. During those frightful, awkward days of adolescence, when her nose had seemed to wander willy-nilly across her face, she had longed to be beautiful. Eventually, though, she had made peace with her shortcomings. Her looks were pleasant enough; and, as they had been sufficient to attract and hold William's attention, she had no complaints. She considered herself a fortunate woman, blessed by God, and she preferred to prize what she had rather than weep for what she lacked.

Not that she considered beauty a "curse," as she had sometimes heard it said. Her mother clearly demonstrated otherwise. Still, she could not see that it had done Lily any good: had she been plain, Edmund Farel never would have thought to approach her. In any case, her looks had as often brought envy and resentment as praise, for if she was open and loving, full of warmth and good humor with those she cared for, in general she had not the knack of unfailing graciousness, of undiscriminating concern, that won hearts for Rosaline's mother. And if Lily could be charming when she put her mind to it, when she did not, when preoccupied with her work or lost in one of her depressions, she could appear remote and superior, so that many attracted initially by her beauty, put off by her seeming indifference, came in the end to think her proud, and to dislike her for it.

As for herself, though the never-ending compliments heaped on Lily had occasionally caused Rosaline to behave with a peevishness that had surprised (and possibly even hurt) her friend, her jealousy was always fleeting. What she felt for Lily, above all, were love and admiration and a deep sense of trust. Their quarrels had never lasted long.

The mystery, thought Rosaline, was why Lily, who never deigned to notice when someone was smitten with her, had paid any attention at all to Edmund Farel; why she had responded to him, but to none of the other far more worthy men who had tried over the years to court her. That was what Rosaline could not understand. Why Edmund? Certainly he was handsome, and had a roguish sort of charm, and a glib tongue, but if good men had wanted her, there had also been a fair number of cads throwing themselves at her feet. She had stepped over the bodies and gone on her way. What in Edmund had caught her attention and made her stop? Why had she chosen him to love? And why, so soon after their marriage, had she stopped?

None of them would ever know. Not that it mattered. All that mattered was that Lily had suffered, and now, if God were truly merciful (and Rosaline chose to believe He was), her suffering had come to an end.

Restless, Rosaline stood. Henrietta was still asleep, her mouth slightly open, her breathing deep and even. Deciding that there was no harm in leaving her for a few minutes, just long enough to freshen up, Rosaline crossed quietly to the door and slipped out into the hall. She climbed the staircase and turned left at the landing. How many times had she done this on her way to Lily's room for an afternoon of play with her friend and her dolls and tea sets? hundreds? thousands? happily certain that even the worst of sorrows would cast their shadows no more than a day or two. Now, she hesitated at the closed door, but could not enter. The silence, the emptiness — she felt unable to face them. Yet, when she came out of the bathroom, instead of returning to the library, drawn by an impulse she did not understand, she continued on to the tower door, opened it, and climbed the stairs to the studio.

A square room with a pitched ceiling and plastered walls painted white, the studio was set above the roofline of the main part of the house, so that there were windows on all four sides giving a full view of the surrounding countryside, each window hung with heavy curtains that could be drawn to control the light. There was a battered plank table, every inch of it covered with drawings, sketchpads, tubes of paint, boxes of pastels, watercolors, jars of brushes. Shelves holding more supplies stood against a wall beside the fireplace. By the window overlooking the river, there was a burgundy velvet chaise longue and next to it a round table covered with a paisley shawl. A tapestry chair with a frame of intricately carved wood sat with no clear purpose off-center in the room. Blank canvases and finished paintings were stacked against the walls. One, covered by a large piece of tattered cloth, sat on an easel in a corner. This was Lily's domain, and no one had ever dared enter without an invitation, except her father, and even he had not done it lightly.

How pleasant it must be to have a room that was entirely one's own, thought Rosaline, looking longingly about, a room where no one could come uninvited, not one's husband or children or parents, for if the Cannings had given Lily a lot of leeway (at least so long as she was safe at home), Violet had had no compunction about entering her daughter's bedroom whenever she liked; and certainly now, with a growing family in a small house, Rosaline had no space to call hers. Even the sewing machine on which she made the children's clothes stood in the dining room, covered by an embroidered cloth, doubling as a sideboard when she and William entertained.

She went to the chaise and sat, staring out at the river, not really seeing it, or the bright smudges of sail in the distance, the black wisps of birds against the blue sky, but remembering the times she had lain in this very spot, striking attitudes for Lily until she was satisfied sufficiently to begin to draw. They were happy times, for the most part, with the two of them sometimes silent, but more often chatting about school and friends and clothes, exchanging confidences as Lily worked, sitting in the tapestry chair, facing her model, sketching rapidly, page after page, and later, standing at her easel, laying in colors on the canvas with quick, bold strokes. Rosaline had wanted to marry and have children and, in her spare time, to write. (How was she to know then that there would be no "spare time"?) Lily had wanted the reverse. She had wanted to be an artist. Husband and children could come later. First, she had to make a name for herself. That was possible for a woman now, she had said. "Look at Mary Cassatt. Or Anna Lea Merritt, how popular she is, though I don't like her work at all. Too sentimental. But Rosa Bonheur! No one painted animals as well as she, except perhaps Stubbs." Unlike Rosaline, Lily had never taken more than a cursory interest in the suffragist movement, nor in any kind of politics. Art had absorbed her completely. Encouraged by her father, by her teachers, by the friends and acquaintances who posed for her portraits and bought her paintings, she had believed her talent would carry her through, that success would be hers. How confident she had been. How full of hope.

That portrait Lily had done of her, in the peacock-printed dress, lying on this very chaise, when was it painted? Rosaline frowned, and then remembered, surprised to have forgotten even for a moment. Not only was it the year of her parents' twentieth wedding anniversary (Rosaline had wanted the portrait as a gift for them, commissioning Lily for the price of the canvas and paints), but also a time of high drama in the usually placid Canning household. It was the summer of 1907, a few months before hers and Lily's sixteenth birthday. "I've learned everything I can here. Everything," Lily had said over and over, day after day, as she begged and stormed and threatened, no longer the well-behaved young miss, but reverting to conduct she had long since given up, reminding everyone of the mischief of which she was capable, until her weary parents had finally agreed to let her leave school to enroll in the Art Students League in New York. Off she had gone with them in the autumn (her going alone was out of the question), to the city, to stay at the Pelham Hotel, coming home most weekends, though her father, who had business to tend to, returned to Minuit more often.

Rosaline had missed Lily terribly while she was gone, her loneliness made worse by the fear that friends in New York would supplant her; but most of the students at the League were older, and faster. Lily had found the men worrying and the women intimidating, both in the city and at the League's summer session in Woodstock, which she also attended, again accompanied by her parents. Even later, no matter where she went off to on her studies, or how many friends she made along the way, she had seemed always as happy to return to the comfort of her relationship with Rosaline as Rosaline was to welcome her back.

She got to her feet. Really, she ought not to remain longer, she told herself. Henrietta might need her. Still, she lingered. Suddenly curious to see if she would now be able to detect in Edmund Farel's handsome face a hint of the trouble he was to cause, she went to the stacks of canvases leaning against the wall and began to sort through them, hoping to find a portrait of him; but there was not one among the wide assortment of paintings — portraits, landscapes, seascapes, some remembered, some new to her — in a bewildering variety of styles.

She had found her friend's constant experimentation unsettling, as had almost everyone. "You'd do better to stick to what you know best," Titus Canning had often told his daughter and, when Rosaline heard him, truthfully, she had not disagreed. Though she adored the early work, however derivative (or so Lily had called it) of Sargent or Eakins or Monet or whomever, she was not sure she at all liked the more recent paintings. They seemed too flat to her, the perspective awry, the color arbitrary.

The one she was looking at now, for example: on the one hand, it was comfortingly familiar, a scene like many Lily had painted, of the Hudson viewed from Riverhall's back porch; on the other, there was nothing peaceful or serene or even beautiful about it. There were few details, just shapes laid in with thick strokes, in odd colors, a great white moon setting to the west, its rays reflected in the dark, wind-ruffled water, the hulking Highlands in shadow beyond, unaccountably menacing. No, Rosaline could not say she liked it.

As she let the canvas slip back into place, the easel caught her attention. Wanting to know what Lily had been working on when she left for New York, Rosaline went to it, pulled off the cloth covering the painting, and breathed in sharply.

It was a portrait — but what a portrait! In a flat plane, with bold outlines and broad patches of color, the two sides of the face seemed unrelated, though they were unified by the symmetrical arrangement of the hair above and the overall pattern of the dress below. The left side was recognizably Lily, looking much as she had when Rosaline last saw her just a few days before — young, vibrant, beautiful; but the right, that seemed a nightmare vision of all one feared about growing old — the thinning hair, the loose folds of hanging skin, the sharpened nose, the drooping mouth and eye. It was terrible to look at, terrifying. Rosaline felt the tears start again. Lily must have painted it in the depths of a depression. There was no other explanation for it.

No one else must see it, certainly not Aunt Etta. Taking the painting down from the easel, Rosaline replaced it with a still life of some flowers in a copper pot, covered it with the same cloth, and carried the portrait to the fireplace. She would burn it. Resting it on the floor, she placed her foot on the bottom of the stretcher and grasped the sides firmly, intending to break it to fit the canvas into the grate.

But she could not do it. Trembling, she let the painting fall and backed away. How could she be sure she was right? What if it was a masterpiece she intended to destroy? Wiping away the tears, she looked around the studio for a place to hide it. In among the other paintings was one possibility; or, better, in the cupboards set into the wainscoting on either side of the stair railing. There was just enough room in one, she found when she opened it and pushed out of the way the bits of broken stretcher, torn pieces of canvas, and other rubbish that ought to have been discarded ages ago. Returning to the painting, she picked it up, carried it to cupboard, and fitted it in, covering it with a tattered smock retrieved from the floor. The painting would be safe there, for a while at least, until she could think what to do with it.

At the steps, she stopped for a last look around. But the comfort she had only moments before found in the studio had fled. It seemed suddenly to reproach her, not for what she had almost done, but for what she always failed to do. The stacks of canvases, the brushes, the paints, all the signs of Lily's industriousness, her ambition, her dedication, seemed to accuse Rosaline of slighting her own talent, of wasting it.

But I'm probably not any good at all, she thought, in her own defense.

"What's important is to keep working." She could almost — not quite — hear Lily's voice, feel her presence. "What's important is not to lose heart."

How often had she heard Lily say those words? Oh, why had she not heeded them herself? thought Rosaline. A wave of the anger that had plagued her the day before came surging back. "Don't you dare lecture me," she said to the empty air. "Not after what you've done." But the anger passed quickly, leaving grief to fill the void left in its wake. "Oh,

Lily," she said, her voice soft and full of pain. Then, she turned and went back down the stairs and out the tower door, closing it behind her.

FLORENCE

Though Florence awakened on Wednesday morning with no greater expectation of the hours ahead but that they should pass with a minimum of fuss, an argument with Andrew over breakfast confounded even that small hope. There he sat, nose buried in his newspaper, and just as she was about to draw his attention by complaining about the quality of the marmalade, he looked up and, in much the same tone he might have used to inform her that he would be late to dinner, told her that he was going to enlist. Just like that.

"But you can't!" she said, without stopping to think whether there might be a more politic response. "You're far too old. In any case, you've done your bit." He had served in the Spanish-American War and come home safely. What was the point in his pushing his luck?

Lowering the newspaper, her husband cast her a somber look. "The President's talking about a draft, but that will take time to organize. Meanwhile, the war effort will be dependent on volunteers. I don't see that there's anything else I can do." As always when he thought he was in the right, there was no reasoning with him, though Florence did her best in the next few minutes to appeal to his sense of responsibility — to his family, to her family, and, above all, to her, his wife. "It's not as if we have children," he countered, unwittingly twisting the knife in her wound. "I can't claim an exemption on that count. My health's perfect. And you'll be well looked after, no matter what," he added, supplying substance to the ghastly scenarios already running through her mind: Andrew wounded, Andrew dead, worst of all, Andrew maimed, returning home a shell of a man. The newspapers were filled with such stories, awful tales of British casualties on the western front. "It's my duty, Florence," he continued in his firm, no-nonsense way. "I have no choice."

She should have seen it coming, she supposed. Andrew not only had a very strong sense of honor, but a craving for adventure that Florence found truly terrifying; and, as she listened to him going on about patriotism and the like, she could not help feeling again somehow betrayed, for he had turned out to be a quite different husband from the one she had set her cap for when Titus Canning brought him home. He had known Andrew Macleod from the Harvard Club and, impressed by his intellect and character, had enticed him to Minuit with the offer of a partnership in his firm, which, if small by city standards, nevertheless boasted an impressive array of influential men (and some women) among its clients. To Florence, when she met him, Andrew had seemed the quintessential staid lawyer, a sturdy, compact man, one who was utterly dependable. And though he was certainly that, he was so much else, for Andrew did not just speak of mountain climbing, bear hunting, and white-water rafting, as did so many young men who had grown up admiring Teddy Roosevelt, he actually did those things. By the time she had understood that, however, and begun to suspect that she had little hope of changing him, the banns

123

were read, the ceremony planned. It was too late to call off the wedding, though it was hardly likely she would have done that given the chance. Minuit did not have a large supply of eligible bachelors, nor had Florence had much luck attracting a suitor when traveling with her parents in pursuit of one. Andrew was about as good as she could do, and, while in the five years of her marriage she had accumulated many complaints about her lot in life, overall she could not regret marrying him. Her husband was a sober man, intelligent, hardworking, respectful of her and her family; and though still drawn to go adventuring with his friends, he was less able to do so since her uncle's death. With the increase of responsibility that had come with taking over the firm, Andrew had little time left for pleasure. But duty? That was another matter. Though Florence might on occasion be able to talk him out of enjoying himself, she never could convince him not to do his duty.

Yet, she intended to try. As she sat doing the household accounts in the back parlor later that morning, her mind kept running through arguments, considering stratagems, trying to find one that had a chance of breaching the wall of her husband's convictions until, finally, with a cry of frustration, she slammed the ledger shut, replaced the cap on her fountain pen, and looked up almost with relief when Fanny, the housemaid, entered to tell her that Nuala had come from Riverhall and was asking to see her.

"Oh, let her come in," said Florence; but, as she waited, her irritation gave way to a pleasurable sense of expectancy, for when Nuala came it usually was to deliver an invitation to a dinner party at Riverhall, and those were always a welcome diversion, with an interesting array of guests likely to be served up with the food. Last time, Mrs. Dowling had appeared, wearing the most spectacular diamond earrings.

But standing there on the threshold of the Macleods' back parlor, her hand lifting to offer a square, cream-colored envelope, Nuala looked quite unlike her typical self. There was no hint of impudence in her green eyes, no smile on her freckled face. One glance at her and Florence knew something was wrong. Aunt Etta was ill again, she imagined, despite recognizing her neat handwriting. Dr. Roeder could say what he liked about her being fit as a fiddle, but really how much longer could she go on before her heart gave out? Though Florence would be very sorry when it did. As a child, she had thought her aunt the nicest grown-up she knew, and her opinion had not changed over the years.

Obviously impatient to get away, Nuala (with no more than a brisk "It's all there, in the note," in response to Florence's query) said she had more errands to run, and hurried off before Florence had quite finished slitting the envelope with her silver opener. She read the note quickly, then again, not quite able to take in its contents. An accident. Lily drowned. It could not be true. She wished Nuala had not gone so quickly, so that she might have answered at least some of the questions teeming in Florence's brain. Breathless with shock, she sat heavily in the chair behind the desk and read the note again. Lily. Opening the envelope, Florence had never given her cousin a thought, though it really would not have been so strange if she had, given the troubles of the past six months, that scandalous marriage and Lily's subsequent breakdown.

Lily. Dead.

How peculiar, thought Florence, I'm not crying. I wept buckets when Uncle Titus died. And I was always so fond of Lily!

After a minute or so, Florence felt better, steadier somehow, capable of movement. Getting to her feet, she hurried upstairs to her bedroom and changed into the new black day dress she had (fortuitously, she now realized) bought on her last visit to Lord & Taylor's. She tidied her auburn hair (a lovely color, really) into a coil at the nape of her neck, took her black tricorne hat from its box, and put it on. From a drawer full of neatly arranged gloves, she chose a suitable pair. Then, after stocking her black handbag with a clean lace-trimmed handkerchief, a tortoise-shell pocket comb, and a change purse, she checked herself in the cheval mirror, and frowned at the full-figured young matron, with her completely satisfactory if unremarkable features, who regarded her with equal discontent. No matter how new or stylish the clothes, she never quite managed to look just right, the way Lily did, even when spattered with paint.

Before leaving the bedroom, Florence pushed the bell to summon Fanny, and then impatiently called her name as she hurried down the stairs. Stopping in the hall at the Chinese lacquer table, she picked up the telephone and was about to tell the exchange to get her husband's number when she thought better of it. You never knew who was listening in. "Sorry," she said into the round mouthpiece and hung up abruptly, just as the operator wished her a good morning. It would be much better to send Andrew a note. Hearing footsteps behind her, she put down the telephone and turned. "Oh, there you are. I'll be at my mother's for a while," she told the housekeeper, a thin, dark figure scurrying toward her along the hall like a twig caught in the wind. She was all the staff the Macleods had at present, though they never hesitated to hire extra help for dinner parties and the like. "Then, we'll be going on to Riverhall. You can reach me there, if you need me," she added, however unlikely it was that Fanny would trouble her for anything short of a calamity, and there could hardly be another just yet.

"Is everything all right, Mrs. Macleod?"

"No," replied Florence, though she did not truly feel as if anything was wrong. She was breathless, yes, and a bit dazed perhaps, but not . . . *heartsick*. How peculiar, she thought again. "There's been an accident." She said the words as if rehearsing them, trying to find the sufficiently solemn, compellingly dramatic tone to take over the next few days. "My cousin. Lily. The poor thing has drowned."

The color drained from Fanny's narrow face and her eyelids fluttered rapidly, as if battling back tears. "Oh, dear Lord . . ."

"A terrible accident," said Florence, pulling on her gloves, shaking her head sadly as she stepped out the door the housekeeper held open for her.

It was a lovely day, Florence noticed with a twinge of guilt, if somewhat cool. The forsythia shrubs bordering the house were coming into bloom. She would have to speak to Walter about trimming them back, as she could see they were growing too wild for her taste; and here and there she could see stray bits of unruly green poking up through the soil. Clearly, the morning he spent each week working for the Macleods was not enough. She would just have to ask her parents if she might borrow him another, she decided. Tiny as it was, the garden was an endless source of concern to her. She wanted it to be perfect, like the ones she saw illustrated in the ladies' magazines, but, though she did her best to keep on top of things, there was always some dying plant, fallen tree limb, or recalcitrant weed to spoil the effect she wished to create. And the autumn! That was pure torment. No sooner did one get all the leaves swept up, than along would come a breeze, sending another million or so showering down in a blaze of red and gold, all turning to a sodden mess in the first rain.

Built by her parents for Florence and Andrew as a wedding present, the house was a small, but pretty two-storey folk-Victorian, painted yellow and trimmed in white, with a porch running the width of the facade. It was only a block away from the town's main street, and a short walk beyond that to the Allens, which had been the site's chief virtue. Mother and daughter still spent a large part of each day together.

Today, her house, like all the others Florence passed, was flying an American flag, set out by Andrew before he left for work, a patriotic gesture in support of the president and the war. What a great fuss over something that's really none of our business, she thought irritably, recalling her husband's mad plan and the chaos into which it was bound to throw her life. Then, adding to her sense of being put upon, she saw coming toward her, on the opposite side of the street, Mrs. Jeffers, the wife of the president of the Union Bank, no doubt on her way to visit her daughter who had just had a baby girl. Ordinarily, Florence would have felt it necessary to cross to speak to her, but this time she merely inclined her head in greeting, smiled, and walked on. As difficult as it was in normal circumstances for her to summon sufficient enthusiasm for announcements of impending births and discussions of recent deliveries, today it would be impossible, bursting as she was with her own news. Surprised, the banker's wife cast an affronted glance at Florence, who nevertheless had enough restraint to resist the temptation to politeness, for she knew it would not do to say anything to Mrs. Jeffers before her own mother was informed of Lily's death. Without looking back, Florence hurried on to the intersection and crossed Center Street, which at this point was completely residential, its commercial end starting a few blocks farther west and continuing on until stopped by the railroad tracks. To her relief, she reached her parents' gate without encountering another soul.

One of the grandest in Minuit, the Allens' house was in the Italianate style, which had been all the rage when it was built by its previous owner, a banker who later lost his money in unwise speculation (a lesson Florence's father had very much taken to heart, thereafter avoiding all trading in futures, confining his investments to the safest of industrial securities). It had an octagonal cupola, decorative brackets supporting the overhanging eaves, and elaborate window crowns. Bounded by a low iron fence and overlooking the communal garden square, the house had a broad walk lined with neat shrubs leading to a colonnaded porch. An American flag, mounted on one of its columns, rippled in the breeze, while pansies in giant terracotta pots set on each side of the wide steps nodded along in tempo, not one dead flower visible amid the blooms. The whole of the garden was impeccably maintained. Edith Allen was even more of a perfectionist than her daughter.

Florence rang the doorbell, and then waited impatiently for one of the staff to come open it, for once regretting that the time had passed when, in possession of her own key, she could enter (though not leave, it's true) as she pleased. She rang again, just seconds before the door flew open. "Sorry to have kept you waiting, Mrs. Macleod, but I was that far away," said Deirdre apologetically, "and everyone else is about their chores." In addition to Deirdre and the cook, the Allens had two maids and Walter, who doubled as gardener and chauffeur.

"Good morning, Deirdre." With corn-silk hair, deep blue eyes, and flawless skin, she was far prettier than her sister, thought Florence, and far more agreeable. She was polite and eager to please, unlike Nuala who, no matter how outwardly respectful, always gave the impression of impertinence. "Have you seen Nuala this morning?"

"No. Not since yesterday, as it happens, ma'am." Deirdre looked suddenly worried. "Were you wanting her for something?"

"No," replied Florence, with a shake of her head. "I saw her just a while ago. She brought news. Sad news, I'm sorry to say. It's Lily. There's been an accident."

"Miss Lily? She's hurt?"

"No." Again, Florence searched for the right tone. "She's . . . dead, I'm afraid. Drowned." It sounded so awful put like that, so cold.

Deirdre's eyes filled with tears. "Oh, no," she said. "Not Miss Lily."

That's what was needed, thought Florence: tears. She blinked, but the tears that came so readily to Fanny and Deirdre eluded her. Still, she dabbed at her eyes with her handkerchief. It must be the shock, she thought. That's why I can't cry. "It's such heartbreaking news. I don't think I've taken it in yet. I'm just . . ." She could not say quite what she was.

"And Mrs. Canning? How is she? Oh, the poor lady," said Deirdre, sniffing, brushing her cheeks with the heel of her hand. "Such a terrible thing, and her with her bad heart."

"Nuala said she was well, but I am anxious to get to Riverhall to see for myself. Is my mother in her room?"

"No, she's gone to her study, to write letters, she said."

Though the girl undoubtedly knew well enough to do it without being told, Florence called, "You'd better tell Walter we'll be needing the car," as she started along the hall toward the small room her mother had claimed as her private domain. What a perfectly dreadful day, she thought, opening the door into the study. Overlooking the side garden, it was full of the deep-carved wood furniture, the fringe-trimmed velvet chairs, the globe lamps, originally from Riverhall. Lace curtains framed by red silk draperies covered the windows, through which sunlight splashed across the mahogany writing table where Edith Allen sat, her head bent, moving her pen carefully across a sheet of white bond paper. "Mother?"

Surprised, Edith looked up. She had a lovely oval face framed by auburn hair, highlighted with a few strands of gray. Her eyes were a light brown, her features delicate, her skin only lightly lined and still radiant. Except for the similarity of hair color, mother and daughter looked nothing alike. Rather, Florence resembled her father, who, though tall and rather elegant in appearance, had a nose too long and eyes a fraction too close-set to be called handsome. "Oh, Florence, are you here already?" said Edith. "I'm in the middle of a letter to your Aunt Mildred. I should have replied to hers weeks ago, but it's just been one thing after another."

Wondering how it could be that her mother failed to notice something was terribly wrong, Florence walked to the table and, leaning down to kiss her, caught the scent of lavender water. "Will you let it go for another while? I need to talk to you."

Edith frowned. "I do want to finish it this morning. Your father has been plaguing me about it for days. You know what he's like when he thinks I've slighted his family."

"Please, Mother," insisted Florence, with a hint of resentment. If her brother, Louis, had come into the room demanding attention, he would have had it with no objection.

"Really, you'd think by now you'd have learned some patience," replied her mother, who nevertheless screwed the cap onto the pen and put it down. "I suppose it can wait a while longer." Getting to her feet, she crossed to the sofa and sat again, carefully arranging the skirt of her striped cotton dress on the velvet upholstery. "Why, you're all in black," she said, suddenly noticing. "What on earth has happened? Florence, is it Henrietta? You haven't come to tell me that Henrietta—"

"No, it's not Aunt Etta," said Florence, sitting beside her mother, taking her hand. "Mother, it's Lily."

Edith looked at her with blank eyes. "Lily?" It was as if she had no idea to whom her daughter was referring. "Lily," she repeated. Then, she understood, and her eyes filled with pain. "Oh, no! Oh, heavens, no," she murmured, and the tears started, running down her cheeks, leaving shiny trails in the powder. "No. . . ."

Tears, thought Florence, but still felt none of her own. Putting her arms around her mother, she held her close. "It's the most terrible thing," she said. "Aunt Etta wanted me to tell you myself. She was afraid . . . oh, please, Mother, you mustn't . . ."

⨖

While Edith changed into her black silk, which took little time as she was too upset to fuss, Florence wrote notes to her husband and father and sent one of the housemaids off to deliver them. Lost black gloves caused some delay as they were not in their usual place, and it was only after a lengthy search that they were discovered to be still in the pocket of Edith's coat. When the two women were ready, finally, to leave, Walter had long since brought the Packard around from the garage at the back and was waiting for them at the curb. Deirdre must have told him the news because he did not venture a smile, but only nodded solemnly as he opened the rear door for them and helped them inside.

"You'll be going to Riverhall?" he asked in his light, lilting voice, that of a young man, despite his sixty-odd years. The Allens had heard him sing once, with the choir at Queen of Heaven, where they normally never set foot as it was a Catholic Church, though of course they were forced to make exceptions from time to time, in that instance for Rosaline's wedding. He had a glorious voice, not unlike John McCormack's everyone said, and the entire Allen family, hearing the compliments heaped upon him, could not help but feel pleased with themselves for having a man of so many talents in their employ.

131

"There's no need for you to wait, Walter," said Edith, as the Packard turned into Kirkby Road. "We'll be some time, I expect. And Mr. Allen will want the car later, if he's to join us."

"As you like, ma'am," replied Walter, a hint of relief in his voice. "I do have a fair bit of work to be doing back at the house." When they arrived at Riverhall, he helped the ladies from the car and then, waiting only long enough to see Nuala open the front door for them, drove hastily away, as if fearing Edith might change her mind given the chance.

Which was too bad, really. A moment later, Florence would have insisted on going back with him, had he still been within hailing distance.

"Not home?" said Edith, in response to Nuala's statement. "But where has she gone?"

"To see Reverend Moreland," replied Nuala, taking the ladies' hats and coats and hanging them carefully on the clothes rack, her manner easy, cordial, and quite irritating, thought Florence, lacking as it did any perceptible hint of deference as she saw them into the parlor, where she knew Edith liked to sit.

"Alone?" Her tone made clear how foolish she thought that contingency.

"Mrs. Schuyler went with her."

"Rosaline?" said Florence. She hoped she did not sound as annoyed as she felt, but really it was infuriating the way Rosaline managed to intrude in matters that were not at all her concern. Though she seemed often not to realize it, she was not family.

"They're gone a while now," said Nuala, "so I'm thinking they won't be too much longer. Would you be wanting some coffee? Maybe a little something to eat?"

For a moment, Florence toyed with the idea of telephoning to the Allen house with instructions for Walter to return to fetch them, but quickly realized that it was better just to sit and wait, or she would spend the day chasing back and forth from town.

"Thank you, Nuala. Coffee would be very nice," said Edith, settling herself on the deep-cushioned sofa. "And perhaps a little bread and butter," she added, "though I'm not sure I can manage to eat a thing."

"Nothing for me, thank you." But no sooner had Nuala left the room than Florence was aware of being hungry. The quarrel with Andrew had put her off her breakfast, and she had not had a thing since. Well, the girl was sure to bring more than enough, she thought, sitting in the armchair opposite her mother and surveying the room. "The coffin will be in here, I suppose."

Edith nodded. "As it was for Mother and Father, and dear Rupert." She opened her purse and removed a handkerchief. "And Titus, of course." She sniffed into the linen, then she, too, looked around, letting her eyes take in the worn upholstery, the faded curtains, the spots of damp and buckling paint visible where not hidden by Lily's paintings. "Though I have to say, your uncle would not have rested easy in this room, as it is now. He did like everything just so. And even the piano was out of tune the last time I heard Henrietta play. She has let the place run down."

"Yes, it is awful the way she's neglected it," agreed Florence. It had been such a pretty room, done in shades of cream and gray-green, with printed cotton fabrics and a silk rug from Persia. Now, it just looked shabby.

"Although we must remember that life hasn't been easy for her these past few years," said Edith firmly, changing tack as she always did whenever someone else dared to criticize a member of her family, even if that someone was her own daughter.

"It's only a matter of calling in the decorators, after all," replied Florence, who did not like to be put in the wrong. "I would have been happy to help."

"Of course you would have. We all would have. But what with Titus dying, and her own ill health, and all the trouble with Lily. Oh, my . . ." It was as if, diverted by the appearance of the room, she had forgotten for a moment the purpose of her visit. Tears again filled her eyes, and she brushed at them with her handkerchief. "I don't know how Henrietta will stand this."

"No . . ." It did seem unlikely that she could survive this blow for long, though it would not do to underestimate her. Henrietta Canning was an amazingly strong woman. Florence had heard all the stories (told to comfort her, she had no doubt) about her aunt's lost babies, the months of grief after each death, her determined effort to rebuild her life, her happiness when Lily was born, when she lived.

Florence's heart went out to her aunt. It truly did. How awful it must be, she imagined, to watch your children die—though sometimes she thought her own case perhaps even more dreadful, for she had not managed in all the years of her marriage to become pregnant. Surely that was the most terrible calamity in a woman's life, to be perceived—no, to *be*—barren, like Sarah, in the Bible, only with little hope of God's intervention to put things right? "Trust in the Lord," Reverend Moreland had counseled her, but she had prayed and prayed, to no avail. "Sometimes God withholds His blessings, through no fault of our own, but according to His will," Dr. Roeder had told her when she consulted him. "God's will be done, on earth, as it is in heaven," she whispered as she knelt in church during services, and at night before getting into bed, hoping by her acquiescence to get Him to change His mind. But it did occur to her, sometimes, when she was filled most with despair, that having her child die might not be so terrible a price to pay for proving herself able to conceive one.

"We will have to be very strong for your aunt," said Edith. "We will have to put everything else aside these next few . . . however long it takes, to help her through. She has no one but us now."

"And Rosaline," said Florence, unable to keep the bitterness from her voice.

"Yes indeed. Rosaline, and Erich too, of course. He always had a soft spot for Henrietta," she continued, as always oblivious to her daughter's mood. "I was considered the pretty one, though I know you must find that hard to believe now," she added, never able to resist being coy.

"Why, no, Mother, not at all——"

"Anyway," she went on with a dismissive wave of her hand, "all the young men around came courting me, but not Erich. He never had an eye for anyone but Henrietta. I think he was shattered when she married Titus. But soon enough Violet came along. Stunning, she was then. A real beauty. Prettier than me, I have to say, if quieter than a mouse. And all that family money. I don't think he's had too many regrets."

"I shouldn't think he's had any," said Florence.

"Well, you know men," said Edith, "always a little bit silly about their first loves."

Was it true? wondered Florence. Was there someone Andrew was still a little bit silly about? She felt an unfamiliar pang of jealousy. It had not occurred to her that there might have been a girl in his past whom he had once loved deeply, devotedly. Through her mind paraded the women she had met over the years at various gatherings. No, there was not one among them to whom her husband seemed especially drawn, she decided with some relief, not even Lily (and most men had managed to make themselves fools over her), though of course he could not help being involved in that business with Farel and then, annoyingly, would not tell even his wife what he knew. In any case, Andrew did not seem the type to fall head-over-heels. A good, steady caring, a sensible devotion, an unfailing courtesy, that is what he was capable of, what he demonstrated to her, day in, day out. She was a fortunate woman.

But, then, why could she not be happy?

But of course she was happy, she admonished herself immediately. What was she thinking? It was all this business with Lily. It had upset her, understandably, leading her mind to dwell in unquiet, unhappy waters, as it were.

"Not Father," protested Florence, as she was expected to. "I can't believe there's anyone in his past——"

"Oh, no, not your father," said Edith. "He always tells me I was his first and only love, and I do believe him. A woman can sense such things, don't you think?"

"Yes," agreed Florence. She hoped it was true.

"Although there are those who prefer not to know, who turn a deaf ear . . . Your aunt, for example—"

"Aunt Etta?"

"I gathered from Rupert there was a girl," said Edith, her voice lowered to a confessional note. "In Boston. Her family whisked her off to Europe when Titus' attentions became a little too pronounced. He had no money, few prospects . . ."

Florence's eyes went to the portrait of Titus Canning hanging over the mantle. Painted by Lily when he was forty-eight or so, it showed a man in evening dress, with silvering hair, brilliant dark eyes, a full mouth and broad chin. One tended not to notice such things about one's uncle, but he really had been amazingly good-looking, she thought.

"Only a handsome face and a good mind," continued Edith. "Which was not enough to suit some."

"But Grandfather didn't object?"

"Oh, he saw how to make everything right. That was Father's way. He got himself an eager young partner; he gave Titus a hand up in the world; and, above all, he made Henrietta happy. She was always his favorite." She said the last without any rancor at all, Florence noted. She would have minded very much being relegated to second place. Indeed, she did mind. "And it was all for the best," continued her mother. "Titus made an admirable husband. He could always be counted on to be discreet, which is the main thing."

"Are you saying he didn't love Aunt Etta?"

"I'm not saying anything of the kind," replied Edith, a touch of irritation in her voice. "There's all the difference in the world between a youthful fancy, however deeply felt at the time, and the committed love it takes to make a good marriage."

Oh yes, thought Florence, vastly reassured, all the difference in the world.

"It was a great, great pity that Titus died so soon. Not only for Henrietta, but for Lily. He would have put an end to her relationship with that Farel person, before it went so far."

"But no one knew about it."

"He would have," responded Edith with conviction. "Lily could never have kept it from him." She seemed ready to continue this train of conversation for some time, which suited Florence, who did not often find her mother in such a confidential mood, but the parlor door opened and Nuala entered, putting a stop to the gossip.

"I thought you might both be wanting a little something by now," she said, placing on the low table in front of the sofa a tray laden with a silver coffee service, china cups and plates, pieces of fruit, and neatly cut triangles of ham, cheese, and tomato set between slices of white buttered bread, thinly sliced and trimmed of crust.

"That's lovely," said Edith. "Thank you, Nuala. Though I really haven't any appetite."

Acknowledging the compliment, the girl inclined her head in a way that Florence found particularly annoying, graciously, as if she were the hostess and they mere guests, as if Riverhall might actually be hers! "That will be all, thank you. We'll ring if we need you." Nuala repeated her irritating nod, turned, and made her way slowly from the room, as Florence watched her with a frown.

"These are excellent," said Edith, taking a second bite of a tomato sandwich. "I don't know how Nuala manages to make something so simple taste quite so good."

"It's the bread, I expect," said Florence, turning her attention back to her mother. "She makes it herself."

"Well, so does our cook, but it's not the same, is it?"

Unable to resist, Florence helped herself to a cheese sandwich and bit into it. No, it was not at all the same, she thought, but said only,

"What will happen to Riverhall?" Nuala's exasperating attitude had started her thinking.

"Riverhall?" repeated Edith.

"Well, surely Aunt Etta won't want to live here alone?" What she meant was that surely her aunt would die before long, though she did not like to say that aloud.

Edith gave a short hiccup of a laugh and said, "The only way Henrietta will leave this house for good is feet first." Then, remembering what she was doing there, she gasped. With all trace of good humor gone from her face, she continued, "As long as she has Jonas and Nuala, she'll manage."

"Yes, but—"

"I don't think she could bear living anywhere else," interrupted Edith, not wanting to follow the line of her daughter's thinking. "She's always loved this place, not just the house, but the property. She's always loved the river. Like Father. And Rupert. And Lily." Her voice broke. She took a deep breath. "I never cared for it that much myself," she said more evenly.

Somewhere, a clock struck the half hour. Florence stood. "If you'll excuse me for a minute, Mother?" She needed to get away, to think. Edith nodded and reached for another sandwich, while Florence crossed the room to the door, opened it, and stepped out into the hall, where she stood looking around her as if she had never seen the place before, which indeed she had not, from this point of view — that of a prospective owner, for, if she had it right, she was indeed just that. It was a delightful space, open and airy, with light streaming in through the yellow stained glass windows. By its size, its furnishings, its general air, it gave notice that this was the home of a gentleman of means. And his lady. It would be wonderful, she thought, to live in such a house.

Moving quietly so as not to bring Nuala hurrying from the kitchen on the pretext of helping, all awash in a terrible excitement Florence made her way up the stairs. Never before had she thought of Riverhall in this way; but, then, always before there had been Lily.

Without any overt discussion of the matter, it had been understood in the family that when Henrietta passed on, except for a few minor bequests, everything would go to her daughter, her share of the Vanklieft estate, plus whatever Titus Canning had left, certainly enough to ensure that neither his wife, nor Lily, would have any money worries, provided they kept their living style within reasonable bounds. That had never proved a hardship for Henrietta, who required little in the way of diversion but to entertain a few friends at Riverhall from time to time. Nor would it have been for Lily. She enjoyed a shopping spree as much as the next girl, but all she really needed to be happy were tubes of paint and some canvas — though Florence had recently heard her say how she longed to travel, to see Europe especially, and how she regretted not going before the war had made the trip impossible. For that, of course, she really had no one to blame but herself.

Florence had made the journey with her parents in the autumn of 1909. The Cannings had planned to join them, as the trip was meant as a present for the girls' eighteenth birthdays, but Lily had come down with an infected throat in the summer. Though she had not in fact been very ill and had recovered fully by the beginning of September, her father (as overprotective as always) had refused even to consider exposing her to "foreign ailments." In a similar circumstance, Florence would have carried on until she got what she wanted, but Lily had accepted his decision with little more than a perfunctory protest. That was amazing, when you considered the handful she had been as a child. But she had seemed to run out of steam as she got older, challenging her father's authority less and less, defying all expectations by becoming manageable. "I just hate to see him worried and unhappy," she had said when Florence asked why she was not kicking up more of a fuss, adding with a shrug, "and it's not as if my going right at this moment is all that important. Next year will do as well, or the one after." Which only went to prove, thought Florence, that you ought not to let anything stand between you and what you truly want.

Florence herself might have preferred a motor car or a new fur coat, but she had had a pleasant enough time in Europe, if by the end of it she was altogether sick of traipsing through the endless galleries of endless museums, the Louvre in Paris, the Capitoline in Rome, the National Gallery in London. After a while, one masterpiece simply blurred into the next, although she did have some lovely memories of wonderfully luxurious hotels, of mirrored ballrooms, of dancing with handsome young men who were friends of friends from somewhere or other. Nothing had come of those encounters; in the end, she had been happy to return home, to Minuit, where she was destined to meet Andrew the following year.

Her husband had always admired the house, thought Florence, moving cautiously along the upstairs hall, noting with approval its comfortable span, the built-in cupboards, the finish of the wood, how smoothly the bathroom door swung open on its hinges, how it would take only new wallpaper to make the room itself, with its bright porcelain fixtures and shiny white tiles, seem completely modern. He would love living in River-hall as much as she. Almost as much, she corrected herself, for while she was willing to do whatever it took to get it, Andrew would not be diverted from his present foolish course by any worldly temptation she could think of, much preferring to throw his life away on principle than spend it happily living in such a grand house. How was she going to get him to change his mind, to make him see his duty in a different light, to make him understand that his first obligation was to his wife?

A wave of anxiety swept through Florence. Did she have it right? Surely, with Lily gone, when Aunt Etta died, the Canning estate would pass to her sister. Surely, thought Florence, her mother would inherit everything, or close to it, for who else was there? And if her mother did inherit it all, why then, since she always said that she preferred her own home in town to Riverhall, Florence had only to talk her into passing over

Louis and giving the house to Andrew and herself. She was the elder child, after all.

Her husband would know for certain who was to inherit, thought Florence. As the family lawyer, he had recently overseen some small changes that Henrietta had made in her will. No doubt that will lay within some file drawer in the Center Street offices of Vanklieft, Canning & Macleod, Attorneys at Law — so near, yet well out of her reach. And Andrew would never tell her what it said, even if she dared ask him.

But then, she did not need to, for there was really no other way for matters to dispose themselves but as she imagined. She was certain of it. Anxiety gave way to excitement. She took a deep breath, and another.

When she felt calm enough, she left the bathroom and continued along the hall, past the tower door, to her aunt's bedroom and, entering, cast a critical eye over its interior. A lovely space, she decided, though the furnishings were all hopelessly outdated. Everything was exactly as it had been when she was a child. The room would have to be entirely redone.

Closing the door softly, she crossed the carpeted hall to peek into one of the guest bedrooms. Spacious and spotlessly clean (whatever fault one might find with Nuala, it could never be said that she neglected her duties), it, too, showed signs of wear: the window hangings had faded, tiles in the mantle had come loose, patches of paper had begun to peel back from the wall. She would just have to get Andrew to agree to spend whatever money was necessary to do what had to be done, decided Florence. No one could expect her to live in a house so hopelessly old-fashioned, in such disrepair.

Resisting the temptation to peek into the other bedrooms, for her mother must have begun to wonder what had become of her, Florence began to retrace her steps; but then, when she came to Lily's door, she stopped. She could not seem to help opening it. And immediately she was sorry. Though it was neat as could be (another testimonial to Nuala's industry, for Lily never minded where she dropped her things), Lily's presence was palpable in the room. Her paintings and drawings covered almost every inch of the pale mauve walls. Pillows with the embroidered covers she had stitched over the years lay propped against the high bolsters of the bed. On the dressing table lay her brush and comb, a glass box full of hairpins, a bottle of scent, a strand of jet beads she had neglected to put away, and, off to the side, a miniature she had done of her mother. Beside the window overlooking the side garden, a lamp, a stack of books, and a photograph of Rosaline's children sat on a table next to a wicker chair whose cushions still bore the imprint of Lily's body. Through the glass panes, Florence could see the giant chestnut tree, within easy reach, and all at once came the memory of a long-ago afternoon. "Come on, it's as safe as a staircase," Lily had called, bouncing up and down on one of the broad branches to prove her point. How different she had been then, as a child, so bold, not giving a fig what anyone thought, not even her father. "Truly, you'll love it," she had added encouragingly, not in the least making fun of her cowardly cousin, for there was no meanness in Lily, Florence had to admit, though she had felt ashamed of herself all the same.

She had desperately wanted to climb out, but instead stood frozen in the open window, too terrified to join Lily and Rosaline in their flight down the branches to the ground. Which had turned out to be just as well. The two girls were punished for their lark, while Florence was praised by her uncle for being an intelligent and level-headed girl, "not an unruly scamp," foolishly putting herself in danger. On the way home, her parents had stopped at Crawford's Confectionery to treat her to an ice cream, perhaps not the best reward for a child inclined to pudginess, but one she had enjoyed nonetheless, not only for its delicious chocolaty taste, but for the sense of well-being it had given her, and the fleeting feeling of superiority.

A distant sound, one she was not even conscious of hearing, pulled Florence back from her memories. She shivered. Even if the room was stripped down to its bare boards, would it be possible to erase the sense of Lily's presence, she wondered, or would her cousin haunt it forever? Would she lurk there ready to pounce whenever the door was opened?

It would do for a guest room, Florence decided, stepping back out into the hall, pulling the door shut behind her. She would take one of the others, one with a better view, for her own use. Instead of a small corner of the back parlor, as in her present home, she would have a "study" like her mother's, where she might write letters, do the household accounts, attend to all the myriad details involved in running an establishment like Riverhall. The idea of it was very appealing, and she was smiling as she reached the staircase — where she came face-to-face with Nuala, coming from the back landing, her arms filled with fresh, clean-smelling, neatly folded towels.

"Oh, Mrs. Macleod," she said, regarding Florence with what could only be called suspicion. "Would you be needing anything?"

"Not a thing. You've been doing laundry, I see," said Florence pleasantly, though convinced that the towels were no more than a pretext for Nuala's coming to spy on her. In any event, she certainly did not have to account to a servant for her movements about the house, the one her mother had grown up in, Aunt Etta's house, and, with a very small amount of effort, one day to be her own.

"I thought I'd get to it while I had the chance," replied Nuala.

"Very wise," said Florence. "The next few days will be difficult for us all, I imagine." She started down the stairs and then hesitated. Though she disliked asking Nuala anything, especially about family matters when by rights it ought to be herself who was better informed, she could not help saying, "Do you know when . . . when Lily will be coming?"

Clearly startled, Nuala looked at her for a moment, as if wondering if Florence had somehow missed the central point of her aunt's note, the awful, inescapable fact of Lily's death. "Miss Lily?" she said. "Oh," she sighed as she realized what Florence meant. "Dr. Roeder will be meeting the New York train at the station this afternoon, and bringing her home."

"Today?" She had not expected events to move so quickly. "Oh, my . . ." Seeing tears beginning to well in Nuala's eyes, Florence turned away. "Thank you," she said, continuing on down the stairs.

"There you are," said her mother, looking up as Florence came into the parlor. Edith seemed to have done nothing but weep in her daughter's absence: the handkerchief she held was wet through. "You've been gone ages."

"I was talking to Nuala," she said, glancing at the table in front of the sofa. Then she sat once again in the armchair and repeated what she had heard.

"Thank goodness for Erich," said Edith.

The table was bare, which mean that Nuala had come in to take away the tray. She had known very well that Florence had left the room. She had indeed come looking for her. What cheek, thought Florence, satisfaction at having been right mixed with indignation at the girl's presumption. She dearly needed to be taught her place, though Florence doubted her own ability to do it. There was something, and she did not like to admit this, intimidating about Nuala, young as she was. Well, no matter what trouble it might cause with Deirdre, and therefore with the Allens who were devoted to her, when the time came, Nuala would just have to go. "Yes, indeed," she said to her mother. "It's a godsend having a man around to deal with things." She hesitated, wondering if now was a good time to mention her own worries. Why not, she thought. "And Andrew, as you know, is normally so reliable. But this war—"

"Oh no," said Edith, throwing up her hands. "Not the war. Please. Your father was carrying on about it this morning, over breakfast. I can't bear to think of it, especially not now."

"I'm sorry," said Florence. "But when it might affect—"

"Florence, really!" Tears glistened in Edith's eyes. "I'm so overset about Lily. I can't cope with anything more."

Lily, thought Florence bitterly. It was always Lily. When people weren't blubbing over her talent, or her looks, they were obsessing about her problems. It wasn't fair. It never had been. Well, not for much longer, came the consoling notion. A few days more in the limelight and Lily would be gone, relegated to the shadows, only a memory to everyone. Then, or so Florence hoped, she might finally get the attention she deserved, at least from her own mother.

When Henrietta and Rosaline at last returned, pandemonium erupted. They walked into the parlor calmly enough, but Edith let out a terrible cry, which shattered Henrietta's reserve. She broke down completely, collapsing in noisy sobs, until finally she fainted, sending Edith into paroxysms of hysteria, convinced that her sister's heart had given out. While Florence soothed her mother, Rosaline and Nuala managed to bring Henrietta around with a whiff of sal volatile. Embarrassed at her own lack of control, she retired to her room to put herself in order, and when she reappeared a few minutes later, she seemed resolutely calm and determined to deflect every foray by Edith toward renewed outbursts of grief. Nuala brought tea, and the two sisters, seated side-by-side on the sofa, finally managed to talk quietly about the events of the past two days, while Rosaline sat watching them anxiously and Florence seethed at the injustice done her father, her brother Louis (who, after all, was actually on the spot, in New York City), and even herself. They ought to have been the ones called on to (what was it her aunt was saying?) see the police, identify Lily, pack up the contents of her room at the Pelham, that overrated little hotel. Florence certainly would have done what was required of her, though it would have meant missing the weekly meeting of the St. Mark's Women's Auxiliary. In the circumstances, no one would have thought ill of her for failing to attend. No, they would have commended her courage, for of course it would not have been a pleasant business, having to clean up yet another of Lily's messes.

At last the front doorbell rang. The four women fell silent as they listened for the sound of Nuala hurrying to answer it. A moment later, they heard voices. Henrietta got to her feet and moved toward the door, which opened as Dr. Roeder came into the room. All the bounce was gone from his step, the light from his face. "You've brought her home," said Henrietta.

"Yes, my dear." The funeral director, Elisha Polk, along with his wife and his assistant, had met him at the station as prearranged, and the transfer of Lily's body from the train to the wagon had been accomplished with little loss of time. Still, the formalities had to be dealt with, and the drive to Riverhall taken at a stately pace, which meant that it was already past five. The doctor took both Henrietta's hands in his and said quietly, "I've brought Lily home to you."

"Thank you, Erich. Thank you." A slight quaver in her voice was the only sign of her turmoil. "Will you ask Mr. Polk to take her upstairs, to her room?"

"Yes, yes, of course."

He returned to the hall, and Henrietta said haltingly, clearly dreading what was to come next, "I must . . . there are things . . ."

Rosaline got to her feet. "Aunt Etta, would you rather that I—?"

Without letting her finish, Henrietta said, "Oh, Rosaline, dear, if you would, I'd be so grateful. Her new silver georgette, I thought. You know the one I mean? "

Rosaline nodded. "She looked so beautiful in it. And her pearls?"

"Weren't they Mother's pearls?" said Edith.

Henrietta sighed. "Yes. They were. Of course, that won't do." She sat, thought a moment, and then said, "The pearl drop Titus and I gave her for her sixteenth birthday?" Rosaline nodded again, and Henrietta went on, "That, and her pearl earrings. She's a dear, dear girl. A treasure," she added, when Rosaline had left the room.

Florence knew that she ought to go, too. Though of course she dreaded seeing Lily, she truly wanted to go, at the very least to be of help

146

to her aunt, but she could not. However badly she felt about her cousin's death, however much she resented an outsider's assuming responsibilities that rightfully ought to be kept within the family, still she could not force the offer from her mouth, or her body from the chair. For her, it was difficult enough just to be in the house at the moment, just to hear the sounds of Mr. Polk and his assistants going about their grisly work of embalming the body, without having to watch, or — worse — to assist. Let Rosaline . . . Florence was sure she would get a chance to be of use when the mourners came, for she prided herself on how good she was with people.

A moment later, Dr. Roeder returned to the parlor, and Henrietta looked at him anxiously. "Is there anything I—?"

"No," he said quickly, pulling a chair up close to the sofa. He sat and took her hand again. "Rosaline and Nuala will do perfectly well between them." He asked what arrangements she had made for the funeral, and Henrietta told him about her visit with Reverend Moreland. Edith had myriad questions of her own, and so, between them, she and the doctor nudged the conversation along gently, minute by minute, while Florence thought how the next few days were going to be an endless repetition of this one, the same stories repeated over and over, until one could scream at hearing them again.

At last came a knock at the parlor door, but, when it opened, it was only Nuala with more tea and some fruitcake. "It won't be much longer so," she said, depositing the tray on its customary table. "Not more than half an hour, says Mr. Polk."

However, it was closer to sixty minutes (by which time everyone had given up the effort of making conversation and the room had grown quiet) before the door opened again. This time, Rosaline stood on the threshold. Her face was ashen, her eyes swollen, the whites a pale pink shot with red. "Lily's ready now," she said in an unsteady voice.

The doctor extended a hand and helped Henrietta to her feet, as Edith and Florence stood as well.

"Shall I have another word with Polk?" said the doctor. "Tell him what it is you want done in here?"

Henrietta nodded, touching his arm lightly as she moved past him out of the room.

"He'll be in the kitchen, with the others," said Rosaline. "Nuala's giving them a bite to eat."

"Thank you, Erich" said Edith. "We'd all be lost without you."

"You're a dear girl," the doctor said to Rosaline, stopping her a moment to kiss her cheek, not noticing Florence at all as she followed his daughter into the hall.

Her heart pounding, her feet heavy, Florence trailed the others up the stairs, falling farther and farther behind as she climbed. Reaching the landing, she caught a glimpse of Mrs. Polk's black skirt as the woman disappeared through the door to the back landing, an empty basin dangling from her hand. She must have rinsed it out in the bathroom, thought Florence. Looking the other way, she saw Rosaline entering Lily's room. She quickened her pace to catch up with her, but at the threshold she stopped and stood with eyes averted, afraid of what she might see inside. The soft sound of weeping, small whispers of despair, drifted out to her, and she recognized the voices of her aunt and her mother. (Rosaline had no doubt finished with crying for the moment.) Finally, having no choice, she entered.

All the lamps had been lit and the room had a serene, rosy glow very much at odds with the pain and sadness in the air. Hovering over the bed, where Lily was lying on top of the satin coverlet, stood Henrietta, her fingers brushing lightly against her daughter's face, her hair, her hands, murmuring her name over and over, until she leaned down to kiss her, then fell to her knees beside the bed, her arms outstretched across the still body.

For once, Edith did not give way to theatrics, but stood behind her sister, her hands on her shoulders, tears streaming from her eyes, whispering, "Hush, darling. Henrietta, hush . . ."

Her hand pressed against her mouth, Rosaline turned away, as if she could not bear to watch. Remembering with a fresh surge of irritation the infamous trip to New York the preceding day, Florence moved to the foot of the bed and forced herself to look at her cousin. She was wearing a very chic and expensive-looking dress that Florence had never seen before. Her short nails, which she could never refrain for long from biting, had been smoothed and polished. Encircling her neck was a platinum chain, from which hung a single pearl, and, in her ears, were tiny pearl studs. Her hair, brushed into a shining coil on top of her head, lay like a jet crown against the cream-colored bolster. A slight purplish bruise showed through the makeup on her right temple. But though there was only a touch of rouge on her cheeks, a hint of lipstick on her mouth, though indeed she did look beautiful, thought Florence, in no way did she look alive. She looked like a wax figure, something you would see at Madame Tussaud's, in London.

Florence shuddered. She felt all at once as if she were in a dream, so unlikely did all this—the weeping women, the body on the satin coverlet, Lily—so unreal did it all seem. It occurred to her that she might wake at any moment and find herself safe in bed beside Andrew, Lily still alive, planning to join the family as usual for dinner at the Allens after church the next Sunday. How could it be otherwise? How could life stop so abruptly? It seemed impossible. She felt poised on the edge of a precipice, on the verge of a chasm that Lily had inexplicably plunged into. Never before had Florence experienced so profoundly this sudden sharp snap of the thread of life, so quick, so final. It frightened her. She put one hand over the other to stop her fingers pulling nervously at the black silk of her dress. She felt a rush of such sadness. Lily, her cousin, her friend. Lily was dead.

But what was Aunt Etta saying? It was difficult to hear. Her face pressed against the counterpane, her voice muffled, she was moaning . . . it sounded like, "How could you? How could you?" Over and over. "How could you?"

Pushing gently past Edith, Rosaline went to Henrietta's side. "Aunt Etta, please, dear, you must stop." The weeping woman looked up at her. "There are days to go, yet," Rosaline continued. "You have to martial your strength."

"Yes, yes," murmured Henrietta, sounding dazed. She allowed Rosaline to help her to her feet.

"Why don't you go along to your room and lie down for a while? You look exhausted." Though Edith's voice was full of concern, there was not a trace of shock.

"Yes, I think I will." A huge sob wracked her body as she turned away from the bed.

Had her mother heard? wondered Florence. Had she herself heard correctly?

"Florence," said Edith. Lost in thought, her daughter did not respond. "Florence, help your aunt to her room."

As if sleepwalking, Florence took Henrietta's arm. It was no accident, she thought, with a shiver of horror. It wasn't. Lily had killed herself. She had taken her own life. She was damned. *Damned.* With no right to a service at St. Mark's, no right to a Christian burial. They were all in the process of participating in a huge fraud, not merely perpetrated against Reverend Moreland and his parishioners, but against the Supreme Being, who would not take such an offense lightly, if His ministers were to be believed.

"Rosaline and I will see to it that all is done just as you'd like," said Edith to her sister. "You're not to worry about a thing."

Her mother clearly had not heard, or at least had not understood, thought Florence, obediently accompanying her aunt from the room, wondering, as she walked with her along the hall, to whom she might confide this astounding news, for she felt she might burst if she had to keep it all to herself. Rosaline already knew, that much was clear. So must Dr. Roeder. And perhaps his wife as well. Perhaps only the Allens were to be kept in the dark, and about a matter that so much concerned them.

There would be a terrible scandal when people learned of this, and it would affect the entire family. They would all suffer the consequences of Lily's wild act. The sidelong glances, the pitying looks, the endless gossip (as if there had not been enough of that already), Florence could imagine how it would be. Excruciating!

Scandal. It was a sobering thought.

"It's kind of you, Florence, to be so concerned about me," said Henrietta, "but you mustn't worry. I will be all right."

Diverted from her thoughts, Florence protested gently as she helped Henrietta into bed, adjusted the pillows, and smoothed the covers, saying that kindness had nothing to do with it: she could hardly be anything but concerned, and so very sorry, which was true, for she was genuinely fond of her aunt and disliked seeing her so distressed.

"I know," she said. Taking Florence's hand, she held it to her cheek. "Thank you, dear."

Touched by the small gesture of affection, Florence impulsively leaned over and kissed her cool forehead. "Try to rest," she said. Obediently, Henrietta closed her eyes. Florence waited until her aunt had drifted off, and then slipped quietly out the door. What am I to do? she wondered.

Nothing, absolutely nothing, was the decision she came to as she made her way back along the hall, toward the stairs. Nothing, if she wished to spare her aunt further grief, if she wished to avoid a scandal. Her parents would be thrown into a crisis of conscience, if she were to tell them, and who knew but that they would feel obliged to take the matter up with Reverend Moreland? Andrew might well do the same. People with such strong senses of honor could not be relied on to protect their own interests. And Louis? Though the temptation was great to confide in him at least, she knew her brother well enough to be certain that he would refuse to believe it, as he always refused to believe anything unkind of Lily. He was devoted to her. He always had been, since they were children. And all that her honesty would earn Florence would be accusations that she was a bitter, spiteful shrew. She was used to such treatment from him.

No, there was nothing to do, no one to tell, no one she could trust with the news. She would keep what she had discovered to herself, keep it secret, as the others had clearly determined to do. And surely the Lord would not hold her silence against her, since she had only the best of intentions.

At the door to Lily's room, she stopped. Again unable to resist, she opened the door and went in. She stood looking down at her cousin, her beautiful cousin, her parents' darling, the toast of Minuit, the belle of every ball. How could she have done it? Fate had been so kind to her, showering her with gifts that it denied (dare she think it?) to more deserving people. What right had Lily to scorn those gifts? to turn her back on them? to deem them insufficient, unworthy? So Edmund Farel had abandoned her. What of it? Florence had had her share of rejections, of humiliations. Even now she could not think of that frightful trip to Europe without a twinge of pain. The eyes that dismissed her with a glance, the affront of the "duty" dance, the suitors pressed into calling, their failure ultimately to deliver the required proposal — no, the slights had not been easy to bear, yet she had borne them, and with dignity, she liked to think. And while she might have advised Lily, in the unlikely event that her cousin would actually have consulted her, to leave Minuit, to go somewhere she was unknown, to start over where the shame of her failed marriage would not forever dog her, Florence could not conceive of ending her own life for any reason, let alone for a man, least of all for one with no character, no fortune, with nothing to recommend him but his charm. She would have brazened it through. Why, even if she were to lose Andrew (and, if he persisted in his idiotic scheme to join the army, it could happen), she would get on with her life, as Aunt Etta had got on with hers when Uncle Titus died. That, after all, was what people did. They got on with life.

Another thought struck Florence. What if Farel had not been the reason? After all, he was long gone, to Chicago and a job on the *Chronicle*, if Mrs. Dowling was to be believed, and she had seen Farel's byline in that paper during a recent trip to the Midwest. What if — Florence could hardly bear the idea — what if Lily had been pregnant? All those trips to New York, staying away for weeks at a time. Who knew what she got up to there? It was a bad city, a fast city. One might go to the theater, to the opera, to dinner at Sherry's or Murray's Roman Gardens and never notice, but everyone knew nonetheless of the burlesque shows, the gambling dens, the dance halls. On her own, unprotected, clearly susceptible to handsome scoundrels, Lily might very well have been lured into vice.

An awful thought: Lily, pregnant. Yet, it made sense. One heard all the time about girls taking their lives because they were "caught." Wouldn't that just beat the band? Lily destroyed by the very thing Florence herself longed for!

From downstairs came the sound of the doorbell. A moment later, she heard voices: Andrew and her father had come at last. She hurried from the room. So burdened was she by dreadful ideas that she felt heavier as she moved, as if in the course of the day she had gained a vast amount of weight. By the time she made her way down the stairs, the hall was empty, as was the parlor when she peeked into it. The grand piano had been pushed out of the way, and the sofa and chairs turned to face the velvet-draped trestle table that now occupied the center of the room. For the coffin, she thought, closing the door.

"Everyone's gone into the library," said Nuala, who had managed to creep up on her again.

Startled, Florence turned, recovered herself, and said, "I thought I heard my father and Mr. Macleod arrive."

"They're with the others. Is the missus asleep?"

"I think she is," said Florence.

"Well, I'll just go have a look."

Suit yourself, Florence thought, but said nothing, as Nuala would do exactly as she pleased, no matter what. Continuing along to the library, Florence opened the door and saw her father standing at the mantle, deep in conversation with the doctor, and her husband, in the wingback chair, talking to her mother and Rosaline, who were seated on the sofa. Andrew rose when he saw her and came to kiss her cheek. Her father left the doctor's side to greet her. "A terrible thing," he said. "You must be heartbroken, my dear."

"Oh, yes," she said.

"Poor Lily," he murmured.

Yes, yes, she thought impatiently. Poor Lily. It was indeed sad. But how many times over the next few days was she going to have to say it? hear it?

Edith picked up the strands of the conversation and continued on about this worry or that until, minutes later, the door opened, and Henrietta came into the room, an anxious Nuala hovering behind her in the hall.

"What are you doing up so soon?" said Edith.

"Did we disturb you? I'm so sorry," said George Allen. "So sorry," he repeated, folding Henrietta into his arms.

She let him hold her for a moment, turning away finally to greet Andrew and accept his condolences.

"Come, sit, my dear," said the doctor, taking her arm.

"Wait." She pulled away from him; and, from the pocket of her black dress, she drew a strand of pearls and went to Florence. "These were your grandmother's," she said. Not certain what was happening, Florence stood. Summoning a smile, Henrietta extended her hand, offering the pearls to her niece. "You should have them."

"Aunt Etta, really . . ." Her fingers closed around them. The pearls were warm and silky to the touch, lovely . . . no, *beautiful*, a long strand of perfectly matched beads, the color of cream with a pink blush. Never had she thought to get her hands on them! "Oh, thank you," she said, and at last burst into tears.

"There, there, darling," said Andrew, slipping his arms around her.

"Etta, there was no need for that now. The pearls could have waited," said the doctor, leading Henrietta to the sofa.

Florence peered resentfully over Andrew's shoulder at Erich Roeder. He had been her doctor all her life. He had been there at her birth. But never once had he thought it perhaps her turn to come first. Never had he taken her problems seriously or lavished the care on her that he had on Lily. God's will, he had said, as if he himself were the Lord. But what did he know of it? He was only a country doctor, she thought, watching him fuss over her aunt, a man of limited experience. She would go to the city, to consult a specialist. She should have done it ages ago, instead of trusting herself to the expertise of a man who had little. When all this was over, she decided, as Andrew, with great solicitude, settled her again into a chair, when the wake was done and Lily buried, she would do it. She would discover the name of the most renowned specialist in New York City and make an appointment to see him.

Again a wave of excitement washed through her. The pearls were hers. Soon Riverhall would be as well. That her cousin had died was awful. Of course it was. And Florence felt unbearably sad when she dwelt on the thought. Still, there was no denying that Lily's death had changed everything. It had opened up a world of undreamt of possibilities. Why should a child not be one of them? Why should Andrew not be made, somehow, to stay at home? Why should she not allow herself to hope?

LOUIS

Her brother, Louis, was the person who could best have told Florence what Lily got up to in the city. If anyone knew, it was he. When Lily was there, he saw her as often as she would allow, which was not, in his opinion, nearly often enough; but she had so little time to spare this trip to New York, she said, that despite the tempting list of entertainments he had drawn up in expectation of her arrival, they met only once, on the night before she died, a fact he would never later recall without a pang. She had joined him for dinner in the Grill Room at the Automobile Club; and afterward, when he thought about that evening, he would wonder at his cheerfulness, his optimism, his total insensitivity to the disaster looming. Surely he ought to have noticed something? There must have been signs, for how could the world change so quickly, with such devastating impact, with no advance warning? He felt bewildered, cheated, certain he would somehow have made more of their time together, if only he had known he would never see Lily alive again.

But he had not known, so that, as he watched her come through the French doors that Sunday night and hurry across the room toward him, he felt only the familiar surge of pleasure the sight of her always brought him, its brightness hardly tarnished by the wicked flicker of a thought that, were he a proper beau, she would have made more of an effort. She would have worn something other than the old green silk he had seen her in countless times before. Still, she looked beautiful (but then, he always thought that, no matter what), radiant, her skin glowing, her dark eyes alight, all trace of unhappiness, of misery, gone from her face, though her nails were still very short, he could not help noticing, despite the effort she had put into smoothing and polishing them.

"Have you been waiting long?" she said, leaning toward him to kiss his cheek as he stood to greet her. "I'm so sorry. I really couldn't get away. I saw the loveliest Mercer Raceabout downstairs," she added, as he held the chair for her to sit. "All white with a black trim. Very smart."

"Oh, wouldn't I love to have one of those," he said, immediately diverted. Encouraged by her, he rambled on, through the ordering and the appetizers and into the main course, about the Mercer and the Lanchester and the Packard Twin Six and all the latest obsessions of the automobile enthusiast he was, until he remembered his manners and thought to ask what she had been up to since her arrival in the city.

Spending hours every day at the Menlo Gallery, with the great Darius Menlo himself, she told him. "And we still haven't made the final selection of paintings, or chosen all the frames, or finished planning the first night party. The beginning of May seems terrifyingly near, let me tell you. But it's all very exciting," she added with a happy smile. "Even if I am always limp as a wet noodle when I leave there."

"You look lovely."

"I look like a hag."

"You most certainly do not. You look beautiful. But you shouldn't let Menlo wear you out," he went on. He had heard someone say (his mother, perhaps? Or Dr. Roeder?) that overwork had been a contributing factor to Lily's breakdown. "Haven't you had any fun?"

"Oh, yes. Some. Darius bought me dinner at Sherry's the other night. I've gone up to the Metropolitan Museum, and down to West Fourth Street to the Whitney Studio. I've seen a few friends, and Laurette Taylor in a matinee at the Globe, yesterday."

"You went on your own?" He could not help feeling a little aggrieved, as the play was one he had suggested to Lily that they see together. "You should have let me know."

"I didn't plan to go. But there I was, staring at a blank canvas, not a thought in my head about what to do next. So off I went. I thought it might help to clear my mind."

He would have liked to say that he would have dropped everything, even at the last minute, to go with her, but instead he asked, "The way you've been going at it, you can't be short of paintings for the show. Couldn't you ease up a bit?"

"Not just yet," she said, with a shake of her head. "I have to finish at least two more. I really must keep working. You know," she went on, her expression becoming suddenly rather intense, "I feel I'm on the verge of something, a breakthrough of some kind. I want so desperately to find a new direction to take my work after all the fuss is over." And then she laughed. "Now, don't let me get started on that subject, or I'll bore on endlessly."

"Fuss?" repeated Louis, settling on the one concept he absolutely understood. "I thought you were enjoying yourself."

"Oh, I am. Really. Did you think I was complaining? I'm delighted. And grateful." She had only before appeared in group shows in the city. Not that she dismissed the importance of those, she told him, but it was thrilling to be having a solo show at last, and at such a prestigious gallery. Some of the major critics might finally take notice of her, though she hardly expected to cause the sensation in New York City that she did in the "boondocks" (as Louis referred to them), where she had been getting rave reviews and winning gold medals at county fairs since she was a child.

"Don't forget the commissions," said Louis, who — along with the rest of his family — took great pride in Lily's success. Why, even the mayor had asked her to paint him, and that portrait still hung in the lobby of the town hall for all to see.

"Yes, I did start off well," she said, "but everything's changed. The old styles, the old techniques — no one's interested in them anymore. Novelty is what's wanted."

Louis caught a note of anxiety in her voice and tried, though he suspected it was way beyond his abilities, to reassure her, saying that as far as he could see there was nothing much to recommend the work of these modern painters. Why, most of them looked as if they could not draw to save their lives, while Lily certainly could, like an angel, with every detail perfect. "If you ask me, they're nothing but a giant fraud being perpetrated on a gullible public."

She smiled and, with the lift of an eyebrow, said, "I'm not altogether sure one can dismiss Pablo Picasso as a fraud."

Louis could not really argue the point. He did not know with any certainty who this Picasso fellow was; in fact, he really did not know much at all about art. Its subtleties escaped him, no matter how many galleries he accompanied his cousin to, no matter how often she explained to him just what about a painting had caught her fancy. He had no real feeling for the subject itself, and no "eye," as she often pointed out to him, though kindly because she was fond of him, she said, and so found his efforts to please her endearing. Had she been younger than he, rather than older by three years, he might have resented her attitude. As it was, he was simply grateful that she agreed to spend time in his company, for Lily was not only beautiful, she was great fun (at least she was when not in one of her "moods"), always easy to talk to, always interested in whatever a fellow had to say. "Well, you must just believe in yourself," he told her, his final word on the subject. "It encourages other people to do the same."

"That must be what makes you such an excellent salesman," she replied, laughing, all trace of anxiety gone as quickly as it had come.

"I expect it does."

"Well, it's very good advice. I'll do my best to keep it in mind."

After dinner they went to the Strand Roof to dance, but, as Lily said she had to be up early in the morning, they did not stay long. "Are you sure you wouldn't rather I found us a taxi?" he asked as they started back to the Pelham. Her evening coat could not possibly provide protection against the wind howling down Broadway.

"It's not that far! You haven't gone soft, living in the city, have you Louis?"

"It was you I was worried about," he said in the querulous tone he usually reserved for his sister.

"You mustn't, you know." She linked her arm through his. "I've caused you and everyone else enough trouble already. It's time you got on with your own lives, and left the worrying about mine to me."

Louis remained silent a moment, wondering what in the world he could say in reply. To discuss the state of her mind with Lily seemed to him to require levels of knowledge, of understanding, even a vocabulary, he did not possess. Finally, at a loss, he merely patted her hand and blustered, "I'm sure there's nothing to worry about."

At the door of the hotel, she turned to him, kissed his cheek, and said, "Thank you, Louis. It was a lovely evening. You're always such good company. I care about you a great deal, you know."

"I should hope so!" he replied, thankful that she could not see in the dim light of the street lamps the rush of color to his face, or hear the wild thudding of his heart. When he allowed himself to think about it, he knew how foolish it was, how wrong, to react this way to his own cousin, but he usually preferred to pretend that it was the normal response of affection, or, if more than that, if the word "love" insisted on intruding into his thoughts, then only the kind of love he might have felt for Florence, if she had been a bit more agreeable. "There's a dance at the Columbia tomorrow night. Would you like to go? Or shall I get us tickets for something?" he asked, as always wanting to see her as soon again as possible. "There's sure to be something on you'd like."

She was engaged for the following evening, she told him. Seeing his crestfallen face, she reminded him that she would often be in the city in the coming weeks. There would be lots of opportunities for them to meet. "And as soon as the show opens and I have more free time, shall we go back to Coney Island? We had such a glorious day there last summer. Remember?"

"Indeed! Whenever you say." He could hardly imagine anything he would like better.

"I do love the roller coaster," she said, kissed his cheek in farewell, and let the doorman usher her solicitously into the hotel. Reluctant to go, Louis reached inside his coat to his jacket pocket and removed a box of matches and the silver cigarette case his parents had given him for his twenty-first birthday. He took out a Chesterfield and lit it, watching as Lily stopped at the desk to collect her messages and then, as if certain he would still be there, turn to wave.

That was the last time he had seen her alive. She had disappeared out of sight around a corner, and Louis, his head reeling with emotions he hardly understood, had continued on his way through the chill April night, home to his bachelor apartment on Seventh Avenue.

If only, he thought, when his father telephoned to him with the news, if only, as well as dropping off a note the next morning, he had given in to his desire to stop by later to see her, when he finished work. Who knew but that her plans for the evening might have changed? She might have gone with him to the theater, or to Roseland, or, yes, even to the dance at the yacht club. Afterward, he would have escorted her back to her hotel. He might have kept her alive. The thought tormented him. Another night, that was all she planned to stay in the city. One more night. If only he had insisted she spend the evening with him, he would have kept her alive. But instead he had taken no for an answer and had joined his friends, Arthur and Max, at Moretti's, and had sat with them discussing the imminence of war until they were so depressed they had gone to a gambling hell on Madison Avenue, where they had drunk themselves into a stupor and lost money they could ill afford.

"Louis, are you all right?" his father shouted into the telephone. It was Wednesday afternoon. "Louis?"

"I'm here. I'm all right. I'm . . . a bit winded, that's all."

"We all are. It's been a terrible shock. Louis?"

"Yes, Father?"

"You weren't at the Columbia on Monday night, were you?"

"No, no, I wasn't. I suggested to Lily we go to a dance there, but she wasn't free."

"Do you think some of the fellows might have seen her?"

"Oh, God! Someone mentioned a bit of a flap. Johnnie Crawford said someone had drowned. A woman. But he didn't know it was Lily. No one knew . . . I can't think . . . Listen, I'll come home immediately."

"Yes, I think you should. The funeral is on Saturday."

It was inconvenient, but death happens in every family and allowances have to be made for it, so the manager, in whose office Louis had taken the telephone call, agreed with no argument to his having off the next few days.

"I'll make up the time when I return."

"I'm sure you will," said the manager. Louis was by far his best, most dedicated, and hardworking employee.

After leaving the showroom, though not in the least hungry, he went to the nearby Automat and grabbed a quick meal (he knew better than to try doing the long journey home without eating first), then returned to his apartment to pack a bag. Lying on the table where he had left it, he saw the letter Lily had sent in reply to his note. "My dear, it would be lovely to stay on, but I absolutely must get back to Riverhall and work," he read.

162

She must have been dead by the time he got it. The absurdity of that took his breath away, and he began to weep, something he had not done in years. When he got control of himself, he splashed cold water on his face, and then went to knock on a few doors, trying to find among his friends from Minuit someone who had been at the club on Monday night; but even those who had bothered to go outside to see what all the brouhaha was about had nothing of importance to tell him. They had gawked until moved out of the way by the police. They had had no idea that the dead girl was someone they knew, that it was Lily Canning who had drowned, beautiful Lily, whom they were all, at least a little bit, in love with.

Louis had refused either to go to university, or to join his father in the insurance business when he finished school. Instead, he had got a job in Manhattan as a salesman with the Peerless Motor Car Company. Early in 1916, he had moved on to General Motors, where he still worked, in the building at the corner of Fifty-seventh Street and Broadway. He knew he was good at his job and expected to go far, in that company or in some other: it hardly mattered to him which, as long as automobiles were at the heart of it. He was mad about cars — had been since he was a boy — and though he would certainly have preferred to own a sporty Mercer Race-about, or even a Stutz Bearcat, given his present employment, he had thought it best to take advantage of the sweet deal offered and had bought a Cadillac V-8 a few months before. Rather, his father had bought it for him. It had set the old man back close to two thousand dollars, but even that was a bargain, Louis had explained when his father blanched at the cost, compared to the price of a new Packard Six. He kept the car in the garage at the Automobile Club on West Fifty-fifth Street, where he had easy access to it; and while he did briefly consider taking the train home, he decided (as he always did) to drive so as not to be left carless in Minuit, dependent on his parents, or indeed on his own two legs, for the journey back and forth to Riverhall, for he supposed that was where he would be spending most of his time the next few days.

Driving north along Route 9, under a cloudless, star-spangled sky, past the small Hudson Valley towns that lined the river, Louis had plenty of time to think about just how awful those days were bound to be. It had been bad enough when his uncle died, seeing Aunt Etta so cut up and Lily looking like a ghost — pale, silent, too numb with grief even to cry. He had spent endless hours then just sitting around, his every effort at conversation a failure, words of comfort sounding false, attempts to discuss anything but the deceased faltering quickly, seeming inappropriate, in terrible taste. And now that it was Lily . . . He blinked rapidly, fighting back tears. He could not cry; he had to be able to see.

The car had an annoying tremor at forty miles an hour, and Louis was tempted to push it above fifty, where the tremor disappeared, but the road was really not good enough for that kind of speed, its surface uneven, dotted with unexpected holes that his headlamps always managed to reveal too late for him to avoid. Resisting the impulse to go faster, he jogged along at what he considered a reasonable pace, trying to keep his mind alert to danger: bicycles appearing out of the gloom, people crossing the road, small animals darting under his wheels.

It had perhaps not been such a good idea to drive, with his head reeling as it was with images of Lily, with thoughts of the war, with dread of the coming days. Nor had he had much sleep of late. In addition to Monday's all-night gambling session, the president's call for a declaration of war had required another meeting with Arthur and Max on Tuesday, a sort of seminar convened over dinner at the Café Martin. And with so many momentous things to talk about, there was little time to linger for more than a moment on the subject of the nameless woman who had drowned the night before as many of their friends danced nearby. They had to consider their futures, to sort through a welter of ideas and emotions. Did they support President Wilson's idealistic call to make the world "safe for democracy," or the appealing pacifism of William

Jennings Bryan? They had been arguing the question with increasing heat since the sinking of the *Missourian,* an unarmed steamer, on April 4th. Thirty-two American lives were lost. Someone had to teach the Krauts a lesson, and if England and her allies were not up to it, then surely the United States had no choice but to fight?

As was to be expected in a debate among twenty-two-year-olds, especially in view of the fine speech they all agreed the president had made, pacifism went down without scoring a point. But while Arthur and Louis managed to keep hold of some sense of self-preservation and put off making a decision, Max had announced that he was not going to wait for conscription (which they all assumed inevitable), but was going to enlist. That called for more drinks, and a trip to a notch house they frequented on West Twenty-fifth Street, where thoughts of imminent death were forgotten in the arms of Pearl and Cora and Meg.

The memory of himself the night before, reeking of drink and vomit, Cora having to clean him up before getting down to business, filled him with disgust. He had spent the night, or a good part of it, with a whore, while Lily, his beloved Lily, lay dead. It seemed inconceivable to him now that he could have behaved so callously, though of course he had not known; and while that should have made a difference to the way he was feeling, it did not. He still felt like a cad. At the moment, he thought himself no better than Edmund Farel, about whose treatment of Lily he knew nothing, but that it had made her desperately unhappy. Would he ever forgive himself? Louis wondered. Should he? Perhaps, after all, there were some sins that even God's grace could not wash from the soul.

A shadow flitting across the road ended his self-indictment, bringing him back sharply to the present: a deer, but far enough ahead so that he needed only to touch the brakes to avoid hitting it. A little closer and the family would have had to make it a double burial, he thought grimly. If he wanted to arrive home in one piece, he had better keep his mind off the subject of his dissipations, the war, Lily's death, off everything but his driving.

165

Peering through the dark, he looked for a familiar landmark, and saw nothing but a ribbon of road unwinding in the moonlight before him, trees on either side, the skeletons of maples, the graceful swoop of cedars and firs, giant shadows dancing in a light wind. "Where the devil am I?" he muttered, promising himself he would not do this again, undertake such a long trip alone when so distracted. Finally, after what seemed forever, he recognized the gates to Lyndhurst, the Gould estate. He had only got as far as Tarrytown. It would be hours yet before he reached Minuit. "By the light, of the silvery moon . . ." He began to sing. "I want to croon . . ." It was one of the songs he often performed at family parties, with Lily at the piano ("just like Rupert," someone would always remark), and even though Louis hardly looked at her as he sang, directing his glance to his family and friends, basking in their pleasure, still he often felt as if he were singing only for her. "To my honey ..." His light baritone swelled and filled the car. Rolling down the window, he leaned forward to wipe the condensation from the windscreen with his gloved hand. ". . . I'll sing love's old sweet tune...." He would sing to Lily all the way home.

Except for the light in the entry hall and another shining from the window of his bedroom, the Allen house was in darkness when Louis drove his car into the garage at the back of the house. It was after midnight, and his eyes were stinging with fatigue and his voice was hoarse from the effort of keeping himself awake. Though he had stopped often enough at the side of the road to stretch his legs, grab a smoke, and relieve himself, he still felt stiff as he unwound from the car, removed his bag, closed the garage, and made his way to the back door, hoping it had been left open, since he had, in his haste, left his key behind in New York. Damn, he thought, jiggling the handle. What was he supposed to do now? Wake the house? While he stood considering his options, the door opened, and he saw Deirdre, still in her uniform but with her blonde hair falling in a neat braid down her back. She looked no more than a child, he thought. "I forgot my key."

"Not for the first time so," she said, with a hint of a smile, stepping back to let him in.

It occurred to him that she had expected that and had stayed awake, awaiting his arrival. "You could have left it open." Even to himself, he sounded remarkably ungracious.

"For any passing thief to be coming in and helping himself?" she said, locking the door again after him.

"I haven't heard anything about a crime wave in Minuit." It must be fatigue that made him so snappish, he thought. Usually he was very polite to the staff. He was polite to everyone. He had a way with people. Early on, he had realized that and had used it, though not, he liked to think, for nefarious purposes. He simply understood that charm was more likely than arrogance to get him what he wanted.

"Well, you're not here all that much, are you now? Would you like something to eat?" she asked, following him through the back hallway to the kitchen.

"No. Thank you. I had something before I left the city." That, however, had been hours before, and he was hungry, he realized. "Well, perhaps just some bread and cheese."

Deirdre nodded and gestured toward a covered plate on the pine table. "I left you a sandwich," she said, "and there's some cider in the ice box. Just leave everything. I'll clear it all in the morning. Goodnight, sir," she added politely, turning to retrace her steps to the back hallway and the staircase leading up to the servants' rooms.

"Deirdre," he called after her. He did not want her to leave just yet. When she turned again to look at him questioningly, he said, "Have you heard how things are at Riverhall?"

"Your mother said Mrs. Canning was bearing up well, all things considered. She was there all day. Mr. Allen didn't fetch her home until almost nine."

167

"And Lily?"

Deirdre hesitated a moment, as if trying to decide what in all she had heard of the day's events was the most important. Finally, she said, "It was on the afternoon train, she came home. Dr. Roeder was at the station waiting for her. And Mr. Polk. They've put her in the front parlor, where Mr. Canning was. She's looking pretty as a picture so, your mother says."

He tried to imagine Lily lying still in a coffin, but that image had no substance, no reality. It seemed improbable, and it gave way immediately to another, Lily hurrying toward him across the Grill Room on Sunday night, the skirt of her green silk dress flaring behind, her hand reaching out for his as he stood to greet her.

"If that's all, sir?"

"Oh, yes. Of course. Thank you, Deirdre." She had to get up at some ungodly hour, five-thirty or thereabouts, he remembered. "I'm sorry I kept you up."

"Not to worry," she said, and turned away.

He watched her as she left the room, noting again how like a schoolgirl she looked without her braid done up into a tight bun, without that silly cap his mother insisted she wear perched on top. She was young, a year younger than he, but what a lot of the world she had seen compared to him, who had refused his parents' offer of a trip abroad, so eager was he to begin working at Peerless. His entire worldly experience was confined to the northeastern coast of the United States, and it often seemed to him not only limited, but very ordinary, if not what his mother would consider respectable, yet a long way from either interesting or dissolute. (There were a few fellows he knew in the latter category, and felt himself to be well wide of that mark.) When he heard his brother-in-law Andrew speak, Louis understood that no matter how fast he drove, or how often he visited Cora, his life had no real adventure in it. He had never done anything as daring as Deirdre, coming that vast distance across the ocean from Ireland to New York, with no company except for her sister. What courage that must have taken. He could not imagine Florence doing it, or Lily—

There she was again. Lily. No matter which way his mind turned, it always came back to her.

Instead of cider, he poured himself a glass of milk. Sitting at the pine table, his mind a determined blank, he ate his sandwich and swallowed the drink in a long gulp, without really tasting either. When he finished, he carried his plate and glass to the sink, as he would have done in his own apartment, though he stopped short of washing them. That seemed to require more effort than he was capable of at the moment. In any case, he was too used to having people wait on him while he was at home to consider cleaning up after himself. Picking up his bag, he switched off the light in the kitchen, made his way to the hallway, turned off the lamp on the telephone table, and continued on up the grand central staircase, avoiding the places he knew for certain would squeak. The last thing he wanted now was an encounter with his mother. She was an absolute sweetheart, a woman with a heart of gold, as everyone said; but she did have a tendency to wring the last ounce of drama from every situation, which was never pleasant, but tended to be particularly unbearable in the middle of the night.

His room was, happily, at the far end of the corridor from his parents'. And, as he knew every weak spot in the floorboards, Louis had not often been caught creeping home in the small hours (which he had done regularly from just after his fifteenth birthday). This time, too, his luck held, and he arrived undetected at his bedroom, which—despite his years of living away—still felt cozy and inviting and very much like home. It had a narrow brass bed (the bedclothes turned down in anticipation of his return), a chest of drawers with a marble top, and a desk by the window where he had once done his schoolwork. On it was the lamp that his mother or Deirdre or someone had left alight, its rays spilling over a stack of books, some framed photographs, and a handwritten note secured by a paperweight, one of the prized possessions of his childhood, a gift from his Aunt Etta and Uncle Titus. Inside the glass globe was the figure of a boy, skating on a pond surrounded by evergreen trees. Louis had spent hours, when he should have been studying, turning it this way and that to watch the snow drift gently down from the glass heavens onto the miniature earth below.

Dropping his bag onto a flat-topped trunk at the foot of the bed, he lit a cigarette and went to see which of his parents had left him a message. He was not surprised to find it was his mother. "Darling," she wrote, "Welcome home, though I wish you had come for a happier occasion. We are all heartbroken. Your loving Mother." For once, she did not seem to be exaggerating. The ache in his chest, in the region where he knew his heart to be, would not go away. Ever since he had spoken to his father, he had been conscious of it. Heartbroken. Yes, that might very well describe what he was feeling. He dropped the note onto the table and put the partially smoked cigarette out in the glass ashtray.

If he could sleep, the pain would stop, at least for a while, he thought.

Taking his toilet kit from his bag, he went into the adjoining bathroom. When he returned, he opened a drawer of the chest and took out a nightshirt, a garment that these days he wore only when at home. He changed out of his clothes, switched off the light, and got into bed. His body was heavy with fatigue. His eyes closed. Heartbroken, yes. He was heartbroken. "Lily," he said softly; and then he was asleep.

His sleep was restless, plagued by dreams that featured Lily and a body of water that Louis knew to be the Hudson, though it was round and encircled by tall evergreens. In some of them, it was he who nearly drowned. In others, he almost succeeded in rescuing his cousin, before the current caught her and swept her out of his grasp, or dragged her down to depths where he could not find her, no matter how often he dove into the choppy water in search of her, each time surfacing out of breath, his heart pounding with terror. Then, at last, he fell into a deep, sound sleep, free of disturbing images, so that, when he awoke, for a moment he could not imagine what in blazes he was doing at home, in his room, in his bed. The confusion did not last long. Memory came flooding back, bringing with it all the forgotten pain. "Oh, God," he murmured, closing his eyes, turning his head into the pillow, trying to recapture the peace he had just lost.

It was no use. Sleep stayed as far beyond his reach as had Lily in his dreams. The hall clock struck eight-thirty. Throwing back the covers, he forced himself from the bed. He felt even more exhausted than he had the night before.

There was a robe hanging in the closet. He put it on, went into the bathroom, and started the water running into the tub. What he really needed, he thought, as he relieved his bursting bladder, was a cold shower, something to shock him into alertness, but he lacked the will to subject his body to more ill treatment, however beneficial the result might be. Standing at the basin, he stared into the mirror above it, regarding himself with dismay. He had his father's height, but his mother's fair hair and delicate features. Always a pretty boy, he had reached manhood without losing the essential femininity of his good looks, which perhaps accounted for the fervor with which he threw himself into "masculine" pursuits. Perhaps, too, it accounted for his success with women, old and young, respectable and not-so, all of whom claimed to feel so comfortable in his company that they allowed him privileges denied to many of his more robust-looking friends. He had stolen more than a few kisses from young ladies under the noses of their doting mothers — not one of whom would have let him within hailing distance of their darlings this morning. Unshaven, with the whites of his eyes pink from lack of sleep and skin chalky white, he looked more like a hobo on a bender than a respectable young man, gainfully employed. Taking the shaving soap from his toilet kit, he worked it into a froth with a brush. Better, he conceded, when his razor had scraped off the last trace of lather, and half an hour later, fully dressed, his face flushed from the bath, his ash blond hair lying clean and shiny against his scalp, he felt, if not exactly ready to face his mother, at least able to survive it without falling to pieces.

He saw one of the maids, carrying a basket of dirty linen, coming out of his parents' room, and called, "Peggy, is that you?"

She was a wisp of a girl, hopelessly shy. As she turned to him, her face flooded with color and she said, "Oh, good morning to you, sir." Her voice had a lilt to it even stronger than Deirdre's.

"Any idea where my mother is?"

"Oh, yes. In her study. That is, she was a while ago."

"Thank you," he said, setting off down the stairs, his hand resting lightly on the oak banister.

Look at me! Look at me!

It was Lily's voice. Though he knew better, he turned to look for her, hoping to see her whoosh by him, riding the banister to the bottom, her skirts flying, her face glowing with excitement. For a moment, he could see her; he really could, as plain as anything. Then, she was gone. The hall was quiet. Accompanied only by an overwhelming sense of loss, Louis continued on down the stairs.

Who had been there that day? Rosaline and her brothers, he remembered; Florence, of course; himself; and Lily. They had set pillows on the floor just in case, though Marcus had made fun of Rosaline for thinking the precaution necessary. The whole thing had been Lily's idea, and she had insisted on going first. The boys had followed, then Rosaline, and last — after much taunting — Florence, who had missed the pillows, hit the floor hard, and wailed, which had brought the grown-ups running and put an end to the fun. They had been punished, he was certain of that, although he could not recall the penalty. Except for Lily, none of them took their punishments to heart, for their parents were not usually harsh, which was not to say that the Cannings were, but Lily hated making them unhappy, and her father in particular always wore such a worried look when she got up to mischief that she seemed to suffer more over that than having her allowance docked, or doing without sweets, or even having her paints taken away for however long the offense merited.

Lily had been a wild one, all right, but there had come a day, though Louis could not pinpoint it exactly, when she not only stopped being the ringleader, but refused to join in their adventures, no matter how hard he and the Roeder boys coaxed. She had turned into a lady right enough, as dignified and proper as the best of them. Never again had she earned her father's, or, for that matter, anyone's disapproval. Until Edmund Farel. What a to-do there had been over that, thought Louis. Though of course Uncle Titus was gone by then.

Opening the door into the study, Louis saw Edith at her writing table, scribbling away, and said, "Good morning, Mother." She was dressed entirely in black from the silk ribbon braided in her hair to her laced leather shoes.

Such a sweet smile lit her face when she looked at him that, for a moment, Louis was almost able to think it an ordinary day, his visit home an ordinary event, his mother's pleasure untainted by sorrow. "Oh, darling," she said.

Going to her, he took hold of the small, smooth hands she held out to him and leaned over to kiss her, breathing in the familiar scent of lavender. Normally, he would have complimented her, told her she looked beautiful, as young as a girl, but the familiar words seemed wrong in the circumstances, and he was at a loss for something to say. "You seem very busy this morning," he ventured finally, settling into a nearby chair.

"Yes. I'm doing menus for the next few days. Nuala's going to be overwhelmed. Mrs. Dutton will have to help." Mrs. Dutton was the Allens' cook. "Everyone will have to help."

While allowing his mother to ramble on about the system she was working out for ferrying food and services to Riverhall (the best way to keep her calm was to keep her busy), Louis studied her face and saw the ravages of grief. Her eyes were swollen and shadowed; beneath the dusting of rouge on her cheeks, her smooth skin seemed unusually pale. Horrified and embarrassed she may have been by the fiasco with Farel, and its consequences, but she had never stopped loving Lily. None of them had, not for a moment, not even Florence, he supposed.

"Oh, dear heavens . . ." The memory of just why she was busy rearranging her household's schedule seemed suddenly to strike Edith like a blow. Her head rolled with the force of it. Tears welled from her eyes. "It's too awful. Too awful . . ."

"Mother, don't—"

"Sweet Lily. To die so young."

Louis got to his feet. If he let her go on, she would be in full hysterics in no time, and then what would he do? He felt barely able to deal with his own sorrow. How could he possibly cope with his mother's?

"Didn't Henrietta teach her to swim, just to avoid this sort of thing happening? I can't understand it! What was she doing at the yacht club at that hour?"

He went to his mother, took her hand again. "I don't know. I had dinner with her on Sunday; she told me she had an engagement Monday evening." He might have kept her alive, he thought, if only he had convinced her to spend that evening with him. Why had he not insisted on it? How could he have gone to Cora when Lily lay dead? "But no one saw her at the club. None of the fellows had any idea she was there."

"When I think what this might do to my sister—"

"Which is why you need to keep calm, for Aunt Etta's sake."

"If anything were to happen to her—"

"You mustn't think about that."

"Her heart's not strong—"

"Then you need to be strong for her. We all do." How, he wondered, was he able to sound quite so calm when really all he wanted was to indulge in a fit of hysterics himself? "Mother?"

"Yes, yes," she murmured, holding tight to his hand. She took a deep breath.

"Agreed?"

"Yes," she said again. Releasing his hand, she took a handkerchief from her pocket and wiped her eyes. Then, turning a watery smile on him, she said, "Have you had breakfast yet?"

⚏

When he finished the fried eggs and bacon, the buttered toast, the strong black coffee prepared for him by Mrs. Dutton, Louis found that it was still too early to leave for Riverhall. For one thing, his mother informed him, his father had gone into his office to attend to some business he insisted could not wait. For another, his aunt had made it clear that, until the viewing began in the afternoon, she preferred to be alone. "Nuala can be depended on to look after her. And Rosaline will be there as soon as she gets her children settled."

"Rosaline?" It seemed strange even to Louis that Rosaline should be welcome when his mother was not.

She shrugged. "Your aunt seems to like having her there. Perhaps she makes her feel as if Lily were still at home. Truly, Rosaline's been an angel. You know, she went with her father to the city, to take care . . . well, there were the police to see, and Lily's belongings to deal with."

A wave of irritation swept through him. Why had no one thought to ask him to attend to matters? He had been there, on the scene, able to do anything that was required. Did everyone think him still a boy, unable to act responsibly? They were selling him short, if that was the case. "Why did no one telephone to me?"

"But your father did. As soon as we knew, which was only yesterday. Henrietta didn't want to worry us until she was sure. There was some doubt about the identity . . . She wanted to be certain first it was Lily."

"I see." And so he had been left to spend the night with Cora, when all the while Lily lay dead in a police morgue. "I think I'll go for a walk," he said, "if you'll excuse me, Mother."

So preoccupied with his thoughts was he that he brushed by Deirdre in the hall without noticing her. Anxious to avoid meeting anyone he knew, he kept away from Center Street, following the back lanes to the road over the railroad tracks, and was in front of the Schuylers' house before he realized that his walk was not quite aimless. He was heading for the river. For a moment, he considered stopping to see if Rosaline was still at home, but decided against it. Given the demands being made on her, she would no doubt be too busy to spare him more than a minute or two; and, in any case, there would be ample time later, at Riverhall, to talk.

But why was he so eager for conversation? What could anyone say to make Lily's death seem less devastating, more reasonable? It wasn't reasonable. Not at all. It was goddamn unfair. A low blow that fate or God or whatever had dealt Lily, had dealt him, wounding him to his soul.

The wind whipped in off the river, and Louis shivered. He had come out wearing only his jacket, which was not protection enough at this time of year, with winter in retreat, but not yet defeated. The forsythia was not quite out, he noticed. Yellow was the color of spring in the country. In the city, it was pale green; at least it was in the parks as the trees came in to leaf, haloed in clouds of soft chartreuse. He walked to within a few feet of the river's edge and leaned against the trunk of a beech tree. Reaching into his breast pocket, he removed the cigarette case, opened it, and took out the last cigarette. He would have to refill the case before leaving for Riverhall. Today was not a day to be short of smokes.

The sky was overcast, the water a dull pewter in the gray light, its surface churned by the wind, so that it looked as if someone had slung chain mail across the river, from bank to bank. Which reminded Louis of something he had learned in school. During the War for Independence, the Revolutionary forces had barricaded the Hudson against the British fleet by submerging chain link across its span at strategic places, one of them at West Point, several miles to the south. Ancestors of his had fought in that war. One had died a hero at Saratoga. In fact, ancestors of his had fought in every American war. Family folklore, inscriptions in bibles, old photograph albums, all gave testimony — a far distant relative killed in the War of 1812, a grandfather lost at Antietam in the Civil War, his cousins at Chickamauga and Spotsylvania. Most recently, Louis' uncle, his father's younger brother, had been killed in the Philippines during the Spanish-American War.

Was this war to be his? Louis wondered. Was it his duty to enlist and fight for his country? A long tradition of family service weighed in, favoring a resounding yes; but there was a part of him that, despite his desire to bloody a few German noses for their attacks on unarmed American ships with civilians aboard, could not help thinking that this was an entirely European fracas and ought to be left to them to sort out.

A freight train chugged across the mountain opposite. Beneath it, off beyond the barges, the tugs, the schooners, the occasional yacht plying up and down the river, a man in a rowboat was setting a net, no doubt fishing for his family's supper. Louis had done the same many times, usually with Henry Roeder. Inseparable growing up, they no longer spent much time together, with Henry off at university and Louis working in the city. It was only to be expected, he supposed; but, in his present mood, the thought served only to deepen his sense of loss. He wondered if Henry would come home for the funeral, and Marcus? Suddenly, he felt a strong need to talk to them, about Lily, yes, but about the war as well. He wanted to know what they thought, what they planned to do, though he was pretty certain he could guess Henry's reaction to it all.

Dropping his cigarette, Louis ground it out under his heel. Turning away from the river, he began the walk home, hurrying so as not to be late. When he reached the house, he found his father waiting, and lunch about to be served. "I lost track of the time. Sorry," he apologized, extending his hand.

"We're all a bit distracted today," his father replied, pulling him into a hug. He was not usually so demonstrative. "It's good to see you, son," he added, as if it had been months rather than weeks since Louis' last visit. The two men were of the same height and slender build, though George

Allen had such solid presence and grave appearance that it was hard to imagine him, even as a youth, indulging in the kind of behavior his son got up to. "How was the drive home?" he asked, when at last he let go. "That road must be treacherous at night."

"You've certainly got to keep your wits about you," replied Louis, following his parents into the dining room.

While his mother pushed her food around on her plate, and his father watched her anxiously, Louis managed to put away a fair amount of the cold meats, the bread, and the salads provided by Mrs. Dutton, all the while keeping up a steady stream of talk, about the state of Route 9, about his work, his social life, giving his parents a brief, censored sketch of his recent activities, afraid to let the conversation veer into more serious subjects, until finally his father said, "Your mother tells me you had dinner with Lily the other night."

"Yes." They looked at him eagerly, hungry for details. He understood. It was what he wanted from Rosaline, an accounting of her last meeting with Lily, as if the finality of death could be put off so long as the accretion of living memories continued. "The night before . . ." He paused and then went on, "She was in excellent spirits. She'd spent the day at the gallery, planning her exhibition." He paused again. "It's a damn shame," he said finally. "A damn shame."

His father nodded his agreement, while his mother said, "I wonder what will happen about that."

"The exhibition?"

"I imagine they might cancel it."

"Oh, I don't know," said Louis. It occurred to him that, given the way of the world, a recently deceased artist, one who had died in rather tragic circumstances, might attract more interest than one who was (boringly, one might say) just getting on with his or her life and work. Lily's death might provide an angle for the press to take up; the publicity would help sales. It was horrible, certainly, but that was business, though he did not feel inclined to point any of this out to his parents. "Someone ought to talk to that Darius Menlo."

"I don't suppose Henrietta's up to it," said his father.

"Oh, no!" said Edith.

"Mention it to her, Mother, would you, if you get a chance? It would be terrible if Lily were to lose this opportunity. She was so looking forward to it. And it really would be the best sort of memorial for her."

"It would," said his father with a sigh. "I can't imagine anything the dear girl would have liked better. I'll have a word, if Henrietta wants."

"Or I," said Louis eagerly. "I could stop in at the gallery one day next week. Will you speak to her, Mother?"

"Yes, of course. As soon as I think the time is right."

When lunch was finished, the three returned to their rooms to make themselves ready for the long afternoon and evening ahead. Louis added the black armband to the sleeve of his navy suit, gathered up his hat and coat, and was making his way back downstairs when he heard the front bell ring. Florence and Andrew, he thought; and sure enough, as Peggy held the door open, he saw come into the hall his sister, all in black, and his brother-in-law in a suit and armband similar to his own.

"You're home," said Florence. "I didn't expect you so soon."

"I drove up last night," he replied, kissing her offered cheek.

"Terrible business, this," said Andrew, as the two men shook hands.

Searching his brother-in-law's face, Louis thought he saw there the same mixture of shock and sorrow that afflicted them all. Andrew may not have known Lily for as long as the rest of them, but he had grown fond of her, it seemed. "Yes," agreed Louis. "Terrible."

For once, driving arrangements required little discussion. Louis would take his own car, while Florence and Andrew would go in the Packard with the Allens.

"Then, I'll see you there," said Louis, who, before he dismissed the thought with a grimace of distaste, wondered when he would be able to talk his father into buying a new Cadillac for himself. It shamed him that he could think of business at such a time.

"Drive carefully, darling," his mother called after him as he started along the hall, taking his usual shortcut to the garage. He heard the front door open. "I'll send the car back for the food," she went on to no one in particular. "I just hope there'll be enough."

In the kitchen, Mrs. Dutton, a dumpling of a woman, stood at the pine table rolling out a piecrust. Peggy had returned and sat stringing beans, taking them from the bag in her lap, snapping their ends efficiently, and tossing them into a large earthenware bowl on the table. The second maid, Harriet, a chubby girl no more than fifteen, stood at the sink washing the lunch dishes. A large iron pot of soup bubbled on the stove, and next to it was another full to the top with potatoes. A large beef joint and a ham lay on platters on the sideboard.

Harriet, looking around, saw Louis, and rattled one of the plates. "Careful, girl," said Mrs. Dutton, then she, too, saw him. "Good afternoon, Mr. Louis," she said. Her eyes were a little swollen, though the girls did not look as if they had been crying. Well, they had not known Lily for long, just a few months. They both smiled shyly at him.

"Hello," he said. "That was a fine lunch you served up, Mrs. Dutton. Thank you."

"I'm pleased you enjoyed it, sir."

"All this is for Riverhall, I suppose."

"Oh, yes. Mrs. Canning won't want to send anyone away still hungry. We're all . . . well, so very sorry about this. She was a fine lady, Miss Lily."

"Yes. She was. Thank you, Mrs. Dutton." He was reluctant to leave, he realized. There were moments here when he could actually forget. At Riverhall, forgetting would be impossible. "Well, I'd best be going."

"Yes, sir. Your aunt must want to see you, I'm sure. It's a comfort at times like these having loved ones about."

Louis left the kitchen, went through the back hall, and out the door leading to the yard. The wind had come up even stronger, whipping the bedclothes and towels on the line with a sharp snap. At the far end, he could see Deirdre taking in the laundry before the threatened rain started to fall, folding the linen into a wicker basket at her feet. It wasn't one of her usual chores, he recalled as he waved to her. One of the girls should have been doing it. Clearly everyone was pitching in and helping out wherever possible, which was damn nice of them, when you thought about it. It wasn't as if they were paid enough to volunteer for extra work. Though, on reflection, he supposed volunteering had had little to do with it. For all they put the best face on it, they'd no doubt been drafted.

People often moaned about their servants. Florence never stopped. But he had never heard his parents complain, or his aunt, for that matter. Those who did not suit for some reason were sent away quickly so as not to disturb the tranquil running of the house. The others seemed to stay on until they died, or, once in a great while, got married. Deirdre would certainly be among the latter, he thought, as she hurried over to close the garage door for him so he would not have to get out of the car to do it himself. She was a lovely girl, hardworking, considerate. "Thanks," he called, flashing her a smile. With a nod of her head, she turned to go back to the clothesline. Some fellow somewhere was going to be very lucky to get her, he thought, backing the car out of the drive into Elm Street. Very lucky, indeed.

Two ways led to Riverhall. One went along Potter Lane, a narrow dirt track, over Apple Hill to Beech Road, and more or less followed the line of the river. The second was more direct, along Kirkby Road, farther inland, cutting directly through the countryside to the next town, some ten miles away. His parents invariably took the latter but, uncharacteristically opting for scenery rather than speed, Louis always chose to go by way of the lane, weather permitting and the roads passable. It happened also to be the way Lily preferred, though he was not conscious of this fact weighing in his decision.

Without giving it any thought, he turned the Cadillac in that direction, a route that this time took him down Center Street, which was busier today than he ever remembered seeing it, with pedestrians crowding the sidewalks and the cobbled street full of people on horseback, in pony carts, in motorcars. The front of Burdett's Emporium was draped with bunting and flags, as was Crawford's Confectionery and every other building in sight. He saw Morton Hardy putting up a recruitment poster in the gun shop's window. Young men queued in front of the town hall, no doubt waiting to enlist. People stood in clusters, deep in earnest conversation. The majority must be talking about the war, but more than a few, Louis would wager, were going on about Lily. He saw Mrs. Jeffers walking with Mrs. Carmichael, the mayor's wife, and Louis tipped his hat, as he did again a moment later to Winthrop Oates, publisher of the newspaper. Even without looking he knew that their gazes followed him as he passed, and that all who saw him go by would declare sadly that he was surely on the way to Riverhall. They would comment on the tragic news, praise Lily extravagantly, bemoan her premature passing, discuss when they planned to call to pay their respects to poor Henrietta. That was the way it always was when someone died. He had experienced it firsthand with Titus Canning, but it struck Louis suddenly that, then, he had not minded so much. As fond as he was of him, his uncle's death had not touched him so profoundly. Now, Louis wanted to run and hide, to crawl into a dark hole, to deal with his grief unobserved. None of these people had known Lily as he did, had loved her as he did. What right had they to come barging into this private place and witness his pain? Of what use was their sympathy to him? To Aunt Etta? To anyone? Why could they not stay away and leave the mourning to those who had suffered the loss?

He was angry, he realized, as he turned into the lane and immediately hit a rut that rattled the car and jolted him out of his seat. No, what he was feeling was more than anger: it was rage, which was not like him at all.

Usually he was hard to get a rise out of. Affable, that's what he was. While everyone else was getting tossed about in stormy seas, he tended to sail through life on an even keel, minimizing the importance of disturbing events, banishing the thought of them from his mind as quickly as possible, drowning unpleasant emotions in a quantity of beer or wine, in glasses of champagne, in rowdy humor, in dancing the foxtrot, in amusing himself with anything that came to hand. None of those remedies would do a blind bit of good at the moment, Louis was certain, even if available; yet it would not do for him to arrive at Riverhall and give in to this mad impulse to tear someone limb from limb. "Get a grip, man," he counseled himself. "Get a grip."

Too soon to suit him, the Cadillac crossed over the railroad tracks and followed the road along the narrow tree-lined causeway until the spit of land broadened at the stone pillars that marked the Riverhall boundary. As he was in the habit of doing, Louis parked his car at the side of the house, near the garage, to leave room in the drive for others, and then walked back to enter by the front door. Wreaths of lilies hung from the columns supporting the porch and the entrance was draped in black cotton. When he rang the bell, the door opened immediately, and Jonas Walker said, "Oh, Mr. Louis, come in, sir. Your mother was worried maybe your car broke down."

Louis almost failed to recognize the old man. Small and wiry, with astonishing strength and boundless energy, Jonas always seemed years younger than his actual age. Today, however, he looked ancient, with lines of sorrow scoring his face and his eyes dull with pain. He was dressed in his best suit, a dark brown wool that Louis remembered from long years of Sundays. A black mourning band encircled his arm.

"Hello, Jonas. No, I'm perfectly fine. I took the lane."

Jonas nodded. "Always bad, this time of year," he said.

"They've got you on door duty, eh?" said Louis, taking off his coat and hat and giving them to Jonas to dispose of.

"Nuala's busy in the kitchen. We're expecting a houseful today."

It really was a lovely place, thought Louis, looking around the hall, taking in its familiar details, the wrought iron clothes rack, the wood settle, the telephone table, the paintings on the walls. The house was nowhere near as grand as his parents', but it had a spacious elegance, a welcoming warmth that he never failed to notice upon entering. Even today, he could not help responding to it, though he stood as if rooted to the spot, unwilling to take the next step. He felt Jonas' hand on his arm.

"Everyone's in the parlor," he said.

Louis wanted to hug the old man, cling to him as he had when he was boy and had hurt himself, skinning his knee on the gravel, or tumbling off a makeshift swing. "Oh God, Jonas. This is hellish, isn't it?"

"It's that." Again Louis felt a gentle pressure on his arm. "You'd best go in, before your mother gets up a head of steam."

Louis grimaced. "Yes, all right."

He started across the hall to the parlor door, the soft sound of Jonas' voice following after him. "It's best to remember her like she was," he said.

The double doors leading into the parlor were opened wide. At the threshold, Louis stopped for a moment, and then, gathering his courage, stepped across. The furniture had been arranged in semi-circles to face the middle of the room, leaving a clear path to the door and the periphery free for those who preferred to stand and talk. His mother and aunt sat on the sofa, in the first row to the left, holding hands like girls. Behind them, Rosaline and Florence sat at a distance from each other on straight-backed chairs brought in to help accommodate the expected visitors. His father and Andrew stood at one of the windows, talking quietly.

The coffin, in the center, drew Louis' eye: its polished mahogany and bright brass handles, the wreath of white lilies on the closed bottom half, a hint of silver fabric above, a blur of pale skin, a shadow of dark hair. None of it seemed real at all, but like one of those paintings Lily was always dragging him off to see, "An Impression of Death." Oh Lily, he thought, forcing himself across the intervening space to where she lay, so still, not like the cousin he loved at all, but a wax replica of her, beautiful but unreal. Her hands lay crossed just beneath her breasts, her fingers long and delicate, the short nails smooth and polished. Unable to resist, he reached out to touch her. She felt not made of flesh at all, but some other substance, manufactured, like the rubber in a child's toy, and cold, so cold. His hand dropped to his side.

He ought to say a prayer, he remembered, but only questions came: why? Dear God, why? Why Lily? Surely the world was filled with people who deserved to die, whose going would only benefit those left behind, while Lily had so much goodness in her, so much life left to live, so much happiness to bring to those who loved her. Why?

How long had he been standing there? He had lost track of time. Only minutes, he supposed, and he felt at once eager to turn away, to break the spell, and yet reluctant to do so, as if by spending every minute of the next few days, while he still had the chance, looking at Lily, he could somehow delay losing her, as if he had not already done so.

He became aware of someone standing next to him. Turning, he saw his brother-in-law looking at him with concern. Andrew had been sent to fetch him away. Well, at least he hadn't begun to blubber. That would have had everyone convinced he had gone over the edge. Giving Andrew a reassuring nod, Louis went to the sofa and, crouching before her, kissed his aunt's sad face. "I'm so sorry, Aunt Etta."

She touched his hand. "I know, dear. Thank you."

Not knowing what else to say, he stood, a little awkwardly, until his mother asked, "Did you have a problem with the car? It seemed to take you ages to get here."

That was to be the way of it, he thought. Everyone was to keep the conversation as normal as possible. "I came by way of the lane," he said.

"Oh," and she nodded, resisting the impulse to go on about his choice of route.

He saw Florence look at him eagerly, as if wishing him to come sit next to her. What bee did she have in her bonnet? he wondered. She was not usually so anxious to talk to him. He went and took the chair next to Rosaline's.

"Hello, Louis," she said. "When did you get home?"

"Last night. Well, early morning, actually. I drove up from the city."

"Henry will be here later today. Marcus is coming tomorrow."

"I haven't seen them in ages. Since last Fourth of July." There had been a party at Riverhall, the first since Titus Canning's death. Over her mother's protests, Lily had insisted it was time for life to get back to normal. And she had indeed seemed like her old self that day. No, that was not quite right, thought Louis. She had been gayer than ever, and he remembered the relief he had felt to think she was finally recovered from her father's death.

Rosaline smiled. "How long ago that seems."

Louis thought of the crowd of noisy friends, the tables laden with food, the canoe races, the games of croquet, the fireworks at the bottom of the garden after dark, the bright sprays of color against the night sky. "A hundred years at least," he said. Before Edmund Farel, before Lily's breakdown. "Where's William?"

"At school. He'll be by this evening. We decided he ought to spend some time with the children. I've been away so much."

"Do they know?"

"We told them. We did our best to explain, but I'm still not sure they actually understand."

"Do any of us?"

"No," she said. "It's hard."

He was fond of Rosaline. Small and gentle ("a pretty little thing" was the way people often described her), she seemed to bring out a fellow's protective instincts. He had found himself more than once, when they were children, attempting to go to her rescue, though she was years older, to help her down from a tree, say, or give her a boost over a wall, when really she was quite resourceful and able to manage for herself, better able than Lily, he had come to think. "I had dinner with her Sunday, you know."

Rosaline turned to him eagerly. "Oh, did you?" she said, clearly wanting every detail.

He told her how Lily had written to let him know when she was arriving in the city, how he had telephoned to her to arrange a meeting, how she had kept him waiting, how she had looked, what they had spoken about. "She was a bit tired, she said, but she looked wonderful. And she was so excited about the show, so looking forward to it. I asked her to stay on to go to the opera with me, but she sent a note saying she was too eager to get home and back to work. It seems a damn shame that now . . . after everything . . . when finally things were looking up for her . . . such a stupid accident . . . such a waste . . ." He was babbling, he realized. Rosaline had stopped looking at him. She was staring at her hands, watching her fingers as they twisted her handkerchief this way and that. "I'm sorry," he said. "I just can't believe it, that's all . . . Rosaline?"

When finally she did look at him, her eyes were blank. "Yes, such a stupid, stupid accident." She turned her head away for a moment, and, when she looked back, all the pain was there again, in her face, in her eyes. "I'm going to miss her so much."

He asked her when she had last seen Lily. "The day before she left," said Rosaline. "She came to visit the children." As if breathing life into her friend with every word, Rosaline began to sound almost cheerful. "You know what she was like with them, up to anything they wished to do. Though I have to say she was very firm with Will when he brought out his toy soldiers. She told him war was horrible, and little boys oughtn't to play at it. He was absolutely crushed. She's hardly ever said no to him. But he recovered quickly enough when she promised to bring him a present from the city." All the animation suddenly left Rosaline's face. "He was quite upset that she didn't . . . I hadn't realized she felt so strongly about the war."

"I don't suppose many of us thought about it much at all until the past few days. It seemed so far away. Nothing to do with us, really."

"I hope my brothers feel the same."

She had misunderstood him. "The declaration of war has changed everything, you know. We have no choice but to think of it, about where we stand, what we must do."

The trouble in her face was all for him now, Louis saw, for him and her brothers. Reaching out, she put her hand over his, resting against his knee. "You'll consider this carefully? You won't do anything rash? You must think about your mother. And your sister. Think about how what you do will affect them."

Louis looked across the room to Edith, but all her attention was focused on his aunt. Florence, on the other hand, was studying him intently. He could see only curiosity in her face. She wanted to know what he and Rosaline were saying, though anyone with any sense would realize their conversation could only be about the war, or Lily. What else was there to talk about?

Taking hold of Rosaline's hand, Louis squeezed it reassuringly. "No, I won't do anything rash," he promised.

Rosaline sighed. "I don't suppose your idea of rash is likely to coincide with mine."

Nor her brothers', he thought, but did not say, as he had no wish to worry her any more than necessary. Henry, he was sure, would be all fired up to enlist. He had always been a bit of a hothead. Marcus would take things more slowly, like Louis himself. "You know there's not a scrape we can't get out of in one piece, when we put our minds to it."

Her eyes drifted to the coffin. "So I always thought, until now."

"What was she doing at the yacht club?" he burst out suddenly. If only he had called in to see her, he thought. If only he had insisted she come out with him . . . "That's what I don't understand. What in hell was she doing there?"

Rosaline looked at him. "I did wonder if she was meeting someone."

"I don't think so." He told her about his asking Lily to the dance, her putting him off, how none of his friends had seen her.

"She had dinner with Alice and Teddy Berlin that evening. You remember them, don't you? Aunt Etta had a telegram from them today, saying how shocked and saddened they were. They saw the notice in *The Times*." She was quiet a moment, and then asked, "Could Edmund have been there?"

"At the club?" Louis shook his head. "Someone would have mentioned it to me. But surely she would never have agreed to meet him? I had the definite feeling she'd come to loathe the man."

Rosaline nodded. "Yes."

Louis stretched his legs out in front of him and sat staring down at the tips of his shiny black shoes. He needed a cigarette. "I don't understand," he said again. "It makes no sense. Why in hell would she have gone there alone?"

"Perhaps she suddenly wanted to see the river, just from that spot. You know what she was like. She wouldn't have thought twice about it, before setting out."

"But even if she walked right down to the edge of the dock, how did she come to fall in?"

"Oh, Louis, what difference does it make?" Though Rosaline's voice was quiet, there was no mistaking the distress in it. "We oughtn't even to be talking about this," she went on, as if angry with herself as much as anyone for pursuing the subject. "She's gone. That's all that matters. What good does it do to speculate endlessly on how or why?"

"I'm sorry," he said, instantly contrite. "I didn't mean to upset you."

"Perhaps she got dizzy, felt faint. Who knows? It happens."

"Yes," said Louis. He had seen girls at parties suddenly overcome with heat, or excitement, even Rosaline herself, though she had been pregnant with Will at the time. Something about that thought made him uncomfortable, and he pushed it away, seizing hold of another. "She

189

might have eaten something that disagreed with her." He smiled. "Oysters, I'd bet you anything."

"Let it go, Louis. Knowing won't help. Nothing will, except perhaps time. Oh look, the Jeffers have come, and Elsie."

He could tell from her tone that she wished their conversation to end, and Louis dutifully looked across to where Samuel Jeffers, his wife, and daughter stood clustered around his aunt. "This will bring everyone out, I suppose," he said. Titus Canning had handled matters for the Union Bank, as well as for the Jeffers' personally. His aunt and his mother and Mrs. Jeffers had been friends for years. It was not unusual. Everyone in town was connected to everyone else by countless ties, both business and personal.

"Yes," said Rosaline, sounding exhausted at the prospect. "If you'll excuse me, Louis."

She stood, and he followed suit, watching as she made her way out of the room without stopping to talk to anyone. His eyes drifted back to the Jeffers family. Elsie had just had a baby, he recalled his mother saying recently. A year or so younger than he, she was a plain girl with a dazzling smile that lit up her face, positively transforming it, so much so that for a moment one was left feeling confused by the difference, wondering where this beauty had come from. And then, the smile would fade, and Elsie would reappear. For a while, his parents had hoped for a match. Her parents, too, he had noticed with some embarrassment. Louis, however, had not been interested, not in marriage, not at his age, with all he had yet to do; and not in Elsie, as suitable as she was, and a nice girl to boot. She had married last year, a good fellow, Charles Andersen, whose family owned the ice company. He and Marcus Roeder were friends and used to go climbing from time to time during the holidays, and once, as a treat, Louis remembered, all the boys were allowed to ride on one of the barges carting ice south to the city.

People were arriving in a steady stream now, and as Mr. and Mrs. Jeffers made way for newcomers, Elsie saw him and delivered a subdued version of her smile. There was no escaping it: he would have to go and say hello. Taking a seat beside her, he agreed that it was indeed a terrible accident, a tragic loss, so devastating for his aunt. The cloud of gloom around him darkened. It was going to be like this for days, he thought, the same words said over and over, the same sentiments expressed, the same tear-filled glances exchanged. When he could not stand it a moment longer, he mumbled an excuse, got to his feet, and, ignoring his sister's obvious desire to speak to him, exchanging only the most cursory of greetings with friends and neighbors, made his way quickly out of the room. He understood now what Rosaline had felt when she had hurried away from him, a need to escape so great it blotted out any semblance of good manners.

Once in the hall, he hesitated. Nuala was coming along the corridor, carrying a tray laden with food. Behind her, carrying another, came Deirdre, who saw him and nodded before following her sister into the dining room. (Walter must have brought her, and whoever and whatever else were needed, up from the house.) Hearing footsteps, Louis turned and saw Rosaline starting down the stairs. He could make it out the front door before she reached the hall, if he hurried, and Jonas, who seemed to understand completely Louis' desire to flee, opened it and nodded him through without a word. A fine rain was falling. A car approached along the drive — Morton Hardy's Chevrolet, unless he was mistaken — and to avoid its disembarking passengers, Louis ducked around the side of the house. From there he made his way past the kitchen garden to the back porch, climbed its steps, and sat in one of the rocking chairs. Taking the re-filled silver case from the pocket of his jacket, he snapped it open. His hand was trembling, he noticed as he took a cigarette. He was going all to pieces. Making a conscious effort to steady himself, he slid the case back. This day would never end, he thought as he lit the cigarette and sucked what comfort he could from it. And then there was tomorrow to be got through, and Saturday — an endless expanse of time. He felt trapped in a sort of limbo, neither dead himself, nor yet quite alive.

Well, much as he would like to, he could not hide out here forever.

Finishing his cigarette, he flicked it over the porch rail into the grass. Instead of walking through the rain to the front of the house, he opened the door into the library and went in that way. The temptation to linger there, where it was quiet, lasted only a moment, defeated by the memories of the many afternoons spent in the room, playing with his cousin and the Roeders when they were children, all too sad to think about just then. He opened the door into the hall — and came face-to-face with his sister.

"Oh, there you are," she said, sounding pleased. "I was hoping to find you."

"I was out on the porch, having a smoke."

"I have to talk to you."

"Now?" Conversations with Florence, while sometimes necessary, were rarely enjoyable, and if this one could be postponed, Louis was all for it.

She nodded and said, "We won't get much chance to speak privately, I imagine, over the next few days."

Since she was blocking his way, short of pushing past her, he really had no choice. Stepping back inside the library, he said, "What about?"

Leaving him to close the door behind them, she went to the sofa and sat. "Andrew."

"Andrew?" he repeated. What in hell could she have to say to him on that subject? She cocked her head, looked directly at him, but for a moment said nothing. "Well, what about Andrew?" he said to hurry her on.

"I wish you to speak to him."

That was one for the books, that she should think his opinion on any subject would matter a damn to Andrew. "What about?"

"The war," she said. "He's told me he means to enlist."

"Ah," murmured Louis. He sat in the chair facing her. "Everyone's talking about it."

"Yes, but Andrew, as you know, will do it, unless someone talks some sense into him. He would have done it already, except for . . . Well, he thinks he oughtn't to do anything until after the funeral."

That was Andrew, all right, wanting to rush right out and sign up at the first call for help. His brother-in-law had backbone to spare. "He's a brave man."

"Reckless, more like."

There was no point trying to make her see the matter from Andrew's point of view, Louis very well knew. Florence never doubted that where she stood provided the best, the definitive, perspective on any subject. "You've told him how you feel?" he asked. When Florence replied that she had, he continued, "Then, I doubt anything I could say would influence him. Perhaps, if Father—"

"No. Father can't help. Andrew would dismiss his views on the subject as the fears of an old man. As for Mother, well, he would never take her opinion seriously."

"In any case, Florence, if Andrew wants to enlist, I don't think it's anybody's business but his really, when it comes right down to it. It's his life, after all."

"No, it's not, you silly boy," she replied, exasperation flooding her voice. "It's my life, as well. And someone has to make him see that—"

"If you can't—"

"Don't think I haven't tried! But you know Andrew. He doesn't consider it honorable to give in to a woman's fears, even if that woman happens to be his wife."

Louis reached into his pocket, took out the silver case, snapped it open, and ran his index finger along the row of slender white cylinders. There was something infinitely soothing even in the feel of a cigarette. "You don't mind?" he said as he picked one out. Florence shrugged, and Louis took his time putting the case away, finding his matches, touching the flame to the tight roll of tobacco dangling from his lips. What was he going to say? He inhaled, pulling the satisfying smoke deep into his lungs before releasing it, taking care to turn his head so that the gray cloud would not travel in his sister's direction.

"Louis, you will help me?" She had grown impatient waiting for him to say something.

"I would be happy to, if I could."

"You can. You must tell him that if anyone has a duty to fight this war, and I have my doubts about that, it's young men, like you . . ."

It was as if, for days, he had been trying to find his way out of a maze, only to discover that its exit opened to the one place he wished never to go. Yes, he thought, that was exactly right, the war was for young men like him, and Arthur, and Max, and Henry.

" . . . Not for those with responsibilities. Men with wives. With children."

The word drew Louis back from the dark path his mind was walking. Startled, he looked more closely at his sister. No one had mentioned it to him. "You're not . . . I mean, are you?"

Florence blushed and looked away. "It's too soon to be certain. But I hope . . ." She turned her head again and looked directly at Louis. "It would be awful if Andrew were to do something foolish before . . . well, we know for certain."

"You've said this to him?"

"Some of it. But it makes no difference, coming from me. He thinks I ought to be a Spartan sort of wife, glorying in her husband's going off to war. But I can't be that, Louis. In any case, he's already done his share. It's not right that he should have to do more, when others have done nothing."

No, it wasn't right, thought Louis.

"He shouldn't have to put his life at risk again. And my life with it. My whole world. You will speak to him, won't you? And point out to him what his true responsibilities are, where his true duty lies. You must use that word. Duty. It carries a lot of weight with Andrew."

Though not often inclined to do Florence a favor, Louis really could not see that he had a choice. He was her brother, after all. "Yes, I'll speak to him," he said, "though I'm not certain it will do the least bit of good."

"Oh, it will," said Florence. "It will. You have only to make it clear to him that you're determined to go yourself, and so he must remain at home to take care of Mother and Father and me."

Should he tell her, he wondered, that he had not yet made up his mind about that? But, no. He could not explain his own doubts to her, especially in view of Andrew's certainty, without sounding a hopeless coward. "I don't expect he'll listen to me. So, don't go getting your hopes up."

"If only you'll try—"

"Oh, I'll do that."

"That's all I ask." She stood. "You're a dear, Louis. And I will be grateful."

He doubted that. If she got what she wanted, Florence would soon forget she owed it to anyone but herself.

"We'd best get back," she said. "Mother will start to wonder what we're up to."

"Yes," he said, stubbing out his cigarette in a marble ashtray and getting to his feet. It would not do just then for him to remain alone with his thoughts. He followed Florence to the door, but before he could open it for her, she turned again to look at him.

"You won't mention to Andrew that we've talked about this?" she said.

"Not if you don't want me to."

"Or anything about . . .?"

"Of course not!" As if he was likely to bring that up with anyone!

"No one is meant to know yet. In case . . ."

He had a vague idea that the first few months in the process were pretty risky, though he would not have been able to say exactly why. "I won't say a word," he promised.

She thanked him with a small smile, then turned away and waited for him to open the door. Side-by-side they walked silently back to the parlor.

It had filled with people in their absence, the women in black, the men in dark colors, for all the world as if a host of crows had descended on the room while he was gone, thought Louis.

Without a word, Florence left him to join Morton Hardy and his wife. Andrew was talking to Samuel Jeffers, and William had come, Louis noticed. He was with Dr. Roeder and Elliot Carmichael, the mayor.

"Excuse me, sir," said a voice behind him, Deirdre's voice. He turned to look at her. "Have you seen Mrs. Schuyler?"

"No," said Louis. His eyes searched the crowd for Rosaline's slight form. "Oh, there she is," he said, "by the window, with Mr. and Mrs. Oates. Shall I tell her you want her?"

"That's all right, sir. I'll do it myself," she said, moving away from him to thread her way through the knots of mourners.

Well, he could not stand in the doorway forever, he supposed, forcing himself to take a few steps into the room. His mother, he saw, was talking to Mrs. Jeffers, while his aunt, still seated on the sofa, sat with a slender young man, as slight as a boy, who looked very like Rosaline. Henry! He had come.

As if suddenly aware of someone's eyes on him, Henry looked across the room toward his friend. They would speak as soon as he could decently leave Aunt Etta, Louis knew, but no conversation was needed to tell him what that first look had confirmed. Henry might be as shocked and saddened as Louis himself, but he was not confused. No, he was all fired up to embrace his future, risks and all.

And there lay Lily all alone, everyone gathered for her benefit, no one for the time being paying her the least attention. He went again to look down at her, and it struck him how serene she looked, how safe tucked into her narrow satin bed, how far she had moved beyond worry, beyond fear, how far she had moved beyond him. It seemed to him that the world had changed drastically in the past few days, and that change would always be irrevocably linked in his mind to Lily's death. Now, the way ahead for him no longer seemed a clear path in a tranquil landscape, as it had just a short while ago, but a road through hostile territory, fraught with unexpected dangers. The future had become the enemy, lying in wait, eager to do him, and all he cared about, irreparable harm. Painful as it was for Louis to admit, even to himself, he was afraid.

TEDDY

eddy saw it first. Leaving Alice in bed, he had gone down early, as was
his habit, to a café on Sixth Avenue, where he ordered a coffee, lit a
cigarette, and wrote a note to arrange a meeting with his current mistress,
whose husband was conveniently out of town. That done, he lit another
cigarette and opened the *Times*. He did not normally bother with the
obituaries (they did not have much to do with him or his friends, most of
whom were still in their thirties), but Lily's name caught his eye as he
turned the page. So inconceivable was the idea of her dying, that at first
he thought there must be another Lily Canning somewhere, and marveled
at the coincidence; but there was her mother's name, and a mention of
Minuit, and he knew with a growing dread that this poor, dead woman
was his Lily, *their* Lily, Alice's and his. Stunned, he just sat for a moment;

then, he stubbed out his Fatima in the ashtray, folded the paper, tore up the note, threw some coins on the table to pay the tab, and hurried from the café.

With the recent improvement in their fortunes, he and Alice had moved into Bryant Park Studios, on the corner of Fortieth Street and Sixth Avenue. Their apartment had a double-height work space with huge north-facing windows overlooking the park, a tiny kitchen tucked away under the stairs, and a bedroom and bathroom off the gallery on the upper level. It was an immeasurable improvement over their previous quarters, a cramped hole in Greenwich Village with a bath down the hall and no central heating.

Without removing his coat, Teddy made his way across the studio, through the clutter of easels and paintings and tables of supplies, and up the stairs, taking them two at a time. He found Alice still asleep and sat for a moment on the edge of the bed beside her, studying the look of peaceful oblivion on her face, reluctant to wake her and watch as it turned to misery. Then, her eyes opened of their own accord; she blinked, bringing him into focus, and smiled. "Even asleep, I could feel you glowering at me," she said. "What's wrong?" When he did not immediately answer, she sat upright. "If it's what I said last night . . . well, I was angry. And I don't remember your being so very kind about my character."

"No. No, it's not that."

"Then what?"

"It's Lily."

The blood drained from her face as he told her. She sank back against her pillow. "I don't believe it," she said. He handed her the newspaper, and she began to read. When she finished, she looked at him. She seemed dazed, in shock. The full horror had not yet hit her. "Monday night? But that's when we had dinner."

"She must have gone to the club afterward."

"Did she tell you she meant to?" When Teddy shook his head, she said, "Nor me, either."

"Do you suppose she was meeting someone there?"

"I think she would have told us . . . Or maybe not. Lily could be awfully secretive when she chose. But she may just have wanted to go for a walk."

Yes, thought Teddy. Lily liked to walk, especially by the river. If only she had said . . . Instead of returning to their studio, where he and Alice had — what? quarreled? made love? he really could not remember — they would have gone with her. It would not have been the first time they had wandered, the three of them, around the city late into the night, stopping in at the Golden Swan, or some other dive, for a glass of wine, running into friends, falling into a dispute over one thing or another: the world never failed to provide a subject for discussion. Things were changing so quickly, everywhere.

Yes, they would have gone with her, if only she had said; and, afterward, he and Alice would have seen her safely back to her hotel. They often did. Why had they not insisted on it that night?

Alice dropped the paper to the floor. She started to say something, and then stopped. What was there to say, after all? Turning her head into the pillow, she began to weep. "Oh, darling," he said. He touched the tangle of yellow hair, and immediately, as if he had pressed a spring, she sat up and threw her arms around him, burying her face in his neck, sobbing uncontrollably. "Darling," he repeated, holding her close, drawing comfort from her warmth, from her breathing, from the consoling fact that she was there, alive.

Since Alice had classes to teach and Teddy a portrait sitting, the earliest they could get away was Friday, when they took the two-ten train up from Grand Central to Minuit. Frequent visitors to Riverhall, they knew their way about the town. Despite the rain, they refused the stationmaster's offer to call them a taxi and, juggling bags and umbrellas, walked the short distance from the station, through the tunnel under the tracks, past the pretty house where the Schuylers lived, to the Wild Goose Inn at the end of River Road.

Their room was charming, full of lace and chintz, with a splendid view of the river, which at another time would have delighted them. Had they traveled as they usually did, carrying with them all their paraphernalia, they might even have set up easels and painted what they saw framed by the window, as Matisse had done at Collioure, though not with his brilliant palette, of course, thought Teddy, looking out across the dull slate water to the rocky face and tree-studded tops of the mountains opposite. Even in good weather, the light here was softer, the colors more subdued. He could not imagine that even the most ardent Fauve could conjure viridian and cobalt violet out of the restrained browns and grays and greens of the Hudson Valley in early April.

Hearing the bathroom door open, Teddy turned away from the view. Alice had changed out of her tweed suit into a belted dress, its skirt skimming the tops of her high-buttoned shoes. A brimless hat revealed only a fringe of blonde hair. Except for a splash of white silk at her throat, she was all in black.

She looked at him reproachfully and said, "You're not ready."

Stubbing out his cigarette, he picked up the jacket of his dark gray gabardine suit from the chair where he had thrown it, put it on, and slipped the black armband over his sleeve. "I was looking at the river, thinking of Lily, of how she loved it. . . ."

"Yes . . . I suppose one could say that she came to a fitting end somehow, though it breaks my heart to think of it."

They stood silent for a moment, looking at each other bleakly, until Teddy said, "We'd better go," and took Alice's coat from the armoire to help her on with it.

Since it was too wet out to walk to Riverhall, they had ordered a taxi; and, as they came down the stairs into the inn's small, carpeted lobby, with its patterned wallpaper hung with engraved prints of Hudson River steamboats, the front desk clerk peered out from his alcove under the stairs and said, "Your taxi's on its way. I didn't book the return," he went on. "You'll find someone to bring you back. Most everyone from around here will be going. I'll be calling in myself, if I can get away early enough."

"I'm sure you're right. Thank you," said Teddy.

"Miss Canning did a picture of me once." The plate on the desk gave his name as Ben Alferson. He was a likeable fellow, somewhere in his early twenties, with a broad face, wide-set brown eyes, and a small scar at the corner of his mouth. "A while ago it was," he said. "She saw me chopping wood out back, and asked if she could paint me. It won a prize at the county fair the next summer. Second prize, though I think by rights it should have taken first."

"I remember it," said Teddy, who could see, as if the canvas were hanging before him, the sun falling through a gap between the trees onto the young man, his muscles bunching under a plaid shirt as the axe fell, translucent beads of sweat against his throat, the chips of wood flying off to the side, the neatly stacked logs, the tree stump, some forlorn blades of grass, a saw extending at an angle out of the picture plane. Lily had done it in her social-realist phase. "An excellent painting."

"I don't know what's become of it, though Miss Canning gave me one of her sketches to keep." The door into the lobby opened, and a burly man in a worn black suit and bowler hat entered. "Good evening, Mr. Mach," called the clerk. "Your driver," he said to Teddy and Alice.

They followed Mr. Mach outside, where a shiny new Ford waited in the cobbled street. "Going to Riverhall?" he asked, making conversation as he opened its black door for Alice.

"We are," said Teddy, going around to the other side.

Mr. Mach hurried to close the door for him, and then climbed into the driver's seat. "Poor lady. It's a great pity. And Mrs. Canning having to suffer it, and her not well." He kept on in this vein for a while but, with no encouragement, soon switched to pointing out local sights he thought might be of interest: the church where the burial service was to be held, the cemetery behind it, the spot where (apparently Minuit's first event of the kind) a Studebaker had hit an elm tree, a result of the driver's having swerved to avoid hitting a dog.

"Was he hurt?" asked Alice, who seemed to feel that some response was necessary.

"Not the dog. Loomis — he's the postmaster — broke an arm, though," said Mr. Mach with some satisfaction. "Got the car fixed, but it's never run the same, he says."

With that, the three lapsed into silence, the Ford bumping along Kirkby Road through the mist into the gathering twilight, while Teddy and Alice smoked their Fatimas and stared out the cab's windows at the stands of trees lining the route. This must all have been forest once, thought Teddy, before the first Dutch settlers came, home to countless kinds of wildlife, to Indian tribes — hereabout the Wappingers, he would guess. They were long gone, but to where? He had no idea. But even now, the woods stretched away on either side for as far as he could see, broken only occasionally along the way by small farms tucked almost out of sight and the stone gates of mansions well hidden from view. It was all very pretty, he thought, and though the march of civilization could hardly be stopped, still something in him ached for the lost wilderness.

"It must have been so beautiful here, when it was wild," said Alice. She had an uncanny ability to read his mind, which was not an altogether comfortable talent for a wife to possess.

"If you look closely, you can just see half-naked savages running through the trees."

"I don't think I'd call them savages," she said. She turned to him and offered a brief smile. "Though I do know what you mean."

"Our noble Indian brothers, if you prefer."

She turned away again without comment, retreating into her own mind, where she had spent much of the past two days. Unusual for them, two people who — no matter what quarrel lay between them — were never at a loss for words, for ideas to discuss, for opinions to argue, they had hardly spoken at all since learning of Lily's death. Shock had rendered them virtually mute.

The taxi passed through the Riverhall gates, continued along the gravel drive, past the huge cedar tree that figured almost as often as the river in Lily's paintings, and stopped at the bottom of the porch steps. "Here we are," said Mr. Mach. Leaving the motor running, he got out to open the door for Alice. "Will you want a ride back?" he asked, after thanking Teddy for the fare and the tip.

"I'm hoping we can cadge one," said Teddy.

"I expect you will. Well, I'll just park anyhow and come in to pay my respects," he said. He got back into the taxi, put it into gear, and rattled off around to the side of the house.

Alice looked at the festoons of black cotton, the wreaths of lilies. "I think I've been hoping," she said, "that somehow we'd made a terrible mistake; that we'd got it all wrong."

Teddy took her hand and pulled it through the crook of his arm. "We'd better go in," he said. He had been dreading these next few moments for hours now. He wanted them over.

"Who could have imagined that our next visit to Riverhall would be for this?"

He could feel the weight of her reluctance pulling against him as he moved up the steps. "That's the thing about death," he said. "It's always unimaginable." Not abstract death, of course. The death of a soldier in war, the death of all those solders at the Somme, for example, one could imagine that. But one's own death? the death of a loved one? the death of a friend? No. That was impossible. One's mind simply could not grasp the idea that the friend who dined with you at eight, could, before midnight, tumble into the river and drown.

The front door opened, and there stood old Jonas in his worn brown suit, his shoulders stooped under the weight of grief, his lined face pale under its perpetual tan. "Mrs. Berlin," he said, "Mr. Berlin. Come in. I didn't know when you'd be coming."

Along the hall, Teddy could see a large number of people, in couples, in groups, all in dark colors, shadows eddying back and forth among the rooms. The low murmur of their talk hung over the space like the distant rush of falling water. "As soon as we could. This afternoon" he said, pulling Alice gently into the hall, and then letting go of her hand to shake the old man's.

"And no one to meet you at the station." Always before, Jonas had been there with the car to bring them back to Riverhall.

"We managed perfectly well. Don't you worry," said Alice reassuringly, as Jonas took their coats. "We know our way about quite well by now."

Jonas nodded. "I expect you do." The doorbell rang again, and he said, "You'll want to go into the parlor," nodding in its direction. "Miss Lily's there."

He turned away to admit the next caller, and Teddy slipped an arm around Alice's waist, urging her forward. On the threshold of the parlor, he paused again to get his bearings, and saw a blur of faces, some familiar, some unknown to him. When he heard Alice draw her breath in sharply, he allowed his gaze to follow hers and come to rest on the open coffin in the middle of the room. It was odd, he thought, as he and Alice crossed the rug toward it, that while he could remember many paintings of the dead, in none of them did they lie in coffins — on beds, yes; on the ground where they had fallen; in rivers where they floated, flowers twined in their hair; even in the bath; never a coffin. Why? he wondered. Did a coffin somehow detract from the drama of the moment, turning death into something ordinary and dull? After all, it comes to everyone.

Though it should not have come to Lily so soon. He saw the waxy pallor of her skin, the bruise on her temple, the makeup — only a hint, but even that seemed too garish for her pure beauty. A wave of intense anguish washed over him, and a profound sense of loss. He was battling back tears. How young she was, how lovely, the most beautiful woman he had ever known, and talented, perhaps even more talented than himself (though that was not a pleasant thought, and he pushed it away quickly whenever it came). Without a doubt, she had a touch of genius lurking beneath all her uncertainties. If only she had been able to tunnel past them, dig deep to the heart of her being! If only she had been able to get free of the constraints that bound her.

What had she said that last night at dinner? That she had begun a new painting; that it appeared promising; that it seemed to be leading her in a new and interesting direction? What if it was true? What if she had at last found the one right thing that would propel her to where they all longed to be — in the Pantheon, admired, revered, like Whistler, like Sargent, like Manet . . . well, why not? like Velazquez, if not now, then one day. Nothing would have been impossible for her, if . . .

But there was no point brooding on that. Whatever talent Lily possessed was lost, lost to the world forever, a great shame, but there it was, nothing to be done about it. Nothing. And she herself was past caring, which was some consolation. When he thought of the turmoil he had lived through himself, and no doubt would again, the ridicule he had endured from critics, the agony of self-doubt, of frustrated ambition, it was possible to see death as a blessing, to welcome the peace it brought, the oblivion. Good-bye Lily, he thought. Good-bye, lovely girl.

Mr. Mach was waiting to approach the coffin. Teddy tightened his hold on Alice, and, when she looked up at him, he could see the pain in her brown eyes mirroring that in his own. Drawing her away, he steered her toward Henrietta Canning, who saw them and extended her hands. "Alice, Teddy," she said. "How kind of you to come." She seemed completely unaware of the tears that had started in a slow trickle from her eyes at the sight of them. "Edith, you remember Lily's good friends, don't you? Alice and Teddy Berlin?"

They greeted Edith Allen, who assured her sister that she remembered them very well, and then took their arrival as an excuse to slip away. "I must see how they're getting on in the kitchen," she said. "There have been such crowds this afternoon, we must be running out of food."

"Edith always fears the worst," said Henrietta, when her sister had left them, "but then no one copes with it better than she when it comes. Here, sit by me," she added, wiping the tears away with her fingers, then drawing her black skirts close to her, making room for the Berlins on the sofa.

Alice sat next to Henrietta and, taking hold of her hand, bent forward until her dark hat and the gray-streaked head almost touched. "We're so very sorry, Teddy and I," said Alice. There was a quaver in her voice. "We don't begin to know how to express our sympathy. . . ."

"There's no need. You were such good friends to her. You cared for her deeply, I know."

"We're going to miss her terribly," said Teddy.

"You had dinner with her? That night?"

"Yes. We saw each other often when she was in the city."

"She said you were going to Delmonico's?"

Alice smiled. "She felt like splurging, and Teddy and I were happy to agree."

That was not quite true, though Teddy had no intention of correcting his wife. It was he who had insisted they go. Alice was always more sensible about money. She had been poor for so long, that was the trouble; but after years of scrounging a living by doing freelance illustrating, she now had a steady job teaching life drawing at the Art Students League. As for himself, he had been doing well since his appearance in the Armory Show. Though the critics had ignored his existence, others had not. His paintings now sold handsomely, and he had received a number of important portrait commissions (the latest from Duncan Phillips, the collector). They could afford to splurge, he had told Alice, and so Delmonico's it had been.

"It's a lovely place. A great favorite of mine, and Lily's. Titus always took us there on special occasions. How did she . . . seem to you?"

There was note of hesitation in Henrietta's voice, as if she had to overcome some resistance to put her question. Now, why should that be?

207

wondered Teddy. Surely it was the most natural thing in the world for her to want to know how her daughter had passed her last hours?

"Seem?" repeated Alice. "Very well," she said, launching into a description of the evening, what Lily had worn, how she had looked, the meal she had chosen (Blue Point oysters, Hudson River shad, Baked Alaska).

"All her favorites," said Henrietta. She listened avidly to Alice's recital, as if waiting for the one detail that would reveal the secret of the universe. Then, looking away, as if embarrassed by the need to ask, she said, "Lily didn't happen to mention Edmund, did she?"

"Oh no, not for ages," said Alice.

Henrietta turned to them again. "I seem to remember that the Columbia was one of the places Lily and he used to go."

"We all went there with her, one time or another," said Teddy. "She knew so many of the members, friends from here, most of them. We were always asked to dances, to crew for races. . . ." Lily had seemed a bit down in fact, and had complained of a headache. Teddy had thought she was just worn out from dealing with Darius Menlo all day, though, it occurred to him now, her former husband might have had something to do with her mood. "You mustn't think she still harbored any feelings for Farel," he said to Henrietta. However absurd it might be (for what did it matter now?), it seemed important to him that the poor woman not think her daughter had died unhappy. "None but contempt."

"I had thought so, but . . ." Henrietta shrugged. "It's not the sort of thing, I suppose, that a girl tells her mother."

"She never spoke of him at all, I assure you." For the first time, that struck Teddy as suspect. If Lily had been over Farel, would she not have talked of him more openly, airing her grievances, instead of keeping them hidden away, perhaps brooding over them?

"Never," agreed Alice. "Truly, she had hardly a thought to spare of late for anything but her show. And Monday, though she had spent hours at the gallery before meeting us, she was in excellent spirits, only a little tired, which is a marvel when you consider how exhausting Darius can be. Teddy will tell you that."

The Menlo was his gallery, as well. It was he who had introduced Lily to its owner, and encouraged Darius to take her up. Without Teddy's intervention, though he would never even have hinted as much to her, Lily would not have got her solo show, not yet at any rate. "She was a bit anxious about some paintings she wanted to finish." Obsessive was more the word. "And apprehensive, as anyone would be, at the thought of the critics sharpening their knives for reviews. But, above all, she was excited, and hopeful."

"She felt she was showing some very good work," said Alice.

"Excellent work," added Teddy. In a way, that was true. No one could draw as well as Lily. She had an excellent understanding of composition, of form, and her use of color was superb — subtle, sensitive, beautiful really. Surely no one would fail to recognize that, not the public, not the critics. "I'm certain the show will be an enormous success." But, though he could hardly have said as much to Lily that last night at Delmonico's (or ever, in truth), as much as he wished it otherwise, in his opinion her "breakthroughs" had always amounted to no more than a few timid steps forward. Her confidence had inevitably failed her. No matter the effort she made, she had remained stuck in the past, in outmoded ideas, while the world had moved on, decidedly on, leaving behind the likes of her mentors (and his), William Merritt Chase and Robert Henri. For no matter how pretty his pictures, Chase had never really got to the bottom of Impressionism, nor had any of the other Americans who had attempted it (except perhaps for Childe Hassam). They had never delved deep into the effect of light on color, but had only brightened up their palettes, splattering paint like confetti across their canvas. As for Henri, the erstwhile radical, he could never bring himself to divorce art from meaning, to luxuriate in the pure painterliness of painting. Even Sargent, with all his profligate abilities, seemed to have been left standing on the station as the train of modernism sped on into the future. Not that Teddy felt always confident about his own development. Doubt was the dragon with which he (and all artists) had to live. But he was making progress, halting though it might be. He was certain of it. And at bottom he believed that his talent would always ride to the rescue, and slay the beast before it ate him up.

"I don't know what to do about the show," said Henrietta.

"Darius can't possibly want to cancel it?"

"That would be so terribly unfair," said Alice.

"Oh no," replied Henrietta quickly. "Mr. Menlo wrote immediately to say that he was eager to go forward."

"Then you must," said Teddy.

"So Erich Roeder has told me, and Edith. But I can't help thinking how peculiar it will seem. "

"Not at all," said Alice. "It will seem a testimonial to Lily, to her work."

Henrietta nodded and said, "Yes, I suppose. She did work so hard. I wanted her to come away with me last month, just for a few days, to Florida—I thought she needed a rest—but she absolutely would not. She had too much to do, she said, too much lost time to make up. I didn't like to press her, she seemed so pleased to be back at work again. I don't understand . . . I don't . . . ." She bit her lip, as if to stop herself talking.

Alice patted her hand soothingly. "Perhaps this isn't the best time to make a decision. It can wait a few days, I'm sure."

"We mustn't take up any more of your time," said Teddy. There was a queue of people waiting to speak to Henrietta. He rose to his feet.

"You're not going back to the city tonight?"

"No. We're staying over, at the Wild Goose," said Alice.

"You might have stayed here." Henrietta's face crumpled with dismay. "I should have thought—"

"We wouldn't dream of putting you to so much trouble," said Alice as she stood. "And it's a lovely inn."

"We'll be near, if you need us for anything," added Teddy. "You have only to ask."

"I know," said Henrietta. The dismay left her face, and the sadness came flooding back. "I'm so grateful. Lily was fortunate to have such good friends." She forced a smile for their benefit, and then, ever gracious, turned away. "Reverend Moreland," she went on, offering her hand first to a slender, fair-haired man in a black suit and liturgical collar, and then to the pretty dark-haired woman beside him. "And Mrs. Moreland. Thank you so much for coming."

As he and Alice wandered through the crowd, greeting people whom, on their visits to Minuit, they had come to know, Teddy could not help thinking what odd affairs wakes were. For a start, there was Henrietta Canning, beyond all doubt devastated by her daughter's death, still concerned for the welfare of others when by all rights grief ought to have laid waste to her good manners. And Rosaline Schuyler, almost as pale as Lily herself, with a strange, haunted look in her eyes, nevertheless managed an affectionate smile and friendly greeting and a promise to speak with them later, at length. Even Louis Allen, though admitting to being bowled over by the events of the past few days, welcomed them warmly and remembered to offer them a lift back to town. It was all rather like a party that had somehow fallen flat, or where the guests had been warned to keep the noise down for fear of disturbing the neighbors. Only Florence Macleod seemed incapable of putting on a good show, weeping as she spoke to them. "I'm just grateful Aunt Etta's bearing up so wonderfully well," she said.

"I didn't expect her to take it so hard," Teddy whispered to Alice as they moved on.

Alice glanced sympathetically over her shoulder to where Florence now stood speaking to a young couple who, despite the somberness of the occasion, had a jubilant air about them, as if they had just done something wonderful—fallen in love perhaps, or produced a child. Turning back to Teddy, Alice said, "They mightn't have been particularly close now, but they did grow up together. All those years, all those shared memories. Losing Lily must be like losing a piece of herself."

"Yes, I suppose," he said. "If I were to lose Walter . . ." Scratching out a living in one upstate New York town after another, Teddy's parents had moved so often when he was a boy that he and his older brother had never formed any close relationships outside that small family circle, made smaller still when their father had died (from cirrhosis of the liver, a diagnosis left unspoken). Now, despite the miles separating them, and the differences in their interests and temperaments, the brothers remained close. A steady sort of fellow, hardworking, reliable, a clerk with a shipping company in Chicago, Walter was married and had a son and two daughters. "Or," Teddy went on, "if you were to lose Joan." She was Alice's sister.

He felt her shudder. "Yes," she said. "It would be awful."

Teddy's mother had died some time ago, of tuberculosis. He had sent her what money he could in her last years, enough so that she could finally stop taking in boarders to support herself, though by then there had been few enough. The sound of her cough was a deterrent to all but those too ignorant to surmise its cause, or too poor to have a choice.

Alice's parents had passed away when she was twelve, within days of each other, casualties of a pneumonia epidemic. She, however, had a bevy of brothers and sisters scattered across the country, although she was close to none of them but Joan, who had raised her after their mother's death, sacrificing herself doing any number of grueling jobs, from cleaning houses to taking in laundry, so that the talented Alice could study art. Joan had sacrificed herself for the others as well, but since they had all settled into conventional lives, with regular incomes, they tended to think of themselves as deserving, and of Alice as selfish for having taken much and returned little. One of the reasons that steady employment was so important to Alice was that it allowed her to send Joan money every month, though that did nothing to ease the complaints of her siblings. Joan was the only one of them who took pride in what her little sister had accomplished. She had a magnanimous heart, did Joan, and a generous spirit; and though it was difficult for Teddy to believe (and he sometimes imagined her indulging it when she was at home alone, like a taste for opium), she was not at all addicted to self-pity.

"I can't imagine life without Joan," said Alice. "Even now, when I hardly see her, just knowing she's there makes me feel safe. She's like some sheltering cave I know I can run to and hide in until the storm's gone passed. She's the one person whose love I never doubt."

Teddy came to a stop. Frowning, he turned to look at her. "You doubt mine?"

She met his look with serious brown eyes. "Now? At this moment? No. But how long will it last? A month? A year? The rest of our lives? I don't know the answer to that question. I wish I did."

"Don't you think the same question plagues me, about you?"

"I suppose it does," she said and offered him a small smile. "We must hope for the best."

They had come to a stop near the hearth. Someone had earlier lit a fire that now seemed in danger of dying out, which would not be altogether a loss as, despite the damp, the crowd in the room seemed to generate more than sufficient heat. Looking up at the portrait of Titus Canning, hanging above the mantle, Alice said, "It's very like him, isn't it?"

"Yes," agreed Teddy. He knew she was not referring just to the physical resemblance, which was remarkable, but to the way Lily had captured the character of the man. He was seated in a leather chair, wearing evening dress, his black eyes looking straight out at the viewer with an unflinching gaze, a hint of a smile softening his mouth, which was full, like his daughter's. The background was sketched in, books in high cases painted in broad strokes, the suggestion of a landscape painting on the patterned wall, a drape of curtain disappearing out of the frame to the right (anyone familiar with the house would immediately recognize the Canning library), but the face and hands were carefully modeled and illuminated by an uncertain source of light that also picked out the satin of the lapels, the diamond in his stickpin, and the glint of silver in his dark hair. "Lily managed to capture not only his arrogance, but his intelligence, and his charm."

"He was a very charming man."

Teddy turned away from the portrait to look at her. "Did he flirt with you?"

"I suppose you could call it that, but it was never unpleasant. I rather liked it. I thought he was terribly sweet."

"Sweet? Titus Canning?" Teddy looked up again at the portrait. "That's the last word I would use to describe him. I think he was capable of being quite ruthless."

"Teddy, really—"

"Look at the way he dealt with Lily."

"He was just being protective of her."

"You would never have allowed him to mollycoddle you so."

"I might have. I might have liked being looked after—"

Teddy shook his head in exasperation. "There speaks a woman who never had a father to stop her doing what she wanted. Or anyone, for that matter."

"He let her paint; he encouraged her. That was the primary thing."

"That was his hold on her."

"That's one of Lily's," said a voice behind them. "But I suppose you know that."

Turning, Teddy saw Dr. Roeder, who looked tired, worn, and years older than when the Berlins had last seen him, at the Fourth of July party. "Yes, indeed," said Teddy. "We were just commenting on what an excellent likeness it is. How are you, sir?" he asked, extending his hand to the older man. "If I may say so, you look done in."

"It's been a terrible few days," said the doctor. He shook Teddy's hand, but taking hold of Alice's, he leaned forward to kiss her cheek. Then, he stepped back and murmured, "First Lily. And if that wasn't unbearable enough, my boys . . . This damnable war," he muttered.

"Oh, no," said Alice. "They've enlisted?"

"Not yet," he said. "But they will. They've caught the war fever. Nothing their mother or I say seems to make the least impression on them." He sighed. "I can understand Marcus. He's a doctor. He can be of some help. But Henry? Fodder for guns, that's all he'll be."

"There's already talk of peace," said Teddy. "The papers say that the German people are starving, that the country can't hold out much longer."

"To think that there's cause for rejoicing in that! A people starving! One had higher hopes for the twentieth century."

"Indeed," said Teddy. "But the century's young yet. We're still living with vestiges of the nineteenth, with militarism, colonialism, expansionism. Who knows but that the president's right, and this war will be the last one mankind will ever have to fight?"

"I pray you're right," replied the doctor. "Though my familiarity with human nature leads me to doubt it." Then, abruptly changing the subject, he said, "I understand you dined with Lily on Monday?"

"Yes," said Alice; and, once again, she and Teddy launched into their recital of that evening's events.

It was an essential part of the ritual, an act of condolence, thought Teddy, this offering up of memories, but to what end? The combined energy of all their separate reminiscences could not breathe life back into Lily, whose body lay so close, but whose spirit was . . . where? Extinguished, as he feared, a flame doused by the dark waters of the Hudson? Or, as Henrietta Canning no doubt believed, now enjoying its heavenly reward? There came into his mind an image of his friend, buoyed by a billowing cloud, surrounded by a host of admiring putti. She was standing at an easel, smiling blissfully, painting: a happy fantasy, one Teddy wished with all his heart he could believe. Then, perhaps, he could shake free of the sorrow that gripped him, the sense of loss, the anger at the idea of such a promising life blighted by depression, cut short by death.

"So, she seemed well to you?" asked the doctor, when Alice and Teddy reached the end of their tale.

"Oh, yes," said Alice. "Of course, we were all upset about the war. The papers were full of it. And we knew it was only a matter of days before we'd be in it, so it was on all our minds, though I have to say we spoke mostly of Lily's show—"

"She never mentioned Edmund Farel?"

"No," said Teddy. "She hasn't said a word about him since . . . since she told us she'd left him. Mrs. Canning asked us that as well," he added, struck by this sudden resurgence of interest in Farel by the very people who, only a few short months before, had collectively (though without overt collusion, Teddy was sure) decided to act as if the man had never existed, refusing to utter his name, wiping him from their conversations, if not—one suspected—completely from their minds.

"Oh, did she?" replied the doctor. He glanced away for a moment, looking to where Henrietta sat, her sister once again on guard at her side, then returned a serious gaze to Alice and Teddy. "We wonder why Lily would have gone to the yacht club at that hour. If she had planned to meet someone, it might make more sense to us."

"If there was someone, it wasn't Farel, I'm sure of that," said Alice.

For the first time, it occurred to Teddy that his wife knew a great deal more than she had ever said about Lily's relationship with her former husband.

"Louis Allen inquired, but none of his friends saw her there."

"I think she may just have wanted to look at the river," said Alice.

The doctor sighed. "Yes," he said. "That's what it always comes back to. Though I wish to God she hadn't. I wish she had hated that damn river, been afraid of it, as anyone with any sense ought to be. If you'll excuse me." And with that, he turned away and went to join his wife, who looked pitifully haggard, her lovely face drawn with unhappiness. She seemed about to collapse under the weight of attention from Mrs. Dowling, Minuit's grande dame.

"Oh, there you are Erich," Teddy heard Mrs. Dowling say. "I was just asking Violet to help with the draft rally next week."

Once, Teddy had believed himself to be in love with Lily. Only twenty-six, a young painter with few sales to his credit, finding commissions hard to come by, desperately in need of some sort of regular income, he had considered himself fortunate to get a place teaching portrait and still life painting at the Art Students League. At the time, a renewed sense of freedom had reigned there, thanks to Frank du Mond. By insisting there be no entrance requirements to his classes, he had helped revitalize the place, putting an end to the insidious creep of formalism that had threatened to do in the school's radical spirit. Anyone, male or female, with no prerequisite but the ability to muster monthly fees of only a few dollars, could choose an independent path of study and attend classes. The changes had brought back William Merritt Chase after a nine-year absence. The faculty was in general excellent, the students eager. It was once again an exciting time to be at the League

Teddy had been teaching there only a few months when Lily enrolled in his class. It was the autumn of 1907. She was just sixteen, and so lovely, with a slender, gently curved body, and a mass of black hair framing a face that had the purity and perfection of marble. Looking at her, one could not help thinking of the statues of Hiram Powers, of Canova, of Praxiteles. It was difficult, perhaps impossible, not to be smitten with her. Sometimes, it had seemed to Teddy that all of the men were, heterosexual or not, and many of the women, too, drawn not just by her beauty, but by an innocence that made her seem like a precocious child. Naïve, reserved, well-mannered, she was generally popular, though more apt to be treated like a mascot than a peer, for she was too young to take part in the school's (sometimes rowdy) social life: either that, or too well guarded by her parents, who had come with her to New York.

If her beauty was the first thing he had noticed about Lily, her talent was the second. Even at that early stage, her technique was impressive. She had learned the basics from her father, she told Teddy when he asked. After that, she had studied with one of the nuns at her school, and then with Grover Watson, who had enjoyed a brief vogue before retreating to Kirkby, where he augmented the meager living he made from the sale of his paintings by taking on students. Teddy was familiar with his work and, if he did not think much of it, he conceded that Watson was a fine teacher. Lily had learned a great deal from him—drawing, perspective, composition. And if that were not sufficient reason for gratitude, without his help, Lily said, she would never have been able to convince her parents to let her leave high school to study art full-time. They had considered the School of the Museum of Fine Arts in Boston (where Lily had taken a class in watercolor one summer) and the Philadelphia Academy (which both Mary Cassatt and Cecelia Beaux had attended), but had settled on the League, perhaps less because of its reputation, than its nearness to home. Titus Canning had a law practice in Minuit to look after.

"Well, I'm very pleased you found your way here," Teddy had told her. "I think we might be able to make something of you."

When she joined his class, Lily's work in oil was highly finished, but labored. Her style was careful, controlled. She was not inclined to take chances, which, given her age and comparative lack of experience, was hardly to be wondered at. Where she excelled was in drawing. She had absolute control of her line. She rendered detail not only accurately, but with a delicacy that took one's breath away. "He who draws best must be the best artist," William Blake had said; and, as Teddy studied Lily's sketches, he wondered if that could possibly still be true, despite the Impressionist substitution of light for line. His own drawing was nowhere near as good as hers, though of course he surpassed her in other areas, in his handling of paint, for example, in his use of the brush. He had many more arrows in his artistic quiver than she, in almost every sense a novice, while he was established, with several group shows under his belt, a few good reviews among the many slighting ones, and a number of commissions to boast of, including the one he was then at work on, a portrait of Mrs. Esther Newbold, a society hostess who had admired his work at a League exhibition and sought him out. Yet, it had occurred to him that, if she stuck to it, Lily might soon catch him up, might even overtake him. It was not a comfortable thought.

Nor was it an easy thing to do, to swallow one's pride, to keep one's competitiveness in check, to remember to encourage and not squelch the ambitions of one's rivals, which in effect every student was. Teddy believed that, as a teacher, he had succeeded more often than not, and that was especially true with Lily. He had done what he could to foster her talent and bolster her confidence, and he had done it while behaving absolutely as he ought, as a gentlemen. He was certain that she never guessed how his heart raced when he caught sight of her, how he struggled to control his breathing before speaking, how she commanded his thoughts when he was awake and his dreams while he slept.

Tempted to follow her to Woodstock where she was to study at the League's summer school, Teddy got hold of himself and decided that he needed to put some distance between them. With the consoling thought that Lily would be a more suitable age when he returned, he left for Europe at the end of the spring semester, using the proceeds of his commission to fund the trip. He went almost directly to friends at the artists' colony in Pont-Aven, returning in the fall to Paris, where he stayed much longer than planned, and not just because the art he was seeing in the museums, in the ateliers of painters, in the shops of dealers, surpassed even his most avid imaginings. What kept him was that, one night at the home of the ex-patriot collectors, Gertrude and Leo Stein, he met Alice. She, like him, had come with a group of friends.

It was nothing like a *coup de foudre*, as the French call it. Pretty as she was with her lemony hair, pert nose, and eyes as soft as a chocolate mousse, Alice's looks had not stopped his breath. They had not caused his heart to do somersaults in his chest. Not at all, though he had desired her at once. There was a sensual, womanly quality to her; and she had an open, friendly manner that was very appealing. Men admired her, they liked her, and yet she managed somehow to evade them, keeping free of the round of sexual entanglements that characterized the society she lived in. She had the gift of seeming accessible, without appearing loose.

Teddy at that point was neither naive nor inexperienced. His affair with Mrs. Newbold, which had added a certain drama to his painting her portrait, was not his first with a patron. He was attractive to women and he knew it, had known it since a boarder of his mother's had paid for a sketch he had made of her by introducing him to sex. His looks were ordinary enough, but he had charm, and a seductive kind of energy, and, though far from predatory, an innate sense of a woman's availability. Alice was not available, he had sensed, at least not in any casual way. Still, for reasons not always clear to him, he pursued her.

While many men in his position were drawn to wealthy women, seeking recompense in the well-rounded arms of luxury for the deprivations they suffered, Teddy had found himself burdened by what was expected of him in those situations, by the need to be deserving of the largesse bestowed on him, by the need to be grateful. What he liked about Alice was how similar to him she was. He found her easy to talk to, about anything, their reactions to the art they saw, the concerts they went to, the people they met, soon even about their families and the grinding poverty of the lives they had lived. When they went their separate ways, he missed her, missed the way she always seemed to know what was on his mind. He wanted to hear her response to whatever was happening, to tell her his, to measure his views and ideas against her own. They became inseparable, and then, inevitably, they became lovers. He was the first for her, she told him, and the last: he was her soul mate, her pal.

When it was time for Teddy to leave Paris for Munich, he convinced Alice to go with him; and, though he expected their affair to have run its course before their return, by then he was more in love than ever. He asked her to marry him. After studying his face for what seemed an eternity, making him fearful that she would refuse, she said yes. And although they had had their share of problems in the intervening years, for he could not always resist the temptations thrown in his way, nor be certain that she had not, at least once, retaliated for his infidelities, he remained entirely grateful that he had found her, won her. However foolish he sometimes was, however weak, Alice was *his* soul mate, his pal.

They were married in Paris, where they remained to go on with their studies, enrolling in the *Académie Matisse*, which had recently opened. Though Matisse's work had at first rather repelled Teddy, ultimately he came to share Alice's appreciation of it. He began himself to experiment, abandoning his preoccupation with the subject of a painting, with its meaning, to concentrate on its overall design, on the act of painting itself.

Three years later, driven by a need to earn some money, they reluctantly returned to New York. Alice picked up some freelance illustrating work and Teddy began giving lessons. When Lily turned up in one of his classes (alerted to his return by a mutual friend), he realized with a start of surprise that he had forgotten all about her. At the sight of her sitting there before him in her artist's smock, her dark hair lying in a neat braid down her back, he waited for the rush of feeling; but, though she seemed as beautiful to him as ever, his breathing remained steady, his heartbeat regular. With something like relief, he understood that, for the moment at least, the only woman capable of engaging his emotions deeply was his wife.

Which suited Lily very well. Her shyness, her reserve disappeared. She and Teddy, and Alice, too, became friends. And so they had remained.

Fragments of conversation falling about them, the Berlins made their way through the ebb and flow of mourners, along the hall toward the Riverhall dining room. The talk was all of Lily, her mother, the war. Reverend Moreland murmured about "God's will" to the stately Mrs. Jeffers, who seemed disinclined to think He had acted well in this instance; one of Henrietta Canning's friends worried another with her concern that the "dear lady's heart" would never withstand this latest blow; and Winthrop Oates, the newspaper publisher, outraged Andrew Macleod with his tale of the snub Wilson had dealt Teddy Roosevelt, who had called at the White House to offer his support, only to be told that the president was in a cabinet meeting and had no time to see him.

"Don't you think it's odd how everyone keeps asking about Lily's state of mind," said Teddy, in a voice pitched low enough not to be overheard.

"No," said Alice, looking at him in surprise. "It's only natural to want to know every last thing about someone when they're taken away from you so suddenly. Don't you think?"

"Hmm," said Teddy. "I suppose. But are you really so certain she wasn't in touch with Farel?"

"Aren't you?"

"I was, but . . . well, it occurred to me while we were speaking with the doctor that, if Lily had been as over Farel as we thought, she surely would have mentioned him from time to time. If only to heap curses on his head. That is what people tend to do with former lovers, isn't it?"

"Not Lily. She wanted not only to forget, she wanted him never to have been. She wanted him obliterated from her mind.

"You know what happened, don't you?" And when Alice continued looking straight ahead, not acknowledging his question, he repeated, "You know."

She seemed to be waiting to see which way the scales of responsibility would tip, toward the living, or toward the dead. Then, after checking to see that no one was within earshot, she said, "Lily came to the studio one night. You were away, visiting your brother."

"That was in November."

"Yes, about six weeks after she and Farel married. She arrived unexpectedly. When I opened the door . . ." Alice's voice caught in her throat. "She looked pathetic. A bruise on her face, more on her arms. Her wrist was sprained."

"He beat her," said Teddy. He stopped walking and looked at Alice. "Why didn't you tell me?" He was not quite able to keep the note of accusation from his voice.

"She asked me not to. She was so ashamed."

"The bastard!"

"He never did before. Or after," said Alice, a grim note of satisfaction in her voice. "He never got the chance. She left him that night. She stayed with me, until the day before you got home."

"I'd have torn him apart," said Teddy. They started walking again, and, as they entered the dining room, catching sight of Louis Allen and the Roeder boys standing in the far corner, near the window, he added, "Any of us would have."

"She just wanted it over. She told me later that Farel said he wouldn't make any trouble . . ."

"I suppose she meant he'd give her grounds." Adultery was the only cause of action in New York State, and it was a long process, taking years. "I suppose she filed."

"I'm sure she did, though she never said. I didn't like to raise the subject."

"Good evening," said Nuala, going past them, carrying an empty basket. "I'll be coming back with fresh bread in a minute, if you like to wait."

"Poor thing, she looks worn out," said Teddy, watching as the housekeeper scurried out of sight.

"I imagine she's had the running of the place the past few days. More like months, really, when you think about Lily and Mrs. Canning both being ill, on and off."

The table was set with a centerpiece of lilies, lighted candles, and a lace cloth on which lay platters with joints of beef and pork and ham, surrounded by artfully arranged slices of meat. There were bowls of cold salads; there were chafing dishes containing a *poule au pot*, steamed rice, and a variety of cooked vegetables; there were wheels of cheese, baskets of biscuits, assorted condiments — enough to feed a brigade of mourners, though only a very few were making their way around the table, sampling what was on offer.

Having not eaten since breakfast, Teddy was hungry, though guilt made him resist heaping his plate. Surely grief ought to have put him off his food? Alice hardly took anything, he noticed — a few scraps of ham, some salad. "No appetite?" he said.

Alice shrugged. "It feels wrong to eat. Everything, no matter how ordinary, how necessary, feels wrong somehow."

As they walked passed, Louis Allen called out, and they stopped to speak with him. "You remember Marcus and Henry Roeder?" he said, indicating his friends with a bob of his head.

"Indeed we do," replied Alice, offering a smile, extending her hand for Henry to shake.

Marcus, the elder of the two, was taller and broader than his brother, and by far the handsomer, his good looks a reflection of his beautiful mother's, though he had his father's coloring and air of quiet confidence. "We still can't quite believe this," he said.

"No," agreed Alice.

"It takes a while when it's so sudden . . . death, I mean," said Henry.

"Your father said you're planning to enlist?" said Teddy to the brothers. He did not feel up to yet another conversation about Lily.

224

The young men nodded bleakly.

No war fever here, thought Teddy, just a grim sense of duty.

"We all are," said Louis. "As soon as the funeral . . . Monday, I imagine. Listen," he added anxiously, "you won't say anything, will you? I haven't mentioned it to my parents yet. I didn't want to get my mother going while . . . well, she has enough on her mind at the moment."

"You don't think it would be better to wait?" said Alice. "There's talk already of peace, you know. It could all be over soon."

"They need men," said Henry. "A million, according to Senator Williams, as quickly as possible. I don't see how we can *not* go, if we're needed."

"But we both don't have to," said Marcus.

"Fine," said Henry. "Then stay and finish your residency."

"I'm older. If anyone is to go, it should be me."

"You've been saying that to me my whole life, Marcus. Well, it won't do anymore. You don't seem to realize I'm a man now."

Marcus looked at his brother with complete exasperation. "You know doctors are needed more than anyone. It would make far more sense for you to wait. For God's sake, you only have a few more months at Princeton before you graduate."

"I'll finish up when I return," said Henry, sounding as if he had put a great deal of effort into convincing himself and was not about to change his mind.

"You'll have to forgive us," Louis said to the Berlins, his expression rueful. "We've been going on about this since we all got home."

"It's a momentous decision you have to make," said Teddy. "But perhaps the country is full of young men eager to enlist. Why not wait and see? You might not be needed, after all."

"It's a question of honor," said Henry. "Fighting for one's country. Defending its ideals. Proving one is an American, a patriot, through and through."

225

Marcus shook his head in disagreement, but, before he could say anything, Louis picked up Henry's theme. "Yes, honor. And duty. It wouldn't do to be a shirker, to let someone else, someone older, maybe less able, go in my place."

"Some old codger like me?" said Teddy, with a grin.

That got him an embarrassed smile. "The papers say the draft will be for men nineteen to twenty-three," said Louis.

Henry shot a look at his brother and said, "Which means that even Marcus is too old."

Louis shrugged. "Though I imagine they're taking just about anyone now."

"So this is where you've all got to," said Rosaline, joining them. "I should have known I'd find you by the food." Despite her teasing, her eyes remained somber.

"We're not very hungry, actually," said Henry.

Rosaline sighed. "No, no one seems to be." She looked at the table. "When I think of all the work Nuala and the others have put into keeping us fed . . ." She turned her attention back to Alice and Teddy. "They've been carrying on about the war, I expect. There were recruitment parades in Minuit this morning."

Alice nodded sympathetically. "It's been mad in the city all week."

"If only there'd been more brave women in Congress, like Jeanette Rankin, willing to vote against the resolution, no matter what the personal cost!" said Rosaline.

"Brave?" sputtered Henry. "It was the most unpatriotic thing I ever heard of. She and La Follette should be run out of town."

"She was voting as her conscience dictated. She should be admired for that."

"Then why won't you allow my conscience the same admiration," countered Henry, "when it tells me my duty is to enlist? Why do you and Mother and Father insist I don't know what I'm about?"

Rosaline hesitated a moment and then said quietly, "We want to keep you safe, that's all." She looked from one to the other. "We want to keep you all safe. We've lost Lily, so stupidly, and we don't want to lose you, too." Turning, she walked quickly away.

Alice handed Teddy her plate. "I'll be back in a moment," she said, and hurried after Rosaline's retreating figure.

Alice had hardly touched her food, and he seemed to have lost his appetite as well. Teddy put both plates on a nearby sideboard, took his cigarette case from his pocket, and offered it to the others.

"This isn't the time or place for this sort of discussion, I suppose," said Louis, taking a cigarette, as Marcus offered his pocket lighter around. "None of us is thinking too clearly. At least, I know I'm not. The war. Lily. They've both rather knocked me for a loop. Sorry if we've put you off your feed," he added, glancing at Teddy; then, his expression brightened noticeably.

Turning to see what had caught his attention, Teddy came face-to-face with Nuala's sister, Deirdre, who had come to collect the used plates.

She smiled shyly and ducked her head at his greeting. "I've brought fresh bread. Nuala said to tell you it's hot, if you're wanting some, sir."

What a lovely girl, thought Teddy, instantly transposing her perfect features, her blonde hair, her starched cap, the white lace collar hugging her splendid throat, into a painting by Vermeer. Yes, Vermeer, definitely. Deirdre had the same serene, competent quality of the maids who inhabited his paintings, while Nuala, with her red hair, her direct bold gaze and forthright manner, might have sat for Manet. "I'm sure it's delicious, but I'm afraid I'm not very hungry at the moment," he said.

"No one's appetite is up to much, I think," said Deirdre. As she cast a quick glance at Louis, another smile skittered across her face and then vanished. Returning to her chore, she finished piling dirty plates onto a large metal tray decorated with painted peonies and carried it away.

So that's how it is, thought Teddy. She's in love with the fellow. Turning back again, he saw that Marcus, too, had noticed, though not

Henry — or Louis himself, who seemed too preoccupied with other matters to be harboring amorous intentions toward his mother's maid, no matter how beautiful she happened to be.

Or was he? "Quite a remarkable team, those sisters," said Teddy, curious to see how Louis would react. "Any general would be lucky to have them heading his battalions."

"Deirdre and Nuala?" Louis' eyes drifted to the doorway through which Deirdre had just passed. "Yes, you can always count on them to get things done." His tone spoke only of a generalized admiration, nothing more. Which was just as well. It was not pleasant to think of Edith Allen's reaction to her son's tumbling head-over-heels for the hired help.

"Nice girls, both of them," said Marcus. "Are you and Alice staying the night?" he asked, changing the subject.

Teddy confirmed that indeed they were planning to remain for the funeral. Turning to look at the door, he grimaced, and then turned back to the others, saying, "I think I ought to see what's become of my wife."

Henry nodded, "She's probably having a time of it, trying to quiet Rosaline down. My sister's taking all of this pretty hard. I mean, so am I. I was fond of Lily. I still can't believe . . . But Roz . . . I've never seen her like this. I suppose I ought to have kept quiet about my plans until all this was over, but—"

"We both would have been better off following Louis' example," said Marcus.

"I had to tell Andrew," said Louis. "Or Florence would have had my head. But he won't say anything, not till I give him the nod. And at least I got him to agree that it was his duty to stay here to look after the family, and mine to go."

"If you'll excuse me . . ." Teddy put out his cigarette in an ashtray on the sideboard.

"I don't suppose I'll be leaving until the very end," said Louis, remembering his offered ride back to town.

228

"That's fine. That will suit us very well," said Teddy, leaving the three young men, sunk in gloom, to their endless, circular discussions of Lily, the war, the hellishness of what had happened and what was yet to come.

♀

Teddy found the women alone in the small sitting room across from the parlor, huddled together on the sofa nearest the hearth. The walls of this room, too, were covered with Lily's paintings, still lifes most of them: vases of flowers, bowls of fruit, and, above the mantle, a charming pastel of Henrietta Canning at the piano.

"I was telling Rosaline about our dinner with Lily," said Alice when she saw him.

Willing to be spared yet another recounting of the tale, Teddy took a step backward. "I'll leave you then, shall I?"

Rosaline held out her hand to stop him. "No, please, join us, Teddy. I wanted to ask you both about Edmund Farel. Do you know if Lily was in touch with him?"

Teddy glanced at Alice, who shook her head, which he took to mean that Rosaline knew none of the sordid details. "She hadn't mentioned him in months," he said, dropping into an armchair across from them. "And I'm sure she would have, if she'd seen him, or planned to."

"Yes, that's what I think. I feel certain she would have told me. We told each other everything." Rosaline sank back against the sofa's cushions. Her eyes closed. "I was with her when they met, you know. He seemed such a nice fellow." Immediately, her eyes snapped open again. Sitting upright, she looked from Alice to Teddy. "Do you have any idea what the trouble was? Between them, I mean. Lily just said they didn't suit. And that it was better to end everything quickly than to go on with each of them growing more and more miserable. But in what way didn't they suit? You saw them more often than I."

"They weren't together all that long," said Alice.

"No. Six weeks, from start to finish," said Rosaline. "Such a little bit of time, really."

"I think," said Teddy, wishing to put Rosaline's mind at ease, if he could, "that when they got to know each other, it was just as Lily said. They realized they weren't well matched. Farel always had to be out and doing. He was restless, full of grand plans. He wanted excitement. And if Lily liked her fun as much as anyone, still she needed quiet time, and lots of it, to paint."

"But surely Edmund sometimes must have needed quiet to write. In any case, don't all marriages require compromise?" said Rosaline.

"Certainly. And I often think we women are the ones who do the most of it," said Alice, throwing a wry smile in Teddy's direction, before turning back to Rosaline to say, "But there must be at least some basic agreement, don't you think, about goals and ideals, about what constitutes happiness, what a good life is? There must be something vastly worthwhile at stake to make compromise bearable."

"Yes, I suppose," said Rosaline. "She was so good, so lovely. The waste . . ."

"Lily told us she was working on some new paintings," said Teddy. "Do you suppose we might have a look sometime before we leave?"

"Her paintings? Of course. They're upstairs in the studio." With an effort, Rosaline stood. Exhaustion seemed to have completely taken her over. "I don't suppose anyone will notice if we're out of the way for a while." After stopping, as good manners required, to exchange a few words with a group entering the room, she led Alice and Teddy out into the hall and up the stairs. The crowd was growing thinner, he noticed. The long evening was drawing to an end.

Below them, Florence and Andrew came out of the parlor, accompanied by another couple. She stopped in her tracks to watch them, looking as if she would like to demand by what right they felt free to prowl the house.

"Florence seems very agitated," said Teddy, as Andrew took his wife by the arm and ushered her toward the dining room.

"She's worried about Andrew," replied Rosaline. "He was bound and determined to enlist, though I think Louis has convinced him that he ought not to."

"She seems very broken up about Lily as well," said Alice.

Rosaline hesitated a moment and then said only, "Yes."

They followed her along the upstairs hall, past Lily's room, to the tower door. "I came here the other day," said Rosaline as she pulled it open and switched on the light. "I thought it would make me feel closer to Lily," she continued, leading the way up the stairs.

Her presence was everywhere. Her spirit, her aura, something real if indefinable clung to everything in the room, the table littered with sketches, the shelves full of supplies, the scattered furniture, the paintings stacked against the walls. If one listened closely, thought Teddy, one might almost hear her voice.

"So many paintings," said Alice.

"And when you think about the ones she's sold, or given away," said Rosaline.

Teddy went immediately to the easel, removed the cover, and frowned in disappointment at the painting, a simple arrangement of a copper pot, filled with wildflowers, on a polished wood table. "You know," he said, "I think she did this for my class at the League, ages ago. What on earth is it doing on her easel?"

"It's lovely, I think," said Rosaline.

"She had trouble getting the highlights right. You can see where she's reworked the canvas." He pointed to a spot in the paint of the table. "I knew even then she was a remarkable talent."

"I remember her coming home, telling me about you," said Rosaline. "How much she admired you, and how she feared she would never do anything you might like."

Teddy laughed. "I'm sure she was much more in awe of Mr. Chase."

"Oh, indeed. She was quite petrified of him. He was thought to be such a god," said Rosaline, watching as Teddy and Alice began to look through the paintings stacked against the walls. These were haphazardly arranged, a jumble of experiments in style — tonalism, impressionism, social realism — obvious early efforts intermingled with later, more expert paintings.

"Ah, here's that painting she did of Ben Alferson," said Alice.

"Just as I remembered it," said Teddy.

"And the portrait she did of me. We'd gone shopping together, and she sketched me trying on a hat. Of course, I had to pose hours for her later. It's very good, isn't it?"

"A wonderful likeness," said Rosaline.

Studying the painting, Teddy thought of a Degas he had seen in Paris, and wondered if Lily had seen it, in reproduction perhaps. Yes, her painting was good, very good, but derivative. Not that it necessarily mattered. One learned by copying the best. But there came a point . . . He remembered a remark of Sir Joshua Reynolds that he often quoted to his students: "Instead of copying the touches of those great masters, copy only their conceptions . . . Possess yourself with their spirit."

"Do you remember that Degas we saw in Paris?" said Alice, reading his mind as she often did.

"Very well," said Teddy.

"If you'd like to have it," said Rosaline, "I'm sure Aunt Etta would be pleased."

"I would indeed. Very much," said Alice.

As they went through the paintings, a chronicle of the life and people of Minuit, of the changing seasons, of Riverhall and the Hudson, he and Alice were profuse in their praise, tempering what criticisms they had for fear of upsetting Rosaline, certain in any case that they were in complete agreement, both about Lily's talent and their belief that she still had a way to go before living up to it.

"I had thought there might be a portrait of Edmund," said Rosaline.

"I know she did one," said Teddy.

"Perhaps he has it," said Alice.

"I thought if I could see his face again, I might rid myself of this idea I have that he's the devil incarnate."

"It was a very handsome face," said Alice. "With a sort of boyish charm. I don't think he would have come across at all like the devil. Look at this," she said, pulling from one of the stacks a painting of the river, this one by moonlight. She set it on the easel, replacing the still life. "It must be one of the new ones she was doing for the show."

"Now, that's more like it," said Teddy, excitement in his voice and, somewhere in his soul, a touch of envy.

"I thought it seemed different, somehow, from the others, when I saw it the other day," said Rosaline.

"It is," agreed Alice. "One can see hints of a transition taking place in some of her work, but here she seems finally to have found her voice. Direct, powerful . . ." Tears began to trickle down her cheeks. Impatiently, she brushed them away. "So beautiful," she said.

"I found it a little disturbing."

"It is. There's danger in it. But hope, too," said Teddy. "Can't you feel that, as well?"

Rosaline shook her head, but she smiled. "Lily used to say, the moon is God's promise of light in the darkness."

"We must make sure Darius gets this."

"Oh, yes," said Alice.

They were silent a moment, regarding the painting as solemnly as if it were a holy icon. A rush of despair swept through Teddy, a sense of the futility, of the utter wastefulness of life. "She spoke of a self-portrait," he said. "But I don't see one. Is there a storeroom?"

Rosaline thought for a moment. "No," she said, turning away. "There's only what's here." She moved toward the stairs. "I ought to be getting back." At the bottom, she waited for them to cross the threshold,

233

turned off the lights, and followed them out, the door closing behind her with a thud.

Downstairs, the hall was empty except for Nuala and Deirdre and a local girl, taken on temporarily to help, scurrying back and forth from the dining room to the kitchen stairs, carrying huge trays of leftovers. In the parlor, only the immediate family remained, along with William, and the doctor and Mrs. Roeder, all sitting quietly, studying Lily's coffin, lost in thought, or prayer.

"Ah, there you are," said William, unwinding from his chair as Rosaline entered, followed by Teddy and Alice.

"We were in the studio," said Rosaline.

The doctor stood. "I think it's time you got to bed, Etta."

"Yes, it's been a long day, for all of us," she agreed, rising from the sofa.

"And tomorrow will be longer still," said her sister.

"Shall I stay the night?" asked Rosaline.

"No, dear. You run along. Nuala and I will manage perfectly well."

"Oh, we couldn't possibly leave you alone, Aunt Etta," said Florence, a protest repeated by her mother.

Insisting she would hardly be that, Henrietta led the way into the hall, where, as if to prove her point, the ever-prompt Nuala appeared to help Joshua with the hats and coats.

"There's a portrait of herself that Alice would like, if you don't mind, Aunt Etta," said Rosaline.

Henrietta turned toward Alice and said, "Oh, do take it. Lily would want you to have it, I know."

Florence frowned at that, noticed Teddy, though he could not imagine why. The painting could have no possible meaning to her.

"Thank you," said Alice. "I'll treasure it, always."

"And there's a painting that must be sent to the gallery, for the show. I'll see to it, if you like," offered Teddy, "make all the arrangements."

234

Henrietta sighed, and then said, "Yes, I suppose there must be a show. If you'd do that, Teddy, I'd be very grateful."

One by one, they all kissed Henrietta, said their goodnights to the others, and made their way out the door into the chilly night. A thick layer of clouds obscured the sky and a light rain was falling.

"Awful night," murmured Andrew.

"I dread to think of tomorrow," said Edith.

"My car's over here," said Louis, leading the way toward the Cadillac, calling to his parents, "I'm giving Teddy and Alice a ride back to town."

"Drive safely, dear," said his mother, with a wave of her hand.

"As awful as this day has been," said Louis, when the others were settled in the car, Teddy beside him, Alice in the back, "I want it never to end. My mother's right. Tomorrow will be infinitely worse." He turned the car in the gravel drive and set off for town.

"I wonder what became of her self-portrait." Teddy had a great longing to see just where Lily had gone after finishing that wonderful painting of moonlight on the Hudson.

"It will turn up," said Alice.

"Well, perhaps after all it's better if it doesn't," said Teddy, aware suddenly of a great ocean of feeling welling in him. "I think I've had enough of loss for the moment."

"Damn," said Louis, hitting the steering wheel with his hands. "Everything's so fragile. It can all be smashed to bits in a minute."

"Not a bad thing to be made aware of that, I suppose, though I'd rather it was done some other way," said Teddy. He stretched his hand toward the back of the car and felt Alice take hold of it. "We need reminding to cherish whatever good life sees fit to offer." Never before had his wife seemed so precious to him. Never before had he realized how he counted on her, on her being there always, on her loving him. She was the very best life had so far offered him, and he was a fool to risk losing her, as he did so often, and so casually. He must do better. He *would* do better. He would make their little world as safe and secure as he could.

"I loved her, you know," Louis said, as the car hurtled along the causeway into the night.

Teddy clasped Alice's hand more tightly, wanting to convey to her with his touch what he would promise in words as soon as they were alone, that he would, from this day forward, cleave only unto her, until death did them part — a promise that this time he meant to keep.

"Yes," said Alice. "I know."

EDMUND

E dmund Farel was not in Chicago, as Lily's family and friends believed. He was in Washington, D.C., on assignment for the *Chronicle*. At least, that is where he was early Friday afternoon when, scanning back issues of the newspapers to compare coverage of the war news, he came across Lily's obituary in Wednesday's *New York Times*. He must have cried out because, when he looked up, he saw that people at nearby tables were staring at him, some with curiosity or concern, some with disapproval, not liking the peace of their lunch hour disrupted by displays of emotion.

Immediately he paid his bill, left the café where he habitually stopped when in Washington for a glass of wine and a bowl of beef stew, returned to his hotel room to pack his bag, walked the few teeming, bunting-and-flag-draped blocks to Union Station, and from there took a train to New

York. He did all of this without any consideration of the consequences, which was the way Edmund usually did things. It did not, for example, occur to him to wonder what Senator La Follette would make of his skipping their scheduled interview later that day, or what his editor would think of his failure to file a story, or indeed how Lily's family would react to his appearance in Minuit, for that was where he meant to go.

Even during the long train ride, so preoccupied was he with thoughts of Lily, random memories of her colliding haphazardly with one another, sorrow and regret, guilt and self-justification doing battle in his throbbing head, that no other idea had a prayer of intruding. It was only when, having taken the ferry across from the terminal in New Jersey and a taxi to Grand Central, he just missed the last train north that he finally paused to wonder what the hell he was doing. Though not for long. He instantly dismissed all thought of turning back.

Jimmy Brennan, a former colleague at the *Sun*, had an apartment in a bachelor hotel on East Forty-eighth Street, and, after a restorative whiskey in a bar near the station, Edmund walked there to beg a bed. Jimmy, however, was not at home, which was in no way a surprise. Having a good idea of where he might run him to ground, Edmund left his bag with the desk clerk and began scouring the nearby saloons. In the third one he tried, a noisy hole, stinking of stale tobacco and unwashed bodies, he found him. Peering through air thickened with smoke from a long day's run of cigars and cigarettes, Edmund saw his friend sitting at a small table littered with empty glasses — a stocky, ruddy-faced man with thinning brown hair, oblivious to the din inside and the Second Avenue el roaring past outdoors, attempting to drink himself into a stupor, his preferred condition.

Dispossessing a hapless prostitute from a chair, Edmund sat down opposite him and thought, God, he looks ten years older than me, though he knew for a fact that Jimmy was a year younger. The thought caused a prickle of pleasure, replaced almost immediately by a feeling of apprehension. How much longer would it be before his own excesses began to etch themselves on his face? "Hello, Jimmy," he said.

Jimmy blinked once, twice, trying to clear the haze from in front of his eyes. It took a minute, but recognition finally came. "Eddie, you ol' chippy chaser. Good to see you." He waved an arm at a passing waiter. "Bring my friend here a drink," he called. "What you want, Eddie? Whiskey? Bring him a whiskey. Bring two. Damn rotgut!"

When it came, Edmund downed the drink in a gulp and ordered another round. Offering Jimmy a cigarette from his fast-emptying pack of Murads, he explained his plight.

"Stay long as you like," said Jimmy. "Always welcome. Anytime."

"Thanks, pal."

Taking another swallow of his drink, Jimmy waited as a vague green tendril of thought slowly pushed its way up from the murky bottom of his brain and flowered into speech. "Heard you two had called it quits," he said finally. "You and Lily. I'm sure I heard that."

Somehow, he had missed the crux of Edmund's dilemma. "Oh, God, Jimmy, don't you get it? Lily's dead." He could feel the tears pushing at the backs of his eyes. When had he cried last? When was it? He remembered: when Lily left him.

"I never want to see you again," she had said. "Do you understand, Edmund? I don't want you ever to come near me again."

"Dead?" repeated Jimmy. "Not Lily."

"An accident," said Edmund. "A ghastly accident." He could feel the tears making their way down his cheeks, but what did he care? Let Jimmy think him as feckless as a schoolgirl. "Drowned," he said. "The funeral's tomorrow. I have to be there. Oh, Jimmy, isn't it hell?"

His friend agreed that indeed it was. "A lovely girl, Lily," he said. "A real honey."

"The most beautiful girl in the world," said Edmund, as memories rose up and carried him away. "First time I saw her, she just knocked me out. It was on a train. . . ." Jimmy nodded, perhaps to indicate he had heard the story, perhaps as encouragement. "There was a scheduling problem, so I took the ferry across from Albany—I was upstate doing a story—and came down that way from Greenbush. And when I think that I might have taken another route, a different train! Why, I might never have met her." He took another consoling swallow of whiskey and continued, "Or perhaps I would have, on another day, in some other place. Do you believe in fate, Jimmy?"

"Oh, I do. I do."

"I didn't use to. I used to think we made our own. 'Our fate is not in the stars, Horatio, but in ourselves.' That's what I believed. But that train —hell, it's a perfect symbol of what I've come to think life is like. You find yourself on a track headed somewhere, being carried along willy-nilly, not able to get off until some preordained stopping point is reached."

"With death the final terminus," said Jimmy with a solemnity born of booze.

Edmund looked at his friend bleakly, "I thought I'd get her back." Even when Lily would not take his telephone calls, or reply to his letters, he had not given up hope, though he had stopped pressing her. What he had in mind was to let time pass, enough time for him to get his life in order, enough for the good memories to overpower the bad, as they generally do. Then, he would make his move. "I was sure I'd get her back."

"And you would have, Eddie." Jimmy signaled the waiter for another round. "You would have. All that southern charm." He shook his head in wonderment. "Never saw a woman yet didn't give right into it."

"I knew she'd come to forgive me."

Jimmy nodded. "Soft-hearted, women are. Willing to forgive almost anything."

"Almost," repeated Edmund. He sat quietly for a moment, and then added, "You wouldn't have thought, to look at her, that she had so much backbone."

His compulsion to talk was overwhelming. The images of Lily knocking about in his head, desperate for a way out of their confinement, had chosen speech as their means of escape. Whether or not Jimmy was interested, whether or not he cared a toss, indeed whether or not he was sober enough to comprehend anything of what Edmund said, hardly mattered. The need to speak was all. In any case, Jimmy seemed happy enough to sit downing whiskeys, smoking cigarettes, listening to his old drinking buddy recount the story of his grand romance and its tragic end. "I met her when—" he said. "Do you remember? I'd quit the *Sun*—"

"Do I?" interrupted Jimmy, with a laugh. "That was some blowout you had with the boss."

Edmund frowned. A rout was what it had been. If he had not quit, he would have got fired, sure as hell. He had gone to Atlantic City to cover the president's appearance before a group of suffragettes. Fortified by whiskey, he had dutifully taken notes, while Wilson pledged himself to the cause and the four thousand women in attendance cheered. "We have waited long enough to get the vote. We want it now," Dr. Anna Howard Shaw had said, bringing down the house. It was a good story, full of passion and color, with potential for good old-fashioned fun. He had retreated to a bar to write it and somehow managed to miss his deadline. Drunk or sober, Jimmy never missed his.

"I told him where to get off, that's for sure," said Edmund, matching Jimmy's laugh. "A man's got to keep his self-respect, no matter what. Can't let anyone talk down to him, not his editor, not his wife—" He stopped. That was not the tale he wanted to tell. "Anyway, a while after, a month or so before the election, I was working on a piece about Charles Evans Hughes for *McClure's*. He was giving Wilson a hell of a time then, remember? Hughes looked like he was going to grab the presidency, so it was a big story. Tell you the truth, I was shocked myself when he lost. So, there I was, on the train, heading back to New York, reading through my notes, when I heard laughter. It was such a sweet sound. I looked. And there she was, just below my window, on the station platform, about to board the train."

It was Rosaline's laughter that he heard. Lily's, Edmund learned later, was deeper, heartier when it came, which was not often. He hardly noticed Rosaline then, for even got up smartly as she was, she was such a little thing, easily overlooked. But Lily! She was a beauty all right: tall, slender, elegantly dressed in a burgundy-colored wool suit, short enough to reveal slender silk-clad ankles and buttoned shoes. Tendrils of black hair escaped from under a deep-brimmed hat that framed perfect features set in skin as luscious as cream; and her eyes . . . oh, they were magnificent he saw when she glanced toward the train: large, dark, dark as jet, and as brilliant, brimming with intelligence, and with an eagerness as rich as his own (or so it seemed to him) to savor the gifts that Providence tossed one's way. He sat mesmerized, staring out at her, watching as she dealt with a porter and her companion said good-bye to two little girls being left behind in the care of a rather stout nanny. Finally, the two women disappeared out of sight to board the train. Minuit, the station sign read. How often had he gone past and never noticed the place? Even if he had, how could he ever have guessed that it numbered such a glorious creature among its inhabitants?

Settling back in his seat, Edmund waited. Would they come into his compartment, or would he have to go in search of them? But no, there they were. He felt almost weak with delight. Shuffling his papers, he made a great pretense of looking through them, then gazing off into space, as if pondering weighty thoughts, all the time surreptitiously watching the women. His girl was carrying some sort of wooden case with a handle. Burdened only by magazines, her friend kept stooping to look out each window as she passed, her attention riveted to the little girls who stood waving on the station platform.

The seat next to him was empty, as were the two across the aisle. Could it be, he wondered, as the women made their way toward him, could Lady Providence be so wonderfully kind to him? "I started praying," he told Jimmy, begging God to do just this one thing for him, grant

242

him this one favor, deliver this precious gift into his hands, and he would change his life, give up his wild ways, become sober, industrious.

"It's my experience," said Jimmy, "you never get the best of a bargain with God."

"He let me down in the end, that's for sure. But, then, all I knew was I wanted this girl. Crazy when you think of it, isn't it? I had just set eyes on her. Hadn't spoken a word. Had no idea what she was like. I just knew I wanted her to be mine."

"Nice girl, too, I always thought. And not too much a lady to enjoy a little fun."

"They sat down right across the aisle. I couldn't believe my luck."

Edmund offered, in as indifferently polite a manner as he could summon, to put Lily's case up on the baggage rack.

"That's very kind," she replied, in a voice that was not in the least encouraging, though Rosaline bestowed a warm smile of gratitude on him when he completed the task.

"My pleasure," he murmured, retreating to his seat, gathering up his papers, reminding himself from time to time to turn over a page, while he listened to the women's conversation, waiting for another opening, a place where he might interject himself without appearing too forward.

His girl was seated by the window. Her friend was on the aisle, a copy of *McClure's* on her lap, Edmund noticed, certain he would be able to make something of that. Happily for him, both were less concerned with reading than with chatting, about the children left behind, about the day ahead in the city. As he followed the soft flow of their voices, soon he learned not only their names, but their plans: where they intended to go, and when — to the Pelham Hotel so that Lily could drop off her things, to the Ladies' Mile for the shopping spree that had tempted Rosaline to the city, for a bite to eat afterward, before she returned home and Lily went off to an appointment.

He heard Rosaline say, "You know how I'd love to stay on and go to the theater with you, Lily, but I really can't leave William alone with the children overnight."

"Alone? Surely he could manage with Dora and Minnie to help?"

Rosaline responded to the teasing with a laugh, "You know what I mean."

"Perfectly. You can't bear to be away from them for long."

"I can't, it's true. Sometimes I think I make an absolutely hopeless suffragette."

"Well, I don't suppose even Dr. Shaw is advocating that women abandon their husbands and children—"

"Of course she's not!"

"—For I don't think many would consider exchanging their families for the vote."

"But the whole point is, justice demands we have both, just as men do. That we be equal partners, not . . . supplicants begging scraps from the master's bounty."

"As soon I heard Anna Shaw's name, I knew all would be well," Edmund said to Jimmy. "I had only to wait for the right moment."

"You heard her yourself in Atlantic City," Rosaline went on. "Wasn't she thrilling? 'We have waited long enough to get the vote. We want it now.' "

"To think," said Edmund, "I might have met her there, in Atlantic City, months before, if only Providence had willed it!"

"You see," said Lily. "William and the children survived your being gone that night."

"Sometimes I think you don't take this matter seriously enough."

"Oh, but I do, Roz. I assure you. I just somehow haven't the same energy to put into it as you. And how you manage the time to attend meetings, go to rallies, stuff all those envelopes, get out petitions, and who knows what else, with a husband and children and a household to run, I can't imagine. But I admire you for it. You know I do."

244

"You really don't mind my not staying?" said Rosaline, a touch of guilt in her voice. "I must say, I'd have enjoyed it. It's been ages since we've had a night together on the town."

"Now, don't be foolish. You know I'd love it if you felt free to keep me company. But I manage perfectly well on my own. Sometimes I think I prefer it, odd as that may seem to you."

With a wry smile at Jimmy, Edmund said, "But she wasn't going to be on her own if I could help it!"

Gathering his courage, he leaned across the aisle to Rosaline. "Excuse me, ma'am, forgive me for intruding—I couldn't help overhearing—you were in Atlantic City for the suffrage convention? I was there myself, covering it for the *Sun*. I'm a newspaperman, you see." Both women turned to look at him, and if Lily's expression was hardly welcoming, he knew that he had interested her friend. "And now I'm doing a follow-up story. Not for the *Sun*. For *McClure's*," he pressed on, gesturing to the magazine resting in her lap. "I'm going about interviewing women like you, ordinary women, women with husbands, families. . . . You are married, aren't you?" Again, he directed his question to Rosaline.

"Well, yes, I am," she said, "though my friend isn't," which, of course, Edmund already knew. Lily wore no ring.

"Indeed," he said, nodding soberly, "it's to the likes of you I need to talk, not to fire-eaters like Alice Paul, but to sensible family women, feminist to the core. You're the ones who'll make the case for the suffragist cause."

"But surely the case has already been made?" said Rosaline. "By Mrs. Catt and Dr. Shaw and so many others. Over and over."

He knew then he had the friend, Edmund told Jimmy. He had got her to engage in conversation. Soon, the beauty would follow.

"It has," he said. "Most eloquently. And yet many men remain unconvinced."

"And you, sir? Are you convinced?" asked Lily.

He could have crowed with pleasure. "Indeed I am," he said, his voice ringing with conviction. "That's why I'm writing this article, doing my bit to try to convince others. For wouldn't it be splendid if, in the elections next month, in the states where it's on the ballot, woman suffrage were to win?

"Oh, it would," said Rosaline.

"Do you think it likely?" asked Lily.

Edmund considered his options, and decided on the truth, or as near to it as it seemed sensible to go. "Quite honestly, I don't." He could see disappointment in Rosaline's face, and curiosity in Lily's. "But I don't consider that a reason to stop trying, do you? After all, Montana gave women the vote in '14, and now there's Jeanette Rankin running for Congress. Other states will follow. It's inevitable. And each article I write on the subject, I think of as a drop of water wearing away the stone of resistance. And that drop, combining with others, with like-minded pieces from many journalists, with the activities of Mrs. Catt and Dr. Shaw and all the women in their estimable organization, well, it turns into a veritable waterfall, a Niagara Falls, shall we say? Whether or not women are added to the rolls in West Virginia or South Dakota in November, there's no doubt at all in my mind that they'll soon get the vote in all the states. And, when they do, they'll use it wisely."

"You weren't afraid of seeming a wee bit over the top in your enthusiasm?" asked Jimmy.

"I was," replied Edmund, with a laugh, "but once I got going, I couldn't seem to stop." He paused to light another cigarette, and then went on. "It did the trick, you know. I had them both utterly convinced of my sincerity." Weaving another trail of smoke into the saloon's heavy air, he added, "Hell, I was being sincere. I do think women ought to have the vote."

"Even if it means you'd never taste another drop?" asked Jimmy, with a wave of his glass.

"You think they'd bring in prohibition, given the chance?"

"I do. And so does the entire liquor industry, or they'd have the vote already."

"Lily was no teetotaler," said Edmund. "She liked wine all right. She liked champagne. Not whiskey, though. I could never get her to drink it after the first time. It made her sick; it turned me into a lout, she said. Never could get her to see the fun of it."

"Women usually don't. Not Lily's kind, anyway. Now, that kind . . ." Jimmy gestured toward a table where an overweight, untidy woman with a flushed face and a genial air of dissipation sat drinking with an equally disreputable looking man. ". . . is another story. But not one to interest you, I expect."

Edmund glanced at the woman, then quickly away. "Lily was like a dream," he said. "Like a goddess, cool and chaste. Like Artemis. Her look pricked my heart like a silver arrow."

"Love," said Jimmy in a mournful tone. "Never felt it myself. Except once. When I was a boy—"

At another time, Edmund might have listened willingly to his friend's own tale of love and heartbreak, but he had not yet finished his own. "I interviewed them both, all the way to New York, just as if I were truly doing a story on the subject," he said, interrupting. "I kept them talking all the way to the city. Picked up some valuable tidbits, too. Rosaline knows Elizabeth Cady Stanton's daughter . . . what's her name?"

"Blatch?" supplied Jimmy.

"Yes, that's it. Harriet Blatch. And by the time the train pulled into Grand Central, I'd decided—what the devil? I might as well write the damn article. And I did, eventually. Sold it to *McClure's*. They ran it instead of the Charles Evans Hughes piece."

"Read it," said Jimmy. "Not bad. Liked the bit about women not being willing any longer . . . how'd you put it? 'To be crucified on the cross of male egotism.' "

Not willing to be distracted, even by praise of his work, Edmund pulled the narrative back to the main story. "When we got to the city," he

247

said, "I got Lily's case down from the rack, thanked the ladies for supplying me with so many invaluable insights, tipped my hat, and hotfooted away."

"You didn't!" said Jimmy.

"I did. It was my masterstroke. I told them I had an appointment, and off I went."

"You crafty devil. You'd worked out how to find her."

Edmund nodded. "It wasn't hard. I'd heard Lily say she was going to some gallery later that afternoon, the Menlo, and it was my plan to run into her again there, by accident, so it would seem. The next few hours were hell. I was in a fever, I can tell you. Tried to work and failed. I couldn't think about anything but her. I was obsessed with her. I looked up the address of the gallery, and near to the time, I stationed myself where I could see the entrance to the building. To be honest, I feared I'd be disappointed, that she would be less lovely than my memory of her, but if anything, when she arrived, she looked even more beautiful. I had no idea how long she'd be, and it was cold waiting. It was October and there was a bite in the air. But I couldn't leave. I paced up and down, trying to keep warm, cursing myself for being seven kinds of fool, until finally she came out, looking so pleased that I knew the meeting had gone well. I had only to hurry to the corner and cross. 'Miss Canning,' I said. 'Is it really you? Fancy running into you again.' She looked at me in amazement, as if she couldn't quite believe her eyes, but then she smiled. She smiled. And the rest was easy."

꧂

Despite the amount of whiskey he was knocking back, Edmund did not lose sight of his objective. He had a train to catch in a few hours time. Not only that, but it was important to arrive in Minuit looking reasonably presentable, at least no more done in than befitted a grief-stricken widower, which is what he considered himself, whatever the current legal

248

status of his relationship with Lily. When he finished his tale, or as much of it as he could bear to tell, he pushed himself away from the table and got unsteadily to his feet. "I've got to dope off for a while before heading north," he said to Jimmy. "You coming?"

His friend hesitated a moment, waiting for the import of the question to present itself in a coherent form to his befuddled brain. "Might as well," he said finally, staggered up out of his chair, and, cheerily bidding goodnight to the serious drinkers he was leaving behind, followed Edmund to the door.

The trains had long since stopped running and the night was silent. From under the el structure came a lone taxi, turning the corner in tandem with the two friends, its driver slowing for a moment in hope of a fare and then moving on when they took no notice. It was raining, and, in the light of the electric lamps, the streets glistened as if paved with gray marble. Sheltering from the wet, guarded by worn burlap sacks full of his worldly possessions, a hobo lay sleeping in a shop doorway. "There every night," said Jimmy. "A home away from home."

A block farther on, the two men passed a policeman walking his beat. He regarded them with suspicion for a moment, trying to gauge the potential for trouble in their wobbling gait, and then smiled when he recognized Jimmy's round face. "Good evening, Mr. Brennan," he called.

"Good morning, rather, Officer O'Rourke. And how are the wife and kiddies?"

"Never better, sir. Never better."

By the time they reached Jimmy's building, refreshed by the night air and the rain on his face, Edmund felt almost sober.

His friend's place was a sty. There was a typewriter covered in ash on a battered desk, papers and books in piles everywhere, clothes strewn over the backs of ramshackle bentwood chairs, dirty dishes in the sink, remnants of half-eaten meals on the stained cloth covering the table. His housekeeping was not much better, so Edmund paid little attention to the mess. Ignoring the filth of the bathroom, he used the toilet and borrowed

249

Jimmy's Dr. Lyon's powder to brush his teeth, then stripped down to his underwear, wrapped himself in a blanket, and, retiring to the lumpy sofa, prayed — as Homer had put it — for the gift of sleep.

It came quickly enough, though it was followed immediately by disturbing dreams in which Edmund searched through mysterious houses, unfamiliar train stations, desolate streets for something, someone, never quite certain who or what, never quite able to give up the hunt, no matter how exhausted he felt, how near to collapsing, however convinced that his efforts were futile. After only a few hours, he awoke, the dreams slipping away like figures in a fog. Only the feeling of frustration, of failure, remained. Luckily, he looked a lot better than he felt, he discovered, surveying his face in the bathroom mirror. A bath and a shave improved matters further, as did a glass of Jimmy's whiskey, just enough to get him going. He refilled his flask from the bottle, knotted his black tie expertly, slicked back his dark hair, put on his topcoat and hat, stuck his head into the bedroom to call a completely unnecessary good-bye to his oblivious friend, and, leaving his bag behind, left to catch the train to Minuit.

Though the morning remained overcast, the rain had stopped, and he walked quickly through streets where every building (or so it seemed) sported a billowing flag and every lamppost a recruitment poster. Outside Grand Central Station, paperboys stood calling the news in their piping, street-tough voices: Spies arrested, German ships seized, William Jennings Bryan (patriotism trumping pacifism) volunteering to enlist as a private. Edmund bought copies of the morning editions to read on the train.

It was a Saturday and, absent the bustle of daily commuters, the vast vaulted hall of the station seemed quiet as a church. Having bought his ticket the day before, he made his way directly to the platform, chose a compartment, and settled in. The train was one of the new steel models. Electric lamps ran the length of the ceiling, and the seats, covered in a patterned mohair fabric, had cast-iron supports. It was plain, with few decorative details, but comfortable enough — and far safer than the old wooden passenger car it was gradually replacing, far less likely to burn at any rate. Within minutes the motor started, and the train jerked to life, beginning its journey through the dark tunnels beneath the city streets. Looking around, he surveyed his few traveling companions: a young man in naval uniform; an elderly woman with a child, a boy of seven or eight; two girls, dressed plainly, servants perhaps, having a day off in the country. The journey was going to be hell, he thought, closing his eyes. If only he could sleep.

But he could not. Memories chased each other through his head, as if in a game of hide-and-seek, vanishing and reappearing, calling out, teasing him.

To Edmund, the compelling part of the story was always his meeting with Lily and the subsequent heady days of his courtship, culminating in their wedding two weeks later. Those fourteen days, far and away, were to him the happiest of his life. Not even seeing his first story in print, an irrefutable sign that he was on his way to making a name for himself, had caused him such a rush of giddy pleasure as watching Lily fall in love with him. She had seemed, this heavenly girl, both a blessing and a reward, both an undeserved gift from God and a prize for an accomplishment he had yet to achieve. She had seemed to him everything that he had ever desired in a woman and had despaired of finding in one creature. Intelligent as well as beautiful, she was sweet natured, but with courage and character to spare, eager if inexperienced, passionate but very much a lady. He could hardly believe the luck that had got him to the right train that fateful day. He had longed to please her, to make her proud of him, and, for a brief while, he had succeeded. For a brief while, love for him had flowed from her like honey, and he had felt as if he might drown in the heavy sweetness of it.

"Marry me," he begged after knowing her just three days.

It was a mad thing he was doing, he realized, even as he spoke the words, but he wanted her so desperately and he knew there was no other way to have her. Of course, she refused. She needed to accustom herself to the idea, to accustom herself to him.

Day after day, she put off her return to Minuit. She had shopping to do, friends to see, museums and plays to go to, meetings at the Menlo Gallery about the exhibition that she was to have there in the spring: her first *solo* exhibition, she told him, to explain its importance to her. But whatever she said, whatever excuse she made, to Edmund it was clear that it was he who held her in the city.

Ruthlessly suppressing the tiresome voice of conscience, ignoring the many reasons he ought to leave her alone, Edmund spent as much time with Lily as she allowed. He escorted her to galleries to look at paintings, and pleased her with his reactions to what he saw, though in truth he picked up his cues from her. He took her to The Brown Betty for southern waffles, to Mouquin's to dine, to the Café Boulevard to hear the Gypsy band, to Roseland to dance, and each night, as their kisses in the taxi on the way back to her hotel grew increasingly more eager, he repeated the request. On the tenth night, after a dinner of oysters and venison and Baked Alaska at Murray's Roman Gardens, after innumerable glasses of champagne, as they sat beneath the twinkling electric stars, he said to her again, "Marry me, darling, please," and to his amazement, she said yes.

Her face was flushed; her dark eyes glowed; she seemed to radiate light. "I must be crazy," she said. There was a note in her voice that he recognized. It was the same tone he used to urge himself on when he was contemplating something foolhardy, but irresistible.

"You won't regret it," he promised. "I swear I'll make you happy. I love you with all my heart."

Four days later, in Haines Falls, New York, they were married by a justice of the peace. The beginning of the end—

But, no, he did not want to think about that.

Opening the *Times*, Edmund began to read, noting with increasing irritation as he did so the lack of outrage, in the coverage and in the public, to the widespread assault on civil liberties. The navy was planning a takeover of radio stations, and no one so far was complaining. Senators who had voted against the war were being asked to resign from committees they chaired. By order of the attorney general, without reference to the courts, men of German birth, some even citizens, were being arrested as spies, sixty in New York alone. At Rectors the night before, a crowd had attacked a lawyer and his dinner companions, two suffragettes, for refusing to stand for the national anthem.

What would he have done, had he been there? he wondered. Would he have gone to the women's aid, or stood on the sidelines and watched, taking notes for a story? It was hard to be sure, though he liked to think he would have gone to their rescue, for he could not, after all, help imagining the suffragettes to be Rosaline and Lily. How terrified they would have been in the face of such unreasonable hostility, how brave in (this case) sitting for their beliefs.

It occurred to Edmund that all it ever took to push a group of sensible people over the edge was a bully with a gift of gab. Crowds were always mobs-in-waiting. Perhaps, next, meetings would be banned as threats to public order. Where would it all end? In martial law? In a police state? Surely it was possible to be patriotic without losing all objectivity, all sense of fair play, all common decency?

A sense of unease gripped him, a feeling of embarrassment. Who was he to sit in judgment on the shortcomings of others? A glass too far and did he not lose all sense, all decency, turn into a tyrant, a bully? Was he not himself contemptible?

He let the paper drop and looked out the grimy window. The train had emerged from the tunnels and was now running north along the east side of the Hudson. The day was overcast, the sky a relentless gray, the water a sheet of lead, the railroad terminals, the warehouses, the industrial works at the foot of the Palisades on the opposite bank no more than shadows in the heavy mist. How different everything looked from the way it had on that brilliant October day when he had ridden the train down to New York in the company of Lily and her friend. Then, the sun had blazed in a cerulean sky, sails white as angel wings had scudded across the choppy blue water, the rock face of the Palisades had sparked light, and the trees had flamed heavenward in bursts of orange and yellow and red. Was it only six months ago? How hopeful he had felt that day. No, more than hopeful—confident.

All his life, Edmund had not had much luck. Things had a way of not turning out for him. He would set his heart on having something, only to find it, at the last minute, snatched away: the eighth grade English prize that ought to have been his, for example, given to Johnnie Barker instead, not because Edmund had failed to study sufficiently hard for the exam, as his father insisted, but because Mr. Armitage, the teacher, was sweet on Johnnie's widowed mother. Jobs Edmund wanted often went to others less qualified but better connected. Those he got usually turned bad, sooner or later, as witness the debacle at the *Sun*. Business schemes he became involved in, real estate deals, mining shares, railroad options, no matter how promising, inevitably turned out to be some sort of flimflam. As for girls, well, Edmund had a handsome face and a winning manner: girls liked him; they liked him a lot. Their parents, their fathers especially, were another matter. Good looks and a keen mind never weighed as much with them as money, or at least the prospect of getting some, and if a strong-willed girl might hold out for a while against her father's wishes, in the end she always gave in.

But that October, after a long bad patch, things had seemed finally to be turning around for him. From a friend moving on to a job at the *Examiner* in San Francisco, Edmund took over a room in a boarding house near Madison Square. It had no view, but what was that compared to a private bath and a cost of only six dollars weekly, a considerable savings from the fifty a month he had been paying for his apartment. Then, there was *McClure's*. Thanks to a relationship with one of its editors (with whom he had enjoyed many a jolly night exploring the city's seamier dives), he got an assignment to write up Charles Evans Hughes, the former governor of New York, who was challenging Woodrow Wilson for the presidency. Finally, there was Lily herself, the chief prize of that benevolent

254

Providence who had deigned at last to smile upon him, putting in his way a woman of incomparable merit, whose father happened to be fortuitously deceased.

Not that Edmund allowed his good luck to go to his head. However certain that, if otherwise unopposed, he would manage to win over her mother, he was still not inclined to take any unnecessary chances. Though not an adage he had previously taken to heart, discretion did indeed suddenly seem the better part of valor, and he determined, if at all possible, to put off meeting the lady until matters between him and Lily were settled. And that did not prove difficult. For one thing, their relationship moved along at a pretty smart pace. For another, Lily herself seemed to be in no hurry to carry him home to Minuit and introduce him into her circle there — there or anywhere. He did not meet even her cousin Louis, or Teddy and Alice Berlin, until after the wedding. While Edmund might, in other circumstances, have been affronted by Lily's willingness to keep what was happening between them secret, as it suited his purposes, he chose instead to view it in the best possible light. She was caught up in the romance of the situation, that was all. She wanted this wonderful, joyful time to be solely theirs; she wanted to be spared the need to consider anyone's pleasure but her own — and his, of course. It never took more than a few careful words from Edmund to divert her whenever a guilty conscience seemed to be prompting her to confess.

The closest call came on the train to the Catskills on the way to their wedding. Edmund watched as, mile after mile, the radiance drained from Lily's face to be replaced by a dismal, anxious look. He knew very well what she was thinking and considered broaching the subject himself, but dismissed the idea as soon as he recalled that "discretion" was his new watchword. Trying to appear absorbed in the book he was reading (not an easy task, given that it was George Gissing's *New Grub Street*, picked up secondhand in the Boni brothers bookstore, and a particularly depressing choice in the circumstances) he silently offered up a prayer to Providence that Lily would refrain from speaking her mind until it was too late.

But it was still far from that when she said, "I'm feeling awful about my mother."

Closing his book, he summoned a concerned look. "You don't think she'll just be happy for you? Once the shock is passed, I mean?"

"Oh, yes. But she'll be terribly hurt at first."

"Darling, look, if you really wish it, all we have to do is get off the train at the next stop and go back. There's no great harm done, is there, if we have to wait a little longer to get married?"

"No . . ." she said, though Edmund could see that she did not like the idea of delay any better than he. "You really wouldn't mind?"

"Well, obviously I want to marry you at once, as quickly as can be. I love you — too much to go through with it now, though, if it's going to make you unhappy. If you like, we'll get off the train in Newburgh. And you'll take me home to meet your mother. I'll make certain to charm her. And we'll let her plan the sort of wedding every mother dreams of for her daughter."

Leaning back against the seat, Lily closed her eyes and rubbed a hand across her forehead.

"Are you getting one of your headaches?"

"No." She opened her eyes and smiled. "Well, maybe just a little one."

Reaching out, he removed her chic new hat. "Come here," he said, pulling her toward him. She closed her eyes and rested her head against his shoulder. "All I want is for you to be happy."

"I am happy," she replied.

The train pulled into the station and shuddered to a stop. Should he say anything? Yes, he decided. Why not? Luck was definitely on his side. "It's Newburgh," he said softly.

Again, her eyes opened. Tilting her head up, she looked at him and said, "Let's go on. I don't want to wait. I'm tired of waiting for life to begin. I want to marry you now."

256

His heart soared in his chest. Never had he felt so wonderfully happy. Oh, yes, Lady Providence was definitely smiling on him. "If that's what you want," he said, kissing the top of her dark head.

$$\mathcal{L}$$

At Minuit, three other passengers left the train with Edmund. He recognized none of them, which was just as well since it put off the moment when someone might ask him what the devil he thought he was doing there. Retreating into the station's waiting room, he went into the public lavatory where, after making himself comfortable and neatening up his appearance, he unstopped his flask and took a long swallow. The chill seemed to have settled in his bones.

Coming out again into the thick gray light, he encountered the ancient stationmaster whose lined face creased further in puzzlement at the sight of Edmund, who hurried on before he could be recognized. Why had he bothered to come, he wondered, if he was going to allow every nonentity to make him feel like an intruder?

"To hell with that!" he muttered as he reached the cobbled street beyond the station gate. He had every right to be here. Love had given it to him, for certainly no one loved Lily as he did. He adored her. Still. She was the wife of his heart.

To its citizens, Minuit might be the center of the universe, but to Edmund it was no more than a whistle-stop town with a geography similar to all such places; and though he had visited with Lily only twice, he had no difficulty making his way from the station to Center Street, which — like the main street of every village and town and city in the nation, he imagined — was a picture in red, white and blue, hung with bunting, decked out in flags, and papered with posters urging eligible young men to enlist.

The street was busy, with conveyances of one sort or another clogging the road, children playing on the wooden sidewalk outside of Crawford's Confectionery, women with shopping baskets over their arms hurrying past, a cluster of potential recruits in serious discussion in front of the Town Hall. Occasionally, someone would turn to look curiously at Edmund as he passed. The church was farther on, beyond the town's commercial center, and he quickened his pace, not as much in a hurry to reach his destination as anxious to avoid any pretext for conversation with those inquisitive passers-by. Burdett's Emporium was open, but the gun shop was not, he noticed. Neither was the newspaper office, nor George Allen's insurance agency. Each had a sign in the window announcing that it was closed for a funeral, and the lawyers' office as well, which was hardly surprising. "Vanklieft, Canning and Macleod, Attorneys at-Law" read the stenciled shingle above the door. The practice had belonged to Lily's father, and grandfather, Edmund remembered. Had he been a lawyer, it might have come to him, he supposed. But Providence had not led him in that direction (which seemed yet another opportunity he had somehow been cheated of) and so the firm had passed to the husband of Lily's cousin. What was his name? Andrew. That was it. No doubt it was to him that Lily had gone running for legal advice.

Edmund had met them all, family and friends, at the reception Henrietta Canning had held for him and Lily at Riverhall to celebrate their marriage. And what a happy day that had been! Whatever her initial reservations, Henrietta had put them aside and allowed herself to be charmed. She had introduced Edmund to everyone as warmly as if she had chosen him herself for her daughter. The women had all followed her lead, appearing quite taken with him. Rosaline had hung on his every word. And Lily, having forgiven him his bender of two nights before, had been absolutely radiant with love and excitement and happiness, while he felt as if he might well burst with pride.

Only the men had looked at him with something like suspicion, and he could hardly blame them for that. In their places, he would have been just as wary.

His breathing was becoming labored, Edmund noticed as he reached the end of Minuit's business district. To be done in by such a comparatively short walk, what a comedown for LaGrange High's football star, for Louisiana State's varsity champion, which he had been before dropping out. Why, there had been a time when he could run for miles with no more effort than it took most people to stroll through the park on a Sunday afternoon. Too many late nights, too much alcohol, too many cigarettes, he thought as he stopped to light another, too little exercise, that was the problem. He rarely even ate well these days, grabbing food, when he remembered, mainly at lunch counters and in hash houses. It was time to repent his misdeeds, he told himself; time to turn over a new leaf. True, he had tried before and failed, but if he just put his mind to it . . . That's what his father had always said, before he had given up in disgust. "Just put your mind to it, Eddie. You're a bright boy. There's nothing you can't do, if you just put your mind to it."

Ahead of him, Edmund could see St. Mark's, an impressive (for Minuit, at any rate) stone church set in a large expanse of lawn, with a pointed steeple and an east window of Tiffany stained-glass portraying the Risen Christ. He had gone there for services with Lily once, and had been disturbed by a certain dissonance, a sense of both strangeness and familiarity. It had less gilt and fewer statues, perhaps, but the high altar, the carved pulpit, the soaring arches, the flickering candles, were much the same as in the Catholic churches he had attended as a child. Yet, he could not escape the feeling that it was wrong of him to be there, that it was a sin for him to be kneeling among heretics, though he had to smile at the idea when he considered the general blackness of his soul. But then, could one ever be sure of the weight of one's sins on God's scale? Perhaps intemperance and fornication were not, after all, so terrible as blasphemy.

Turning his eyes from St. Mark's, Edmund looked around and, seeing the street empty, ground his cigarette under his heel, reached into his pocket, and removed the flask. Whatever his good intentions, today was not a day he could reasonably expect to see them through, not when he needed all the courage he could get, and whiskey its most reliable source. He took a long swallow, screwed on the silver top, flipped the lid shut, returned the flask to his pocket, and, feeling ten times better, resumed his walk.

As he drew nearer the church, he could see a horse-drawn funeral coach waiting in the drive, along with several parked automobiles. Edmund's pace slowed. Suddenly, his thoughtless dash from Washington to Minuit seemed mad to him. What had he hoped to gain by coming? Lily was gone, and with her his chance to mend his ways, prove his love, win her back. Her family and friends, gathered to mourn her, would certainly not receive him kindly. However few reasons Lily might have given them for leaving him (and he knew her well enough to be certain that she would have said as little as possible), no one would ever have believed her to be the least at fault. He had seen it happen time and again. A woman could be a veritable she-devil and never get blamed for the failure of her marriage, while a man, as guiltless as Joseph with Potiphar's wife, would be held solely responsible.

In all the world, thought Edmund, perhaps only his mother had mustered the faith to believe him the injured party. Not that he was, of course. Except . . . well, his mother did have a point. Lily was spoiled, though he could not blame her (at least, not very much) for that. From the day she was born, she had been looked after and fussed over. Never had she wanted for a thing. Her parents had served life up to her neatly packaged and tied with bows. All their energies had gone into making her happy. Was it any wonder that she had never learned to return the favor? Indeed not. Still, to live with someone so dismissive of your needs, so completely unable to cope when things did not go her way, so little inclined to be patient or forgiving — it had been punishing. At times, it had been infuriating. Lily might have been beautiful and intelligent and many, many other wonderful things, but it would have taken a saint to put up with her moods, her headaches, her nightmares, her intolerance. And she had been sadly lacking in the common virtues of any ordinary housewife. Why, she could not even cook a decent meal.

Slowly, Edmund made his way along the gravel drive toward the two broad steps leading to the church door. "You for the funeral?" he heard a voice call. Turning, he saw the coachman on his high seat, holding the reins slackly while his horse stomped and snorted and tossed his black plumes to protest the wait. When Edmund said he was, the coachman added helpfully, "They've gone 'round to the churchyard."

Edmund thanked him and headed in the direction of the pointing finger, but, when he reached the wrought iron gate, he hesitated. Half-concealed by the forsythia flowering beside it, he could see them all, a short distance away, black-clad figures, shadows against the gray light, standing amid a field of weathered gravestones, under the hovering branches of a budding chestnut tree. The minister, in his black chasuble, stood at the foot of the open grave, into which Lily's coffin had no doubt recently descended. On the far side, Henrietta Canning was weeping inconsolably, the weight of her grief-stricken body supported by Dr. Roeder and her nephew, Louis.

As he looked from one pale, doleful face to the next, Edmund was surprised at how many of them he recognized, though he had met them only briefly all those months ago. These were Lily's family and friends; and, no, there was not one among them who would welcome him should he open the gate and pass through to join them. He would be asked to leave, perhaps *made* to leave. Louis and the Roeder brothers, who had been jealous of him from the start, would see to that. No doubt Teddy Berlin would be glad to lend a hand; and that Andrew Macleod, though years older than the rest, he was by far in the best shape. Edmund knew it was unlikely he could stand against one of them, let alone all.

But it might not come to that. None of them would wish to mark Lily's burial with a brawl. There was a chance, thought Edmund, that cooler heads would prevail, that propriety would win out, that they would suffer his presence among them in silence. They might feel inclined to show respect for his grief and allow him to say good-bye to his wife, as was his right, his duty.

As he stood there, hand on the gate, riven by grief and remorse, frozen with indecision, warily watching the mourners, one of them, standing at the rear of the group, turned and looked directly at him. It was Nuala, the Cannings' housekeeper: there was no mistaking that red hair, peeping out from under the worn black hat. Surprise registered on her face. She must have sensed his presence, though she had not really expected to see anyone when she turned, he supposed, or certainly not him. Recognition followed quickly; and then, immediately, a look of such intense hatred that Edmund's hand dropped to his side and he took a step backward. Dear God, if Nuala felt that way, what must the others . . . ?

When he gathered his courage to look again, he saw that she had turned her attention back to the service. The blonde woman standing next to her whispered something, but Nuala shushed her; and then the minister began the Lord's Prayer, and the voices of the mourners rose and mingled with the breath of the wind and the sad calls of the birds nesting in the churchyard's trees.

Edmund had more than once put his life at risk covering a story; he had never yet walked away from a barroom fight; and, if the whiskey he had downed had sufficiently fired his blood, he might have found the courage to brave Nuala's hatred, to face the withering contempt of one and all. He might have managed to walk through the gate. At that moment, however, he could not do it. His sense of shame was, after all, too great, as was his fear of embarrassment. Turning away, he retraced his steps, and, seeing the coachman's look of surprise, called up to him, "It was a mistake. A mistake . . ."

As he crossed the road and headed back toward the train station, he seemed incapable of a complete thought. Coherent sentences eluded him. I shouldn't . . . perhaps if . . . not my fault . . . if only she . . . All at once, he became aware of a pain so searing that everything else he had felt since learning of Lily's death dwindled to insignificance, a cigarette ash fallen on

262

his hand, not this red-hot poker through his chest. "Oh Lily," he murmured. "Oh, dear God."

There was a saloon across the street from the train station, and Edmund stopped in to brace himself for the return journey to New York. It was empty except for the burly bartender and a reed-thin man in shabby clothes and a battered cap seated at a table in the corner. A brightly lit, cheerful place, it was one that even the more respectable citizens of Minuit might not hesitate to enter, though probably not so early in the day. The oak paneling gleamed, the brass fittings shone, the chandeliers' green glass sparkled, the sawdust on the floor had been laid down fresh that morning. Despite its being technically spring, a fire burned in the grate. Above the mantle hung an oil portrait of a jolly pink-cheeked man with a fringe of white hair, his round stomach stretching the fabric of a shiny black suit.

The barman saw the look Edmund cast its way and said, "The owner," as he poured the requested whiskey.

"Put on a bit of weight since then," called the man in the cap, his voice slurred. The town drunk, Edmund surmised, for did not every town have at least one?

"Nice painting," said Edmund.

The barman shrugged his narrow shoulders. "He likes it. That's what counts, I guess."

Edmund beat back the temptation to ask who the artist was. He knew the answer, and really what was the point in provoking the conversation that would inevitably follow his question? What was the point in endlessly prodding the same open wound? Instead, he lit a cigarette, ordered another drink, and, after inquiring about the departure time of the next train to the city, asked the bartender to refill his flask, then settled himself at a table to wait. Half an hour later, he paid his shot, hurried across to the station, bought a pack of Murads and a copy of the *Hudson Tribune* at the newsstand, and got to the platform just as the train roared in and shuddered to a halt.

"Your ticket, sir?" asked the stationmaster.

Startled, Edmund stopped. He patted his coat. It was there, somewhere. "Yes, yes, I have it," he said. He pulled it from his pocket. "Here, it is."

The stationmaster took the ticket, looked at it, then at Edmund. The frown that flittered across his face was followed immediately by a look of triumph. He's recognized me, thought Edmund. "Short visit, sir," the stationmaster said.

"Yes." Edmund held out his hand, wanting the ticket, impatient to get away.

As if considering whether or not to say something more, to mention the funeral perhaps, the stationmaster hesitated a moment. Discretion won. "Have a good journey," he said, handing back the ticket.

Small chance of that, thought Edmund as he boarded the train. He found his place, removed his coat and hat, put them on the luggage rack, and sat down, dropping the newspaper onto the seat beside him, where it would remain, forgotten.

Casting a quick glance around, he noted that the car was almost full. By the look of them (and the number of bags in the racks), his travel companions were on their way into the city for an evening at the theater, the opera, perhaps a variety show, he imagined, followed by supper at Sherry's or Delmonico's, a night at the Belmont, or some other grand hotel. With all his heart, he wished that he had the prospect of such innocent pleasures before him, rather than what would surely be his own itinerary, a series of dives in the company of Jimmy and a cohort of newspaper hacks. How had he come so close — not just to happiness, but to respectability, and let them slip away? Why had Providence, after offering him such hope, after dangling such riches before him, turned her back on him again?

Edmund heard a whistle. The train jolted forward and slid out of the station. He had again sat on the river-side of the car and, looking out, saw a sloop heading north to Albany, a barge going south loaded with timber, a yacht under sail, charcoal smudges he took to be fishermen in rowboats working nets in the choppy gray waters, and, in the distance, the Highlands looming out of the fog. It all looked familiar to him, eerily so, and not from his previous trips along this stretch of track, but from Lily's paintings, so many paintings, of the river.

He thought of the portrait over the mantle in the saloon, the luster of the hair, the glint in the eye, the sheen of fabric over the paunch. There was such vitality in the painting. It was trite to say it, perhaps, but one really would not have been surprised to hear its subject speak, to invite one to have a drink, say, or a meal.

If he had taken Lily's work more seriously, he wondered, would things have turned out differently? Would he then have been more inclined to forgive her for what he considered her obsession with it? More importantly, if instead of thinking of her as an amateur, a dabbler (which he did, whatever Darius Menlo and Teddy Berlin had to say to the contrary), he had seen her as an artist, would she have been more inclined to forgive him? But then, how could he have been expected to know? He could see she had talent: any fool could see that. But talent is a flexible concept; and if Edmund was familiar with Mary Cassatt, the much-admired Impressionist painter, and Cecelia Beaux, and a handful of others like them, Lily seemed to him to be of a different order entirely. In his mind, such women ranked with the Carrie Chapman Catts and Anna Howard Shaws of the world, with muckraking journalists like Ida Tarbel, if not quite on a par with mythic Amazons and Valkyries, women at least far out of the mainstream, devoted (some fanatically) to a calling, a "cause." He could not imagine them to be anything like his beautiful Lily.

So, despite her obvious abilities, Edmund had found her dedication to painting to be exasperating rather than admirable, and could not help but feel offended when she seemed to put it before all things, including

265

him. Even in the first, heady days of their courtship, only once had he coaxed her into leaving her paints and brushes when she meant to work, and he doubted she would have done it then had he not wrangled them an invitation to see the Henshaw collection. Lottie Henshaw and he had briefly been lovers. Kindred spirits, understanding of each other's ambitions, financial and otherwise, they had parted the best of friends when she married Nelson Henshaw, the financier, and she was always happy to help Edmund, even to further a new romance, if an invitation to tea could do it.

Watching as Lily moved slowly from painting to painting, saying almost nothing, Edmund knew that he had pulled off a coup. He saw tears in her eyes. There was one painting that seemed especially to move her, though he saw no particular merit in it. By someone he had never heard of, an Alfred Sisley, it was of a snow-covered village street in France. There was hardly a trace of color in it, only duns and whites and a stroke here and there of black, but Lily seemed to find it beautiful. "Nelson bought it in Paris, ages and ages ago, before I was even born," Lottie said. "The painter was a particular friend of Monet's, though nowhere near as successful."

"If you ever think to part with it," Lily replied, "I'd be grateful if you'd let me know. I'd pay almost anything to have it."

Encouraged by his success, Edmund had tried tempting Lily with other treats, but she never again succumbed. Until she finished her day's work, she would not meet him, no matter how he coaxed. She was feeling overwhelmed, she told him. She had paintings to complete, new ones to begin, if she hoped to be ready in time for her show. When he himself was having so much trouble concentrating on the story for *McClure's*, when he seemed totally incapable of writing it, so infatuated was he with Lily, so unable to think for long of anything but her, he could not help but resent her ability to forget him for hours on end, and for what seemed to him no more than a pastime, for she was not the one who had to eke out a living by spilling her guts onto a piece of paper. She did not have to worry about paying the rent. Why, she even took a suite (a suite!) at a hotel to have an extra room in which to paint, when he so often had nothing but a table in a saloon to serve as a desk. She had money to spare, lavishly supplied by a doting mother. If Lily had only known what it cost him to write!

If, in the weeks before they were married, Edmund managed to accept Lily's refusals to accompany him on outings with a good-natured bow to her wishes, during the few days of their honeymoon, he foolishly became convinced that all would be well in the future, for they seemed to reach a kind of balance. He would sit happily enough reading, or just watching her, as she sketched the view from wherever they found themselves after a breath-taking hike; and she would willingly put aside her sketchpad to accompany him wherever he wished, which was — more often than not — to bed in their room at the Catskill Mountain House. However, once back at the Pelham (where they had decided to stay until they could find an apartment that suited both their needs and their pocketbooks), Lily returned immediately to her routine, insisting on painting for endless hours each day, no matter what else Edmund might want to do. She refused even to go with him to LaGrange to meet his parents (not until after her exhibition in the spring, she insisted), forcing him — so eager was he to show off his prize — to invite them to New York, where, he had to admit, Lily was perfectly delightful during their brief visit, captivating his father entirely, though perhaps not totally winning over his mother. "This is not a holiday, now, this is life," Lily would say, as he dangled one enticement or another in front of her. "And for life to be good, it's essential to work." He would plead, he would argue, he would tell her that a husband had a right to expect his wife to put him first, and sometimes, to keep the peace, Lily would give in, going along and giving every appearance of enjoying herself. But inevitably she would get one of her headaches; and though she protested that she was prone to them, Edmund could never help feeling that somehow he was to blame, that it was he who had caused the pinched, pale look of her face, the pain in her eyes. He would promise himself never to bedevil her again, but the next day would come, and having her with him just then would seem far more important than the possibility of a headache later, and he would badger her until either she said yes, or he sulked off in a temper.

When he looked back and considered the evidence, he could not help thinking (while in no way trying to escape his share of the blame) that many of the problems in their marriage could have been avoided if only Lily had been a bit more malleable. His benders, for example — three absolute beauts in six weeks — if only she had kept him company, he would never have got so completely soused. And though, to be fair, she might have relented if he had given her the reasons for his feeling so low and needing to get out, he could not really reproach himself for not wanting to confess his fears and his failures, for not wanting to tell her, for example, just how intimidated he was by the prospect of going to Minuit to meet her family and friends (which prompted that first binge); or about *McClure's* not running his piece on Charles Evans Hughes (which brought on the second).

He had missed his deadline, a catastrophe as it turned out, since by the time the following issue of the magazine was ready to go to press, Wilson had won, and no one cared at all about his former rival for the presidency. Edmund's pal, the editor, had been most decent about it, understanding about Lily, about the wedding, but "Yesterday's story isn't worth the stock it's printed on," he had said. "Sorry, bud."

It was a blow. Edmund was counting on the money, not only to keep him from sinking further into debt, but to retrieve his grandfather's pocket watch, pawned to buy Lily a wedding band. He had to find work, but where? The sad truth was, he had acquired a reputation in the newspaper world for being difficult. With an article in *McClure's* to his credit, assignments from other magazines would have been easier to get, but he doubted that his friend, for all his understanding, would offer another anytime soon. How was he going to get his hands on the money he needed to live until he managed to earn some? That was the question worrying Edmund. No, panicking him. How was he to get some money? He had not yet repaid Jimmy and his other pals for what he had borrowed in the aftermath of losing his job at the *Sun*, and the loans from his parents that he had always relied on to tide him over in dry spells could not possibly stretch to support a wife. His father earned a decent amount managing a hardware store, but there was not a lot of cash to spare. In any case, of the four children, Edmund was far from the favorite. A man of limited aspiration, his father neither understood his son's ambitions, nor approved of them, and took each of Edmund's failures as further proof that he was right to be skeptical. A cautious, steady man, a man of narrow vision, he could not see that failure was the necessary short-term price the talented, the courageous, had to pay for future success. He would think that his son, having taken a wife, ought to be able to keep her himself.

There seemed to be nowhere Edmund could turn, but to Lily; and while certainly she had enough income to do for them both, he could not see how, after all his bragging to her about his prospects, he could admit that they had all come (even if temporarily) to nothing.

With desperation nipping at his heels, he could not, just then, do what Lily suggested and stay at home. "Alice and Teddy work together all the time. It's easier for artists, I suppose, because we're so used to it from class. But if you can write in a café, surely you're not worried about being distracted here? I promise I'll be quiet as a mouse."

Thinking how much more troubled she would look if he told her his upsetting news, Edmund — without another word — slammed out. After looking for Jimmy, who was nowhere to be found, he ended up with strangers, drinking through the whole of the afternoon and late into the night, telling and re-telling his hard-luck story, getting advice from one and all, most of it having to do with the necessity of standing up to "the little lady," of letting her know who's "boss". Fired up to do just that, he reeled back to the Pelham, but when he saw Lily, wrapped in her dressing gown, sitting up waiting for him, her lovely face pale with worry, the flame of his anger sputtered and went out. Collapsing at her feet, he buried his face in her lap and confessed the sorry truth.

"How terrible," she said, stroking his hair. "You should have told me. My poor darling, of course you were in no mood to work after such news. You needed cheering up. I would have gone with you, if only you'd said."

"I'm so sorry," he murmured, over and over. "I'm so sorry."

"You mustn't be too hard on yourself. After all, if it hadn't been for me, you would have finished the article on time. I've been a terrible distraction to you."

"You've been wonderful to me. For me. Oh, Lily, God knows I don't deserve you. If you only knew the things I've done . . ."

She told him that she loved him, coaxed him out of his clothing and into bed, held him until he fell asleep. The next morning he awakened not nearly as hung over as he ought to have been, and imbued with a sense of well being, grateful that he had somehow managed not to do himself or his marriage any great harm.

"There's one thing I don't understand," Lily said, watching him as he downed cup after cup of black coffee. They were seated, having breakfast, at the small table in the parlor that functioned as sitting room, dining room, and studio.

"What?" Edmund said, wondering if he could manage a piece of dry toast.

"I thought the article you were doing for *McClure's* was about women and the vote?"

"Oh, no," he replied, without thinking. "Charles Evans Hughes. That's why the timing was so damn important." And then he remembered. He hesitated a moment, trying to find something to say that would redeem the situation, that would redeem him, but for once his ready tongue failed him.

"It was a lie," Lily said.

Edmund shrugged. "I wanted so desperately to speak to you." Reaching across the narrow table, he took hold of her hand, which was plucking absently at the tablecloth. "From the moment I set eyes on you, I loved you."

He thought that would be enough, but she looked away. "A pretty face isn't everything," she said, though he was not sure whether at that moment she was referring to her own or to his. Gently, she extracted her hand and stood up. "I need to clear the table. It's time to get to work."

For once, it did not even occur to Edmund to argue. Gathering up his papers, he decided to go to a nearby café and try to work himself — on the suffragette piece. It was hardly a dead issue, despite the election results in West Virginia and South Dakota, for the women were up in arms, and Montana had, after all, sent Jeanette Rankin to Congress. Getting it published would go a long way toward soothing Lily's ruffled feathers. "I love you," he repeated as she turned her head away, offering only her cheek for him to kiss.

"I know," she replied.

By the time he returned, brandishing the pages he had written, she seemed to have forgiven him. But she had never completely trusted him again, of that he was sure. And if his whole marriage came to seem to him later like shooting the rapids in a canoe, it was at this point that his fragile bark plunged over the falls and began its pell-mell tumble to the rocks below.

♫

Edmund emerged from Grand Central Station onto Forty-second Street and hesitated for a moment, not sure in which direction he wished to go. Everywhere he looked, flags provided cheerless splashes of color in the solemn gray day. The street was dense with traffic — taxis, automobiles, trolleys, wagons, vying for the right of way. The ubiquitous paperboys stood calling out the headlines, expertly catching tossed coins as

271

people snatched the papers from their ink-stained hands. Crowds of young men seemed to be heading east, toward the Navy Recruiting Center to enlist, Edmund imagined.

Though he had meant to go immediately to find Jimmy and join his friend for a consoling night on the town before heading back to Washington in the morning, instead Edmund turned north, threading his way through the traffic in the streets and the pedestrians on the sidewalks, block after block, until finally he stood across from the Pelham Hotel.

There was the canopy under which he had so regretfully said goodnight to Lily in the weeks before their marriage, the doorway he had entered so happily with his new bride, and exited again such a short time later, forlorn and desperate. What a mess he had made of things!

He had been foolish to come, and he cursed himself for not having resisted the impulse. If attempting to attend Lily's funeral had been a futile and demeaning exercise, it at least had held the promise of some sort of consolation, the consolation of ritual, if nothing else; but what did he hope to gain by revisiting this scene of so much bitter disappointment?

She had left him without even a good-bye, without giving him a chance to make amends. It was Mr. Locke, the hotel's manager, who told him, when he gathered the courage to ask, that Mrs. Farel had departed some hours before, taking her things with her in a taxi. She had also paid the bill, he added. It was his understanding that their rooms were to be vacated that day. But perhaps Mr. Farel intended to stay longer?

Of course he was not staying, Edmund replied, the one true thing he said to the discreetly impassive Mr. Locke. "My wife has had to rush home. Her mother isn't well. I'll follow on later. I have some errands to run first. I'm sure you won't mind, if I just leave my things here while I do."

It was a delicate situation; the manager could only agree; and Edmund hurried off to Alice and Teddy's studio where the doorman told him no one was at home, to the Menlo Gallery, to the car showroom where Louis Allen worked, to everywhere he could think of to ask, with as much subtlety as he could manage, where his wife had got to, returning finally to the Pelham to find his bags (humiliatingly) packed and awaiting him in the lobby.

A few days later, *McClure's* bought his piece on the suffragettes, and for quite a handsome sum. Armed with the courage of success, Edmund plagued Alice, whom he was certain knew where Lily could be found, to arrange a meeting, which she did, though he knew it was hardly to please him. In the Edwardian Room at the Plaza, he and Lily sat at a table near a window overlooking the park, with Alice nearby, keeping watch. That was the agreement.

"I'm sure you mean well, Edmund," Lily said, after listening to all his entreaties, "but you have no strength of character, no self-control. You're a bully, and a liar. You're incapable of telling the truth, of keeping your word. It makes me very sorry to say that, but it's true. No, there's no point trying to change my mind. It's made up. I never want to see you again." She reached into her purse, took out her wedding ring, and dropped it on the table. "Do you understand, Edmund? I don't want you ever to come near me again."

Her bruises were gone by then, most of them at any rate: there was only a slight hint of purple on her left wrist, visible beneath the sleeve of her dress. The sight of it made Edmund deeply ashamed. He let her go without more argument. Another chance to make things right would come later, when time had done its work, when Lily had acknowledged her own faults and forgotten the worst of his, when she remembered how deeply he loved her, how deeply she loved him.

But even now, though he could see that there had been no excuse for what he had done, and that matters might have turned out otherwise if only he had stopped his drinking and dealt with her more honestly, he could not help feeling that their relationship might have survived, in any case, if only Lily had been a bit more . . . well, womanly; if only she had been kinder. She had said such heartless things to him: that he was wasting his life, drowning it in drink, and though she might not be able to stop him from squandering his time and dissipating his talents, she was damned if he would get her to do the same.

What he had needed was not scolding, but warmth and encouragement, and if she would not give them, then what choice had he but to get them from friends, or if need be, from a glass of whiskey? And though she might protest until her voice was worn to a whisper that she believed him to be enormously talented and capable of doing very fine work indeed, what he saw always (and never more so than when he was, of necessity, lying to her about where he had been, what he had done) was the doubt in her eyes when she looked at him, and, finally, the complete contempt.

A taxi drew to a stop in front of the hotel, and the doorman emerged from inside to open its rear door for a middle-aged couple, looking very like several who had accompanied Edmund on the train down from Minuit. He recognized the doorman, Walter, an ambitious lad who dreamed one day of working in a hotel much grander than the Pelham — the Waldorf, say, or the new St. Regis, though it was likely that he would first trade in his fine blue livery for a khaki uniform. Turning away before he was noticed, Edmund continued on, walking west. Just beyond the Sixth Avenue intersection, he saw the small French café, the *Alouette*, where he had often come, alone to write, or with Lily, sometimes just the two of them for dinner, sometimes with Alice and Teddy, or other friends. They had had some happy times there, he recalled, hesitating for a moment before deciding to go in. It was after six already, and he had not eaten all day.

"*Monsieur* Farel, hello, how good to see you again," said the owner, a heavy-set man with gray hair and a bushy moustache beneath a narrow nose. "It's been a long time."

"Yes, it has," said Edmund, offering his hand, explaining that he now worked for the *Chronicle* and was temporarily on assignment in Washington.

"I was sorry to hear—" he said, and then stopped abruptly. "A great pity," he added.

It had been a mistake to come in, thought Edmund, but there was no help for it now. "Yes," he said. "Thank you, Jean-Pierre. If you'll bring me a carafe of the house red," he went on, taking his seat at one of the round tables neatly laid with a white cotton cloth, an intricately folded napkin, and silver cutlery, "and a steak with *pommes frites*, that will be fine."

In the past, when business (or the lack of it) had permitted, the two of them would sit together for a while, enjoying the chance to discuss matters of interest to men of the world like themselves, their conversations often in French, though Jean-Pierre sometimes had difficulty following Edmund's Cajun accent. This evening, however, neither of them felt inclined to pick up the relationship where they had left it months before; and, as Jean-Pierre hurried off with his order, Edmund got up and went to where the selection of newspapers lay in stands against the back wall. As he looked through them for ones he had not yet read, it occurred to him that Tuesday's *New York Times* might contain a news item that would perhaps give more details concerning Lily's death than her obituary had. He found a copy, returned with it to his seat, lit a cigarette, and began to skim through it, effectively blotting from his mind the scurrying waiters, the clink of glasses, the murmur of voices, the cheerful diners, appearing happy with their lot in life, as once he must have done sitting here, full of hope for the future, laughing among friends.

On page nineteen, he found what he was looking for, one short paragraph, which read:

New York, April 3. The body of an unidentified young woman was retrieved from the Hudson River near Eighty-sixth Street shortly before midnight, last night. A vagrant told police that he saw the woman leap into the river, and plunged in after her, in a rescue attempt which failed. An investigation is in progress.

Stunned, Edmund reread the piece. "Young Woman Drowns" was the lead, followed by the subhead, "Suicide Suspected." He remembered seeing the story, but it was a common enough one, with nothing in it to hold his attention (except perhaps for the courageous vagrant) even when the world was not at war. His eyes had slid right past it, on to the article about Russia's promise to restore independence to Poland. Even the next day, when reading her obituary, he had not connected the item to Lily. How could he? It would not have occurred to him that his Lily, his beautiful girl, his willful, pampered darling, might have wanted to take her own life.

What he was thinking was too awful. It was wrong. It had to be. "Your wine, *monsieur*," said a waiter, filling Edmund's glass from the carafe and setting it on the table. "Your dinner will arrive momentarily." Edmund nodded, reached for the glass, swallowed its contents in a gulp, and then poured another. Could he be mistaken? He returned to the collection of papers, found Wednesday's *Times*, and, taking it back to his table, opened to Lily's obituary and compared it to the news story.

Could two different young women have drowned in the Hudson, accidentally or otherwise, on the same night, at the same time? No, he was not mistaken. Lily had killed herself. "Oh Christ," he murmured, stung by the horror of it. Not that he was concerned for her immortal soul, for he had long since stopped believing in hell, or at least a hell not of this world and of one's own making. It was the waste of such a life thrown away that appalled him. A surge of grief washed over him — grief, and guilt in its wake. Was he somehow responsible? Had his actions brought Lily to such a desperate deed? But no, he reassured himself. They had lived apart for months; and though it would flatter him to think that she had still cared so much, she had made it only too clear how relieved she felt to be rid of him. No, she would not so much as crossed the street to avoid running into him, he thought, grief and guilt giving way to anger, let alone take her life in despair for having lost him.

How could she have done it? How?

The steak arrived, perfectly prepared, and the potatoes fried to a crisp golden brown, but all desire to eat had fled. Hurriedly, Edmund downed the remainder of his glass, paid his bill, made his excuses to Jean-

Pierre for having left his meal untouched, promised to return the next time he had business in New York, and escaped into the street. In the grip of conflicting emotions that tore at his heart, pounded in his head, without making a conscious decision, Edmund continued walking west.

Had Lily come this way? he wondered as he crossed under the Ninth Avenue el. It was unlikely. Even bent on self-destruction, she would not have chosen a route through Hell's Kitchen. The worst of the gangs had long since been brutally dispersed by the New York Central's private police, and the meanness of the neighborhood had now more to do with its abject poverty than with crime, but still it was not the sort of place a well-brought-up young woman would have felt happy to wander through alone. The buildings looked ill kept, run-down, with facades in need of repointing, doors in need of paint. There were no flags here, just windows flying a tattered piece of lace for a curtain. On every corner, servicing the inhabitants of the tenements that lined the streets, was either a candy store or a saloon. From a particularly seedy one (its faded sign proclaiming it the best alehouse in the city), emerged a man carrying a bucket of beer. At another time, Edmund might have stopped into the place, driven by a craving for drink, for the pleasure of exchanging a few words over a glass. Tonight, however, armed with his flask, he was not even tempted to linger. Continuing on across the railroad tracks, he wended his way up West End Avenue, where the tenements gave way to handsome homes of three or four stories, and then west again to Riverside Drive and its elegant array of row houses and villas, with their bow fronts and balconies, dormers and gables.

Avoiding Riverside Park itself, he kept to the street until he reached the plaza of the Soldiers and Sailors Monument, which rose out of the dark like a giant wedding cake at Eighty-ninth Street. He walked to the perimeter wall and stopped. There was a wind coming off the water and a chill dampness in the air. Edmund shivered. Wishing he had a warmer coat, he stopped and lit a cigarette.

Night had come on. Overhead, a few stars and a faint shimmer of moon could be seen behind a cover of fast-moving cirrus clouds. Behind him, on opposite corners, the red brick mansions of Edgar Rice and Mrs. Alfred Corning Clark (the latter complete with its own bowling alley, he had read) commanded a view of the drive, the park, and a wide sweep of the Hudson. From that vantage point, however, their owners could not see what he could: the landscaped grounds dropping away steeply to an industrial waste of rail depots, garbage dumps, and gravel pits, with the Columbia Yacht Club's two-storey bungalow, its tiny square of lawn, and its boat docks, a small oasis of luxury. He had spent several evenings at the club with Lily, guests of friends of hers, fortunate young men with money to spare, who issued invitations to this event or that, and vied for his agreement to crew for them in the spring when they would begin again to race their yachts. How he had hated them. Envied them. Admired them.

Would he ever have such carefree days again?

A freight train hurtled past below, spewing noise and belching smoke, taking a long while to disappear from sight, restoring the night to silence. Beyond the tracks, the river lay like a length of black silk, fading into the distance. It looked cold, forbidding. How could she have done it? The river was dark as the mouth of hell. He could not imagine himself capable of plunging into it, no matter how great his despair.

And what had she to despair of? Nothing. From infancy, the pleasures of the world had lain at her feet, waiting for her to stoop to pick them up. She had been loved, cared for, her person admired, her work praised. Though not rich precisely, she was well-to-do, lacking for nothing; and had she wanted more — hell! Edmund had seen the way men looked at her, that wealthy old roué Henshaw, for example, who would have traded in Lottie in a flash, if Lily would have had him. But Henshaw had not interested her, nor had any man, as far as he could tell, but himself. She had loved only him. She had given him her heart; and what had he done in return? He had broken it. What a wretch he was! A liar, a drunk, a man without principles, a scoundrel with nothing to recommend him beyond good looks and a clever tongue, and those surely would not withstand the assault of much more alcohol. No wonder Lily had come to despise him!

"Oh, Lily," he said, as the memory of that night, that other dark, terrible night, their last together, pushed past all his usual defenses and came flooding into his mind. "I'm sorry. I'm so very sorry." His breath was a wisp of vapor in the air.

Once again, Lily had refused to go with him, to — where was it? To nowhere in particular, that was the thing. He was restless. He had sent in his piece on the suffragettes and was waiting to hear from *McClure's*. He could not bear being cooped up a moment longer. A walk. He just wanted to take a walk. Lily, however, was working on a portrait, one of him, as it happened. She wanted it for the show. She almost had it, she said. She was very close, if only he would sit still for her a while longer. But he could not. And when, ignoring first his pleas and then his shouts, she absolutely refused to stop painting, he slammed out on his own. He stopped at the café for a glass of wine, and then continued on, calling in from time to time at his favorite haunts, places where he knew the bartenders, where he had friends, connecting with Jimmy finally, and another pal from the *Sun*, who knew of a gambling hell near Madison Square, where there was always a good time to be had. Edmund could not remember much after that, except that he had lost the little money he had on him. There might have been a late stop at a dancehall, but of that he was not sure: it might have been some other night. Finally, Jimmy, who had started later and could hold his liquor better, put him into a taxi, paid the driver, and sent him home. A mistake. The truly friendly thing would have been for Jimmy to have taken Edmund back to his place and lent him the sofa for the night.

Once again, Lily had waited up for him, and that, too, had been a mistake, for perhaps if he had been able to go right to bed, things might have turned out differently. But she had waited up. Fully dressed, she was, looking like an avenging goddess, waiting to pronounce judgment. Overcome with guilt, with loneliness, he went to her, his hands outstretched. But she slapped them out of the way. "Sweetheart, don't," he murmured, reaching for her again.

"Don't touch me," she said. "You're drunk."

"What did you expect?" The contrition in his voice gave way to a snarl. "If you'd just come with me—"

"Why must your bad behavior always be my fault? Why can you never accept responsibility for what you do?"

"Lily—"

"You had a visitor while you were gone. A woman. Amy, she said her name was. You'll find her at the Hermitage Hotel."

His hands dropped to his sides. "Oh, my God. Lily. I can explain."

"I don't think I can bear to hear any more lies."

She started for the door, and he noticed then that her portmanteau and box easel were there, packed and waiting. A wave of panic washed over him. "Lily, don't go! You can't go!" But she seemed not to hear him. It was as if he had ceased to exist for her. A flash of rage obliterated the panic. He went after her, grabbed her by both arms. "You married me! You promised!"

"Let me go," she said. "You disgust me!"

He hit her then, backhanded, across the face. "Shut up," he warned.

"You're a liar." Her voice was like that of his own conscience. "A cheat. A coward. You have no sense of decency, no honor. "

"Shut up," he said, shaking her again and again, taking hold of her wrists, twisting her arms as she fought him, dragging her to the bed. He pulled up her skirt, ripped off her knickers, and forced himself between her legs. But it was no use. "Oh, Jesus," he murmured. Now, alcohol had robbed him of his manhood, he thought, with a flicker of amusement at the irony of it. Rolling off her, he turned away and passed out.

When he awoke, she was gone. So were her belongings. Even her canvases were missing. She had left behind only a brief note on the dining table. "Edmund, I'm leaving you," she had written. "And I hope you will at least be good enough not to try to contact me. I never want to see you again."

In the grip of a terrible despair, he wept then, but by the time he bathed and shaved, he began to feel the first stirrings of hope. He was truly sorry for what he had done, and when Lily understood that she would forgive him. She loved him. She had told him that, over and over. She was proud, arrogant even, but when she cooled down a bit, she would forgive him. She had before. And, most encouraging of all, Lily had taken his portrait with her, a good omen, if ever there was one.

After their meeting at the Plaza, Lily went home to Riverhall. Edmund managed to get a job on the *Chronicle* and moved on to Chicago. Unable not to, from time to time he telephoned her; he wrote her. He told her that at last he had settled matters between himself and Amy. Lily never responded. In January, he heard from an acquaintance of hers he ran into in Chicago that she had had some sort of a breakdown, and he thought, viciously, that it served her right, that it was just payment for the anguish she had caused him, the damage she had done to both their lives. But though he could not help but count, over and over, the many ways she had fallen short of his ideal, still she remained the prize he coveted above all others. And always beneath his anger, his regret, his shame, lay the belief that in time, somehow, he would win her back.

"I never want to see you again," she had said. And now, of course, she never would.

What was he to do? he wondered, turning away from the river, crossing the plaza to the drive. All his plans for the future had involved Lily. Since meeting her, all he had ever wished to do was to please her. Except for his drinking, he might have; but he could not seem to stop. And was it such a great failing? Everyone he knew drank too much. Taking his flask from his pocket, he took another swallow. He would never have hit her again, of that he was sure. He had learned his lesson. If only she had given him another chance, he might have saved both their lives. If . . .

Now, before him stretched an endless desert of days, of scrounging to make a living, of running down leads on stories, of convincing wary editors to give him another chance, a wilderness of nights spent in drunken debauchery, trying to relieve a loneliness that had no cure but love, and where was he to find that again? He took another swallow, emptying his flask.

It was a long way back to Jimmy's, he thought, returning the flask to his pocket. He had better get a move on. He was tired, very tired. He needed to sleep. He would take the train back to Washington in the morning. On Monday, sounding bright and full of enthusiasm, he would call his editor.

Leaving the park, he began to retrace his steps along Riverside Drive. The lights in the houses were on. People were snug in their homes, enjoying the comforts of the good life. Peering into one window, he saw a man bent over the keyboard of an upright piano, a young woman beside him, singing. Lovers, he imagined; newlyweds, perhaps. Did they know, he wondered, how fragile happiness was, how life could smash it in an instant, without a second thought?

He would walk to Ninth Avenue and take the el, he decided. He doubted he had the stamina left to walk the distance to Jimmy's place. After a few more steps, he doubted he had the stamina to walk anywhere at all. His legs were weak. He felt sick. He staggered, righted himself, then gingerly lowered his body to the curb and buried his head between his legs to calm the waves of nausea.

Aside from him, there was not a soul on the street, and only an occasional automobile rattled past. Too ill to care, Edmund did not bother to look when he heard one come to a stop nearby. "Buddy, you all right?" someone asked.

As he reluctantly raised his head, the moon moved from behind a cloud and illuminated the troubled face of a taxi driver, peering out of the window of a black Ford. "I could use a lift," Edmund said. "My legs seem to have given out."

Like a delivering angel, the driver emerged from the cab to give Edmund a hand. "Anyplace in particular you want to go?" he asked, settling him in the back seat.

Edmund gave him Jimmy's address. "But first," he said, "if you could stop somewhere I can fill my flask, I'd appreciate it."

The man grunted his assent, and Edmund leaned back against the cushions, eyes closed, luxuriating in the feeling of comfort, of safety, of satisfaction. He would not be spending his night in the gutter, after all. He became aware of a small flicker of . . . something, not quite hope, he was too sad and it was too small for that, but it did occur to him that perhaps his luck had again begun to change. True, a taxi with a beneficent driver was not much of a sign, but to one as adept as Edmund at reading fortune's hieroglyphs, it seemed that, after having kept her back relentlessly toward him for months, Lady Providence had deigned to turn and bestow her beautiful smile on him once more. He felt his spirits begin to lift. Yes. Absolutely. He was certain of it. She had just held out her hand to him, and now he had only to extend his own and take it.

LILY

The headaches had started again. They came and went haphazardly, brought on by unknown causes, cured by time: an hour, a day, two days. She never knew for certain how long one would last.

Worse than the headaches, though, was the fatigue. Even when she was free of pain, she could not sleep. Hour after hour, she would lie awake, restlessly shifting position on the soft mattress, her mind teeming with unpleasant thoughts, wracked with worry about this and that (her mother, her work, her future), tormented by voices urging her to one mad act or another; and when she did manage to drift off, it was not into a restful sleep, because then the nightmare would come, the same nightmare that had plagued her for years. In it, she raced through the dark streets of an unfamiliar city, not even a real city, but a painted one, like a stage set, empty of people, full of blind alleys and shallow doorways, with no place to hide, trying to escape someone, a sort of Jack-the-Ripper figure. She never saw him, but she knew he was there, close behind her, pursuing her with a single-minded purpose, not wanting to rape or kill her (she was very certain about this, even while she dreamed), but to put out her eyes. The meaning of the dream was clear to her (she had discussed it at length with Dr. Bettelman), but understanding had not robbed it of its terror. She would awake with a scream, out of breath, drenched with sweat, her heart pounding. Mornings, she would lie in bed as if pinned to the mattress by an elephant's foot, and it took every ounce of will power she possessed to summon the strength to push it away and get up. Worst of all were the panic attacks. Like the headaches, these too came intermittently, without apparent cause. One moment she was fine; and then, suddenly, she would feel her heartbeat quicken, her throat begin to close, her breath become shallow. She felt as if she were suffocating. She felt like an accordion being squeezed shut, the music of her life fading away with a sigh. Usually these attacks passed quickly, for which she thanked God: she really did not think she could bear them for longer than a few hours at a time.

On some days, though (often for several days in a row, and perhaps because she had somehow managed to get just enough sleep), she felt like her old self; or, more exactly, like her "well" self. She could not only rise without much of a struggle from her bed, bathe, and dress, but carry on in spirits good enough to fool even her mother, who had taken to watching her warily while pretending to be unconcerned. It was irritating to be looked at in that way, and Lily could not help resenting it, especially as it made her have to stop and assess her feelings, her behavior, to be sure that she was indeed as "all right" as she professed herself to be.

On the day that was to be the last of her life (though of course she did not know then it would be), she awoke in her room in the Pelham Hotel feeling as well as she ever did these days. There was no sign of a headache, she could breathe easily, and it took only a little effort to get herself up and into the bathroom to begin the morning's ritual.

Staying at the Pelham, however, had certainly been a mistake, she thought, as she turned on the faucets and watched the water splash into the porcelain sink. Now that she was about to leave (the following day, to go home), she was willing to admit it. She had hoped to lay its ghosts, to rid it of all its associations with Edmund and her time with him, for why should a few weeks of folly put off limits forever a place that otherwise held only happy memories for her? But she could see now that she had been foolish to return. Only a few months had passed, and for most of those she had not been well. She should have given herself more time.

Her mother had said as much, but Lily had dismissed her concerns. "Really, Mama, I'll be perfectly fine. There's nothing at all for you to worry about," she had said. But, in truth, her doubts about her decision had started building on the train ride down from Minuit. When the taxi stopped in front of the hotel, it had taken a major effort of will for her not to ask the driver to go on to the Astor; she had barely managed a smile for the welcoming doorman and desk clerk; and, though she was shown to a suite she had never before stayed in, absent any associations, good or bad, still she burst into tears the moment the bellman left her alone in it. The sense of Edmund's presence had knocked her flat and cold, like the drift of snow that had broken loose and engulfed her once when she was a child, playing in the garden at Riverhall. She had cried then, too, but her father had been nearby and had lifted her up into his arms, literally before she knew what had hit her. "Now, now," he had said, "you're all right, aren't you? Still all in one piece? There's no need for my brave girl to cry." But if being held by him was enormously comforting, it was so only for a moment, she had to admit, remembering the incident. However reassuring his voice, he was frightened himself: she could feel it, and so had to battle not only her own fear, but his — and her dismay for having caused it. He had handed her off to her mother for a

warm bath to ward off the effects of the cold, and Lily had not been allowed out of the house for days afterward.

If only she had taken his fears more to heart, Lily thought, brushing her hair until it shone, twisting it into a coil that she pinned at the nape of her neck, if only she had learned from his example over the years how to care for herself, she might have escaped the avalanche of misery that had engulfed her these past months. As it was, adding considerably to that misery was the knowledge that her father's concern for her, unlike her mother's, would have been laced with impatience at her folly. Nor could she have concealed from him (as she had from everyone, but Andrew) the full extent of it. He would have been so disappointed in her. As guilty as the thought made her feel, it was a relief sometimes to know that he was dead and could no longer be hurt by anything his wayward daughter did.

Since she meant to work that morning, Lily put on the old gray dress kept for that purpose, and then went down to the lobby. There, clusters of people were entering and leaving in a steady murmur of conversation, while others lounged in the brocade-covered chairs, quietly absorbed in the morning papers, coffee in handsome china cups within easy reach on nearby tables. Everyone seemed so normal, so carefree, which was very much how she felt right at that moment. She stopped at the newsstand to buy a paper, and at the desk to collect the morning mail. "You should have left word last night, Miss Canning," said Thomas, a middle-aged clerk in the hotel's blue livery, always eager to be of help, and the soul of tact. (She had counted on the staff's tact when booking the suite in the name of Canning, not Farel.) "I'd have sent these up to you."

"Oh, I quite like to come and see how everyone's getting on," she said; and, indeed, on her good mornings, it was a pleasure to find herself in this commonplace assembly and to stop perhaps for a chat with some of the guests whom she had come to know.

She lingered so long in the lobby that the maid had been and gone by the time Lily got back to her rooms. She set the mail and the newspaper down, then opened the doors of the cooking closet to make herself some

287

coffee and buttered toast, not that she had much appetite, but she had sense enough to know that she must eat, whether or not she felt like it. When her breakfast was ready, she carried it to the table near the window and sat looking out at the busy street below, watching the men in their trilby hats, the well-dressed matrons in their loosely belted coats, the shop girls in somber colors, the raggedy boys running errands. It was going to be another dreary day, she thought with a pang. For heaven's sake, it was spring. Was a little sunshine too much to ask?

Turning away from the window's gloomy prospect, she began to read through the mail as she ate her breakfast. There was a letter from Rosaline, filled with news of William and the children; another from her mother, insisting she was fine and all was well with the world; a confirmation from Alice that she and Teddy would be at Delmonico's at eight; and a note from Louis to tell her how much he had enjoyed seeing her the previous evening and to ask if she would care to stay in town an extra day to hear Caruso sing in *Aida*: if so, he would be happy to get tickets. She could not help smiling at that. Her little cousin had become quite the man of the world; he always knew what was worth doing. But he was a little in love with her (she could hardly help noticing), and she knew she ought not to encourage him by seeing him too often. For the most part, she felt that she struck the right balance in their relationship, not trying to conceal her genuine fondness, but keeping him at a certain distance, treating him like a very dear younger brother, though she hoped without the condescension she thought Florence sometimes showed him.

In any case, while she had enjoyed much about her stay in the city, Lily absolutely had to return to Riverhall. However exhausting she found the idea, she needed to complete one, perhaps two more paintings before the opening of her exhibition, so that she could (if only Darius Menlo would agree!) substitute them for some of the earlier works she had come to dislike. Of course, Darius might absolutely hate the direction in which she was moving. She herself was not at all sure it was the right way to go. A landscape she had recently finished had a certain something, she was sure; but the new self-portrait . . . well, she had her doubts about it. Though not quite certain yet, she thought she might have to abandon it, and begin something else. One had to experiment, to change, to push on into the unknown, no matter what the resistance in one's self and others. One had either to grow, or wither away and die.

If only she had not lost so much time — first those weeks with Edmund, with their endless distractions, and then afterward at the hospital. She had to try to make it up. She *would* make it up. She would work night and day if she had to. And if the new paintings were as good, as full of interest and energy as she hoped to make them, she would insist on Darius' including them in the show.

Not even Caruso could tempt her to stay in the city longer, she wrote Louis in reply, with a thank you for his offer. Sealing the envelope, she left it propped conspicuously on the mantle, so that she would remember to take it with her to mail when she went out later in the day. Then, returning to the table, she took an apple from the cut-glass bowl and bit into it. Opening the *Times,* she began to read closely, from front page to back, as she had every day for weeks, though she knew it would be wiser not to since it was impossible to avoid becoming at least a little depressed by all the horrid news. Some would, she supposed, be cheered by the success of those poor boys fighting in the battle of the Somme, who had at last managed to push the Germans back a few miles, but she found it difficult to take any pleasure in what had to have been a bloodbath. The Germans were starving, but she could not seem to rejoice in that either. The Dutch, too, were short of food. Rioters had broken up a pacifist meeting in Washington the day before. Troops were on the move to secret destinations. The United States entry into the war seemed inevitable. Why, even Brooklyn's Plymouth Church, that bastion of liberal politics, had declared in favor of it. She thought of Louis, of Marcus and Henry, of all the young men she knew, of the sweet doorman downstairs, the bellmen in the hotel, the waiters in the restaurants she frequented, and what war would mean for them. Death and destruction were everywhere. The entire world was in turmoil.

But it was pointless to worry about it, she told herself firmly, closing the newspaper and disposing of it in the basket by the hearth for the housekeeping staff to take away. There was nothing she could do to alter the course of events. More profitable by far, she knew from her endless discussions with Dr. Bettelman, was to concentrate on keeping control of her own life. She resolved again, as she had every morning since her arrival in the city, not to get the paper the following day. Instead, on the train journey home, she would read magazines, though perhaps even that was not such a good idea, she thought, as her eyes drifted to a copy of *McClure's*, lying on the coffee table. What had prompted her to buy it was the most recent installment of Edith Wharton's new novel, *Summer*, which unfortunately seemed to be moving in a very gloomy direction. While it was impossible to muster much sympathy for the book's grudging and self-important young protagonist, still one did not really wish her to end up with all her hopes crushed. Even such a silly girl did not deserve to be deceived, betrayed, and left alone to suffer the consequences of her folly, for surely it was a pardonable offense in one so young to believe that her beauty would suffice to hold a weak and greedy young man? Of course, thought Lily as she tidied the stack of magazines, burying the *McClure's* (which she ought not to have bought, it brought back such unhappy memories) beneath copies of *Harpers Weekly* and the *Saturday Evening Post*, she could be wrong. All might yet end happily. She hoped it would, though she was not certain she would buy the coming issues of the magazine to find out. Edith Wharton was a novelist Lily admired, but perhaps not one it was wise to read when one's spirits were low. Somehow things rarely turned out well for the women in her stories.

Now, there remained only her breakfast things to clear, which Lily did at once, throwing away the remnants of toast and apple, washing the dishes and cutlery in the cooking closet's tiny sink, drying them, and returning them to their proper places. Though she could leave most rooms any which way, for others to pick up after her, she found it impossible to work in a space that was untidy. She put away the bread, cleared the crumbs, folded the towel, and turned to survey the room. Even Nuala could not find fault, she thought. It was time to get to work, though now she did not feel like it at all. She rarely did of late. In anticipation, yes, but not when she finally got down to it. She went on only out of habit, and in the hope that afterward she would feel better, as she often did, the relief at having done something lifting her spirits sufficiently to carry her through the rest of the day, giving her the energy to face the world with a smile.

She put on her painting smock and stood for a moment studying the tulips she had bought a few days before. Their colors were already fading, but their long stems had begun to dip and swoop in the most elegant way. Well, why not? she thought. Moving the round pottery vase from the sideboard, she placed it next to the bowl of apples on the lace-covered dining table. Stepping back to study the effect, she found it wanting and went again to the cooking closet. Returning with a cream-colored china cup and saucer, she set them on the table. Again she studied the arrangement, and again went back to the closet, took a plate from the shelf and a silver knife from the cutlery drawer. With the knife, she cut a section from an apple, placed the apple on the plate, and added them and the knife to the collection of items on the cloth. That was much better, she thought, as she adjusted the curtain of the window to the right of the table. Often when she was sketching, as an exercise, she narrowed her focus, concentrating on a bouquet of flowers, or a bowl of fruit, on a bare table against a plain ground, but she had something more adventurous in mind today. She would include the window, or part of it at any rate, and a hint of the building across the street.

At home, especially of late, Lily worked long hours, going on, over her mother's protests, until she was worn out. In the city, where she had so many other demands on her time, she had to moderate her pace. It was not the number of hours, in any case, as she well knew, but the degree of concentration. This afternoon, she had an appointment at the gallery at two, but she pushed that thought from her mind. She opened her box easel, a neat contraption with a drawer for paints and equipment and a carrier for canvases, all of which folded up into a lightweight case. A present from her parents on her twelfth birthday, it was the most useful gift Lily had ever received, and one she would not have traded for all the pearl pendants and diamond earrings in the world. Only once since getting the box had she gone anywhere without it, and that was to the hospital. Dr. Bettelman had thought it unhealthy for her to work. Her poor, tired brain needed rest, he said. She would get well much more quickly if she could simply allow herself to do nothing for a while. And so she had, and here she was, as well as could be.

Though she carried her sketchbook with her everywhere and used a pencil to test ideas and work out problems, when settled at her easel, in front of her subject, Lily preferred to do what she had learned from William Merritt Chase at the Art Students League (and he had learned in Munich), to draw with paint and brush. If the technique was forgiving of a lot of defects, it nevertheless gave immediacy to the work, Lily felt; it plunged one right into the heart of the subject. She chose her colors, squeezed the paints from their tubes into neat little patches on her palette, and began to sketch rapidly in oil, trying to capture the image before her, so that, when she returned to her studio at Riverhall, she would be able to reproduce on a larger canvas what she saw now: the tulips weeping over the apples; the cup off-balance on its saucer; the knife projecting out of the picture plane; the curtain billowing like a sail; the building opposite, a monolith set against the sky; the unifying grays and greens; the bright notes of red and yellow; the joy of warmth, of plenty, within; the gloom outdoors. If she got the finished painting right, she would insist that Darius take it in place of one of her earlier ones. If she got it right . . .

While she worked, the issues troubling her mind fell away. She forgot the war, her mother's bad health, the failure of her relationship with Edmund, her fears that the show at the Menlo would also fail. She forgot everything but the problems presented to her by her need to transfer what she was seeing, what she was feeling, to the canvas before her. She worked quickly, steadily, stopping from time to time to substitute another canvas as the light through the window changed, so that she could catch the differences in the shadows, in the highlights, in the values of the colors. That is what Monet had done, sitting in a field, studying haystacks, or in a boat drifting on a river, attempting to capture the play of light in the heavens, on the water, on the trembling trees and grasses of the bank.

A blare of horn from the street broke her concentration, which meant that she must be getting tired, for noise never bothered her when her mind was fully engaged in her work. She looked at the clock on the mantle. Though it hardly seemed possible, she had been painting for over three hours. If she wished to be on time for her meeting at the gallery, she had to hurry; but, as she propped the sketches against the furniture to dry, her pace slowed. She found she was not at all pleased with what she had done, not that there was anything obviously "wrong" with the sketches. In fact, most people would have found them to be very well done indeed. Still, to her critical eye, they seemed bland, boring. A competent painter might have produced them — a Grover Watson, for example — but not one with the mark of genius.

Feeling her spirits begin to plummet, Lily began to lecture herself silently as she returned the tulips to the sideboard, the dishes to the cooking closet, as she cleaned her brushes and palette and closed her box easel. This was a familiar feeling, she told herself, one she often experienced, and it was no more to be trusted than the wild elation that sometimes gripped her when she looked at her work. She was no doubt a better artist than she believed herself to be at her worst moments, though perhaps not quite as good as she imagined at her best. In any event, what did it matter? History was the only accurate judge of genius, which is why it would be wise of her not to think about such things, but to soldier on in the hope of improving. As she changed into her navy suit, Lily called to mind what Vasari had said of Raphael: always a good painter, he had become great only after recognizing his inferiority to Michelangelo, when he set himself to learn from and surpass the master. Not that he had. But his failure had not disheartened him, or at least not for long. When he realized there were things he would never be able to do even as well, Raphael had concentrated instead on those areas where he could, if he tried, at least equal Michelangelo's accomplishments. And the result? Some of the greatest masterpieces of western art, the *Virgin and Child with a Book*, for example, which Lily had seen in reproduction. If only she had not been ill, forcing her father to cancel their trip to Europe. If only she had managed to go another time, before all this dreadful business with the war. Another lost opportunity, among so many others.

But there was no point brooding on what could not be helped. It was much better to do as Dr. Bettelman always advised: concentrate on the present and how to make the most of that. The important thing, Lily told herself, is never to give up

As a rule, Lily enjoyed the time she spent at the Menlo. Everyone at the gallery was always so enthusiastic and complimentary. They made her feel successful and important, hopeful, too, that others would view her work as admiringly as they. In the presence of the dashing Darius Menlo, caught up in the wave of his zeal, she could not help but feel excited by the prospect of good reviews and healthy sales — and the conviction these might bring that she was not, after all, a fraud; that she was, in fact, contributing something valuable to the world of art, to the world at large.

Today, however, the enthusiasm of Darius and his minions seemed strained to Lily. Their opinions of her paintings seemed more nuanced. She detected hints of dissatisfaction that she had never before noticed. Because all the paintings she had submitted could not possibly be shown, the winnowing process had been going on for some time, but now there were only a few weeks left until the opening. Final decisions had to be made, and inevitably that meant frank talk. Not that anyone said anything at all terrible, far from it; but anxious about the reception her work would get from the public, and the critics, Lily heard every comment as a criticism. Any suggestion that a painting was not perfect (though she knew far better than anyone that it was not) pricked her like a pin. She found the process excruciating; and, when it was over, when she conceded to Darius' wishes about which works to include, gave in to his "suggestions" about their framing, and won his agreement to consider at least two new paintings for the exhibition (her only victory), she had a raging headache. Assuring him that whatever plans he made for the opening night reception would be acceptable to her, she took the box of engraved invitations meant for her personal guests and fled. As she rode down in the elevator, an image of one of those Renaissance paintings of the martyrdom of Saint Sebastian came to her, and she saw herself in his place, naked flesh quivering with arrows, punishment for the folly of believing herself possessed of any talent at all.

She knew she ought to go back to the hotel to rest, but in the time it took the elevator to descend from the tenth floor, where the Menlo was located, to ground level, Lily decided to keep to her original plan and return to a gallery she had visited on her previous trip to the city. If she could have left it for another time, she might have, but she had to have another look at a painting on show there before returning home. She needed to rekindle the excitement she had felt on first seeing it, and perhaps to have answered some of the questions that had arisen since, though she was not too hopeful about the latter, for it seemed to Lily that, for the past four years, there had been only questions, no answers. She seemed to exist in a state of perpetual confusion, as indeed did many of her contemporaries, thanks to that confounding 1913 Armory Show. It had thrown them all for a loop.

As vividly as if it were only yesterday that she had strolled through those eighteen galleries, beneath the yellow tenting, accompanied by the sound of a brass band and the scent of potted pine trees, Lily could remember the feelings aroused in her by that first cataclysmic encounter with paintings by Gauguin, by van Gogh, by Matisse, by Picasso, the amusement, the bewilderment, the horror. Standing in front of Duchamp's *Nude Descending a Staircase*, studying its flat planes, compressed space, cubist forms, she had wondered what all this meant for herself and her undeniable skill at perspective, her ability to represent reality faithfully on canvas, to render the perfect apple, the perfect rose, the sheen of silk, to reproduce the exact face, to capture character with a brushstroke? As she left the Sixty-ninth Regiment Armory that bitter February day, she had felt that all the rules had changed without notice, that everything she had learned from her first art lesson on, everything she had believed without question to be true, had been declared nonsense. She had come away as well with a headache that raged on for days.

She had not been alone in her fear. It had afflicted almost every artist she knew, though experimentation was hardly unknown to them. All but the most hidebound had always eagerly explored new styles and techniques. Lily herself had moved away, over time, from the highly finished surface of her early work to a broader, looser brush stroke, to impressionism, social realism, the moody atmospherics of tonalism; she had tried out whole new vocabularies of color. Whatever she attempted had brought praise from some, and resistance from most, which was disheartening, especially when it came from her father, whose criticism always cut deepest because, really, there was no one in the world who thought more highly of her, and her talent, than he. Nevertheless, she had kept going, trying to see each change as a positive step, an evolution in her work.

But the Armory show had presented something else entirely, not an evolution, but a *revolution*, a brutal severing of the ages-old connection between painting and its subject matter.

In the months afterward, Lily's sense of bewilderment, of fear, had grown steadily worse, for the whole art world had seemed to descend into a state of anarchy, with no consistent standards, with opinions flying about like leaves in a storm, no one more weighty or likely to settle than any other. But while the public laughed, the critics scoffed, William Merritt Chase ranted, Kenyon Cox (that strict adherent of academic principles) raved, and even the erstwhile radical, Robert Henri, dug in his heels and refused to budge, people were buying the new art, people who mattered, like Albert Barnes and Lillie Bliss; and while the Old Masters, and even the Impressionists, could hardly be said to have fallen out of favor, they were definitely yesterday's news. The post-Impressionists — the Cubists, the Fauvists, the Orphists, the Synchromists — they were the ones being talked about. They were the Moderns. Her father might advise her to stick to her guns, but Lily, like her friends, could not help feeling the necessity of climbing on the bandwagon or getting left behind. But which one? And to what end? Those were the perplexing questions, and most perplexing of all: if art no longer had to represent reality, what *was* it supposed to do?

Eventually, the black mood enveloping her began to lift. As her eye grew more comfortable and more acute, she came to see things to admire in the works of this new generation of European artists, whose paintings were suddenly everywhere. It was hard to resist the exuberance of Matisse or Vlaminck or Derain, for example, or the decorative way they filled their space with color, even if the arbitrariness of that color did jangle the nerves a bit; it was impossible not to admire the monumental stillness, the austere power of Cézanne. Once again, Lily set to work experimenting, but even as she explored the uses of design, or the geometry of form, she was aware of a resistance in herself, a reluctance to relinquish the techniques she had prized for so long. She could not, she discovered, let go of the figure (or it could not let go of her). And she had no wish to paint ideas. Places interested her, and people, and things. All she wanted was to use line and color to capture reality as she perceived it to be. Yet, she could not proceed as if nothing had changed, for everything had.

"We'll find our way," Teddy had said. "When things get tired and dull, revolution is necessary. Chaos is inevitable. But the dust is bound to settle, and when it does we'll be able to see the road ahead." But he had

297

been to Munich and Paris, as had Alice. Neither of them had been knocked quite as flat by the Armory Show as was Lily. They had already absorbed the shock, considered the questions, and chosen their answers, throwing in their lot with the Fauves. Teddy had even had two paintings in the Armory Show. "It may not be the same road for all of us, but what does that matter, if it takes us where we need to go?"

But where was that? How could one possibly know? Or be certain when one had arrived?

From time to time, Lily would think she had found . . . if not the way, then at least another clue, a coded message, as in a treasure hunt. She had uncovered one the previous May, when she went with Teddy and Alice and a few other friends to an exhibition of Georgia O'Keeffe's drawings at 291. Afterward, they had taken the artist out for a celebratory drink, for most in their crowd had been together at the League in 1907. Then, awed by the older student, with her bobbed hair and boyish swagger, the timid sixteen-year-old Lily had rarely dared to speak to her. And, if less tongue-tied by hero worship nine years later, she still regarded her former classmate with something like reverence, and more than a dash of envy, not for her success, because in truth she had had almost none as yet, but for her sureness, her authority. Someone seeing a drawing by Georgia O'Keeffe could dislike it certainly, but no one could doubt for a moment that the artist knew what she was doing, and was doing exactly as she pleased.

Drinks had turned into dinner, with the talk going on for hours, what O'Keeffe had to say seeming, then, only a part of the general call for a "truly American art." What was necessary was to break free from all one has learned, she said. "There's no point, is there, in simply repeating what every one else has done, no matter how competently one does it?" What was necessary was a personal aesthetic.

The next morning, Lily had awakened to the sound of O'Keeffe's words echoing in her head. In a blinding flash, she had realized *that* was the answer: she had only to remain true to herself, to her personal vision.

Only, it soon occurred to her, she did not yet have one. And, in the months since, a personal aesthetic had proved elusive. Though she sometimes felt that she was near to finding it, that she had only to struggle through the underbrush a while longer to get to that clearing in the forest where all would be revealed to her, so far she had failed to reach it. No matter how powerful she felt before beginning to paint, how certain that she could do anything, afterward the work always seemed derivative to her, or frightened, tentative, small. And so she went on seesawing between hope and despair, high momentarily on praise, on prizes, on the promise of a show of her own, before falling back down into self-doubt.

Then, a few weeks ago, at loose ends for an hour, she had strolled into the Modern Gallery to have a look at the exhibition, and had found a painting that seemed to her to hold the final clue.

The Modern showed only European art, in recent weeks a show of paintings by Pablo Picasso, Juan Gris, and Georges Braque. Unusual for a gallery, it had large windows fronting onto Fifth Avenue, and that asset combined with its location at the intersection of Forty-second Street, just a few blocks from Sherry's and Delmonico's, drew crowds of the affluent and the curious — though today, Lily noticed as she approached it, people seemed to be less interested in the art on display than in the wares of the paperboy stationed at the corner, touting the *World*. She stopped to read the headline, but it only offered more of the same: rumors of war. Resisting the temptation to buy a copy, she turned away and went into the gallery.

The fresh air and short walk had done her good. Her head felt better. She smiled at the assistant, a dapper young man who reminded her of Louis. Clearly remembering her from her last visit, he asked expectantly if he could be of help. "I haven't come to buy a thing," she told him. "I'm not even sure I like any of it very much. But I do want another look, if you don't mind."

Though not vain in any real sense, Lily nevertheless had a very clear understanding of the effect she had on men and was in no way surprised by the warm smile she got in response. "By no means. Please, feel free to stay as long as you like."

She did not wish to see everything again, just the one painting that had drawn her back. Casting only the most cursory of glances at the others as she passed, she walked directly to it. It was by Picasso. And though the painting's surface was broken into flat planes of essentially rectangular forms in shades of brown, its subject was clear enough. It was of a seated girl, playing a guitar.

Lily had not exactly *liked* the painting when she first saw it, but it had cast a sort of spell on her. It had intrigued her, though she was not immediately certain just why. It was not its palette, which was dull, or its handling of form, which she found grotesque, even ugly.

But it was not ugly, she had decided finally; there was an underlying harmony among its elements that precluded ugliness. It had monumentality, too, grandeur. The girl's pose was classic. One might have seen it in a painting by Bronzino, or Leonardo. Was that what made this work feel so familiar, despite seeming so disturbingly new? She had had a sense of its artist simultaneously reaching back and pushing forward, struggling to achieve some sort of synthesis, attempting to reconcile opposing forces with the power of his genius (for she was certain that, like him or not, he was a genius). All you who have grown tired of looking at things in the same old way, he seemed to be saying, try looking at them from my perspective for a change. Aren't they exciting from this vantage? Isn't this how Adam and Eve might have seen the world when they were made to leave Eden? Not as a series of broken planes perhaps, but as something fresh, new, thrilling.

Here is someone willing to dare, Lily had thought, someone afraid of nothing. She had found that fearlessness inspiring and returned to Riverhall determined to give herself free rein to try — well, anything. Rejecting the pull toward the conventional or the pretty, she had quickly painted a landscape, quite different from any she had done before and more interesting by far, she believed. Then, she had moved on to what she intended

300

to be a self-portrait in the truest sense of the word, not just a picture of her face and body as in so much of her early work, but a representation of her interior self, her true self, the Lily that only she knew. Yes, Rembrandt had done that, and sublimely; but why should that stop her? He had found his way. Now, it was up to her to discover her own.

Imbued with a sense of power, Lily had taken her portrait of Edmund and painted over it. The past was done with, she told herself. Only the future mattered. Sorting through fragments of thought to find the underlying harmony of her vision, she began to lay in form and color, and was thrilled by what she could see taking shape on the canvas. Her work seemed to have a new vitality, a spirit of adventurousness. She was convinced that this new path would lead to somewhere wonderful. Then, as always, doubt had set in.

But now, standing once again before the Picasso, Lily felt a sort of exhilaration, an incipient comprehension of the possibilities of fusion.

A sense that she was no longer alone broke her concentration. Turning away from the painting, expecting to find at her side the young assistant, who might be forgiven for thinking he could sell her a work that seemed to captivate her so completely, she saw instead a man of about forty, with a neat moustache, wearing a knee-length coat of brown waterproof wool and a bowler hat. When he saw that he had her attention, he smiled. "What do you make of it?" he asked.

She assessed him coolly for a moment, trying to decide what his intentions were. Not that it mattered. He could be the Archangel Gabriel himself and her response would be the same. Edmund Farel had cured her forever of daring to put her trust in strangers. This man, in any case, was no one she wished to know. "Not as much as I'd like," she said, without a smile. She took one final look at the painting, and then turned and headed for the door, directing a nod at the assistant, who shot her a look of intense disappointment as he ushered her out politely and begged her to come again. "I'm sure I will," she said. "The exhibitions here always give me so much to think about."

Outside it was damp and threatening rain. Along Fifth Avenue, businesses were closing for the night, the lights in their windows going out, the last of the customers spilling into the streets, followed by the shop assistants, the managers, the businessmen leaving their offices, heading for their clubs or their homes. As Lily made her way through the crowds thronging the sidewalk, she could feel the expectation in the air, the apprehension. The war. Everyone was waiting for the next awful step to be taken. She tried to find consolation in the thought that, at the moment, everyone was as fearful of the future as she; and indeed there was some comfort in finding that her fear again linked her to others, instead of isolating her from them as it often did. The truth was, however, that the war accounted for only a small fraction of the dread that plagued her. She had other bitter worries, some known, some nameless, and the anxiety they inspired took possession of her mind like an invading army when she was awake, and haunted her dreams while she slept.

Her headache was coming back. Think about something else, she commanded herself; and immediately the painting left unfinished at Riverhall came into her mind.

She had imagined a sort of Janus, not looking forward and back, but facing the viewer in a flattened plane, the past and future self, all one's different selves, existing simultaneously: the adventurous girl who had dreamed of being a painter possessing the same soul as the woman who stood before the easel, or that sad creature moping about the hospital, or the old woman she would one day become. But what at first Lily believed a significant breakthrough had finally seemed merely pointless and grotesque. The face staring back at her from the canvas was not interesting, but terrifying. She could not bear to look at it. Was this really the way to go? Losing heart, she had stopped, convinced she had reached another dead end.

As someone wounded might require an infusion of blood to survive, Lily had felt in need of another shot of inspiration. Had she got it from this return visit to the gallery? she wondered as she made her way north along Fifth Avenue. Well, she would know soon enough, tomorrow, when she got home. She could imagine the trepidation she would feel as she stood again before her easel and reached to remove the cloth draped over the painting. She felt a little sick to her stomach at the thought, yet excited too. She felt suddenly eager to get back to work.

The question of inspiration aside, what she had come away with this afternoon, Lily thought, was something much more pragmatic, but equally important, a sense of how to proceed. Alone at Riverhall, she had lost the way, but now she was sure she had found it again. Picasso had shown her that at least. What she had to do (and she hoped she might already have begun) was take the elements that appealed to her, break them apart, and recombine them in a new way, keeping at it until she had achieved an art that was truly personal — and truly American. For though the Europeans were riding high, revered by critics and collectors alike, it would not do to imitate them slavishly, so Lily believed, with Teddy and Alice, with Georgia O'Keeffe and Edward Hopper, with so many others among her peers. They had to bring something unique, something homegrown, to the table. And as Darius Menlo (who showed only Americans) liked to point out, money followed interest; and, as the appetite for the new and exciting grew, it was expanding to include painters who had never set foot in the "Old World." What attracted collectors now, no matter its country of origin, was the art of the twentieth century. Her century. She had to keep that in mind, for while she dismissed the notion that it was essential to cut free of the past to succeed, still she did not wish to get stuck there. One had to take what one needed and move on.

So deep in thought was she that Lily was at the Plaza Hotel before she realized that she had missed her turning. As she retraced her steps to Fifty-sixth Street, she felt suddenly chilled through. A cup of tea would do her a world of good.

The Pelham's doorman, Walter, who generally seemed to find life a fine thing, was barely able to summon a smile as he held open the door for her, wishing her a good evening. Inside, there was a feeling of tension in the air. The desk clerk did not quite meet her eyes as he handed her the messages awaiting her. She had thought she might take tea in the lobby, but decided against it, given its present atmosphere. The war, she thought. It's like a disease, infecting everyone's mood. Even Luther, the elevator operator, normally the most cheerful of men, seemed in a funk. His long face was bereft of its usual smile and his green eyes looked as flat and dull as pond water after a storm. Instead of making conversation, he stared straight ahead. At the third floor landing, he opened the door for the one other passenger, an elderly gentlemen with a bright pink face and white moustache, and let him go without a farewell; and when Lily, as she got off, remarked that she would see him again in a bit, he replied that he was finished for good in half an hour.

"But why are you leaving?" She would be sorry to see him go. The Pelham had a very good standard of service, but Luther's willingness to run errands for her always seemed to have less to do with the tip he might earn than with a genuine desire to be of help.

"It's the accent, miss."

"Your accent?" She was so used to it that she hardly heard it anymore; but of course, she suddenly realized, it was German.

"Some people, they don't think it's right."

"That's horribly unfair," Lily said. As well as a wife, she remembered, he had two boys and his mother to look after.

He shrugged and said, "It's the times." There was no anger in his voice, just a terrible resignation.

She reached into her purse and pulled out some bills. When he refused them, she said, "Don't be silly. Think of your children." And she hurried away so that she would not have to deal with his gratitude, which would be too much for so little. Could some of the hotel's guests have complained? Once she would have thought it impossible, but one only had to read the newspapers. People these days seemed capable of the most appallingly small-minded behavior. She would lodge a protest with the manager in the morning, she decided. Perhaps others would as well, other guests who found the idea of Luther as a spy as ridiculous as she; and if sufficient numbers did speak up for him, his job might be saved. *Vox Populi*. It could do good, as well as ill. Really, she counseled herself as she entered the suite, she must try harder to follow Dr. Bettelman's excellent advice and not take such a dismal view of matters, until she was certain they could not be put right.

She walked through the dark sitting room to the bedroom, and turned on the lights. According to the clock on the night table, it was six-forty — later than she had thought. There was no time for tea, no time to rest; but she would have a bath. That would relax her. She removed her hat and coat, and laid them on the bed. Taking the invitations from her tapestry purse, she put them on the dressing table. Tomorrow, on the train, she would draw up her guest list. (She would ask no more than twenty, she thought). From the drawer, she took enough money to replace what she had given to Luther, and dropped the purse on the boudoir chair. Then, she opened the telephone messages she had collected from the desk. There was one from her mother, another from Darius Menlo. The latter could wait for the morning, she decided: she had had enough of him for one day. Her mother she would call before leaving the hotel to meet the Berlins. Going into the bathroom, she started the water running, and then returned to the bedroom to choose something to wear. Her new beaded black silk she had worn for dinner one night with Darius; the green silk for dinner with Louis; which left the silver georgette. She loved how gracefully the fabric fell against her body; how tiny the belt made her waist seem; how the uneven hem, revealing her ankles, gave the dress an aura of daring despite the high neckline and elbow-length sleeves. She hesitated a moment (it seemed a pity to waste that particular dress on Alice and Teddy, who would not care at all how she looked), and then chose the green silk. It would do perfectly well; and Alice would not be wearing anything new. Despite the improvement in their fortunes, money was still an issue for her friends, as it was not for her in any significant way. Thanks to Edmund, Lily now understood that money was something one had to keep in mind, if one hoped to stop friendships from spoiling.

A thought struck her. Perhaps she ought not to have suggested Delmonico's? But surely Teddy and Alice would have said no, if they considered it beyond their means. They must know they did not have to stand on ceremony with her. Well, it was too late to worry about it, thought Lily, as she returned to the bathroom to test the temperature of the water. She added a bit of cold and tested it again. Perfect. Stripping off her underclothes, she left them in a silken heap on the tile floor and stepped into the tub, easing herself into the steaming water. There were many things she liked to do, many places she enjoyed going that were not expensive. Next time, she would keep her friends' finances in mind before suggesting an entertainment. Her head was a dull ache from forehead to nape. Leaning back against the white porcelain of the tub, she closed her eyes.

By the time Lily bathed, fixed her hair into a neat coil, donned the silk dress, slipped pearls around her neck and into her ears, and, in place of a hat, tied a narrow bandeau sporting a green feather around her head, it was close to seven-thirty. She had been looking forward to seeing her friends, but now that it was time to leave to join them, she found herself reluctant to go. She regretted having told Alice and Teddy that she was in town, regretted making the appointment to dine. A quiet night was what she needed. Since arriving in the city, she had been running around far too much.

She considered sending a message that she could not make it. Her headache would be excuse enough. Surveying herself critically in the dressing table mirror, she saw that she did indeed look a little pale. She hesitated. Could she do it? But no, she could not. They would worry, Alice especially. They would think she was on the verge of something awful, when she was just a little tired. It was exhausting, really, having to expend so much time and energy convincing everyone that she was perfectly well. Taking the cake of rouge from her cosmetic purse, she applied a bit to her cheeks, rubbed off the excess with the heel of her hand, and dusted her face with powder. Much better, she thought, as she pulled a few wisps free from the tight roll of her hair, softening the effect. She ought to get it bobbed. Now that her father was no longer here to protest, she could not imagine why she hesitated. Keeping it long was nothing but an endless chore, washing it, drying it, pinning it up; and the pins made her head ache even more. She would get it cut tomorrow, before catching the train home, she decided. Her mother, bless her, would only smile and tell her she looked lovely.

Taking her velvet evening coat from the closet, Lily put it on, put some money, a handkerchief, and a comb into her beaded evening bag, and made her way through the dark rooms to the door. She knew very well why she was reluctant to turn on the light. She did not want to look at the sketches she had left out to dry. Sooner or later, she would have to, of course, but not yet. When she returned, if her head felt better, she thought as she closed the door firmly behind her, she would look at them then.

When the elevator came in response to her call, it was John operating it, not Luther. So he's gone, thought Lily. A feeling of weary inevitability crept over her, for John, too, who was no more than eighteen, would no doubt soon disappear, called up by the threatened draft, if he did not volunteer first. His boyish face lit with admiration when he saw her. "Good evening, Miss Canning," he said.

"John," she replied, nodding agreeably, before stepping to the back of the elevator out of his line of vision. Usually she liked to chat with the staff, but tonight she could not muster a thing to say.

Sensing her mood, John remained silent. When the doors opened again on the ground floor, his good-bye was barely audible.

Crossing the lobby, Lily saw Mr. Locke, the hotel's manager, who surely ought to have left by now; but perhaps he had been so busy firing people all day that he had found it necessary to stay later than usual. He saw her and smiled; and though Lily felt a great reluctance to do the same, she forced herself. After all, he had always been enormously helpful to her, assisting her through some of the worst moments of her life with great discretion. She also thought it not a particularly good idea to alienate him, if she hoped to change his mind about Luther. "Good evening, Mr. Locke," she called. For a moment, she considered broaching the subject with him then, but decided against it. There was no time, for one thing, not if she wished to speak to her mother before leaving the hotel; nor, when she thought about it, did she feel up to having the conversation. It would require more stamina, more coherence, more firmness of purpose than she believed herself capable of just at the moment. "I'd like a word with you in the morning, if you don't mind," she said, more to confirm her intentions to herself than to give the manager advance notice. Once she made a commitment, she stuck to it—if she possibly could, she corrected herself, as an image of Edmund flitted through her head.

"Any time that suits you, Miss Canning," the manager replied. "I'm completely at your disposal."

"Thank you," she said, continuing on across the Oriental carpet toward the telephone, which was located in a glass-fronted booth off a small salon. She closed the door behind her, sat on the low stool, picked up the black receiver, and gave the operator Riverhall's number. In what seemed to her, as always, an amazingly short time considering the distance involved, she heard Nuala on the other end of the line and called into the mouthpiece, "Nuala, hello—"

"Miss, is that you?" Her voice, crackling over the wire, sounded far away and hollow, like the voice on a phonograph record.

"Yes. Can you hear me? Is everything all right there?"

There was a slight hesitation, which Lily found troubling; then, she heard Nuala say, "Yes, it's all very well, miss."

"Could I speak with my mother, please?"

"She's gone to bed, a while ago now. I just looked in on her and she's sound asleep."

"But it's so early. You said everything was all right!"

"It is, Miss Lily. Mrs. Canning was feeling a mite tired, that's all."

"Did she have any pain?"

"Not that she mentioned."

Lily sighed and then asked, "Do you know why she telephoned me?"

"No, miss, sorry. Though she was wanting to know if you was still coming home tomorrow."

"Yes, but I don't know yet what train I'll be taking. I'll telephone again in the morning, when I've decided."

"I'll tell her so, when she wakes."

"Thank you, Nuala."

"Bye, miss."

As she replaced the receiver, Lily became aware that her heart was racing. Remaining seated, she breathed deeply, holding each breath for a long while, in the hope that her heart would slow, her throat would stay open, and the anxiety lurking nearby, waiting to grab hold of her, would be held at bay. Her mother was fine, she told herself; if anything was wrong, Nuala would have urged her to come home immediately; she would never have dared to take responsibility for keeping her away if her mother were—

No! Everything at home was all very well, just as Nuala had said.

Someone was waiting to use the telephone, Lily noticed, a rather round man with a fringe of gray hair encircling his bald dome like a Roman hero's laurel wreath. He was in evening dress. With a murmured greeting, he bowed slightly as she walked past him out of the booth.

"Good evening," replied Lily with a smile. He looked a sweet old codger, in town on holiday, she imagined as she walked away, from somewhere like . . . oh, Sioux City or Twin Falls. Yes, there was his wife, the small dowdy woman in the plum-colored gown and matching turban, seated in the salon, clearly waiting for someone. A match, if ever Lily saw one. They were no doubt on their way to the theater — no, the opera, and after that to a late night supper somewhere splendid, like Sherry's. It was their anniversary, she went on fantasizing, their fortieth; and they could, if they liked, afford to commission a portrait of themselves to commemorate the happy event, to hang above the mantle back home in . . . where was it? Wichita Springs? She almost wished to offer to do one. There was something about them, her idea of them, she found touching, and enviable: their long happy years together, the children, the grandchildren, the good health, the successful business, the placidity of their spirits, the regularity with which all their dreams came true.

It was a foolish thing to do, to envy people whose lives, for all she knew, might be completely diabolical. Why was it, she wondered, that she was able to imagine the happiest of circumstances for total strangers, while for herself, too often, she could foresee only the bleakest of futures? It seemed so unfair. She ought to be able to do better on her own behalf.

"Taxi, Miss Canning?" asked Walter, as Lily swept out of the hotel.

"Yes, please." Here was another boy destined for the war machine, she thought, watching as he raced beyond the parked automobiles and waiting drivers to the corner in search of a cab.

The damp made it seem colder than it was, and Lily pulled her thin coat tight about her as she waited. People were coming out of the hotel on their way to a night's entertainment, the men in top hats, the women wearing jeweled combs and fur wraps. Some of the men set out on foot; many of the couples got into the waiting limousines; a few stood grumbling about the absence of the doorman and the lack of taxis. Finally, Walter returned with a cab, helped Lily into her seat, relayed her destination to the driver, and wished her a good evening, before turning his attention to the impatient couple next in the queue.

She must try to have a better attitude, thought Lily. She really did not want to go on always expecting the worst. It was too exhausting. It wore her out. And it was not as if, looked at from a wider perspective — as Dr. Bettelman always suggested she do — her life had been so very awful. True, terrible things had happened to her, but who did not lose a father to death at some point? She at least had had hers until she was into her twenties. As for Edmund, well, she ought to be grateful that she had been able to extricate herself from a bad situation so quickly, instead of having to endure it for a lifetime as so many women did. Her quickness to act had shown great strength of character, or so Dr. Bettelman had said. Not only had she taken a stand and delivered herself from danger, she had insisted on her right to lead the life she chose, the life she needed to live, a life devoted to her work, free of domestic entanglements and petty tyrannies. She ought to be proud of herself; and she was, sometimes to the point of elation; but at other times she feared that escaping Edmund had used up what strength she had, leaving her with no reserves to cope with even the most trivial setbacks, let alone major ones, like . . . A painting she had done once came into Lily's mind. It was of a gazebo, perched on a cliff overlooking the Hudson. An outpost of a house belonging to friends of her parents, it was a pretty thing, all Victorian gingerbread, with a wonderful view of a long stretch of the river. Late one summer, the cliff had given way in a storm. The gazebo had slipped off its foundation and into the water. That's how she often felt, like a fragile construct teetering on the brink, its supports, worn by the relentless assaults of time and circumstance, giving way slowly, threatening to send her hurtling down . . . down . . .

Within minutes, the taxi covered the short distance to Delmonico's, did a swooping u-turn, and drew to a stop behind a long line of cars in front of the Fifth Avenue entrance. Though she had been in the area only a few hours before, the place seemed transformed to Lily, the busy hustle of the daytime street replaced by the night's lamp-lit elegance, the serviceable wool of clothes exchanged for luxurious taffetas and silks. The rich came here often, along with the famous, even the notorious, for dinner in the main restaurant, for more select gatherings in private salons, for grand affairs in the ballroom; but the less affluent came as well, if not so frequently. Lily's parents had celebrated their anniversaries at Delmonico's; and they had hosted parties for her there on her eighteenth and twenty-first birthdays. She, however, saw no reason to wait for such special occasions. Not that she was profligate with money, but the restaurant was not so expensive, and it was awfully good. It was entertaining, too, watching the people in such a place. But its major attraction for her, what she liked best about it, was how close it made her feel to her father. He had loved the city, its luxury and its entertainments, often going off on his own to enjoy them. Though Lily had sometimes resented that (and never more so than when he died there, instead of at Riverhall, where he ought to have been, with her mother and herself), after his death, when she began to go about alone, she had come to understand and, she believed, to share his pleasure; and when she was at Delmonico's, enjoying the fine cuisine, the French wines, the luxurious decor, she felt close to him. Even now, she sensed him near as she made her way through the familiar, crowded lobby, and it was for his sake as much as for her friends' that she forced a smile to her face when she caught sight of herself in the mirror of the ladies' lounge. After checking her coat with the uniformed attendant, she smoothed her hair, adjusted her dress, closed her eyes for a minute, then took a deep breath, which got enough wind into her sails to carry her from the lounge to the restaurant, where Teddy and Alice were already seated.

"You look lovely," said Teddy, standing to greet her. He took her hand and ducked his head to kiss her cheek, though not before Lily caught sight of the worry in his eyes.

It was there in Alice's, too, as she kissed Lily hello.

"Have you been waiting long?"

"Long enough to have sampled the Madeira," said Teddy. He reached for the bottle to pour some of the chilled wine into her glass, waving off a waiter, who instead held Lily's chair as she sat.

She took a sip. "It's lovely. Just what I needed. It's been quite a day."

"You were at the gallery?" asked Alice.

Lily nodded and grimaced. "You should have heard Darius picking out every little flaw in my sorry little work. It was deeply discouraging."

"I'm sure it was, and that isn't even the worst of it," said Teddy. "Wait until you return to hang the damn paintings! Darius inevitably insists on putting the one you most loathe right up front."

Alice laughed and said, "Remember Teddy before his last show? Or me, for that matter? You seem a bastion of good sense in comparison."

"I did convince Darius to let me give him two new ones. Perhaps they'll revive his enthusiasm. And mine."

"New paintings or not," said Alice, "wait until opening night. When you hear him speak of you then, you'll begin to think you're this century's answer to Michelangelo and Rembrandt combined."

They all laughed, and the conversation paused while Lily studied the menu. "Do you know what you're having?" she asked. When Teddy said the crab and lobster en casserole, she considered changing her mind, but then decided against it. What was the point in coming here if not to order her favorite foods? "I'll have the Blue Point oysters to start," she told the Maitre d', when Alice had made her selection, "and then the Hudson River shad. I used to go fishing for shad, with my mother," she said when he had gone. "That is, Mama fished. I sketched mostly, unless she needed my help." She thought of the spring mornings in the rowboat on the river; the sun rising over the wooded hills; the songs of the ovenbird, the veery, the wood thrush, hidden in the trees along the shore; her mother's skillful fingers handling the linen net; the iridescent rainbow colors of the shad as they came out of the silver water.

"Your mother?" said Teddy.

Lily laughed. "Well, she does do a very good imitation of a lady, but at heart she's a complete tomboy. She grew up on the river. She knows it the way you do the street where you live. The winds, the tides, the best places to fish. My poor father!" she added, with a rueful laugh. "How he worried when we were out in the boat. Always afraid of sudden storms, or some such disaster. And when Mama took me skating, in winter . . ." She grimaced. "You never saw such a look of pure terror on a man's face, if he got home early and caught us at it."

"I'm surprised she had the courage to try an end run around his wishes," said Teddy. "He was absolutely charming, your father, but a formidable man, not one I'd think of crossing."

"Oh, she didn't, often. Not unless she was absolutely sure of her ground. And to her," said Lily, with another little laugh, "the river was terra firma, so to speak. He was a cautious man, at least where I was concerned, but not unreasonable. Never unreasonable. He was so good. One really wished only to please him."

"You knew he had your best interests at heart," said Alice.

"Oh, yes," said Lily. "Always. He was a rock I knew would never give way, no matter how fierce the storm." There was a small tremor in her voice. "I do miss him."

"I know you do," said Teddy. "He was a fine gentleman and the best of fathers, I'm sure. But, really, Lily, when you total up his hopes for you, and his fears, not to mention your desire to please him, don't you think that perhaps all of that constrained you somehow? Isn't there a wonderful freedom in having no one to answer to but yourself?"

"Freedom," repeated Lily. "Everyone always talks about it as the most desirable thing in the world. Everyone wants it, or claims to. I do, certainly. But haven't you found it can be quite terrifying?"

"Terrifying, perhaps. But exhilarating."

Lily thought of the times when, even as a young girl, she had wished to be off somewhere, completely alone, owing nothing to anyone. Sometimes, she had imagined that, if she could just get away, her headaches might stop. "Do you suppose anyone is ever completely free?" she asked.

Teddy glanced at his wife, turned back to Lily, and said, "Not *completely*, I suppose. Alice and I, for example, here we are, bound to each other by ties of love and law, and the rules of the society that fashioned us, some of which we can't quite manage to escape. Or don't want to

314

escape. Rules of civility, of good manners, which require us to be considerate of one another. But I never think of her as standing between me and freedom."

"No?" countered Lily. "Yet I've heard you disagree, and vehemently. To make it possible to stay together, one of you must surely have to give in to the other. And doesn't that represent a surrender of freedom?"

"A small one, perhaps," said Teddy, "but for a greater good. If one only acted in self-interest, freedom wouldn't be the result, but anarchy."

"Or is it that you feel so completely free because you do just what you please, and it's Alice who compromises?"

"I don't think—" began Teddy.

Rushing to her husband's defense, Alice said, "In fairness, both Teddy and I make compromises, Lily. As you said, it's what makes life together possible. But only in small matters—small to us, at any rate. Because one can't truly be a person and choose . . . well, bondage, I suppose. One can't willingly agree to have the movements of one's mind or heart or soul dictated by another. Though at times it would be much more comfortable just to give one's self up entirely without a struggle, just to say yes." She smiled at Teddy, a bit ruefully, Lily thought, and added, "Especially when one is in love."

"Yes, yes, I know. One can't do that. But surely it's not a question of giving one's self up entirely?" said Lily. "To anyone, or anything. But we do have to trim our sails to the wind. No matter how much we may want freedom — as you said, there are rules. There *have* to be rules. Without them . . . why, it's like trying to find one's way through unfamiliar, even treacherous territory without a map."

"Yes. Still, that's how the most amazing discoveries are made," said Teddy. "The Americas, for example, found by explorers who were hopelessly lost."

"They were the lucky ones," said Lily.

"And the only ones Teddy allows himself to think about." Alice smiled. "There are no shipwrecked sailors in his philosophy. Everyone makes it to the new world."

"Not everyone. No," said Teddy. "If there were no risk, there'd be no glory. But what's the point in dwelling on the *idea* of failure?"

The conversation had shifted somehow. It was no longer about relationships, but about work. Teddy was lecturing her, realized Lily, and she could not help feeling that he was being unfair. It was not a simple matter to find one's way in these new and confusing times. "But surely it's important to consider one's mistakes, to learn from them?"

"By all means. But one can't allow them to destroy one's faith, sap one's energy, rob one of the will to go on."

"No, certainly not," said Lily. "But it's very hard, especially now when everything seems so topsy-turvy."

"It does take courage," said Alice. "But one can usually find a scrap of it lying around somewhere."

"Usually, repeated Lily. "Not always, though." But the turn of the conversation had brought to mind her visits to the Modern; and, when the waiter had settled their appetizers before them and opened the bottle of Muscadet, after she had sampled the oysters and pronounced them delicious, she told her friends about her experiences there. "Looking at the painting," she said, "I began to see that it's Picasso's understanding of the rules, his mastery of them, that gives him the courage to throw them away. No," she corrected herself, "not throw them away. Transform them. I began to see allusions, connections . . ."

"I suppose even radical change must be somehow linked to what came before," said Alice, "though the relationship might not be obvious at first."

Lily nodded. "Exactly. When I realized that, I felt . . . well, as if my talents hadn't after all been pushed so ruthlessly aside, reduced to complete irrelevancy. I felt it was at least worth trying to do something original. I finished a landscape, and began work on a self-portrait. It's unlike anything I've done before. At first, I thought it was amazing; and then, a complete failure. Now, I'm not sure which it is."

"None of us understands where we're headed," said Teddy. "We're all stumbling around in the dark, looking for the door into the future."

"I'll have another go at it when I get home. I'll finish it if I can. If I can't, I'll start another. When I think about my exhibition," Lily went on, "about the paintings I've done, they all seem so insignificant somehow. I must have something new."

"You mustn't push yourself too hard," said Alice.

"No, but I must have at least two more, all the same."

"Lily, it will hardly matter—" said Teddy.

"I must," insisted Lily.

"Your paintings are wonderful. You have to hold on to that idea."

He spoke forcefully enough, and Lily wished to believe him; but she could not help feeling, as she often did, that Teddy's praise lacked conviction. She shrugged. "If only the critics would be so kind to me—"

"It's not a question of kindness!"

"And if they're not," continued Lily, "I'm afraid I'll dissolve into a pool of self-pity. Dry up like a puddle in the sun."

"Rubbish," said Teddy. "You'll do what we all do when the critics draw blood. You'll patch the wound, give it time to heal, and set to work again, because really you've no choice."

"You're apprehensive about the opening," Alice said. "Anyone would be. Remember me, before mine? And that was a group show. I could hope to be overlooked. But you'll get through it all right. Everyone does, one way or another."

"Yes," said Lily. "First-night nerves." A memory lightened her mood, and she smiled. "I remember you very well. You spent most of the evening in the ladies' room, being sick."

"I did."

Lily shook her head. "What we do to ourselves!"

"The show will be a great success," said Alice.

"I feel that sometimes, too," said Lily. "Sometimes I know that I'm incredibly talented, that my work is sublime, and that the critics will tremble with awe to see it."

Teddy raised his wine glass. "To success."

"To success," echoed Lily and Alice, as the three tapped their glasses for luck.

"You haven't finished your oysters," said Teddy, as the busboy appeared to clear the table for the next course.

"I'm not really very hungry," said Lily, setting down her wine glass. "Darius gave me a bit of a headache today. Though it's better now." She closed her eyes for a moment as if trying to banish the pain behind them. When she opened them again and smiled, she did indeed seem to be completely well. And then the next course came, and the conversation shifted to talk of war.

"It was delicious, truly," Lily insisted a while later to the Maitre d' when he remarked on how little of the shad she had managed to eat. "I'm just not very hungry, though I will have the Baked Alaska for dessert. I can never resist that."

Nor could Alice and Teddy, though they had cleaned their plates. "And coffee for us all," said Teddy.

Gossip carried them through to the end of the meal; and, as they came out of Delmonico's and sheltered from the rain under the canopy, Alice said, "What shall we do now?" It was early yet, and there were clubs where they might go to hear music, others where they might dance.

"President calls for declaration of war!" shouted a newsboy, causing a rush of passersby toward him, all wanting the late night extra.

"Oh, no," said Lily.

"So it's come at last," said Teddy, tossing the boy a coin in return for a paper.

"What does it say?" Alice peered over her husband's shoulder for a look at the headline, as the boy repeated his cry, over and over, selling out in a matter of minutes.

318

"If you don't mind," said Lily, "I think I'd like to have an early night."

"Your head still bothering you?" asked Alice, returning her attention to her friend.

"It's more a matter of the train I want to catch in the morning."

"We'll see you to your hotel," said Teddy, folding the paper and tucking it under his arm.

"That's foolish. You go on and have a good time. Try to forget the news, horrid as it is. I intend to. I'm just going to pull the covers over my head and go to sleep."

"If you're sure," said Teddy.

"Absolutely."

"Goodnight, darling," said Alice as she and Lily exchanged kisses. "Let us know when you return to town. And if not before, we'll see you next month at the opening. Remember, you're not to worry. Everything will go splendidly."

Lily nodded, and then tilted her head for Teddy's kiss. "It will, you know. You'll be a great hit," he said.

A taxi drew to a stop at the curb, the doorman opened its door, Teddy handed him a tip, settled Lily inside, and gave the driver the hotel's address.

They stood waving for a moment, and then Teddy put his arm around Alice, pulling her close. To be so much in love must be a great comfort at times like this, thought Lily, as she watched them through the taxi's rear window. She faced forward. The cab's headlamps threw up brief glimpses of Fifth Avenue, pieces of a puzzle the daylight would solve. Yes, her friends had disagreements; she had been present when they argued; she had felt tension between them at times, over what she had no idea, though she thought Teddy sometimes patronized Alice, and that she demeaned herself unnecessarily by accepting without question the superior value of Teddy's work. But, just as they said, nothing seemed to undermine the foundation of their relationship, its essential solidity. They trusted each other. Trust. That, to Lily, seemed the key. But perhaps it was not. Perhaps it was just that their love was strong enough to stifle doubt — or to live with it.

She wondered if things might have turned out differently if she had not caught Edmund in that first lie. It had not even been such a terrible lie, as he had been quick to point out, just a man's ploy to capture the attention of a woman who interested him. There was no great harm in it, he had said. And yet, there had been, for it had robbed her of her blind faith in him. It had planted seeds of contempt in her mind, which had required only a little nourishment from other small lies to grow, like the bindweed that her mother worked so diligently to keep out of the garden, putting down deep roots, its delicate tendrils sprouting relentlessly, curling around her heart, smothering every trace of the tenderness, the *love* she felt for him, so there was none left to come to his aid when he begged her to forgive his last, great lie.

She now knew she had the strength of character not to succumb to deceit, to cruelty, to force; it was kindness she could not resist, and love, true love, not the mirror image of it that Edmund had felt, seeking only his reflection in her eyes, not the fever in her blood that had blinded her to his faults. Love had been her father's hold on her: he had known her completely and cared for her beyond reason. She would have stayed in thrall to him forever, had he lived; but from Edmund she could not escape quickly enough; and never, in all her life, had she felt more free than at the moment she fled from him.

❧

Lily opened the door to her suite and stood on the threshold, reluctant to enter. Then, impatiently, she stepped inside, closed the door behind her, and, urging herself not to be such a complete coward, turned on all the lamps.

There they were, the sketches she had made earlier in the day, scattered around the room like enemies waiting in ambush. The air seemed charged with danger. With great reluctance, she walked from one to the other, studying each for a moment, before picking it up and adding it to the growing pile in her arms. Not one of them was worth a damn, she thought. Oh, yes, they had their redeeming features. They were well drawn. The composition had promise. But there was nothing new in them, nothing interesting. They had no life.

When she picked up the last, she considered tossing them all into the trash, but she hesitated. They might not seem so bad to her in a few days. She might find a way past the flaws. They were only sketches, after all. Without looking at them again, she placed them in the holder of her box easel, got the brushes she had left drying by the sink and put them away as well, closed the case, and left it on the floor by the dining table.

It was only then that she realized she was still wearing her velvet coat. Going into the bedroom, she took it off, draped it over the back of the boudoir chair, removed the bandeau from her head, and, taking her grandmother's long pearls from around her neck, looped them over the edge of the dressing table mirror. As she removed her earrings, she caught sight of her face. Dropping the studs into her jewelry case, she sat on the stool and stared at the image looking back at her with such troubled dark eyes. Once again, as she did more and more often, Lily caught sight of the old woman she would one day become.

She shivered. Yes, she was afraid of growing old, though she could see, in her mother and Aunt Edith at any rate, that it was nothing so terrible, that each age brought its own afflictions, and each could be borne with resolution and humor. Nevertheless, the fear remained. Among the things she had been trying to capture in her most recent self-portrait was this, the terror beneath the surface calm, and the sense of loss, not of youth so much, as of hope, its hallmark. While recently she had put up a good show for the benefit of others, and managed sometimes to fool even herself, it seemed to Lily that she, who had been such an amazingly brave

321

and self-assured child, had somewhere along the way lost confidence in everything: in her looks, her judgment, her nerve, her resiliency, and — above all — her talent. Instead of the endless possibilities that had beckoned to her so tantalizingly when she was younger, what she saw now in her future was a narrow road leading to a predictable and dreary end.

Did she wish to keep to that road? Did she have the strength to do it? The courage? Could she sustain the interest year after year? No matter how often she pushed them from her mind, shoved them out of the way, refused to consider their implications, the questions kept returning to torment her. Do you really wish to go on? Do you? Surely there's no point, some wicked inner voice kept repeating.

Her throat was tightening, her lungs closing. Her breathing was coming in short, painful gasps. She would never be able to sleep. She needed air. Quickly, without thinking, she picked up the wool coat from the bed where she had thrown it earlier in the day, and slipped it on, tugging impatiently to free the silk sleeve of her dress caught against the wings of the butterfly pin in the lapel. Snatching up her hat, she put that on as well, grabbed her tapestry purse, and hurried through the rooms to the door, not bothering to turn out the lights as she left. After jabbing the call button twice, she waited impatiently for the elevator's arrival, and then entered with barely a nod to John, who looked at her with some surprise as he greeted her. But she certainly did not have to explain her comings and goings to him. *Let* him wonder where she was off to. In any case, she did not know herself. "Goodnight, John," she murmured, as the door opened again. Crossing the lobby, she took no notice of the few men still gathered there, drinking brandy and smoking cigars, who stopped their huddled conversations to watch her curiously as she walked by. Passing the desk, she nodded to the clerk. He, too, looked at her strangely, she thought. But what did she care?

Despite the rain, Lily refused Walter's offer to fetch her a cab, and started walking east, taking deep breaths as she went, sucking the cool, wet air into her lungs. One breath, two, three. But they were doing no good. She felt as if a giant hand were slowly squeezing her shut, forcing all the air from her body. What was she to do?

Company might perhaps help, friends to distract her. Turning south on Fifth Avenue, she considered going to Teddy and Alice's. They would not at all mind her turning up. They would understand. Though they might not have returned to their studio, but stopped off somewhere to dance or listen to music, despite the awful news, or perhaps because of it. Well, what about Louis? Would a young man be at home at this hour, or still out with his pals? She would stop by to ask, for he above all would be delighted to see her. He would not even think it strange that on her last night in New York, with the war about to snatch away all their good times, she had changed her mind and decided to have a bit of fun.

At the next corner, she turned west again, heading toward Seventh Avenue. She walked quickly, breathing deeply, trying to ease the tightness in her chest. It would go — she knew that, but when? She did not think she could stand it for long.

It was after eleven and the streets were quiet, with only an occasional taxi or automobile rumbling by. Young couples, absorbed in each other, took no notice of her at all; but middle-aged ones, on their way home after an evening's entertainment, eyed her as she passed; and young men in groups called out, but let her be when she did not respond. What must she look like? she wondered, with her clothes bedraggled, her poor hat a sodden mess. Someone demented? someone to be pitied? despised?

At last she reached the building where Louis lived, climbed the few steps to the door, and went in. A clerk was on duty behind the desk in the lobby, an older man, very thin, with spectacled, deep-set eyes that looked reluctantly up from the newspaper he was reading. Too old for the draft, thought Lily. He's safe. "Is Mr. Allen in, do you know?" she asked.

"I'm afraid not, miss," he said.

"Ah," she sighed and turned to leave.

"May I tell him who stopped by?"

"You needn't bother," she said, over her shoulder. She doubted the clerk would remember to mention her, which was just as well. Louis would mind having missed her. "Goodnight," she called politely.

Where to now? she wondered when back outside again. She walked uptown for a while along Seventh Avenue, but this street was more crowded, full of young revelers, and she found their boisterousness helped neither her head, which ached dully, nor her labored breathing. She considered going back to the Pelham and at least trying to sleep, but dismissed the notion, for she knew she would not be able to until she could breathe more easily; and then, almost certainly, the nightmare would come. God help me, she thought.

Behind her, she heard the rattle of a taxi and stepped to the curb to flag it down; and because she did not look quite as disreputable as she imagined, it stopped.

"Where to, miss?" asked the driver, as Lily opened the door and got in.

"The river," she said, though she had not known until that moment where she meant to go.

"The river?"

"Riverside Drive," she said more calmly. That sounded far more reasonable.

Often at home, when she could not sleep, she would go out onto the porch and sit in the dark, looking at the river. Sometimes, she would even walk down the sloping lawn to its edge. The river was treacherous, of course she knew that. Not only had she had heard stories her entire life about just how treacherous, but she had witnessed it do its worst. She had seen schooners run aground, sailboats keeled over in storms. Yet, she could not think of it as dangerous. Ever-changing and mysterious, yes, but not dangerous. Watching its movement, as graceful as a dance, hearing its sound, more soothing than music, calmed her mind, lifted her spirits. "Cast your bread upon the waters," the Bible said, but what Lily cast were her troubles, and the river bore them away.

"Do you have an address, miss?" asked the driver.

"Just a bit farther on." A moment later, in front of the entrance to one of the row houses, she said, "Here will do. Thank you." She took some coins from her purse, paid him the fare, tipped him, and then waited until, with a last perplexed look at her, he turned his taxi around and disappeared in an instant around the corner. Gazing for a moment up at the house, Lily saw that all the lights were out. Everyone safe at home, she thought, in bed, dreaming sweet dreams. Such peace seemed a small thing to want, and yet, though it came easily enough to others, to Rosaline, for example, dear Roz, who inhabited her own busy little world with happy contentment, whatever way Lily turned looking for it, always it eluded her, slipping out of her grasp before she could quite grab hold, before she could get her arms around it and hold it fast.

Crossing the street, Lily entered the park, keeping to the lighted path, taking the steps down toward the river. Somewhere behind her, she heard an automobile come to a stop, voices speaking in hushed tones, a stifled laugh carried on the night air, a door slammed shut. More happy people coming home, she thought, as the sound of the car receded into the distance.

Soon, she came to the stone wall that kept strollers like herself from wandering down onto the railroad tracks. As always, she felt a surge of irritation. A law had been passed ages ago giving people the right-of-way to the river, but the Dock Commission and the New York Central together had managed to thwart it, keeping the riverfront for commercial use. As happy an invention as the railroad was, surely a better route for it could have been found, somewhere inland. It seemed a desecration to her, all this despoiled beauty.

A train roared by below, and hurtled off again. The quiet rose up and enfolded her. It had stopped raining. When she stood still, she could hear the wind soughing through the trees, animals rustling among the bushes, opossums perhaps, and raccoons; above all, she could hear herself fighting to breathe. She suspected there might be rats and wished she had changed into more sensible shoes, not that she felt herself in danger of attack, not from the animals who passed so near, or the vagrants who were no doubt hoping to evade the police and catch some sleep on the park's benches, which were at least free, if not comfortable. Nothing, no one, outside herself wished her ill; she knew that. She had only herself to fear, herself and her aching head and ragged breath and the troubling voices within.

Beginning to walk again, she followed the path that bordered the wall. The way was familiar, for she had often come here with friends, with Edmund, or alone to sketch the river, sometimes wandering as far north as Inwood Hill Park, finding new perspectives to interest her, new problems to solve in color and composition. She had tried to capture the changing play of light on the broad span of water; the elegant ease or storm-tossed trouble of the schooners hauling fruit and coal and all manner of freight; the glint of sunlight on the Jersey Palisades, stands of evergreen and birch, alder and maple crowning their broad heads, railroad terminals and factories clustered like giant carbuncles at their feet.

When she reached the bridge leading to the Columbia Yacht Club, Lily realized she must, after all, have had a purpose in coming this way. Below her, the club sat on the far side of the railroad tracks, a small civilized patch of land jutting out into the river, a suggestion of the uses to which the shore might be put, were it not for John D. Rockefeller and his like. The bungalow was lighted, and Lily could hear music. There was a dance going on. Yes, she remembered, Louis had wanted them to come. People were already leaving, but wrapped in an alcoholic fog, they took no notice of her as she slipped past them, entering before the gate slammed shut and locked. She crossed the bridge over the tracks and went down the stairs to the patio. As she made her way around the building, she caught glimpses through the windows of flags and bunting and balloons, of an orchestra playing, of young people in smart clothes, but not Louis among them, and she had no wish to speak to Johnnie Crawford, or any of the others she recognized.

326

At the balustrade on the far side of the lawn, she stopped. A lighted battleship went past, heading for its mooring down river, leaving the idea of war in its wake. She looked up, hoping to see at least a glimpse of the moon, but there was not a trace of it. A solid layer of ashen clouds hovered like a floating carpet above the world, obscuring the sky and casting a pale eerie light that turned the trees in the park above into ominous charcoal shades, while the river, so beautiful in moonlight, spread out dully before her in a vaporous expanse. Her breathing was easier now, she realized. Inhaling deeply, she savored the cool air. The mist settled on her face like a soothing balm. The worst of the panic had passed. It was not, after all, Louis she had come for, but this. The river was working its magic, and, however temporary, it was welcome.

This had been the pattern for years now, from her adolescence: periods of despair — marked by headaches, nightmares, panic attacks — followed by stretches of normalcy, during which hope gradually returned, and then a few, wonderful weeks of such pure happiness that Lily could believe her misery to have been an aberration, endured and conquered, gone forever. That, however, had always proved a foolish belief, a forlorn hope. Since her father's death, the bouts of despondency had grown worse, the time between them shorter. Last December, just weeks after she left Edmund, her condition had become so severe that she had entered Bloomingdale Hospital, in White Plains, for treatment. There, Dr. Bettelman had helped her to understand that her depressions were a retreat from a reality she found too painful to bear, that the euphoria she sometimes felt was simply another manifestation of the same dilemma. He had encouraged her to think that she might, with knowledge and fortitude, be able to overcome her affliction. For a while, she had felt a brief flaring of . . . optimism perhaps, or possibly just a wistful longing for his words to be true. Then, the headaches had begun again.

Her hands were cold. She had forgotten to put on her gloves. Her purse dangling from her wrist, Lily put her hands into the pockets of her coat, leaned against the balustrade, and stared into the dark, not seeing the river at all, but her future, the long desperate years that lay ahead of her.

She could put an end to it now, right now, put a stop to all the pain, all the fear.

The thought, which at other times had rushed at her with the force of an attacking Mongol horde, came to her calmly. Before, her father had been near, or her mother, Dr. Bettelman, a kindly nurse, someone. She had called out and they had come running. Now, though she did have the strangest sense that her father was hovering somewhere just out of sight, she knew he would not come to help her — no one would; still, amazingly, she was not in the least afraid. The idea did not terrify her as it had in the past. Instead, it comforted her. For once, she did not feel herself to be helpless, at the mercy of hostile forces whose movements she could neither understand, nor predict. She felt in control of her fate. She could put an end to all her wretchedness, all her dread, if she chose. If she chose . . .

But did she? That question, too, came to her more calmly than usual. She had been arguing it with herself for a long while, weighing the different elements of the problem — the moral issue (which she could not quite ignore), the effect on her mother and friends, the work she had yet to do, the possibility that Dr. Bettelman might be right, the probability that he was not — watching as the scales dipped first this way, then that.

Below her, she could hear the soft, rhythmic lapping of the water, a soothing sound, and into her head came some lines from Tennyson: "And at the closing of the day/ She loosed the chain, and down she lay./ The broad stream bore her far away . . ." She thought how lovely it would be to find herself in a boat in the middle of the river, rocked gently to sleep by the movement of the waves. But there were none moored below, for it was still too early in the season. I'll just have to play Ophelia, she thought as the image of the Millais painting came into her mind — the young girl, the pale skin, the loose hair billowing behind her, the arms half open like those of a priestess invoking the spirit of peace, the flow of the embroidered dress, the tranquil horizontal lines of the picture plane, the jewel-like perfection of the roses on the bank, the forget-me-nots in the water. "I would give you some violets," quoted Lily to the night, "but they withered all when my father died."

She had loved her father dearly; she had felt bereft at his death, frightened, too, for he had been the anchor of her life and suddenly she was cut adrift. Yet, to be absolutely honest with herself, as she could not be with Teddy when he raised the issue, she had felt a certain excitement as well, not at first (the grief, then, had been too overwhelming) but later, when her soul had begun to heal. The prospect of freedom had dazzled her. The world had seemed suddenly full of tempting possibilities. She might skate on the river, swooping and spinning till her nose reddened and her toes tingled with cold, till she dropped with exhaustion. She might travel —- to New Mexico like Robert Henri, to Tahiti like Gauguin, to Paris like Mary Cassatt. She might ramble for long hours through the world's great galleries, feasting her eyes on their wonders, never worrying that she might be tiring herself out. She might do anything she damn well pleased.

Now, she knew that it would have been far better to have stayed at home, safe at Riverhall, where her father had wished her to be. Surrounded by what she knew and loved, she might have warded off some of the attacks, and survived those she could not with better grace, less fear. Instead, like a fool, she had given in to the urge for excitement; she had let herself be dazzled by a man with little to recommend him beyond his easy charm. Entranced by his smooth finish, she had failed to look deeper. She had said yes to Edmund Farel; and, by that act, she had completely undermined her trust in her judgment. She had proved her father's point: she really was not able to take care of herself.

To be sure, her relationship with Edmund had not been a total loss. Though she had not got the soul mate she dreamed of, the companion in arms, the dauntless knight able to slay the dragons that lay in wait along the road through life, she had nevertheless come away much wiser, with a

329

deeper knowledge of human nature, of hers in particular. She had learned this truth: however much she might envy the connection between Teddy and Alice, between Rosaline and William, however much she might love Willy and the twins, she did not want a husband; she did not want children. That was why, though she was as given to falling in love as the next girl, she had not seriously responded to Teddy's regard all those years ago, or to anyone's, until Edmund. And why him? She was not sure, though Dr. Bettelman had suggested that it had to do with some need for comradeship, for safety, for someone who could keep her storm-tossed world on a steady keel. Well, she had certainly chosen the wrong man for that!

But what if some day, Dr. Bettelman had asked, she were to find the right one? Her complaints about Edmund were genuine enough, but specific to him. He was a liar and a bully. She had answered that, even had he been a man of impeccable character, hardworking, sincere, and kind, she still would not have wanted to be married to him. Though she had found the physical part of marriage, the lovemaking, wonderfully exciting and satisfying, she could not otherwise bear his presence (not his, or any man's, she was convinced), his always being there, his incessant demands, both spoken and silent, the sense of his need hanging over her like a pall. She had felt stifled by Edmund, desperate to get away. And if she had not stayed in that evening, that awful, wonderful evening, when poor, wretched Amy had come to call, Lily knew she might never have found another such splendid reason to go. Edmund might have found a way to conceal his worst duplicity from her forever.

The memory of that night remained fresh, and painful. Never had she thought to live through such a scene. Never had she thought such a thing could happen to her, Lily Canning. Well, she had wanted real life, and she had got it, sure enough.

Mr. Locke himself had come to tell her that a woman was at the front desk insisting on seeing Mr. Farel. She was acting rather wildly, he said, and ought to be sent away, but he did not like to do it without permission. Later, Lily was not sure why she had told Locke to bring the woman up:

curiosity, she supposed. When the knock came, she had opened the door expecting to see some haggard, mad creature, but instead found a pretty blonde woman, a girl really, surely not yet even twenty, respectably dressed, although not in the latest fashion. "Is Edmund here?" she asked.

"I'm afraid not," said Lily. "He's gone out for the evening."

"Oh," she said, and staggered a little. She glanced at Mr. Locke, who had escorted her up. "I'm sorry. I thought you were lying." Returning her attention to Lily, she went on, "I thought Edmund had refused to see me. That's why I made such a fuss. I've come all this way, you see, all the way from Mobile."

"Won't you come in?" asked Lily. Mr. Locke started to protest, but Lily thanked him and waved him off. She did not believe the girl meant her any harm. "I won't ask you to wait," she said, ushering her into the parlor. "I have no idea when Edmund will be back. But you seem a little unsteady on your feet. You'll want to rest a minute before you go."

"I am very tired," she said.

"Perhaps you'd like a coffee?"

"Just a little water, please." Then, she noticed the portrait. "Why, that's Edmund."

"Yes. I'm painting him. I've almost finished now."

"It's a very good likeness." She seemed on the verge of tears.

"Please, sit down," said Lily. She went to the cooking closet, turned on the tap, filled a glass, and offered it to the woman. She had lovely blue eyes, Lily noticed. "May I ask your name?"

She drained the glass and said, "Amy. Amy Farel."

Thinking how odd it was that he had never mentioned her, Lily dropped into a chair across from her, and said, "Are you related to Edmund, then?"

She looked Lily squarely in the eye. "I'm his wife."

"Wife?" echoed Lily. She felt as if she had suddenly tumbled down the rabbit hole into Wonderland.

"These two years," said Amy. "He left me in Mobile when he came north to find work, you see. And though I minded terribly, I agreed it was best, until he got a little ahead. But he stopped writing, and I didn't know where he was. Then, I ran into a friend of his."

"Two years?" said Lily.

"Mr. Locke said you're his wife. But you're not. I am. I didn't say that to him. I don't know what Edmund's up to, you see. I didn't want to get him into any trouble. But I am his wife. "

"You poor dear," Lily had managed to say. "I'm so sorry."

Never for a moment had she doubted Amy's story. For one thing, she did not seem clever enough to have made it up. And then, there was a sweetness about her, an innocence, and though, at that point, Lily ought to have questioned her ability to judge character, she did not. What she was hearing was the truth, she was certain of it. In any case, Amy had duly produced the marriage license, for what it was worth. There might have been a dozen more Mrs. Farels scattered about the country, yet to be discovered. The strange thing was, though Lily was shocked almost speechless and furiously angry, though she was suffering the same pangs of pain and humiliation at being deceived and dishonored that she saw in Amy's eyes, even then, in those first few moments, Lily was aware of a growing sense of release. She was not married to Edmund. She was not married at all. She was free.

She listened patiently to the whole predictable story of the innocent young typist and the handsome reporter. As soon as she decently could, she ushered Amy out with a promise to send Edmund to her at her hotel as soon as he returned. When the girl was gone, driven by a need she did not stop to examine, Lily began packing her things. If her marriage had been a true one, like most women, happy or not, she might have stuck it out, she supposed later. But there had been no need to. No need at all. Not only was she free to go, she was honor bound to leave.

Without any clear idea of what she would do after taking this next fateful step, Lily had a bellman tie up her canvases and carry them down to the lobby with all her bags but her portmanteau and box easel. Then, still in a welter of conflicting emotions, disappointment and sorrow vying with rage and shame, and, pulsing beneath them all, a terrible sense of relief, she had sat and waited for Edmund's return. And as she listened to him curse the unsuspecting friend who had given Amy his address in New York, listened to his promises to get a divorce, reform his ways, never lie again, Lily had felt the relief flowering into elation. Gladly would she have suffered a much worse beating to earn her freedom back!

Yet, that freedom had not brought with it happiness. Elation had given way again to sadness, which was only to be expected, she had thought at the time, for how could one be duped so badly and *not* be saddened by it? And while the sadness itself had then turned into a sort of wild, singing joy, it too had passed quickly. In its place had come the most abysmal sense of loneliness. She had felt detached, isolated, as if locked in a tower, her tower, her studio at Riverhall, where she spent most of her time, trying to paint meaning back into her life. Then, her mother had suffered another attack. Sitting by her bed when she slept, studying the beloved face, the pink tinge of the closed lids, the aristocratic nose, the skin still smooth except for the fine lines around the eyes and mouth, Lily had wondered what she would do were her mother to die. She would certainly be free then. There would be no constraints on her at all. But, oh, how alone she would be. She found the idea suddenly terrifying. Mama, don't leave me. Please, don't leave me, she had begged, the words tumbling over and over in her mind, endlessly repeating. Once, she must have spoken them aloud, because her mother's eyes had flickered open. "I won't, dear," she had said, her voice barely more than a whisper. She had recovered, and Lily again had felt full of hope, full of energy, as if she could do anything. But soon the sense of dread had returned, and the headaches, and the panic attacks, worse than any she had ever before experienced. It was then Dr. Roeder suggested that a few weeks in White Plains might do her a world of good.

The darkness of depression mitigated by brief, too brief, flashes of joy — that was the set pattern of her life. That was how it would be for her until she died. It was a terrible thought, and Lily waited expectantly for the panic to seize her again; but her breathing remained regular, easy. She felt perfectly calm. No, beyond calm. She felt peaceful.

There was only one way for her to keep hold of this peace. For the price of a little courage, she need never be miserable again. Never. And it was not such a fearful thing, she told herself, remembering the many times she had leapt into the river, from a boat, from a rock on the bank, from a pier. "My little fish," her mother had called her, as Lily swam in the waters below Riverhall through the long, happy summers of her childhood. That was all she had to do now, cast herself upon the water and let the river bear her to the other side, where her father waited.

Her mother, of course, would be left behind, alone and acutely miserable. Did she have the right to inflict so much pain on her? "Poor Mama," she murmured. But her mother's heart was bound to fail any time now. Whatever pain she felt, however great, would be brief. But for Lily, if she failed to act at this moment, while she had the courage, rather than just a few months, there would be years of sorrow and loneliness ahead, especially if, as she feared, the war was to do its worst, taking the men who were like brothers to her, Louis, Marcus, Henry. She could not stand to think about it.

As for the others who would care if she were to die, care deeply, Teddy and Alice, Rosaline, Aunt Edith, all her family and friends, even Nuala, that indomitable girl, her death would not affect them in any profound way. They would not forget her — she hoped they would not — but losing her would not cause them lasting heartache. The powerful current of their own lives would carry them quickly away from their grief.

Moving from the balustrade, she went to the ramp leading to one of the docks and took hold of the rope rail. The ramp rocked beneath her as she walked, and the dock swayed as she went to its end and crouched to dip her hand in the water. It was cold, so cold.

In a short while, she thought, they would all be together again, her father, her mother, herself. Oh, she knew what Reverend Moreland would say, that committing such a terrible sin would doom her to hell: she would be separated from her parents for all eternity. But, if there was a God, and she wanted to believe in one, a God of justice and mercy, He would not be so cruel. And if, after all, there was not, well, in that case, what would it matter?

Wondering whether she should remove her hat and coat, she stood up again. But, no. The more weight, the better. Her wet clothes would drag her down quickly. She would hold her breath. If she was truly lucky, she would pass out before she gasped for air and not even feel the water rushing into her lungs to drown her. Either way, a few moments, that's all, and it would be over.

Thinking she heard a voice behind her, shouting, she turned and looked, but there was no one; then, gazing again out over the water, she imagined she saw her father, his arms open wide.

"Miss, wait," called the voice.

"Lily, come, dear," said her father.

She knew neither was real. Her mind was simply having one last argument with itself.

The image of her father faded, but the idea took hold that she might see him again from the water. She closed her eyes and imagined herself at Riverhall. It was summer, and she was standing in her bathing costume on the bank above the river about to jump in. Yes, she thought, as her feet left the dock and her body sailed through the air, hitting the water with a splash. Oh, it was cold! As she surfaced, she could feel the water reaching for her again, tugging at her clothes, but she resisted it, turning so that she could float on her back. She thought of the self-portrait she had left undone at Riverhall, of all the paintings left undone. But they were no great loss to the world. God knows, she had tried to convince herself otherwise, but she had failed miserably. Had she believed in herself more, that might have made a difference. A great talent might have made living, however painful, worthwhile. But she was no Velazquez, no Michelangelo, no Raphael. The idea was laughable. She had nothing to add to the history of art, not even a footnote.

Looking at the sky, she saw its blank, ashen face staring back at her. If only she could see the moon, she thought, the moment would be perfect; but it was hidden from her. From a distance came the sound of splashing, of muffled cries. The water lapping against the pier, she thought; gulls she had awakened from their rest. Poor gulls. She hoped they would be able to get back to sleep. She closed her eyes, held her breath. Lifting her hands, she let the river take her.

APRIL 1922

NUALA

&

Nuala was on her knees in front of the Canning gravestone, working a small patch of hard earth with a hand claw. She wore a wide-brimmed hat of plain straw, a shabby beige wool cardigan over a printed cotton dress, stout shoes, and gardening gloves. Overhead, the sky was blue and unclouded, and a mellow spring sun, filtering through the branches of the budding chestnut tree, cast dappled shadows on the ground and gilded the forsythia that lay scattered in unruly clumps about the churchyard. Beside her lay a canvas satchel, a watering can, a bag of mulch, and nursery boxes full of tulips, wood anemones, and some lovely pink ladies smock, all of which she meant to plant as soon as she had finished preparing the soil. It was the fifth anniversary of Lily's death, and Nuala had come, as she did every year on this day, to repair the ravages of winter. Every few week over the season, she would return. If the weather held, she could keep the grave looking fine until well into November, when the last of the roses died.

That had been Henrietta Canning's ritual, for as long as Nuala, or anyone, could remember, tending the grave from early spring to late fall. Until her heart started giving her trouble, she had come on her own. Afterward, Lily had always accompanied her, or Nuala; and then, only Nuala. Jonas had driven the two of them to the churchyard with spring flowers to plant within days of Lily's burial, when the grave was a fresh wound in the earth, and again a few weeks later to put in the dog rose and forget-me-nots. Mrs. Canning had, as always, insisted on doing most of the work herself. "I need to be doing something," she had said in response to Nuala's protest, adding with a brief smile, "As for Dr. Roeder, what he doesn't know won't trouble him, will it?"

By early summer, she, too, had gone. She had lain down for a nap after lunch and never awakened. Heart failure, Dr. Roeder had said. The answer to her prayers is what Nuala had thought. From the moment she buried her daughter, Henrietta Canning had wanted only to die.

She should have known sooner, she supposed, but only then, when Mrs. Canning was gone, had Nuala realized that the respect and admiration she had felt for her, almost from the beginning, had somewhere along the way turned into love. She had not expected it to happen. All those years ago, as she and Deirdre trailed down the steps of that employment agency in New York City a respectful distance behind an imperious Edith Allen, Nuala had thought she would remain, no matter how smiling a face she put on, at bottom always resentful of any employer. That was a servant's lot, it seemed to her, unless blessed with as sweet a disposition as Dee's, to be spoiled by poverty and eaten up by bitterness. But Titus Canning had charmed her; and his wife, with her trust, her affection, and, ultimately, her frailty, had slowly worn away the hardness in Nuala's heart. Henrietta Canning had burrowed in and made a place for herself there, where she would remain for as long as Nuala drew breath. She was so very grateful to her.

Her relationship with Lily had been more complicated, of course. They were near enough in age, but so different in circumstances and temperament that Nuala had sometimes found it hard to conquer the resentment, the jealousy, she was ashamed to admit she felt. At times, she would gladly have slapped her young mistress for being so miserable when she had everything a body could need to be happy. Nuala herself would have managed to be ecstatic with a deal less, she was sure.

But, if she had not quite conquered those feelings, she had, at the very least, backed them into a corner where pity and affection kept them at bay, for Nuala had come to see that Lily's moods were beyond her control. They were an illness, like a fever that had to run its course. Besides, there was not any meanness in her. Though she could look right through you at times, pass you by without a flicker of acknowledgement, that was not from arrogance, as Nuala had at first taken it to be. It was . . . she was not sure what, but it was as if Lily was absent, off somewhere ("preoccupied with work and this and that," she would explain apologetically, if called to attention). And while it was possible to think her spoiled, leaving her clothes strewn anyway about her room, calling Nuala to fetch what was easily to hand, taking it as her due that everyone about should try to rearrange the world to suit her, she had never tried to lord it over others. When Lily was not lost in some dark place, wrapped up in her own wretchedness, she had faced life with an easy grace, treating everyone she met as an equal, treating a servant like a friend.

Sitting back on her heels, Nuala drew the sleeve of her cardigan across her forehead and surveyed her work. The soil still looked lumpy and hard. She took a deep breath, and could smell spring itself in the air, the scent of freshly turned earth, of wet grass, of her own sun-warmed body. How good it was to be alive, she thought. Then, as quickly as it had come, the joyful feeling passed. Nuala jabbed the claw into the earth. "Oh, you foolish, foolish girl," she said, anger and sorrow mingled in her voice, as they always were in her mind when she thought of the dreadful act that had marked the end of Lily Canning.

The gravestone was a simple granite marker inscribed with the names of the dead, their dates, and the words, "Together in death, as in life." It was a nice enough sentiment, Nuala felt, at least with regard to Titus and Henrietta Canning. It did seem off the mark, though, when it included a child; well, perhaps not the babies, for so many little ones died before they took their first steps, said their first words, that it almost seemed in the nature of things. But certainly Lily ought not to be here. She should have had a long life and great fame. She should have had a husband and babies of her own, and only then a grave, but not here, not yet.

Impatiently, Nuala brushed at her cheek to wipe away the tears. Five years had passed and still she let herself get bothered. Did a body never forget?

But she knew the answer to that. Images of her mother, father, brother, Jamie Ryan, all flitted through her mind, joining the Cannings who had been having the run of the place all the morning long. "I'll never be done, if I go on like this," she murmured, lifting her arms above her head to ease the tightness in her back. At least the soil was looking better. Opening the bag of mulch, she added it slowly to the turned earth and worked it in, saving some, as Mrs. Canning had taught her, to pack around the roots, to give the plants a good start.

She had almost finished with the tulips when she heard someone say her name. Looking up, she saw Florence (or Mrs. Macleod, as she liked to be called) and Edith Allen, a bouquet of spring flowers in the crook of her arm, moving toward her through the field of gravestones. Once upon a time, Nuala would have scrambled to her feet, but she saw no need for that now. Instead, she stayed where she was and called out, "Good morning to you both. Now, if only you'd come a while later, I'd have had it all just so."

"We're expected at Mrs. Dowling's," said Florence, coming to a stop beside her mother at the foot of the grave. "In any case, it hardly matters."

"It's so good of you to do this, Nuala," said Mrs. Allen.

"Though you really shouldn't go to so much trouble," said Florence, with something approximating a smile. She had slimmed down in the intervening years, and it was possible to see now a certain resemblance to Mrs. Canning, not in her looks exactly, but in the way she carried herself. She had something of her aunt's dignity, if not her grace of manner. "Walter could do the planting. He has such a gift for it."

Nuala laughed, discounting as she always did the implied criticism. To have taken it to heart would have given Florence the upper hand, and that Nuala would never do. "He'd have to fight Jonas for the privilege," she said. "I do myself, though how he thinks he would manage is beyond me. The poor man can hardly walk some days, his arthritis is that bad. Anyway, I like to do it."

"Still," said Mrs. Allen, "it's very kind." The brightness of her skin had faded, and the weight she had lost left her looking gaunt and worn. After all her years of fearing that it would, the sky had indeed fallen on her, first her niece dying, then her sister, and finally, most terribly, her son, Louis.

The war was over quickly for the United States, not even two years from entry to end, but still not quickly enough. Henry Roeder had fallen at Chateau Thierry; Louis two weeks later, at the Marne. A monument in memory of them, and all of Minuit's young men who had lost their lives in Europe, would be dedicated in November, on Armistice Day. It was to be set in the small park by the river, across from the inn, the statue of a Doughboy in front of a scroll inscribed with the names of the dead.

So many gone, thought Nuala, and in such a short time. It had been hard, families and friends not recovered from one loss, having to deal with a second, a third, too many. It set you wondering, it did, what the Lord was about.

After Henry's death, Dr. Roeder had lost all his blustery good humor; the flesh had melted from his bones; in under a year he was gone. Cancer, they said, but Nuala was certain that grief had played its part. His wife had faded to a small silent thing, a shadowy presence, easily overlooked. Rosaline, too, had been in a bad way, but, while William waited patiently for her to heal, Willy and the twins had clamored for attention, and her suffragist friends had begged her to get back to work with the movement. Before she knew it, Rosaline was out marching and giving speeches. She even got arrested once and spent the night in jail — a horrid experience, she said, but a small price to pay: women finally got the vote in 1920. By then, she had started writing, articles sometimes, books mostly, about the adventures of two friends growing up together in a small town closely resembling Minuit. The three published so far had been a great success. Very popular they were with young girls.

Nuala dropped her trowel, got to her feet, stretched a little, and extended her hand to Mrs. Allen. "Will I take those? I'll set them in a jug with some water, so, and arrange them nicely before I leave."

"Oh . . ." Staring at the gravestone, lost in thought, she seemed to have forgotten the flowers she was holding. "Why, yes, thank you." She fixed her sad eyes on Nuala's face, and said, as she handed the bouquet to her, "Sometimes I think the awfulness started then, when Lily died, that her dying somehow set everything in motion."

It was a sign to Nuala of how much had changed, how far she had come, that Mrs. Allen should speak so familiarly to her, and she could not suppress a small glimmer of satisfaction as she answered quite honestly that, to her, the world seemed an endless cycle of good and bad, joy and sorrow, with no beginning and no end, "But that," she said, pointing to the grave.

"Mother," said Florence. Her voice was full of impatience, and Nuala would not have been surprised to see her tug at Mrs. Allen's sleeve like an unruly child. "We'll be late to lunch at Mrs. Dowling's, if we don't hurry."

"Yes, Florence, in a minute."

Mrs. Allen closed her eyes and bowed her head. Reminded of what was required, Florence followed her mother's example. Even Nuala, who had been talking to the occupants of the grave on and off since her arrival, did the same.

"Tell Deirdre I miss her badly," said Mrs. Allen, her prayer finished. "Tell her to come see me when she can."

"I will. I'll surely tell her. And you know if you need Dee, or myself for that matter, for anything, we'd be only too happy to oblige."

"Thank you. That's very kind. Well, we must go."

She said good-bye, her daughter gave a brief nod of farewell, and, as the women turned and walked away, Nuala heard Florence say to her mother, "I should think they would be delighted to oblige, considering how much this family has done for the two of them."

Nuala shrugged away a flash of anger. However irritating Florence might be, and inclined to feel aggrieved, she was right this time, though it was not the "family" who had done so much, but Mrs. Canning herself.

The women stopped at Louis's grave, prayed quietly for a moment, and then continued on out of the gate to where Walter was waiting for them, parked next to the old Packard that Nuala had bought secondhand from the Canning estate. Taking a pottery jug from her canvas bag, she walked across the winter-worn grass to the spigot on the church wall to get water for the bouquet. Poor Dee, she thought. Her sister had taken Louis's death hard. Head-over-heels in love she had been with him, and he, certainly on the verge of falling for her. Nuala had seen the way he looked at her sister and had come to believe that, with Lily gone, Louis would soon get over his infatuation with his cousin and turn to Deirdre. How could he not? Who else was so good and so beautiful, and capable as well, if a little too apt to let herself be pushed around? No doubt the Allens would have been upset, but it was the twentieth century after all, and the United States of America. People were free to follow their hearts,

345

though perhaps it remained an open question whether Louis would have been brave enough to follow his.

Ah well, thought Nuala, it would have made a grand story had fate not written it otherwise.

Leaving the jug of flowers resting on the flat top of the gravestone, Nuala knelt again and began planting the anemones, remembering the days following Lily's death, everyone still aching from that, when Louis announced his intention to join the Roeder brothers and go off to war, causing a new round of fear and grief. No sooner had the boys departed, it seemed, than Henrietta Canning had died. The following spring, there had come the awful news about Henry, and then Louis. What a terrible time it had been; but at least Nuala had been able to get her sister out of the Allen house and away to where she was free to mourn openly, for by then, with the money she had received as a legacy from Mrs. Canning, Nuala had bought the old Wild Goose Inn on River Street. Had she needed to, she could certainly have managed it on her own, but she had convinced Deirdre she could not; and it had turned out to be a very good thing indeed to have her sister working by her side — and Jonas, who helped out a bit with the handy work, though his own legacy had left him with no need to lift a finger. The inn had twelve guest bedrooms, a cozy parlor, and, overlooking the river, a dining room where breakfast and dinner were served to anyone who cared to drop in. Outside, a bright new sign proclaimed it "The Innisfree House." A thriving business it had become in the years since, and Nuala smiled with pride, as she could never help doing when she considered what a grand success she had so far made of her life.

Of course, there had been moments when she doubted, when she was afraid. The afternoon she had found Mrs. Canning lying in her bed (icy cold to the touch, yet looking so peaceful, as if she were still only asleep), mixed with Nuala's sorrow had been dread. Though she would rather have died than admit to it at the time, she had felt the same sort of thing on the ship crossing the Atlantic, and through the endless immigration process, and when saying good-bye to her brother Seamus. He had come to Ellis Island to meet her and Deirdre, for women on their own would not be admitted to the country. They had planned to go with him back to Kentucky, where Liam was as well, but Seamus had said that opportunities were better in New York, as was the pay, settling the matter for Nuala. "We came this far for the best chance," she had said to Dee, "so why not take it?" But still the knot of dread had remained tight in her stomach, until she got to Riverhall and saw that it was not so bad.

With Mrs. Canning gone, to Nuala, the future had once again seemed terrifying. What would become of her? Where would she find work, or for whom? How would she manage if she had to leave Minuit and her sister behind? And she had heard stories, told by girls she knew, other Irish girls like herself, who worked for people mean as the devil, or had friends and relatives in even worse situations, humiliated by the women who employed them, beaten sometimes, raped by the men, and, when their bellies began to swell, thrown out on the streets with no way to earn a living but prostituting themselves. Not that she would ever stoop to such a thing, Nuala was sure. But what she would do, she had no idea.

As it happened, she had no cause for worry. Life had a way of turning out right for her, she thought with some satisfaction as she put the last of the anemones into the earth, and she was forever grateful to the Lord and His Blessed Mother for that, and for settling Deirdre and herself in this pretty part of the world, among decent, God-fearing people.

It was Dr. Roeder who had put her mind at ease, even as Mr. Polk and his assistants were upstairs at Riverhall, going about their business. Though stricken terribly by Mrs. Canning's death, and worried sick about his sons, he had seen past his own troubles to Nuala's. "You're not to fret, my dear," he had said. "Mrs. Canning's made provision for you in her will. She was so grateful to you for your goodness to her, and to Lily. You'll be well taken care of, so you can rest easy on that score at least." Nuala had started to cry, and the doctor had patted her shoulder awkwardly, murmuring, "Ah, now, don't. We're all counting on you to be strong, to see us through this, as you always do."

Dr. Roeder and Andrew Macleod (good men, both of them, even if Andrew could be a bit pompous at times) were the trustees of the Canning estate. With complete confidence in their judgment, Nuala had left it to them to handle the details of her legacy, and the subsequent purchase of the inn, keeping in the background as much as possible, mostly to keep out of Florence's way. To this day, she was not at all pleased by her aunt's generosity (as she put it) to one who had only been doing her job, and getting well paid for it, too. Though why it should make any difference to her was beyond Nuala, for Florence had ended up with Riverhall.

It should have gone to Louis, of course. After Lily's death, Mrs. Canning had revised her will, leaving the house to her sister, Edith, who had announced at once, when they were all still gathered for the reading, that she meant to give it to Louis when he married. That had caused a huge row, which Deirdre and all the rest of the staff had overheard. Florence had thrown a fit, protesting that, as she was the elder, it ought to be hers, especially as she was already married. Still awaiting orders to go overseas, and home on leave to attend his aunt's funeral, Louis had seemed pleased at first with the idea of having Riverhall, for he had always loved the place; but soon he was agreeing that it should go to Florence "in the circumstances," though he did not say which circumstances he meant, his sister's or his own. No one pressed him, for if it was the possibility of his death he was considering, his fears — everyone's fears — were best left unspoken. In an attempt to put an end to the battle once and for all, Andrew had said that he could not, in good conscience, even consider depriving Louis of his inheritance, but his had been far from the last word.

The argument had raged for months, Florence harrying her mother at every turn, and poor Mrs. Allen sick with sorrow and worry. She had stuck to her guns, though. Riverhall was to go to Louis, and that was that, she declared. And then Louis died.

Though she had said nothing to Deirdre at the time, in those months between Mrs. Canning's death and her nephew's, Nuala had often imagined her sister as mistress of Riverhall, living there with Louis and a bevy of children. It was just as well that she had kept her daydreams to herself, for, instead of Dee, it was Florence who now was mistress of it, having the ladies in for lunch when her husband was away hunting or climbing or shooting rapids (or one mad thing, and another), throwing grand parties when he was at home, doing what she could to fill the house with life. The child she wanted so desperately had not come, despite the many specialists she had consulted over the years.

She could not imagine Florence a comfortable mother, thought Nuala, taking time to stretch again while considering the placement of the ladies smock. But then, who was she to judge? Disliking the woman surely did not give her the right. "God forgive me," she murmured. Florence might be a much better person, far more thoughtful and generous, if she got what she wanted. Happiness brought out the best in some people.

In most people, Nuala acknowledged with a smile. And, as she set the ladies smock amid the tulips and the wood anemones, she indulged in one of her favorite daydreams, that Riverhall was hers. She imagined herself and . . . and, yes, her children, three — no, maybe four — playing on the lawn, the busy Hudson streaming by below them, a lovely sight on a sunny spring day. Though she sometimes chided herself for wasting time on daydreams, deep in her heart she believed that the best way to get ahead was to know where it was you wanted to go. And this particular fantasy could very well come true, for with no one left to inherit, perhaps the Macleods one day would be of a mind to sell the place, and herself in a position to buy. What with the fine meals she served at the Innisfree House attracting all the locals, and a bit of advertising bringing in tourists off the steamships and railroad, she stood in the way of earning a fair bit of money; and, though she had left it late (but better late than sorry, she always said), now that she was to marry Joseph Burdett, her future seemed even more secure. True, his family was kicking up a bit of a fuss, they being Protestant and she, Catholic, but Nuala was confident that they would come round, for Joseph and she made a formidable pair, not one to take no for an answer. The Burdetts owned the local dry goods store, but (no matter the money at stake) Joseph had no real interest in the business. He had political ambitions. He planned to run first for mayor, and then, as soon as could be, for the United States Congress. A decorated war hero (a bayonet wound had almost cost him his life — but that did not bear thinking on), with looks and intelligence to spare, he could get himself elected to whatever office he chose, Nuala was sure, especially with her by his side to help. To think of it, herself an immigrant, married to a member of Congress! Her Ma would be that proud of her!

If only she could get Deirdre settled, Nuala's mind could be easy about the future. Well, all in good time, she cautioned herself, remembering how long she had taken to get over Jamie. Her sister was beginning to heal, and there was, as always, no shortage of men interested in her. Marcus Roeder, for one. Since returning from the war to Minuit, to take over his father's practice, he had become a regular at the inn, bringing family and friends to dine, sometimes just wandering in on his own. Even at Mass, he could not seem to keep his eyes from Dee.

With a laugh at herself for imagining such a happy, untroubled future for them all, Nuala put her trowel aside and got to her feet. The planting was done. The flowers looked a bit droopy, but, given some water, they would soon perk up, and the grave would look as pretty as could be. After carrying the empty nursery boxes to the trash, she took the watering can to the spigot and turned it on. While she waited impatiently for it to fill, she heard footsteps on the gravel behind her and, turning her head, saw the smiling face of Reverend Moreland. "Ah, Reverend, good morning to you," she said. There were a few strands of silver in his hair, she noticed, and a tracery of lines in the corners of his eyes and on his brow. The young minister was at last beginning to look the part.

"Good morning, Miss Costello," he replied. Though she was not a parishioner of his, he could hardly help recognizing her, with all the time

350

she spent in the churchyard, and it was a source of pride to Nuala that he always addressed her formally. "I see you've been hard at work again. The grave is looking very fine. I'm certain Mrs. Canning is smiling down on you this moment, delighted with how lovely you've made it."

"It's the anniversary of Lily's death today," said Nuala, after acknowledging the compliment.

"Ah, so it is," he said, his smile fading.

Turning off the spigot, she held the watering can with both hands, feeling the weight of it tugging at her tired arms, and said, "I still do get angry when I think of it," as if it were the most natural thing in the world to be confessing herself to this minister of an alien religion, which perhaps it was, since he had known Lily. Nuala's priest had not. "Her life cut so short. I wonder what God could have been thinking to let . . . to let it happen."

"Oh, I'm afraid there's not much comfort to be found in questioning the Lord's motives," he said. "Or anyone's, for that matter. Acceptance is what makes things easier to bear. We must just pray for the courage to endure what we must, and leave it to Him to sort out the whys and wherefores, the right or wrong of things. It's His mercy we must count on, not His reasonableness."

Did he know? she wondered. But he could not, for then surely, just as Father Duggan had when she confessed to him, the reverend would not be speaking of God's mercy, but of His punishment.

"May I help you with that?" he asked, pointing to the watering can.

"No, thank you, Reverend, I can manage."

"Then, you leave me no choice." He was smiling again. "It's back to writing my sermon. Good day, Miss Costello."

Watching him as he limped back toward the door to the church office (he had broken his leg skiing in Vermont in February), it crossed Nuala's mind that it might possibly be a sin to like him, as she did, far better than Father Duggan. But no, she decided finally, for Reverend

Moreland was a kind man and, Protestant or not, that must count for something.

Returning to the grave, she sprinkled the flowers liberally with water, found a place for the jug holding Mrs. Allen's bouquet, and then stepped back to admire her handiwork. Yes, the reverend was right: Mrs. Canning would be pleased. Pretty as a picture, it all looked. As she turned to begin packing up her tools, she saw someone moving across the churchyard toward her. Recognizing Rosaline, Nuala waved. "You've come just in time," she said. "I've finished.

"Oh, it looks gorgeous," said Rosaline, drawing near. She was carrying a wreath of lilies and a small bouquet of daffodils. As she lay the wreath on the grave below the newly planted flower bed, she said, "It's from Alice and Teddy. No matter where they are, they never forget."

"They're still in Paris?"

"Yes. For the moment. They'll be taking their girls to Cannes for the summer. Little Lily is four now, and Joan almost a year. Can you believe it? Their letter said they're all having a bang-up time. Paris seems to be the center of the world."

"For artist types, at any rate."

Rosaline laughed. "You're quite right. There's certainly nowhere I'd rather be than here." They stood for a moment, as if on a street corner in town, exchanging news about the children, William, Dee, the inn, until Rosaline said, "Oh, I forgot a jug for the flowers."

Nuala stooped to rummage in her satchel, pulled out a glass jar, and offered it to her. "Will this do you?" she asked.

"Yes, very well, thank you. And now for some water." Turning away, she retraced her steps through the row of graves to the church wall.

By the time she returned, Nuala had packed up her things and was ready to go. Rosaline crouched down, settled the jar of daffodils, and then looked questioningly around to Nuala, who nodded and said, "It's grand."

Straightening, Rosaline took a step backward and, with her eyes fastened firmly on the grave, said, "That's another thing Lily missed out on.

Paris. I know she regretted not going to Europe when Florence did. And it sounds like such fun now."

How different it is when old folks die, thought Nuala. Then, no matter how deep the sorrow, the talk is happy, memories hit back and forth like shuttlecocks, everyone enjoying the game. With the young, it's different. Talk of them is mostly a sorry catalogue of lost opportunities, endlessly repeated, each item breaking your heart all over again.

"Reverend Moreland would say she's in a better place," Nuala said, more to comfort Rosaline than because she believed it to be true. What she believed — no, not quite believed — what she *feared* sometimes, when she could not help herself, was that Lily was in hell, suffering the torment of the damned, burning in everlasting fire. It was a terrible thought. She felt the tears start again, and brushed them away.

Rosaline turned and looked at her. "Do you believe in hell?" she asked.

"Yes."

"So do I, though I try not to. It seems a terrible punishment, no matter what the sin."

Their eyes met and held for a moment. For the first time, Nuala was aware of the unspoken knowledge, the terrible dread that linked her with Rosaline.

How many others knew? Nuala wondered. How many others carried that awful secret in their hearts? But what was it the Reverend Moreland had said? That we must trust in God's mercy? Yes, she had always believed that. Perhaps He had found a way to save Lily, when no one else could. "Oh, I think some be deserving of hell fire," Nuala said, "but then it's not for us to judge. Only God can do that, and there's no telling who He'll think it right to spare."

Rosaline nodded. "So William keeps reminding me," she said, turning her attention back to the small plot of earth before them. "'In this grave doth lie/As much beauty as could die,'" she went on, quoting a poem Nuala did not recognize. "She was so good, and so very talented. I thought more would be made of her after her show."

It had been a success, so everyone said. Mrs. Canning had returned to Riverhall from the opening feeling a little cheered by the reception her daughter's work had received, and the few newspaper reviews had been complimentary indeed. From the standpoint of sales, however, the show had been a disaster.

Nuala had not been invited to the opening, of course; but on her next day off she had traveled to the city and gone on her own to the exhibition, and a revelation it had been. After years of not paying any attention whatsoever to those on the walls at Riverhall, seeing Lily's paintings hanging there, in the gallery, with nothing to distract the eye, Nuala could at last see what all the fuss was about. The paintings had a presence, a power. They called out to her, even the ones she did not much like. She would have bought one, if it had occurred to her she might, but it did not. Nor to many others. Only four were sold: two had gone to strangers; Alice and Teddy had bought one; Edmund Farel, another. And that was it.

The man had a nerve, Nuala thought, remembering how upset Mrs. Canning had been to see Farel's name on the list of buyers sent by the gallery, more bothered by that than the sorry number of paintings sold. Nuala had not mentioned his being at the churchyard the day of Lily's funeral to anyone but Deirdre, for her mind could have been playing her tricks, and what was the point in adding to the general upset? But when Mrs. Canning showed her the list, she knew that indeed it had been himself, not some specter she had conjured, though she could not imagine where he had found the gall to put in an appearance, however sorry he might be for all his evil actions, whatever they were. Lily had never said, not even to her own mother. "I made a mistake" was all anyone could get out of her. "And I'd rather correct it at once than live with it all my life." All her life. A few months, that was all she had left, and whose fault was it, if not Edmund Farel's? And him? Well, he had made a name for him-

354

self as a war correspondent, and had won some sort of prize—a Pulitzer, that was it—for writing against the Palmer raids, which just went to show there was no justice, not in this world at any rate.

"I heard Mr. Berlin say that with the war just starting, no one was paying any attention to art. Who knows, but at another time—"

Rosaline shook her head. "I doubt there ever can be another time now."

The women looked at each other bleakly, remembering the day, three years before, when Lily's paintings were destroyed, all their lovely colors turned to smoke and gray ash.

Walter had told Jonas, who had hurried back to the inn as fast as his arthritic legs could carry him to tell Nuala. She, knowing she could not save the paintings on her own, had run up the street to Rosaline's house to ask for help. Without even bothering to tidy her hair or put on her hat, Rosaline had called to the children to behave, told Dora to fend for herself, taken her coat from the stand in the hall, picked up the keys to the Ford, and led the way to the garage, where the car was parked.

"We'll be there in no time," Rosaline had said, driving along Kirkby Road at a speed her husband would have deplored. "I have four of Lily's paintings . . . no, five; and there must be at least half a dozen more at my parents' house."

"I've got that miniature of Mrs. Canning that Mrs. Allen gave me." It was the one of Henrietta, looking prosperous and regal, that Lily had kept on the dressing table in her bedroom. In Nuala's much smaller room at the Innisfree, it sat on her chest of drawers, next to the faded photograph of her own care-worn mother. She would have told anyone who asked that, as she saw it, she owed both women her life. What she might not have admitted quite so readily was that the portraits were a constant reminder to her to beware, for though she had taken long steps in the right direction, she could still as easily end up like one as the other, well-off and respected, or poor and ignored. She had to be vigilant. She had always to make the right choices. "There's the portrait of Louis in Mrs. Allen's study," Nuala went on. "And the landscape in the hall."

"Alice and Teddy have some. And let's not forget the ones that Lily sold over the years."

Trying to make the numbers mount, dismayed by the pitiful sum, they continued the inventory until the car crossed the causeway to River-hall, where they saw a plume of smoke rising over the cedar tree. "Oh God," Nuala murmured. "She's done it."

The bonfire raged in the gravel drive at the side of the house, a safe distance from the garage. The new gardener was throwing paintings from the pile at his side onto the flames, while Florence stood away from the heat, watching. Rosaline stopped the car, set the brake, and clambered out. "Florence, what on earth are you doing?" she called, racing toward her.

"Have you lost your mind?" shouted Nuala, who never, from that moment on, gave another thought to keeping her place.

"Not at all," Florence said calmly, turning to greet them, as cool as could be. "What else was I to do with them? I'm redoing the house. I'm tired of them covering simply every wall. The attics are full. And I can't sell them. They have no value at all, as you well know."

'You can't burn Lily's paintings!" said Rosaline.

"I can. And I have. That's the last of them," she went on, gesturing to one of the housemaids, who was carrying a large painting from the house.

"No," said Nuala, running to the girl and grabbing hold of it.

Florence chased after her. "Let it go. Let them get on with it!"

"No," said Nuala, pushing her out of the way.

"How dare you!" shouted Florence. And then, suddenly aware of her dignity, she shrugged and said quietly, "Very well, have it. I certainly don't care."

"Florence, how could you?"

"Don't be such a ninny, Rosaline. What does it matter?"

356

It was a question to which neither Rosaline, nor Nuala, had an answer. They just knew what Florence had done was very wrong. It was as if she had killed Lily's babies.

"We should have gone to Mrs. Allen's first. She might have stopped her," Rosaline said now, neither her anger nor her regret diminished a whit by the intervening years.

"It's hard to stop Florence any time," said Nuala, "but when she's got her steam up?"

"Andrew would have, if only he'd been home."

"Which, I don't doubt, is why she waited until he was out of the way."

"At least you saved the one."

"Yes." It was of the river, by moonlight. One of a continuing series that Lily had done over the years, unlike some of the others, this particular painting had a sense of peace, of tranquility. It seemed to promise that all would be well. Nuala had hung it over the mantle in the inn's parlor. "All together, there might be enough, should that Mr. Menlo ever think to do another show."

Rosaline laughed. "Always the optimist, Nuala. But you're right. You never know what the future will bring." Then, the laughter left her face and she said, "I really shouldn't be so hard on Florence. She's such an unhappy person. And I almost destroyed a painting of Lily's once myself. A day or two after she died. It was a terrible painting, a frightening one; I didn't want Aunt Etta to see it. Or anyone, then."

"But you didn't."

"No. I thought, what if I'm wrong? What if it's a masterpiece? I hid it instead. I got it away from Riverhall as soon as I could. It's in my attic now. I suppose, one of these days, I ought to show it to Teddy and Alice, to see what they make of it." Again her eyes met Nuala's. "At least Lily's beyond knowing what's become of her work."

"Or caring, at least." Nuala shrugged. "I suppose the truth is, that not a thing the rest of us did, or didn't do, mattered a fig in the end. Not a thing mattered, but what Lily did." And if that was true, then what of Edmund Farel? "Don't you think that's the way of it? Try as we might to blame others, in the end no one's responsible for what becomes of us but ourselves?"

Rosaline thought for a moment and then said, "It's true we must answer to God for our actions. Come Judgment Day, excuses won't do. There'll be no escaping blame, I grant you that. Yet, I can't help thinking we're all connected somehow, that we influence each other's lives whether we mean to or not, as if each life is a river and every person encountered along the way a pebble tossed into it, making ripples that spread and spread, out to infinity. If Lily hadn't died . . . well, she'd be living at River-hall now, wouldn't she? Not Florence. And perhaps you'd still be the housekeeper there, not the owner of an inn."

"I'd gladly—" said Nuala.

"Oh, I know," interrupted Rosaline. "I know you'd never wish to get ahead at another's expense. I didn't mean to imply that. Or that Lily's death could in any way make you happy. It's just, I can't help thinking how different everything might have been for all of us, in ways I can't even begin to understand, if only Lily had lived."

The conversation died between them. Soon, they would have to return to their lives, their duties, their pleasures, but for the moment they stood looking at the gravestone with its names and dates and loving inscription, the bed of newly planted flowers at its base, the tulips and wood anemones and ladies smock beginning to liven up after their drink of water, the bouquets of jolly spring flowers in their jars, the wreath of lilies covering the sparse grass.

Nuala thought of the smoke from the fire rising above the tall cedar, of Lily's spirit climbing to meet it, mingling with it, floating out over the Hudson.

"Lamb of God," said Rosaline, "Who takes away the sins of the world—"

"Have mercy on her," said Nuala, joining in.

"Lamb of God, Who takes away the sins of the world, have mercy on her," they repeated. "Lamb of God, Who takes away the sins of the world, grant her peace."

They were silent a moment, and then Nuala picked up her canvas satchel and said, "Come, we had better be getting on."

Acknowledgements

Of the many books I consulted for background and information while writing this novel, I am especially indebted to: *The Hudson Through the Years* by Arthur G. Adams; *Hudson River Memories* by Julian Burroughs; *Painting American* by Annie Cohen-Solal; *The American Century* by Harold Evans; *Painters on Painting*, Selected and Edited by Eric Protter; *New York 1900: Metropolitan Architecture and Urbanism 1890-1915* by Robert A.M. Stern, Gregory Gilmartin and John Massengale; *The Lives of the Artists* by Giorgio Vasari; and *From Manet to Manhattan: The Rise of the Modern Art Market* by Peter Watson. The internet and its multitudinous resources also deserve a mention.

To my family and friends, who have been unfailingly supportive as I journeyed from the initial idea to the eventual publication of this novel, I offer my heartfelt gratitude.

In particular I would like to thank my agents Lynn Pleshette and Michael Cendejas for their Herculean efforts on my behalf, as well as Nick Lyons, Carla Singer, and Beth Uffner for their good advice and invaluable assistance.

Claudia Ricci, Victoria Sackheim, Marcia Wallace, and Marie Wallace were most generous in sharing their experiences with me.

Without the insightful notes and encouraging words of Norman Boyack, Frank Marshall, Jan Meshkoff, Lucretia Slaughter, and Jeff Young, I would never have made it past the first draft.

Nor would I have got to the point of publication without the long hours so generously spent by Cara de Silva researching resources, editing text, listening to my problems, and putting her keen mind to work helping to solve them.

Finally, to Michael and Victoria Bell, I owe a debt beyond words for their love and support over the years, and, above all, because once upon a time they told me a story.